THE VERY BEST PEOPLE

By Elizabeth Villars

THE RICH GIRL

THE VERY BEST PEOPLE

The Very Best People

Elizabeth Villars

Coward, McCann & Geoghegan, Inc.
New York

In memory of
Ruth and Sina

In appreciation of
Russ's memory

And again and as always for
W.C.B.

In Boston they ask, How much does he know? In New York, How much is he worth? In Philadelphia, Who were his parents?

—MARK TWAIN

In the first generation thee must do well, in the second marry well, in the third breed well, and the fourth will take care of itself.

—A QUAKER FORMULA FOR
FOUNDING A FAMILY

Prologue to Book One

Washington, 1937

It was uncommonly hot that night in September when Tyson Enfield asked Kathryn Owen to marry him. It was a pity he hadn't waited another week. By then the weather would have broken and it would have been twenty years to the day since she'd fallen in love with him.

But Ty had never had much respect for the proprieties of time. His seven-o'clock telephone call on that hot September morning reminded Kate of that, as if she needed to be reminded of anything about Tyson Enfield. The army, Ty used to say, had stripped him of the last vestiges of tolerance for schedule. Never again, he announced when he arrived home from France early in 1919, would he eat, sleep, make war, or, for that matter, love by the clock.

Kathryn supposed the seven-o'clock call was a reaffirmation of that resolution, though she knew without being told that Tyson Enfield must have been doing a great many things by the clock for a good many years now. He must have taken the morning train to town by the clock, lunched at his club by the clock, worked by the clock, played by the clock, eaten, slept, and, she supposed, thinking of Amanda Enfield with less satisfaction than might be expected at this moment, made love by the clock. But Ty had telephoned from Philadelphia at seven o'clock this morning as if to say that he would no longer live according to schedule.

Kathryn, however, had her own schedule, and after Ty's phone call she was a quarter of an hour behind it. On her way out of the apartment she stopped in the small pullman kitchen, took a bottle of gin from the cupboard, another of vermouth, and placed them in the icebox. Ty had taught her that.

By the time she reached her cubicle in the ballroom of the old McLean mansion that had been converted to accommodate the Federal Arts Project, the thin cotton of her dress clung to her back damply.

"Do you think old lady McLean used to keep an army of footmen around to fan the guests when it got this hot? Or don't the rich feel the heat? I know they don't sweat." Arthur Lasher stood next to her desk wearing his familiar wrinkled trousers and short-sleeved white shirt open at the collar. His pockmarked face, the reminder of a grim youth, bore a sour expression. Like the trousers and shirt, it too was familiar. "This place was designed to keep the heat in—except in winter, of course. Then we freeze. Typical of the powers that be to put the Writers' Project in this barn of a ballroom. Ornate as a bordello and twice as uncomfortable. Shows what they think of the arts. Writers' Project, hell. Writers' penance is more like it. The WPA is the bureaucrats' revenge on the artist."

"At least it's a job."

"Are you reminding me to mind my manners, Katie?" He gave her a wolfish smile revealing tobacco-stained teeth. "Because you should know by now I don't have any manners—or gratitude. You can call it a job, but to me it's still charity. Of course, that's the difference between us. You left a job, or maybe it was a *position,* to come here. I left only my poetry, poetry you wouldn't understand, but poetry nevertheless. I'm an on-the-skids poet earning fifteen-sixty-five a week to compile a carefully whitewashed history of our country. You're an administrator earning a lot more than that to oversee this joke. Tell me, what *are* you pulling down for counting Midwestern church records?"

"Not nearly so much as you imagine, Arthur."

"But a helluva lot more than fifteen-sixty-five a week, Katie Owen. Owen. That reminds me. Seems to me I heard something about a connection between you and Senator Owen, something about some Philadelphia politicians named Owen. You wouldn't be one of those Owens, would you?"

still couldn't get over what had happened to the old mansion. At the corner she let the streetcar pass. It would be faster to walk. Kate smiled to herself at the thought. That was one of the first things she'd noticed about Washington when she'd arrived two and a half years ago. No matter where you were going, everyone always said it would be faster to walk. Now that she said it too, she supposed she was a native. But of course she wouldn't be for long, because Ty was back, and Ty meant Philadelphia.

Every memory she had of Ty had something to do with Philadelphia. Even during that time almost two years ago, when he had come to Washington every week to see her, she had always been aware he had come from Philadelphia, and would return to Philadelphia. The thought that she herself would not return should have made the city at the other end of Ty's journey more distant, but somehow it only served to make it more intrusive. When she went to Union Station to see Ty off, standing with him in the steam and noise and crowds on the railroad platform, she had always been painfully aware that the train was taking Ty not only away from her but back to Philadelphia. The train was taking Ty home.

Philadelphia had been her home too, until she had lost it. No, not lost it, thrown it away. She remembered her mother's words just before she'd left. "You could have had so much, Kathryn, but you threw it all away gambling for everything."

She'd be going back to Philadelphia now, though she knew it would never be the same for her. Just as she knew Ty would never be the same for her. Kathryn told herself she was foolish to think about it now. She had Ty. He was all she'd ever wanted. But as she showered and dressed and made herself ready for Ty, a part of her mind kept going back to Philadelphia.

he was waiting for Kate when she returned to the apartment that evening. He still wore the dark riding jacket, the cream-colored trousers, the white silk stock. She'd had a long day at the Writers' Project office, and she couldn't help thinking it was an absurd costume to be wearing at that particular moment in history. But at the same time, she couldn't help thinking how well Ty carried it off.

He was sitting in the small living room with a whiskey before him, and Kate knew the moment she saw his face that something was wrong, more wrong than her mere refusal to attend the horse show. Kate wasn't surprised. Like the telephone call this morning, she had been waiting for something to go wrong without knowing she was waiting. If it hadn't been the baby, it would have been something else. He had talked of divorce all that summer, and she had pretended to believe him, but she hadn't believed him then any more than she had years earlier when he had spoken of marriage.

It seemed she had always known she could never have Tyson Enfield. But that was a lie, a lie of hindsight. Years ago she had believed they would marry. Years ago when she'd had Ty, she'd never believed she could lose him. It was only now, after she had lost him, that she could tell herself she had always known she would.

But of course she hadn't lost him after all. This morning's telephone call proved that. Tyson Stratford Enfield had done the unthinkable, the unreasonable, the unacceptable. Tyson Stratford Enfield had divorced his wife and returned to Kathryn. And he had waited until it was absolutely, irrevocably final to tell her. There would be no disappointments this time. He was free and he was coming down on the four-o'clock to see her, to ask her properly and formally to marry him. "I'll even get down on one knee"—he'd laughed on the telephone—"if that's what you want."

He knew exactly what she wanted. Tyson Enfield kneeling, standing, walking, crawling. Tyson Enfield any way he came.

Kathryn began watching the clock on her desk a little after three. At four when she checked it against the gold wristwatch Ty had given her for her birthday—how many years ago, now? fourteen, fifteen?—Lasher laughed and said the clock wasn't broken. At four-thirty he commented without any particular kindness that she must have a big evening planned. At a quarter to five he suggested she leave. Kathryn knew he'd be both pleased and angry if she did.

"No, thanks, Arthur. I keep the same hours everyone else does."

As the minute hand took the last stroke to five, Kate was out of the ballroom, down the great staircase, past the sullen doorman who

"There are a lot of Owens in Philadelphia."

"But not all of them are in politics."

"I scarcely think you'd call this job being in politics, Arthur."

"In other words, you're telling me you're not that Owen after all. Just a coincidence about you and Senator Owen. And here I was thinking you owed your position here to the honorable senator from Pennsylvania."

"I can assure you, Arthur, I owe nothing to the honorable senator from Pennsylvania. And I owe this job to my hard-nosed ability as an administrator"—Kate flashed Lasher one of his own sarcastic smiles—"so let's forget my family tree and get down to work. Are those the pieces for the second anthology?" She indicated the stack of papers he carried.

"And a pretty watered-down lot they are."

"You mean they're socially irresponsible, Arthur? In that case we'll have to include some more of your poetry. To raise the tone. Or at least its social significance."

"Am I supposed to be grateful to you for that too, Katie? For putting one of my poems in the first anthology?"

"I don't want your gratitude, Arthur. Only your professional expertise."

Lasher pulled a chair close to hers, and they began to go through the articles. He smelled of tobacco and sweat. Arthur Lasher prided himself on being a man of the people. He also, Kathryn suspected, enjoyed offending her. He hated the Writers' Project and the paltry salary it paid him with the same fierce hatred that inflamed his socially conscious poetry. And he hated her, Kathryn knew, as the living embodiment, for him at least, of the WPA.

What Kate never guessed was that Lasher's hatred of her as a woman exceeded his distaste for her as a symbol. Her presence aroused him, and because it did, it served as a constant reminder of the women he had loved and lusted for and never possessed. Moreover, he knew that Kate never worried about money, and he suspected—just as he suspected a connection with Senator Owen—that at some time in her life she'd had a good deal of it. His political convictions conspired with memories of an impoverished childhood to make him rail against the ease of Kathryn Owen's life. And as if all that were not enough, Kate had a pride that Arthur Lasher and his hard-boiled sarcasm could not penetrate. Kathryn Owen was everything that Arthur Lasher wanted to possess, but he could not possess her and as a result he hated her. Kate would not have believed for a moment that Arthur Lasher felt these things about her, but neither would she have doubted that such feelings could exist.

The ringing of the telephone on her desk interrupted their concentration. Before the long-distance operator could say that Chicago was calling, Peter Lynnquist's voice came rushing over the wire. "We settled it, Katie! We settled it without a strike. A real coup these days."

"Congratulations. I don't know how management and labor feel about the settlement, but you sound euphoric."

"Exhausted is more the word. I'm coming off what the evening editions are going to call 'round-the-clock negotiations.' "

"You need a vacation."

"My thought exactly. I'm going to get the eleven-o'clock out of here tonight—it would be faster to fly, but I have a feeling that's bad form when you've just settled a labor dispute for the railroads, and anyway, I can sleep on the train—and I'll be in Washington by seven-thirty tomorrow morning. I'll pick you up for breakfast and we can drive down to Virginia for the weekend. It'll be cooler, if nothing else. What do you say?"

What she had to say was not for Arthur Lasher's ears. She covered the mouthpiece of the phone with her hand. "Arthur, would you excuse me for a minute?" Arthur skulked off, looking annoyed. "I'd like to, Peter, really I would, but I can't. I'm sorry."

"If you're worrying about my behavior, don't. I'm harmless, remember. I proved that in Vermont. Worst campaign swing I ever made. Lost the state for the President—and the girl."

Kate wished he wouldn't joke about that weekend. It was almost a year ago, but the memory of it still made her uncomfortable. "You know it's not that. It's just that I have other plans. I'm sorry."

"If you mean the office and that band of misguided aesthetes you monitor, we can wait until tomorrow night to leave. It will still give us Saturday and Sunday."

"It isn't the office. It's something else."

He was quiet for a moment. "Don't you mean someone else, Katie? Someone from a long time ago?" He sounded tired, as if he wasn't quite up to the battle.

"Yes, Peter. I'm sorry."

"Listen, Katie, stop saying you're sorry. There's nothing to be sorry about. I can't say you didn't warn me. You've done nothing but warn me ever since I met you. So there's no need to be sorry. And Virginia was a bad idea, anyway. I really ought to work this weekend. Things have piled up while I've been out here. There's talk of another steel strike in two small plants in Ohio. And you know they can't settle it without Lynnquist."

"I'm sure of that. And congratulations again—on the railroad settlement."

"Thanks, Katie. Thanks for everything. And good luck."

Kate was surprised. She'd expected more of an argument. "You don't have to sound so final, Peter. Call me when you get back from wherever the steel strike is going to be."

"Sure thing, Katie. I'll keep in touch." It was exactly what people said when they had no intention of keeping in touch at all, but she supposed Peter was right. Now that Ty was back, there was no place for Peter Lynnquist in her life. And Tyson Enfield was definitely back. Permanently and irrevocably, according to this morning's telephone call. The articles on her desk swam before her eyes, commanding only a corner of her concentration while her mind went back to Ty's words.

"Kat, it's Ty," he said, as if she wouldn't recognize his voice. The strange thing was that she hadn't been surprised. Kathryn had rarely thought consciously about the call, but she had always known it would come.

"Kat, it's final. I waited to call until it was final. I thought it would be better after last time." Though they were miles apart, she knew exactly how his face would look at that moment. The gray eyes would be earnest and apologetic, but he'd be smiling slightly, with that careless boyish smile that knew it would be forgiven anything. Even *last time.*

It had been almost two years ago, a year and eleven months to be exact. Ty had come down for the Inter-American Horse Show. He had really come to see her, but the horse show provided the excuse. She hated those excuses. They were more than a reproach. They were a humiliation.

He'd come down on the seven-o'clock the night before, and when he awakened in the morning and found her dressed in the navy-blue linen with the white collar he called her "career-woman dress," he looked disappointed, as much by what she was wearing as the fact that she'd got up and dressed without waking him.

"Aren't you coming to the show with me?"

"You know I can't."

Ty sat up in bed and lighted a cigarette. He looked sleepy and more innocent than he should have, Kathryn thought. "They can get along without you for a day." As she walked past the bed, he caught her hand and pulled her down beside him. "At least they can get along without you better than I can."

"It's more than the office." She took his other hand, which had been toying with the buttons of her dress, in hers. "Washington isn't that far from Philadelphia, you know."

"You're wrong there." He laughed. "Baltimore isn't that far from Philadelphia, Virginia isn't that far from Philadelphia, but Washington—especially these days—is miles from Philadelphia."

"And you thoroughly disapprove—of Washington, I mean."

"I don't disapprove half as much as you think." He reached an arm around her waist. "Just because I live in Philadelphia doesn't mean I *am* Philadelphia." It was a familiar argument.

"Did you know they turned down nineteen million dollars in federal aid because it came from this administration?" she demanded.

"Mother was very proud of the fact."

Kathryn stood. "Your mother isn't unemployed."

"You're right there, though a lot of people in Philadelphia who are still hate Roosevelt. But that doesn't mean I hate him. I approve of what he did with the banks. And he's got a lot of good men working for him. All the same, he's a little hard on business, don't you think?"

"I think," she said, turning from the mirror where she'd been putting on her hat, "anyone who's a partner in a law firm that represents ninety percent of the steel and coal interests in Pennsylvania would think so."

Ty held up his hand in a gesture of surrender. His arms and chest were as deeply tanned as his face—he'd got in a lot of sailing and swimming and rowing that summer—and looking at him, Kathryn felt as if she were the one surrendering.

"Okay, Kat, I stand convicted. Now, let's forget politics and promise me you'll go to the horse show. I could only get away for two days, and I don't want to spend one of them away from you."

She crossed the room and sat on the edge of the bed again. "You know I can't, Ty. Someone will see us."

"What if someone does?"

She wanted to remind him that he'd promised Amanda they'd be discreet until after the divorce, but she hated to mention Amanda, so she merely leaned over and kissed him and said he'd better go without her.

He had gone off alone, looking a little hurt that she had refused to accompany him, and he must have left the horse show early, because

Book One

Philadelphia, 1917—1924

1

Kathryn Owen was born with the century, and in the autumn of the year they both turned seventeen and four million American boys were marching toward war. Kathryn started out on the first stage of what she had come to think of as her real life. It was to be the beginning of everything. Nothing before this counted, she told herself. But of course those past seventeen years counted a great deal.

Charlie Finney arrived early that morning to drive Kathryn and her mother out to the college in Will Owen's Maxwell. Charlie always drove for Will Owen and his family, though he wore no livery to indicate he was Mr. Owen's chauffeur. "Imagine what the boys down at City Hall would say if Mayor Owen had a driver with a uniform," he told his wife, Margaret, when she suggested it. "Why, they'd split their sides laughing." But Margaret knew, without being told, it would be no laughing matter to her husband. It would be around the wards in no time that Will Owen was putting on airs. And the one thing Will Owen was not permitted to do was put on airs. He knew that. He knew also, with a sixth sense, exactly where the line should be drawn in each case. Even in his younger days as a ward heeler he had been careful about such things. The Eighth Ward included not only that few blocks of jungle called the Neck, that same area where Will had grown up, but also the silk-stocking district, and his laws for dealing with one segment of his constituents were as carefully drawn as his rules for the other. As mayor he would no more stop one of his old cronies from calling him Sweet William—a name he'd won in his first political campaigns, less for the spell he cast over his listeners at that time than for quantities of rock candy he consumed to soothe his throat between rallies—than he would permit one of his upper-class supporters to patronize him with the name. And he would no more turn up at a ward club party in a dinner suit, though he owned one, than he would climb the steps to the Philadelphia Club. Will was familiar with the club because it, like all its members, was within his old ward, but that did not mean he would choose to enter it. His sons might, his grandsons would, but Will Owen knew the limits of his life. And so Charlie Finney would drive his daughter, Kathryn, and his wife out to Bryn Mawr College, wearing Will's old brown suit.

The college had not been Will's original choice for his daughter. He would have preferred a season, a proper Philadelphia season with teas and a coming-out ball, and though he knew he could not hope for it yet, the final seal of approval, an invitation to the Assembly, but search as he and Margaret might, they could not find a dowager to sponsor their daughter. Those in a position to put Kathryn forward for a season shuddered at the idea of presenting the daughter of a politician and a former servant girl to their friends. Those who were eager to do the mayor a good turn would not be able to carry it off. There were few things Will Owen could not arrange in his city, but it seemed a proper debut for his daughter was one of them.

Just when Will had given up hope of arranging a season for Kathryn, she came to him with the idea of Bryn Mawr.

"What makes you think you want to go to college, Katie?" he'd asked.

"Bill and Chris are going."

"It's different for your brothers." And of course it was precisely the difference that presented the difficulty. Will had planned his sons' futures with care. On the day William Jr., Bill as they called him, was born, Will put his name down for the University of Pennsylvania, and a year later, when Christopher came along, he had been duly registered for Princeton.

There were those at both schools who had been reluctant to list the offspring of a man with neither an impressive name nor a fortune, but Will's ability to maneuver people, his pure political instinct, got his sons' names recorded at the schools of his choice. And he had chosen deliberately. Bill would go to the University of Pennsylvania and its law school. He would be an educated man, but also a man rooted in the city whose politics he, like his father, would dominate. Will had never wanted to be more than the mayor of Philadelphia—it was the greatest city in the world, and he would be satisfied to be its greatest mayor—but Bill would be a senator or perhaps more. It was time there was a Philadelphian in the White House.

Christopher would go to Princeton. Though it was located in New Jersey, it was a Philadelphia school. There he would meet the sons of the old families and the newer moneyed people. Will hoped Chris would choose to study medicine. It was an old and respected Philadelphia profession. But if the boy showed no aptitude for science— Will was neither an unreasonable nor a stupid man, and he knew he could not plan every aspect of his children's lives—he might take up the law. Unlike Bill, however, he would not go into politics. Christopher would be a gentleman, and his legal practice would be beyond ethical question.

Kathryn's future proved more difficult to arrange. With a daughter it was not merely a matter of choosing the right schools and launching the right career. With a daughter it was a matter of launching the girl herself, and that, as the mother of every debutante knew, was best done at a season, but since a season had eluded him, Will was willing to consider Kathryn's request.

"Your brothers will have to do things, Katie, so college is necessary for them. But for you, why?"

"Because I want to do things too, know things and do things. Bill and Chris get to do everything, but all anyone ever says to me is, 'No, Katie, it isn't ladylike.' "

"Well, I'm not saying a girl shouldn't go to college, but it's not necessary for her to. She ought to know a little about music and art, enough to get along in polite society, but I can't see how all the rest is going to help. You don't need a college degree to preside over a tea table."

Kathryn wanted to say that she had no intention of spending the rest of her life presiding over a tea table—she wasn't sure what she planned to do instead, but that was where college entered the picture; it was a beginning, and anything might follow—but she knew that was exactly the argument that would lose the day. And she knew too exactly what would win her point. "Well, Daddy, if it's tea you're worried about, then I think I ought to go to Bryn Mawr. According to Linda Travis, every girl there has her own tea set. It's almost a requirement—like athletic bloomers."

The point was not lost on Will. He knew that few of the old Philadelphia families sent their daughters to college, but when they did, it was to Bryn Mawr, located firmly and securely on their own Main Line. Though he worried that the school, too intellectual by half for his taste, might encourage certain bluestocking tendencies in his daughter, he reasoned that it would also give her access to the circles he felt certain she must enter.

Margaret Owen would have preferred a more direct approach through one of the fashionable country day schools, just as she would have liked the boys to go to boarding school in the English manner, but there Will had drawn the line. College was one thing, private secondary schools another. To take his children out of the public high school would have been impolitic, and Will Owen was never—or almost never—impolitic.

"It doesn't do to go too far one way or another, Maggie. Now, if we didn't have any driver at all or refused to let the children go any further in life than we have, everyone would know I was only playing at being one of them. That or I was a darn fool. Like old Pennypacker. I'll never forget the laughs he gave the boys back in '03. He took a trolley from his house on Fifteenth Street and then a train to Harrisburg. He carried his own suitcases—wouldn't even let the conductor on the streetcar help him. I wonder if he let them carry his bags when he got to the governor's mansion? Well, Pennypacker went to one extreme, and Senator Penrose, smart as he is, went to the other. He thumbed his nose at the people, and it cost him. Remember the election he lost after the papers carried that picture of him coming out of a bawdy house."

"I should hope we don't have to worry about that with you, Will."

"Now, you know very well you don't, Maggie, but you do know what I mean. This is my second term as mayor, but it isn't going to be my last. Like Senator Penrose, the only office I've ever really wanted was mayor, but unlike Penrose, I won it." Will permitted himself a smile of satisfaction. It pleased him to think he had picked off the single plum that had eluded the legendary Pennsylvania political boss, the huge man—huge of body, appetite, and spirit—whose early blessing had started Will on his way to power. "And I plan to hold on to it for as long as possible. I'm going to set records in that area, make no mistake about it."

So with deliberation and a careful eye for pacing, Will had decided to enroll his daughter in college and hope for the best. Not that Will was leaving much to chance. Years ago he had begun planning for Kathryn's future. Bryn Mawr might give her options, but just to be on the safe side, Will had taken out insurance.

It was, however, the options, not her father's but her own, Kate had in mind on this bright September morning that promised one of those autumn days almost too perfect to bear. As the car crossed the Schuylkill, she looked down at the river that ran like a smooth satin ribbon between the grassy slopes. Two rowers in single sculls sent ripples along the fabric.

"Do you remember," Margaret asked, "that day your father took you down to the river to watch the rowers? For weeks after that you begged to be taken rowing."

"I was just thinking of that," Kate said. They had already moved from the tiny house in Kensington to the larger one with the big front porch in Mount Airy, but Kate didn't think she could have been more than seven. It was a Saturday morning and she was sitting alone at the kitchen table. Her mother had said she could not leave the table without finishing her breakfast, and as a result her brothers had escaped—Bill eagerly, Chris a little guiltily—without her.

"How would you like to go down to the river with me, Katie, and watch the rowing?" her father asked as he sat down at the breakfast table.

Kathryn could see the question surprised her mother, busy at the stove, as much as it did her. Katie nodded eagerly and began to attack her unwanted egg.

"What is it you have on your mind, Will? I've never known you to be one for rowing. Especially on a Saturday afternoon when the clubs in the wards are likely to be busy."

"Perhaps not, Maggie, but I know someone who is keen on rowing. Mr. Samuel Enfield won the President's Cup two years ago. You know what the President's Cup is, Katie?" She shook her head. "It's a prize they give to the man who has rowed more miles on the river than anyone else. Now, Mr. Enfield rowed somewhere over fifteen hundred miles that year." Kathryn looked confused. "I'm not much impressed by the idea either, Katie, but Mr. Enfield and his friends seem to be. And I think today we'll go take a look at those fine gentlemen in their endeavors."

"They're not going to like your going into one of their rowing clubs, Will."

"Not *one* of the clubs, Maggie. *The* club. Nothing less than the

University Barge Club for Mr. Enfield. But don't worry. I'm not going in. Just going to stroll along the river for a bit. Now, if I happen to run into Mr. Enfield while I'm strolling, I'd be awfully happy to have a few words with him. I don't imagine Mr. Enfield is eager to see me this morning, but he'll talk to me, all right."

"I don't see why you want to take Kathryn along."

Kate stayed very still.

"Well, I think Katie deserves a treat. And I don't think it would hurt Mr. Enfield to be reminded that there are good God-fearing people in this city who are trying to raise families."

"In that case, why don't you take Bill and Christopher too?"

"Because the boys are just old enough to understand, and I want to be able to speak to Mr. Enfield freely. You'll let me talk to some of the gentlemen, won't you, Katie? And say how do you do and curtsy when I tell you to?" She nodded eagerly. "Yes," Will Owen said as much to himself as his wife, "I think Katie lends just the right touch."

There was rarely a mistake in Will Owen's calculations. He and Katie arrived at the willow-shaded spot on the Schuylkill a few yards from the University Barge Club just as Samuel Enfield was emerging from it.

"Good morning, Mr. Enfield. Fine day for a row, isn't it?"

"Yes," Samuel Enfield said as Will approached. "A fine day."

"That's exactly what I said to myself when I got up this morning. And I decided to bring little Katie here down to the river so she could see one of Philadelphia's grandest and oldest sports. I'm only sorry she missed you, Mr. Enfield. You're quite a legend, you know. As I hear it, you're going to walk off with the President's Cup again this year. Didn't even give the other fellows a chance. Now, your brother, Mr. Nicholas, he doesn't row, does he?"

Though Enfield had clearly been expecting it, he stiffened a little at his brother's name. "No, my brother's passion is horses." As soon as the word "passion" was out, Samuel Enfield regretted it. "He hunts. And shows them."

Will Owen permitted himself a smile at the word "passion." "So he does. It seems to me I've read of his exploits in the paper. Excuse me, Mr. Enfield, perhaps that was a poor choice of words. But you can be sure that nothing of last night will appear in the papers. You have my word. You might extend my reassurances *and* my apologies to your brother. Of course, O'Reilly and his boys never would have raided that place if they had known your brother was there. I mentioned that to Mr. Nicholas myself when they called me down to the station house. Told him I was most surprised to find him at that particular . . . ah . . . establishment. I suggested that if he stuck to the houses that are, shall we say, acceptable in your circles, this never would have happened. I told him those places in the Neck are simply too dangerous. But Mr. Nicholas just laughed—he's got a fine sense of humor, he has—and said his tastes are—let me see, what was the word he used?—eclectic. He said he has a taste for beauty and doesn't care where he finds it or whether it's white, black, or yellow. I suggested in that case perhaps he ought to go up to New York, but he said if he did he wouldn't have me to pull him out of scrapes. As I said, quite a sense of humor your brother has. But forgive me, Mr. Enfield, I didn't mean to make light of the matter. You can be sure I gave it my personal attention. The newspaper boys were kept out until your brother left the station house by a back door. And of course there'll be no record."

They had been walking along the riverbank, and now Samuel Enfield stopped and stood looking across the Schuylkill to the peaceful landscape beyond. He thought of William Penn and his plans for "a greene countrie towne." The verdant village had become a city of noise and filth, and the good men who had settled it—or so Samuel Enfield thought, since they were, by and large, his ancestors and those of his friends—had given way to the Will Owens. "I assure you my brother and I are grateful, Owen, and if there is anything either of us can do for you . . ."

"Well, now that you mention it, Mr. Enfield, perhaps there is. It has nothing to do with last night, of course. Whatever you feel about my candidacy, my people and I will continue to treat your family with due respect. But I'm planning to run for mayor next election."

"You mean you no longer find the ward a sufficient arena for your talents."

"Now, that's kind of you to say, Mr. Enfield, and the fact is I've done about as much as I can in the ward. The way I see it, I'll be able to do more as mayor."

"I'm sure you will," Samuel Enfield said dryly. "And I'll put a check for your campaign fund in the mail Monday."

"Well, now, that's very generous of you, Mr. Enfield. And if I might ask one more thing . . ." For the first time since they had stopped walking, Samuel Enfield's eyes moved from the river to Will Owen's face. They were filled with disgust. Owen saw the disgust, but did not allow himself to return it. Will had his reasons for hating

Samuel Enfield—reasons that went back a lifetime, and beyond mere envy—but he would not permit himself to give vent to them. Will found vindication preferable to vengeance. "Financial backing is more than welcome, of course, but there are many kinds of support . . ."

"Certainly with Senator Penrose behind you, you don't need me."

"Now, that's where you're wrong, Mr. Enfield. Senator Penrose has a lot of influence, but not among your friends. Oh, there was a time when he was one of you, I'll grant you that, but his behavior has made him something of an outcast." Will hesitated just long enough for Enfield to remember his own brother's behavior. "But your position, of course, is entirely different, so you can imagine how helpful it would be to me if, when the question of mayoral candidates comes up at the Philadelphia Club or the Union League, you mentioned that you were backing me. I can assume you're behind me, can't I, Mr. Enfield? Isn't that what the check means?"

Samuel Enfield knew there was no point in arguing. Owen had the power and the good fortune to be called in last night when Nicholas Enfield had been arrested in a raid on one of the city's most scandalous whorehouses. In any event, it scarcely made a difference to Samuel Enfield if Owen were elected or one of his cronies. They were a pack of rogues, one and all. He took a deep breath. "You have my support, Owen."

"Well, that's very kind of you, Mr. Enfield. And now I won't take up any more of your time on this delightful day." Will knew not to extend his hand to shake Samuel Enfield's, and as he turned to go, he saw Nicholas Enfield walking toward them.

"Ah, Mr. Owen again." Nicholas Enfield shook Will's hand as if he hadn't seen him in some time, though they'd been together fewer than twelve hours ago. He was a large man, taller than Will Owen, heavier than his brother Samuel. His face was full and florid and his substantial abdomen protruded under a bright-colored vest. His appearance told of appetites rarely denied. "A fine day for the river, isn't it? Although not all of us embrace it as fully as my brother." Nicholas turned to Samuel Enfield. "Did you have a good row, Sam?"

"It was adequate, thank you, Nicholas." In fact, the brisk autumn sunshine and light breeze had stirred Samuel Enfield to set a new record for himself—Samuel Enfield never rowed against anyone else, only against his own expectations—but the appearance of William

Owen and now his brother, the twin culprits of last night's disgrace, had dispelled the pleasure of the morning's achievement.

"You don't row, do you, Owen?" Nicholas asked.

"I've never had time to pursue the sport. Much to my regret."

"Well, I have the time, of course," Nicholas said, "but rarely the inclination. Somehow the morning always seems better spent astride a horse than enclosed in a scull. There's a find old Arab proverb to that effect. Let's see, how does it go? 'True happiness is to be found in only two places—on the back of a horse and in the arms of a woman.'" Nicholas's smile was ebullient. He knew both men wanted him to be humble and repentant after last night, but there was no room for either sentiment in Nicholas Enfield's lexicon. He had a sense of himself as well as humor. "But of course if one is forced to stay in town, the next best thing to a good ride is a good row—or at least the sight of one."

"That's why I brought little Katie here along," Will said.

Nicholas Enfield's eyes, as sparkling as the Schuylkill in the morning sunshine, lighted on the girl. "A fine sight for a fine-looking child. She's going to be a beauty, isn't she, Owen? I can see she's Margaret Montrose's daughter all right, with that raven hair and eyes like great delft saucers. Extraordinary-looking! I'd like to paint her sometime." Both his brother and Will Owen looked startled, but Nicholas Enfield seemed to notice nothing.

"Well, Owen," Samuel Enfield said, "if you'll excuse us now . . ."

"Certainly, Mr. Enfield. It was a pleasure talking with you. And it was nice to see you too, Mr. Enfield," Will said to Nicholas. He did not permit himself the pleasure of observing that Nicholas Enfield was looking none the worse for the night before. Will Owen had achieved his end, and anything more would be gratuitous.

"Now, one more stop, Katie," Will said, lifting her into the carriage. "I want a word with Senator Penrose. You can play with Roger Atherton. He's sure to be there. Whenever the senator's in town, there's sure to be an Atherton underfoot," Will added to himself.

"I don't want to play with Roger Atherton. I hate Roger Atherton."

"Now, you know that's not true, Katie. Roger Atherton is a very nice boy. From a very good family. Unfortunately, although it may not be unfortunate for us," he said, looking at his daughter and thinking that Nicholas Enfield was right, she was sure to be a beauty, "the Athertons don't have a penny to their name these days. But a fine family all the same. And Roger's a perfectly nice boy."

"He's horrid and he does horrid things. He captures ladybugs and tears off their wings. And he said when their cat died he cut it open to see what was inside."

"He was teasing you, Katie. You mustn't believe everything little boys say to tease you. Now, I don't want to hear any more about hating Roger Atherton, and when we get to the senator's house I want you to behave yourself and be nice to Roger."

It was a final command, and Kathryn was silent in the face of it, but she knew Roger Atherton was horrid and she hated him, and nothing her father said could change that.

When they arrived at the Penrose house, they found Roger Atherton and his mother as Will had predicted. Sara Atherton was only a distant cousin of the senator's, but in a world where family connections counted for a good deal, Sara Atherton was determined to thrust her son into the senator's presence as often as possible. Her hope and Roger's only chance was that the senator, a libertine who could on rare occasions be as generous to others as he was to himself, would take Roger on and give him the opportunities his lineage demanded.

Sara Atherton greeted Will with that peculiar blend of fear and condescension she reserved for the senator's political cronies and sent the children outside to play. She didn't relish Roger's association with the Owen girl, but it was a necessary consequence of staying close to the senator.

Ten-year-old Roger was no happier with the arrangement. "What do you want to play?" he asked sullenly, ready to veto any suggestion.

Kathryn shrugged her shoulders. She didn't want to play any game with Roger Atherton.

The realization made Roger angrier. What right had she to be disdainful of him? "I bet all you know are dumb girl games anyway."

Kate wanted to tell him how completely her skill had depleted her brother Chris's marble collection, but some instinct told her silence would infuriate Roger more than argument. She shrugged her shoulders again.

"What are you so stuck up about anyway?" Roger remembered a conversation between his parents after their last visit to the senator's house. "You haven't got anything to be stuck up about, Katie Owen. Your mother's Irish trash and your father's just a thief."

The insult broke through her silent defense. "They are not," she screamed. Then, remembering the few words of this morning's conversation she'd understood: "My father's going to be mayor. Mayor of Philadelphia." She recalled the man in the vest embroidered with all the beautiful flowers. "And someday I'm going to have my picture painted."

"Ha! Why would anyone want to paint your picture?"

It was a good question, and one for which Kate had no immediate answer. She remembered the man had said something about eyes like saucers, but that didn't seem much of a reason for painting her. "Because . . . because someday I'm going to be mayor too, just like my father, and then they'll paint my picture and hang it right on Market Street."

"You can't be mayor. You're just a dumb girl. And girls can't be mayor. They can't be anything but somebody's wife."

"They can so," she said self-righteously. "They can be anything they want."

"Success?" Boise Penrose asked as soon as he and Will were alone. He enjoyed taunting the members of the world he had long ago abandoned, much as one feels the need to pick at the scab of an old wound.

"Success, Senator. A fat check—or I imagine it will be fat—and a promise of support."

"I suspect the latter rankled considerably more than the former. Well, it serves Sam Enfield right. The man oughtn't to be so pompous. Not with a brother like that. Not that I have anything against Nicholas. Not a bad egg at all. Shame he didn't stay in Paris as he wanted to. He would have fit in there."

"He's a curious bird, all right, Senator," Will said, taking a less cosmopolitan view. "And I don't mean just that business last night. Everything about him is unpredictable. Oh, he's a likable sort, I'll give you that. But when it comes to business, I'd rather deal with his brother, Samuel. He may be a cold fish, but you know where you stand with him. Predictable to a T. And manageable."

"As long as you don't try to cast his vote for him." There was a wicked light in Penrose's eye. He could be a generous man, but he was rarely a kind one.

Will laughed. The senator's barb was blunted. It was an old mistake of a very young Will Owen.

"I certainly learned my lesson that day. I'll never forget it, Senator. There we were right on Spruce Street, and old Dr. Rodman asked me how he'd voted that day, and I'd just come from the polls and told him he'd voted correctly of course, and the doctor said that was one of the nice things about living in Philadelphia, that even if he happened to be out of town during an election, he knew he could count on me to vote the correct Republican ticket. And then I got so carried away with the joke—Dr. Rodman always was an amiable fellow, God rest his soul—that I told Enfield he had voted correctly that morning too. It was only luck at that point that we hadn't voted Enfield. We'd already cast half the silk-stocking district. You know how gray-looking Samuel Enfield is, that long stringy body and that bloodless face, well, he turned crimson right there on Spruce Street. Swore if he ever caught anyone casting a vote for him, he'd see the man right into the state penitentiary. The way he was ranting, I was glad the doctor was there. In case of apoplexy."

The senator laughed. "You've come a long way, Owen."

Will Owen smiled. It did not do to let Penrose draw the point too finely. "And I plan to go a lot further, Senator."

"The important thing," Margaret Owen said, taking her eyes from the rowers on the river and fixing them squarely on her daughter, "is to take your time. Many girls will be eager to make friends with you, you being the mayor's daughter. But you must choose your friends carefully. Avoid the girls who are too eager, and by all means don't be too eager yourself. If you are, the right girls will say you're a social climber. Remember, Kathryn, the best friendships are not made the first week of school."

Kate wished her mother would be quiet. She knew her parents' expectations as well as her own dreams, but there was no point in talking about them. You spoiled everything by talking about it too much.

"And you will make the best friendships, Kathryn Margaret." Her mother always used both her names when she wanted to emphasize a point. "You are as good as any girl in this school." Margaret's confidence seemed to be dwindling as they drew closer to Bryn Mawr. "Just because your father made his own way—and his own money—it does not speak less of him. And the Montroses are not to be looked down on either. Northern Ireland and Church of England to a man. I didn't come over in steerage like that riffraff of Southwark. As Lady Fenleigh's personal maid I had a cabin of my own. A fine third-class stateroom it was." As often as Margaret told the story, she never mentioned the absence of a porthole. Her eyes misted over

for a moment, remembering the excitement of the voyage. Margaret Montrose had known the minute she saw the great hull of the *Campania* looming out of the sea in Southampton that her mistress's forthcoming marriage in the New World would mean a new life for her. Still, no matter how far one had come, it didn't do to forget where one had been. "And there's no shame in having been in service, Kathryn Margaret. You remember that, because there will be girls here, who, if they know, will try to make you forget it. Your grandmother, a fine Orangewoman if ever there was one, spent her life in service, but it never bowed her. She kept her pride bright and hard, as bright and hard as the fine noblewoman she worked for."

Margaret Owen's pride, however, bright and hard as it was, seemed to flag a little at the sight of the line of dark shining automobiles and liveried chauffeurs before Pembroke Hall. Charlie Finney could barely find a place to park the Maxwell. "Well, Katie"—he smiled his snaggle-toothed smile at her as he began to unload her suitcases—"it looks like you'll be mixing with some pretty fancy people here. Pret-ty fancy." Kathryn could barely return his smile for fear of having the other girls think Charlie Finney was her father—and her shame at the sentiment. For years Charlie had showered her with sweets, fixed her bicycles, and driven her to piano lessons and parties, and now all she could do was wish him far away.

Margaret Owen led the way to the dormitory with Kathryn at her side and Charlie Finney carrying bags at a somewhat less than servant's distance. Ashamed of her shame of a moment ago, Kate dropped back a step and let Charlie rattle on about the more impressive automobiles.

In the archway that separated the east and west wings of the dormitory, a man in livery was struggling to wrest a trunk from the most impressive of all. A small girl with dazzling white-blond hair and an imperious manner issued impatient orders. Kathryn followed her mother past the scene, and though Margaret did not appear to observe it, Kate knew she had.

"There is no rudeness," Margaret said to her daughter, once inside the dormitory, "worse than rudeness to a servant. Because there is no recourse from such rudeness. The way one treats one's lessers is the true mark of a lady or gentleman, Kathryn Margaret. Remember that, if you remember nothing else I have taught you." It was, Kate thought, a fitting farewell speech from her mother.

* * *

The first time Kathryn saw Tyson Enfield, she was sitting on the grass outside her dorm with Roger Atherton, who had come over from Camp Colt to see her. It was also the first time Kathryn had seen Roger in his second lieutenant's uniform, and she was struck by how absolutely right he looked. It wasn't the fit of the uniform, for it was not custom-tailored, much to Roger's dissatisfaction, and in fact did not fit well at all. The tunic was too large for a man of Roger's moderate height, and the jodhpurs flared too wide for his spare wiry body, but for some reason Kate did not understand, the uniform looked appropriate. Her brother Chris had been absurd in his ill-fitting enlisted man's clothes. He had joked that he was the only man he knew who did not look better in uniform. Her older brother, Bill, looked well enough in his officer's uniform. But Roger Atherton was something different. Roger was dark and smooth and sleek, and his looks had always reminded Kate of a sea otter, a cunning quick-moving sea otter, but seeing him for the first time in uniform, she thought him more menacing than that harmless animal. When he crossed the entrance hall of the dorm toward Kathryn, his boots sounded like gunshots on the bare wooden floor.

It was a soft afternoon that felt more like May than October, and after they had walked around the campus they settled under a chestnut tree in front of the dormitory. The sun was sinking behind Denbigh Hall, and in the shimmering heat haze the autumn colors contrasted with the lengthening shadows.

"It isn't as bad as I'd expected," Roger said. "Of course, all the rumors you hear are true. Half the barracks aren't finished and there aren't enough blankets or uniforms to go around, but if you're any good at all, you can live pretty decently. It's a matter of natural superiority, of knowing whom to talk to and how to talk to them."

"It seems awfully unfair—for the naturally inferior at least," Kate said.

"It's a waste of time to worry about them, Katie. Some people know how to get on, and some don't. It's as simple as that."

And Roger Atherton knew how to get on, though even Kathryn didn't know how well he knew how to get on.

When Senator Penrose had not seen fit to fulfill his family obligations as Sara Atherton saw them, Roger, then eighteen, had taken his future into his own hands. Will Owen had once mentioned to Roger that if there were ever anything he could do for him, Roger should not hesitate to ask. Roger did not hesitate. He went to the mayor's office and requested an audience.

Inside the mayor's private office Roger had seated himself in one of the two large chairs directly before Will's desk. The green carpet in front of the chairs had been worn thin by the nervously tapping feet of thousands of petitioners. Roger noticed the threadbare carpet and the portrait of Will, directly behind the man, looking a little more regal and considerably more austere, but he found neither intimidating. When he spoke, his voice was confident. He went straight to the point. "I want to study medicine, sir, but as you know, there's no money."

"I understand perfectly. For a young man without it, money can be an enormous problem. But large as it may seem, it's a problem that can be solved. It would be a crime not to solve it for a young man with your future—and background. I'm sure we can arrange something about your tuition. I expect you'll be living with your mother"—Will thought with pity and some satisfaction of the old Atherton house, now filled with a dozen boarders—"so we won't have to worry about anything more than tuition."

"That's right, sir."

"Well, then, that's simple enough. I think the best way is an account. Twice yearly I'll see that the money for the tuition is there."

Roger Atherton did not ask where the money would come from—Will Owen's pocket, Republican-party coffers, the city's treasury—nor did he inquire if there were any conditions attendant to his acceptance of it. The first question did not interest Roger; the second, if he read Will Owen correctly, and he believed he did, more than met with his approval. If Will Owen wanted Atherton blood surging through the veins of his grandchildren, Roger was willing to provide it. The combination of Kathryn Owen's dark beauty and cool independence had aroused him ever since he had been old enough, and the idea of marriage to her suited his instincts as well as his plans for the future. Without money Roger could hope for no more than the plainest and least popular girls of his own class, and he preferred the shortcomings of Kathryn Owen's birth to the more insistent ones of an undesirable and undesired wife. And with the Atherton name and connections and the career Kathryn's father could buy him, Roger would be able to overlook and, more to the point, force others to overlook the minor accident of his wife's birth.

Roger was aware that Kathryn was innocent of the tacit agreement between him and her father, and knew that it was just as well. She was cool enough as things were. Far from putting Roger off, however, Kathryn's obvious lack of affection only intrigued him. Roger

Atherton did not believe in love, an illusion of the weak, stupid, or merely foolish. A marriage of mutual concern and contentment seemed to him unspeakably boring. Marriage, like the rest of life, he was convinced, ought to be a challenge, a contest of wills, a war of desires. He did not want to win too easily, which was where Kathryn Owen came in, but he would win ultimately, which was also where Kathryn Owen came in. Roger did not doubt for a moment that he could bend her will to his and that he would enjoy doing it. He looked at her sitting beside him now. In profile her nose was sharp and her chin strong but fine. He would enjoy it immensely.

The sound of laughter broke through the afternoon stillness, and Kathryn turned to see three figures emerging from the shadows of the archway into the sunshine. Amanda Wycombe walked arm in arm with two young men.

Amanda Wycombe. The first time Kate had seen her she had been supervising the unloading of a trunk in that same archway. Kathryn had been as surprised as her mother was offended by the girl's imperiousness. In the time since then, Kate had come to know a good deal about Amanda Wycombe.

She was generally agreed to be the cutest girl in the sophomore class. "Cute" was the word people always used when they talked about Amanda. She was continually tossing blond hair so pale it had been called angel hair by more than one ardent admirer, and she had perfected a look of wide-eyed innocence that was reputed to have conquered half the senior and the entire junior class of Princeton. Whether girls liked her too, or whether they merely recognized that Amanda was the honey to which all the drones flocked, her suite, two doors down the hall from Kathryn's room, was always filled with girls and laughter and strains of the latest songs. Except during quiet hours. Amanda Wycombe was a staunch upholder of rules.

But for Kathryn, Amanda's looks and popularity rankled less than her manner. Amanda Wycombe had an air of confidence that she wore like a worldly halo. She seemed to say that whatever she did was correct merely by virtue of her doing it. Kathryn knew where Amanda's sense of sureness came from. Amanda Wycombe's manner was as indigenous to old Philadelphia and the Main Line that stretched out from it as Fish House Punch and cricket. Kate knew she might emulate some things about Amanda Wycombe and win other aspects of her world and her life for herself—indeed, she knew it was what she had been brought up to do—but she knew too that she would never *be* Amanda Wycombe. And on those frequent days when Amanda turned up at breakfast or lunch wearing a dark riding coat and jodhpurs as if they were her second skin, Kathryn hated her more than ever.

Amanda Wycombe walked now between the two young men, turning her head from one to the other and tossing her hair, fluffy under a small red cap. Her laugh was perfectly pitched. Both boys wore beautifully cut officer's tunics and looked as if they had walked directly out of a Kuppenheimer ad for custom-tailored uniforms. One was chubby, with a face like a cherub's, and absurdly rosy cheeks. The other, whose back was to Kathryn, was tall and slender. Suddenly he snatched the cap from Amanda's head. As he turned to face her, running backward a few steps with the cap held behind him, Kathryn saw his face. It was more slender and sensitive-looking than that of the officer in the Kuppenheimer ad, but had the same look of polished perfection. He was exactly the sort of boy Kate would expect to see with Amanda Wycombe.

Kathryn watched them scuffling for the cap. There was a grace and an ease, almost but not quite a laziness to his movements. They held none of Roger Atherton's aggressive quickness. His face, his manner, his movements, the deep laugh that floated toward Kate on the soft afternoon, filled her with a strange longing. She did not understand it, but she felt it as surely as a sharp pain.

Roger Atherton watched Kate looking after the three figures as they moved off across the campus. Never before had he seen that expression on her face, and now he didn't know whether he was glad he had finally seen it or angry because it had been provoked not by himself but by Tyson Enfield.

"Might as well dream of being the first lady mayor of Philadelphia, Katie."

Kathryn turned away quickly. "I don't know what you mean."

"Only that you'd better stick with me. We're a far better match than you know."

Kathryn hated Roger Atherton's assumption that they were a match at all. And she hated his sharp insistent tone and the way it mingled with the soft laughter drifting back from the distant figure Amanda Wycombe's lieutenant had become.

Christmas came with a certain fierceness that year. With all the men sure they would be going "over there" any day now, every party and ball took on a romantic intensity. The old pastels of flirtation had deepened to the brilliant hues of imminent passion. Girls chattered endlessly, in the halls as classes changed, in the dining rooms, over afternoon tea or late-night cocoa. Those from New York or Chicago or the South speculated on which men would be likely to be on which trains. Those from Philadelphia compared invitations and talked endlessly of ball gowns and tea dresses and always that one special officer who must be sent overseas carrying a perfect mental picture of their last moments together.

It seemed to Kate there was no escaping the excitement—and no sharing in it. It hung in the cold December twilight like a glittering Christmas-tree ornament, but it was an ornament that was out of reach. The tree was too tall, Kathryn Owen too insignificant. There was no mystery to the holiday that lay before her. Kate could picture Christmas day as clearly as if it had already occurred. There would be her father's family assembling with that cringing deference they reserved for the successful branch of the family.

Her Aunt Martha, who had married a dentist, would sit at her father's right and condescend to everyone at the table except Kate's parents. Her Uncle Robert, whom her father had managed to keep on the police force for some eighteen years, would be deferential. If he ever forgot to whom he owed his livelihood, the sumptuous holiday meal was a concrete reminder. Her Aunt Mary, who had been abandoned years ago by a drunken railroad worker whose name was never mentioned, would try to make herself useful by helping the girl in the kitchen and would cry over the substantial check tucked into a sensible woolen sweater or flannel wrapper. And so on through the Owen aunts, uncles, and cousins according to their success in the case of the adults and immediate promise in the case of the young people.

There'd be parties Kathryn might go to. The girls she'd attended high school with, many of whom had already married, would want to see her. But she felt that in a single semester she had moved far away from those girls. In the first months of school Kathryn had made a discovery. She had a good mind. It was not a brilliant mind, but it worked quickly and logically and occasionally even imaginatively. That Kathryn should have been slightly surprised as well as pleased by this discovery said a great deal about her upbringing. And when Professor Silva said, after a heated discussion in which he had attempted to back Kathryn into every possible corner, that she was right in her interpretation of innocence in Henry James's heroines and had argued her point well, she had been inordinately pleased. Kathryn felt herself a very different person from the girl who had entered school a few months before. She couldn't see the girl she'd become spending an afternoon with her old friends giggling over wedding photographs and layette purchases.

But there was another world Kathryn had glimpsed in this last semester. She wasn't sure she approved of it, but she knew that almost against her will she was fascinated by it. It was the world her father had in mind when he'd sent her to Bryn Mawr. Compared to talk of coming-out balls at the Merion Cricket Club, weekends at this or that country house, and theater parties in New York, Kathryn's parties loomed paltry indeed. There was no promise of romance in her immediate future, and the lack of it seemed especially bleak against the sea of expectancy surging around her. She quickened her step a little, half to drive away the dissatisfaction and envy, half because it was only five minutes to the dinner gong.

The reading room was deserted at this hour. Here and there where a desk lamp had been left on, the bulb cast a small island of brightness in the gloom that hung from the high vaulted ceiling. Kathryn stopped abruptly in the doorway. Though the room was empty, he had chosen to sit at the carrel where she had left her things. She recognized the sharp profile silhouetted against the lampshade. The collar of his uniform was open and the second lieutenant's bars glowed dully in the lamplight. He was leaning back in the chair, his long arms and legs stretched out in elegant repose. A book was propped up on the desk, and he seemed totally engrossed.

She thought of leaving her things there and coming back for them after dinner, but there was no telling how long he might stay. Besides, he had broken the unwritten rule—books and papers signified possession of a desk—and it angered her. If Kathryn cared little about regulations, she was a great believer in rights.

"Excuse me." Why was she whispering? There was no one else in the room. "Those are my things."

He lifted smoky gray eyes from the book. They combed her lazily. "We could share the desk if you like."

Kathryn reached for the book she had left, but he caught it from her and turned it over to look at the spine. His hands were large, with long slender fingers. "Machiavelli. Tell me, Miss . . ."—he flipped open the cover and glanced at her name printed carefully on the inside—"Kathryn Owen, just what is your intention in reading this? Do you plan to take over the world or merely reform it?"

"You're awfully fresh, Lieutenant—for a nice Main Line boy."

"The word is 'man,' and how do you know I'm either nice or Main Line? This uniform is designed to camouflage a multitude of sins." "And I bet you're proud of each and every one of them." He looked at her closely. "Well, if you're a reformer, you're a clever one." He pulled the chair from the next desk closer. "Why don't you sit down and tell me how you're going to straighten out the world? You've already missed dinner, and I have an hour to kill." "And you'd like me to help you torture it to death. No, thanks, Lieutenant. I can still make dinner if I run." She picked up her things and was out of the room in a few strides.

She learned who he was from his sister. Hilary Enfield was the first real friend Kathryn made at school. Kate had known the wisdom of her mother's advice instinctively and would have followed it without Margaret's warning.

Almost immediately Kathryn had realized she was an outsider at school. As the daughter of the city's mayor she enjoyed a certain fame—one might even say notoriety, given the regard in which Philadelphia politics were held by the faculty and the parents of her fellow students—but she did not belong. The girls who had gone to the right boarding or day schools would not deign to go beyond a casual classroom association, and the few girls on scholarship did not dare to. Hilary Enfield was the exception to the rule, but Hilary Enfield prided herself on being the exception to as many rules as possible.

The dorm had that familiar late-night aroma of coffee and cocoa. In the corner of Kate's room the radiator hissed, punctuating the quiet that hung over the halls. There was a light knock; then a head peered around the door. From beneath a mass of drab brown hair two small brown eyes peered out quizzically. "Friends, Romans, dormswomen, lend me your notes. If you don't, I'll flunk for sure." Hilary arranged her large awkward frame in the window seat and Kathryn pushed aside the book before her. She knew Hilary could talk for hours. Her visitor produced a package of forbidden Fatimas from her chocolate-stained flannel wrapper. She held the package out to Kathryn, who shook her head. "I know I shouldn't, but I can't resist. Even though Muffy McKendrick has turned me in once this week. That makes a grand total of three spoken and two written reprimands for the semester." She puffed away furiously. "Sometimes I wonder what I'm doing here. It's a farce. And my grades are going to show it. I only took Latin so I could translate Havelock Ellis, and

I end up with Ovid. I repeat, would somebody please tell me what I'm doing in this place."

"Didn't you want to come?" Kathryn suddenly realized that to girls like Hilary, Bryn Mawr wasn't a step up at all, it was merely a step.

"Well, sort of. It seemed the best way out. Correction, the only way out. If I were a great beauty"—she tossed the drab brown hair over one eye and struck a mock seductive pose—"I wouldn't have bothered. If I looked like Amanda Wycombe. Darn it, if I looked like you—what I wouldn't give for your cheekbones or that swanlike neck—anyway, if I looked like you or Amanda, I'd find something better to do with my time than conjugate moribund verbs. Men, for one thing. But I look like me, more's the pity. You see, I'm the mistake in the Enfield family. We've been carefully bred for generations —like cattle. The women are supposed to be beautiful, the men smart, and both of them upstanding, utterly predictable specimens of old Philadelphia. Only, something went haywire this generation. Last generation too, for that matter, but Uncle Nicholas is another story. My older brother's *wild,* as mother politely puts it, my baby sister, who incidentally looks exactly like Mae Marsh, shows every sign of outdoing her big brother, and I, I am the worst of the bunch. Not only am I outrageously *outspoken*—that's what mother called it when I used the word 'libido' in front of her two closest friends who practically run the Assembly—but I'm also a flop in the beauty department. I'm the Enfields' real two-headed calf. The outrageous *gaffe* in generations of careful breeding.

" 'Well, perhaps she's a bluestocking,' Mother reasoned, remembering 'libido' with a shudder, so the family decided to pack me off to college. I wanted to go to Barnard. I met a girl from there over the holidays, and she said they have their own canteen. There are officers around day and night—and never enough chaperons. Ah, bliss. But, of course, the family vetoed that. When they do admit New York exists, it's only to say how wicked and vulgar it is. I'm not supposed to know, but that's where Uncle Nicholas keeps his women. So Bryn Mawr it is. Mother doesn't believe in college for girls, but she thinks as long as the college is on the Main Line it can't be too bad. And that explains what I'm doing here." Hilary seemed to realize the monologue had gone on a bit, even for her. "But what about you? Don't tell me you really wanted to come."

"Sort of," Kate said defensively, aware her own enthusiasms would sound strangely out of place next to Hilary's disdain.

"But why? If I were you, I would have stayed home and had the most glorious season ever. And the wildest. With all the men going off to war, you can get away with practically anything." Hilary stopped suddenly. "Lord, what a dunce I am. That's the point, isn't it? You wouldn't have had a season."

"I'm afraid the Owens aren't on the list for the Assembly," Kate said brightly.

"If only I could give you my season. You'd make more of a hit than I am, that's for certain." Hilary was silent for a moment, contemplating the smoke rings from her third cigarette. "Well, I'll simply have to take you up. See you meet the right people and that sort of thing. We'll shock them all."

If Hilary had been watching Kathryn instead of her smoke rings, she would have seen two blue eyes grow wide and dark. "Thanks, but if it's all the same to you, I'd rather not be the scandal of the season. And I would be, you know—eating my peas off a knife and forgetting to tip my hat to the master of the hunt." Hilary looked at her in surprise. "You're wondering how I knew about tipping my hat to the master, aren't you?" Kate laughed.

"Of course I wasn't. And don't be so sensitive. I just phrased it wrong. I won't 'take you up.' We'll 'take each other up.' We'll form a mutual-assistance pact. I'll introduce you to all the Zeta Psi's and Ivy Club tigers I can. That's your first lesson. If he isn't Ivy or Colonial at Princeton or St. A's, St. Elmo's, or Zeta Psi at the University, he isn't Main Line. Oh, he may live on the Main Line, but he isn't Main Line." Hilary remembered the comment about the master of the hunt. "But of course you know all that. Anyway, I'll turn them over to you—the ones who are worth anything don't bother with me anyway—and you can find me some perfectly adorable creature who thinks I'm almost as cute as the Enfield name and fortune."

"You don't mean it, Hilary? You wouldn't really want someone to marry you for your father's money."

"Wouldn't I? The way I look at it, I'm bound to be married for money one way or another. Old Hilary may be a great old gal, but men don't marry great old gals, or haven't you noticed? They keep them around as friends, they come to them when they're having problems with someone like you or Amanda Wycombe, but they don't marry them. So what they're going to be marrying in my case is the family's money and my blue blood. Now, there are two kinds of men likely to be interested in that combination. The scion of some fine old family whose fortune has just about run out and whose blood has begun to run to water, or some eager young fellow on the way up. And maybe if I'm lucky that *arriviste* fortune-hunter won't be too bad-looking and will even have some sex-appeal—don't look so shocked, lamb. So I don't get such a terrible deal after all."

"You make it sound so grim."

"Only for two-headed calves, lamb. And you'll never have to worry about that."

Hilary took her pact seriously. In February she suggested they move into a suite that had been vacated by two juniors. One had married a second lieutenant from Michigan who swore he was to be shipped out any day now. In a fit of jealousy, her roommate, who had turned down a proposal from the same lieutenant only a month earlier, joined the Red Cross as an ambulance driver. It was more than likely she would be shipped out before the lovesick lieutenant.

Hilary was constantly introducing Kate to one or another of the hordes of young men she had grown up with. At a tea dance for officers at the Bellevue Stratford she introduced Kate to her brother Tyson.

On the train into town Hilary had been in high spirits. "It isn't as good as the Barnard canteen, but at least it's better than an afternoon in the library."

"You haven't been to the library for a week."

"That's the problem. I absolutely would have had to go today. But thank heavens I got this reprieve. I can't decide if I feel like Fort Dix, Camp Meade, or Quantico."

"Why play favorites?" Kathryn laughed. "Give them all a crack at that deadly Enfield charm."

"Easy for you to say, lamb. I've got to wage a more concerted attack. The stag line doesn't exactly flock to me."

"Oh, Hilary, you're always exaggerating about that."

"You think so? Last time I went to one of these, I spent the entire time shooting craps with a bunch of my brother's friends from the City Troop. At least I came out ahead. America's first and oldest— and most obsolete, if you ask me—volunteer cavalry troop aren't much good with the ivories. I took them to the tune of four dollars."

Later that afternoon when the dance was in full swing and fifty young ladies two-stepped around the floor with an equal number of officers and gentlemen, Kathryn found Hilary once again on the circular marble stairs. With her were three young men in uniform, but the only one Kathryn noticed was the lieutenant from the library— Amanda Wycombe's lieutenant.

"Hi, lamb. Sit down." Hilary patted the next stair up. "Maybe you'll bring me luck. It seems mine has run out."

"I think mine has just begun to change." The blond lieutenant who had stood to make room for Kathryn eyed her appreciatively.

"That's Johnny Witmer," Hilary said. "The one with the dice—and the money—is Greg Childs. And this is my brother Ty, excuse me, Lieutenant Tyson Enfield."

From under a heavy fringe of lashes the gray eyes took her in carefully. "It's the lady reformer."

"What's this?" Hilary said. "I think I missed something."

"Nothing important." Kathryn tried to make her voice as deprecating as possible.

Then Amanda Wycombe was standing at the top of the stairs with the rosy-cheeked boy Kathryn had seen last fall. "So that's where you disappeared to, Ty. Now I will give your dance to Tim." Amanda's mouth formed a perfect baby-doll pout.

"Sorry, Ty, old man." The boy beside her smiled broadly.

Out of the side of her eye Kathryn watched Tyson Enfield. For a moment she thought he was going to laugh, but the smile stopped just this side of ridicule. "Oh, come on, Mandy." He stood, and his long legs took the three steps to the landing in a single stride. "Don't break my heart that way." He held out his hand, and Amanda hesitated for only a moment before she took it and led him into the ballroom.

"And this," Hilary said as the chubby boy joined them, "is Timmy Wharton. Don't look so glum, Timmy. You've still got us."

"Count me out," Johnny Witmer said. "That is, if Miss Owen will dance with me."

"Trust beauty to break up the fun." Hilary sighed as Kathryn disappeared into the ballroom on Johnny Witmer's arm.

Lieutenant Witmer had soft brown eyes that never left Kathryn's face as he told her about flight school and training flights and life at Hazelhurst Field on Long Island. He didn't mention the war at all, just flying and what it was like. He said when he was up there he felt as if he were almost one with the machine. "I can't really explain it," he said. "It's almost as if I'm part of it and there's something about, oh, I don't know, the speed and"—Johnny Witmer dropped his eyes for a moment—"power of it all. It's not something you can talk about, but you'll see what I mean. When I get home I'll take you up. You'll understand then."

Kathryn listened to Johnny Witmer and liked his combination of shyness and pride in this wonderful thing he'd found. She liked him, but she kept thinking about Tyson Enfield. It was the next-to-last dance when he finally cut in on her. She had almost given up hoping he might.

"Hi, Bryn Mawr."

"In other words, you remember Machiavelli but not me."

"I remember you, all right. Why, I've thought of you day and night, Bryn Mawr . . ."

"The name is Kathryn Owen."

"I like Bryn Mawr better. It suits you."

"And a couple of hundred other girls."

"But you're one in a million. Now, where was I . . . oh, yes, thought of you day and night, night and day. Run off with me now and you'll send me off to war a happy man."

"I hope this is your second-rate line, Lieutenant. I'd hate to think it was the best you could do."

"You won't run off with me, then? Well, will you wait for me? Keep a light in the window and as soon as I get finished cleaning up that mess in France I'll come home to you. And if I don't come home, you can be true to my memory."

"That isn't funny."

"Hey, Bryn Mawr, don't get serious. Nothing to get serious about. I'm a hero, and heroes don't die."

Kathryn pulled herself up. He was right, of course. It didn't do to get serious. "I'll keep the light in the window, Lieutenant, morning, noon, and night."

Johnny Witmer cut in again during the last dance. "I'm shipping out next week." His words came in a rush, as if he were racing for time against the next cut-in. "Would you mind if I wrote to you? What I mean is, would you write back? I know you probably have hundreds of fellows to write to, but if you could find the time, just every once in a while . . ." Whatever power Witmer found in the air, it clearly eluded him on a dance floor.

"I don't have hundreds of fellows to write to at all, Lieutenant, and I promise to answer every letter."

But it wasn't Johnny Witmer she was thinking of two nights later as she lay in a tub gone tepid from long rumination. Nor was she mulling over the Borgias and the essay she should be writing. She was thinking of Tyson Enfield, or rather dreaming of Tyson Enfield.

Kathryn had never really shared her parents' expectations for her. As long as she could remember, she had been hearing that someday she would dance at the Assembly, but the Assembly itself held little fascination for Kate. Her romanticism had a realistic edge, and she knew the ball was only as good as the partner. Emma Bovary had her vicomte, Anna Karenina her Vronsky, but whom did Kathryn Owen have? Certainly not Roger Atherton. She thought of Johnny Witmer, but on the ground at least he was not a figure of romance. But when she remembered her dance with Tyson Enfield, the way his voice sounded soft and teasing when he called her Bryn Mawr, and the flash of excitement when he had drawn her close and she felt the rough cloth of his uniform against her skin, the elusive dream became sharp desire. She had been brought up to want Tyson Enfield's world, but what she really wanted was Tyson Enfield.

Suddenly the dream was shattered by the sound of voices on the other side of the wooden partition. Kathryn recognized Amanda Wycombe's well-modulated tones. Above the sound of water being run, teeth brushed, and hair braided for the night, Kate could hear Susan Simpson extolling the virtues of a naval ensign she had met at the tea dance.

"But where is he from, Susan?" Amanda demanded in that tone that implied a lack of interest in any answer that might be offered. "It's all very well to carry on about what a divine dancer he is, but you still haven't said where he's from."

"Nebraska."

"Oh, Susan, you are a sketch. No one's from Nebraska. At least no one who matters. If it were Wyoming he might be a rancher, or Texas might mean oil, but Nebraska. Really, Sue, you oughtn't to be so easily taken in. He's probably just some pathetic farmboy dressed up in an ensign's uniform. That's the trouble with these tea dances. They'll let anyone in. That goes for the girls as well as the men. What was Kathryn Owen doing there, anyway? That little climber. Mother says it's the war, and of course, she's right. No one seems to care who anyone is anymore."

"Apparently you still do, Amanda." Kathryn emerged from the bathing cubicle smiling, but her color was high and her eyes bright.

"I didn't know you were in there," Amanda said.

"Obviously. But it really doesn't matter, does it? I mean, it scarcely matters what you say in front of me, since I'm not the sort of person who counts. Rather like talking in front of a servant or perhaps a dumb animal."

"All I meant was . . ." Amanda's voice trailed off. It was the first time Kate had seen her embarrassed, and she was delighted, or she would have been delighted if she hadn't been so angry.

"All you meant was the climbers like me had no place at that tea dance. I'm terribly sorry you feel that way, Amanda." Kathryn flashed what she hoped was a condescending smile. "But I'm awfully glad other people don't."

"Of course other people don't," Susan Simpson said quickly. She was still thinking of Amanda's insult to her ensign. "Obviously Johnny Witmer didn't and"—did she dare make an enemy of Amanda Wycombe?—"Tyson Enfield didn't either."

2

"You're a fool to go," Hilary said, puffing furiously on her Fatima. "You don't belong there, Katie."

"Why is it everyone is so busy telling me where I do and do not belong lately?"

Hilary ignored her sarcasm. "Old Hatchet Face—"

"Miss Brockton is scarcely old, Hilary. I'm sure she's under thirty."

"Old Hatchet Face was born old, and you know it. Anyway, she'll be up there doing her imitation of Mrs. Pankhurst and urging every bluestocking in the school on to her idiot cause. I tell you, Katie, a girl, especially a girl who looks like you, ought to have one cause, and that's men. Lord knows I do my best to keep you up to it, but you're simply impossible. I know Roger Atherton called you this morning and wanted to come down. You should be spending the afternoon with him instead of Old Hatchet Face and her henchmen."

"You spend the afternoon with Roger Atherton."

"I'd love to, but unfortunately he isn't interested. You've got him all sewn up. He's bound to ask you to marry him as soon as the war's over and he finishes school."

"Perish the thought."

"What's so awful about Roger Atherton?"

"When we were little he used to pull the wings off bugs."

"I swear, Katie, you're the only person in the world who could find something like that to hold against a perfectly gorgeous creature like Roger Atherton."

"Gorgeous! He reminds me of a sea otter."

"Well, gorgeous or not, I'm sure he doesn't pull wings off bugs anymore, so that's scarcely a reason not to want to marry him."

"But can we be absolutely sure, Hil?" Kathryn, putting on her hat, smiled at her roommate's reflection in the mirror. "What if I married him and came home one day to find he'd pulled off the children's legs to see if they could walk without them? I really don't think I can take the chance."

"I wish you'd be serious for a minute."

"I am being serious. That's why I'm going this afternoon. And if you had a single principle, you'd be going with me."

"Principles! Hell's bells, lamb, you know I don't have any principles. There's nothing I won't sink to, given the chance. The unfortunate part of it is, I'm never given the chance."

"Hilary, I am not talking about sex."

"I know, lamb, you're talking about life-and-death matters."

"A soldier *was* killed."

"They're killing soldiers in France every day now, hundreds of soldiers. And just to keep the record straight, he wasn't a soldier at all, and you know it. Just a cowardly observer."

"The term, Hilary, is conscientious objector."

"Well, anyway, if all those soldiers are dying overseas, I can't see why you're getting so worked up about one old C.O. at home."

"Don't you see, they killed him because he was a C.O."

"They didn't mean to kill him."

"Oh, no, they only meant to teach him a lesson. He refused to fire a gun, so they hung him by his feet and left him out in the rain all night to teach him a lesson. He died of pneumonia, but they might as well have shot him."

"Well, if he had just fired a gun, none if it would have happened."

"Hilary, he was a Quaker, and Friends don't believe in firing guns. That's why he was assigned as a noncombatant."

"All right, lamb, suppose everything you say is true—I don't agree and I still think the boy was a coward—but even if he wasn't and even if they did kill him, what good is your standing around on the steps of the draft center with the worst girls in school—the ones that *don't* matter—going to do?"

"Maybe it will stop it from happening again."

"Oh, sure, Old Hatchet Face and her band of do-gooders are going to reform the army. You're hopeless, lamb. Absolutely hopeless."

Miss Brockton, or Old Hatchet Face as Hilary and half the campus insisted on calling her, had told them they would not be politely received, and on the train into town she reiterated her warnings. "When people are behaving badly, ladies, they rarely welcome being told just how badly they are behaving. Nevertheless, it is our duty to do so." Kathryn wished Miss Brockton sounded a little less smug and a little more concerned. "And remember, ladies, that no matter what happens, you *are* ladies."

A great deal began to happen almost immediately. As the girls, joined by the members of several Quaker meetings, arranged themselves on the steps of the induction center according to Miss Brockton's directions, and Miss Brockton, accompanied by the other leaders, mounted the steps to deliver a few rousing phrases on the civil rights of every American, including conscientious objectors and women, before presenting themselves and their petition to the federal authorities, a crowd began to gather.

"Go back to Germany where you belong," shouted one patriot.

"Hun lovers!"

"Kaiser's cowards!"

A burly man in a cap pushed one of the Friends, and when he did not respond, the man began to push harder. A large woman in a hat with bright-colored feathers began to shake Jean Baker, who was standing in front of Kate, and the small boy at her side kicked at Jean's shins.

"Do not fight back, ladies. Do not fight back." Miss Brockton's clipped tones came down the stairs, but unlike Miss Brockton, the police standing to one side did nothing to stop the burgeoning violence.

Egged on by the others, the more aggressive began to push through the first line of demonstrators. A gray-haired motherly looking woman, or rather a gray-haired woman who would have looked motherly had her face not been contorted into a mask of hatred, rushed at Kathryn and began pummeling her. "Traitor," she screamed. "Cowards and traitors, and my son in danger at the front."

Suddenly two uniformed arms were pulling the woman from her, and Kathryn looked up to see Tyson Enfield. "Now, ma'am"—his words were more gentle than his restraining hold on the woman—"that's no way to behave." The woman took one look at his uniform and backed off grudgingly. He turned to Kate. "This is bound to get ugly. Or uglier. We'd better get out of here."

"I can't run away now. This is exactly the sort of thing we're fighting against."

"That's all very well, but it seems to me you're getting the worst of the fight."

His lightheartedness infuriated her. "I can take care of myself, Lieutenant. Thank you very much."

"It didn't look that way a few minutes ago." But she still refused to budge. "Okay, Bryn Mawr, if you stay, I stay."

"Go away, Lieutenant. I don't need your protection. This isn't your fight."

"Listen, Bryn Mawr, it may interest you to know that I come from a long line of C.O.'s. There's a great-uncle somewhere who paid three hundred dollars to stay home from the Civil War. He may not have been a C.O., but no one ever called him a coward—at least not to his face. So I have as much right to this fight as you. Maybe more."

"Get out of there, soldier," one of the crowd yelled at Ty. "You don't belong with them no-good Kaiser lovers."

Tyson Enfield merely smiled and kept a firm hand on Kathryn's arm. Through her fear of the crowd and her anger at the way he turned it all into a joke, she was terribly conscious of the pressure of his fingers.

"Get out of there, soldier," the man repeated, and others took up the cry. It seemed now that all the hatred was directed at Ty.

"You're a disgrace to your uniform," the gray-haired woman shouted, and lunged at him. It was as if she had set off a charge, and the crowd began to rush them. Kathryn could feel herself being kicked and struck and Tyson Enfield's arms about her trying to shield her body with his. A large man loomed over them and his fist came between their faces. Ty's mouth was bleeding, and still the blows continued.

Gratefully, Kate saw a policeman behind Ty and felt another pulling her from him. "Come along, then. Move it along." The police pushed a path through the crowd and dragged them roughly behind. At first Kate thought they were being led to safety, but when they emerged from the crowd, the police began to push them into a wagon. Inside were several girls from school and a dozen Friends.

"If I were you, officer," Tyson Enfield said, his bloody mouth wearing the familiar smile, "I'd let the young lady go. Miss Owen is Mayor Owen's daughter."

"Sure, kid, and you're General Pershing. Get in and be quick about it."

The arresting officer was nonplussed to find that the young lady was, in fact, the mayor's daughter. And as if that were not bad enough, the soldier was not just some wiseacre doughboy who had made lieutenant, but Mr. Tyson Enfield, son of Samuel Enfield of Rittenhouse Square and Highfield Farm, that vast, unfarmlike estate out past St. David's. The information produced more than a little consternation at the station house. Mayor Owen was telephoned immediately. Mr. Samuel Enfield was not disturbed. The two young people—who should have known better, the captain agreed with the arresting officer—were left alone in a private office to await his Honor the mayor and a retribution higher than any the police force cared to mete out.

"I suppose you're going to say 'I told you so,'" Kate said.

"But I didn't. I was worried about your getting hurt, not arrested. In fact, given that crowd, this is the safest thing that could happen to us."

She noticed the *us*. "I'm sorry I got you into it."

"Don't be, Bryn Mawr. I've been in worse fights. Though I don't imagine your father's going to be too pleased."

His nonchalance infuriated as much as it fascinated her. There was something devilishly attractive about it—and decidedly immoral, in view of the circumstances.

There was a knock at the door, and a young policeman entered with a basin of water and what appeared to be first-aid materials. "The captain thought you might want someone to take a look at that lip, Mr. Enfield."

"That's very kind of the captain. If you leave those things here, I'm sure Miss Owen will be happy to take a look at it. Well, Bryn Mawr," Ty continued when the policeman had closed the door behind him, "aren't you going to nurse me back to health?"

"Don't you take anything seriously?" she demanded.

"A great deal. Right now, for example, I'm taking my lip seriously. And since I won it trying to protect you, I think the least you can do is take a look at it."

Kathryn walked to where he was sitting and looked down at him. "Well, it looks nasty, I can tell you that."

"You don't look too marvelous yourself, Bryn Mawr, with your hat knocked all out of shape and your hair undone and those smudges on your face." He reached up and rubbed her cheek.

"We were talking about your lip," she said, trying to push her hair into her hat.

"Ah, yes, my lip." He took a corner of a towel, dipped it in the basin, and handed it to her. "I think you're supposed to cleanse it first." She began to dab gingerly at the encrusted blood at the side of his mouth. "Gently, very gently, Bryn Mawr," he said, placing his hand over hers. "That's right. Now the antiseptic. After all, we don't want gangrene to set in. It wouldn't be much of a hero's death, would it?"

As she began to apply the antiseptic, he reached an arm around her waist. "You know, Bryn Mawr, you're a born nurse. I think I ought to take you to the front with me."

Then three things happened very quickly. Tyson Enfield stood, so that his face was only inches from Kathryn's. Kate stepped quickly backward. And Will Owen exploded into the room.

"Now, Katie, what is this damn-fool story about you and a bunch of conscientious objectors?"

"We were protesting the treatment of noncombatants on army bases." She echoed Miss Brockton's words, but in the face of her father's wrath, they sounded hollow.

"You were what! Talk some sense, Katie. What were you doing with that riffraff?"

"It was about that C.O. who died at Camp Colt, sir," Ty said.

Will seemed to notice him for the first time. It was not like Will Owen to storm into a room or to fail to take account of who was in it, but it was not like Kathryn to be picked up by the police, either.

"Are you Lieutenant Enfield?"

"Yes, sir."

"Samuel Enfield's boy?"

"That's right, sir."

"Well, I can't understand what you're doing here, any more than I can my own daughter. I suppose you took her to that brawl." Will was hoping the answer would be yes. Another strike against Samuel Enfield was nothing compared to Tyson Enfield's interest in Kathryn.

"More or less, sir."

"Oh, don't be so chivalrous," she said impatiently. "He didn't take

me, Daddy. I went alone. Or rather, I went with a group from school."

"I knew it! That damn school. But that doesn't explain what you were doing there, Lieutenant. I know you're not a Quaker or a bluestocking. And that uniform shows you're not a coward."

"The lieutenant was there because of me, Daddy."

Will Owen hid the pleasure he felt under sternness. "Don't tell me you dragged Lieutenant Enfield to that thing, Katie."

"She didn't drag me, sir. I was passing by, and when I saw what was going on, I stopped."

"The lieutenant was trying to get me to leave when the trouble started, so you can tell the police to let him go."

"Thank you for your permission, Katie, but the police are not the ones who concern me here. They'll let you both go, of course."

"What about the others?"

"That's up to the authorities."

"Then why aren't we up to the authorities?"

"Stop acting like a child, Katie." Will turned to Tyson Enfield and extended his hand. "I want to thank you, Lieutenant, for trying to get Katie out of that mess. I only wish she had as much sense. Of course, there'll be no record of the incident."

"No, sir, I didn't think there would be."

Will was impressed by the boy's confidence in his position. "Well, then, we might as well be on our way. I have my car, Lieutenant. Can we drop you somewhere?"

"Thank you, but I was just on my way home. It's only a short walk."

Will did not permit himself to be disappointed, though it would have been nice to have the city car drive up in front of that austere federal mansion and disgorge Samuel Enfield's son. But there would be other times, Will reassured himself.

When the police had called about Katie, his initial reaction had been alarm, but turning things over in his mind as his car raced across town, Will began to speculate on the arrest of Tyson Enfield as well. If the boy's presence were a coincidence, Will had another knot in the noose he kept ready for Samuel Enfield. If the boy were there with Kathryn, Will was prepared to forget past hatreds in the interest of future plans. To have contracted for Roger Atherton and receive Tyson Enfield was manna from heaven.

In front of the station house Ty took Kathryn's hand. "I trust you'll be more careful after this, Miss Owen. And," he added in a

lower voice, "remember that light in the window, Bryn Mawr. Morning, noon, and night, you said."

"Well, Katie," Will began when they were alone in the car, "I'm very displeased. Not about the Enfield boy, of course, but about your behavior. To begin with, men don't like bluestockings."

Kathryn would have liked to snap back that he was wrong, but in fact she had no assurance Tyson Enfield liked her at all. He was amused by her, he had been ready enough to kiss her, but she wasn't sure he liked her.

"Besides, people like the Enfields are not the sort you find getting mixed up in things like this. And I'm sure they don't approve of others who do. I can't imagine what you were thinking."

"I was thinking of that boy who died at Camp Colt."

"A boy who was unwilling to fight for his country. Tyson Enfield isn't unwilling to fight for his country. Your brothers aren't unwilling to fight for their country. But that boy was."

"He was a C.O., Daddy, a Quaker. He doesn't believe in fighting of any kind."

"He believes in taking advantage of all this country has to offer, doesn't he? For the moment, however, I'm not interested in C.O.'s. I'm interested in you and your future. You're reckless, Katie, reckless and headstrong. Today proves that. And if you're not careful, you're going to throw away everything your mother and I have worked for."

"Like Tyson Enfield, you mean." Her tone was superior, but her heart pounded in fear her father might be right. Ty had stopped when he saw her in trouble, but it was Amanda Wycombe he courted, not Kathryn Owen, and you weren't going to find Amanda Wycombe at anything faintly resembling a protest for C.O.'s.

"Tyson Enfield or any of a dozen young men like him." Will thought of Roger Atherton, but without the old satisfaction. "They want a wife who is a lady, one they can be proud of, not some ragamuffin rabble-rouser. If you could see what you look like now, your clothes disheveled and your hair falling down. Do you think someone like Tyson Enfield finds that attractive?"

Kathryn remembered the feel of Tyson Enfield's fingers as they rubbed the dirt off her cheek.

Two weeks later Hilary returned from a weekend at home with a photograph of a departing troop ship. There on the deck of the *Leviathan*—formerly the *Vaterland,* which had had the misfortune to be in an American port when war was declared—a few hundred young men stood waving jubilantly. Kathryn's eyes combed the rows of identical uniforms and found Ty's face immediately. He was standing a little to one side of the enlisted men with a group of officers. The uniforms were different, but the facial expressions were the same. *Idiots,* Kate thought. *They're all idiots. Smiling and waving as they go off to be killed.* It didn't matter who or what they were, smart or stupid, handsome or ugly, rich or poor. They all wore the same facade of blissful bravado. Kate could almost hear them singing, *"We won't be back till it's over, over there."*

Suddenly Amanda Wycombe was in the room. "I heard you have a picture of Ty."

"My, doesn't news travel fast in Pembroke Hall." Hilary took the picture from Kathryn and handed it to Amanda.

"Where is he?" Amanda demanded impatiently.

"On the left—with the officers, of course," Kate said.

"I'm surprised she didn't want to borrow it to put under her pillow," Hilary said when Amanda had left. "I tell you, that girl will stop at nothing. Amanda Wycombe got her claws into Ty back in Tuesday-afternoon dancing classes, and she isn't about to let go."

"Your brother doesn't seem too unhappy about the situation."

"Oh, Ty likes her all right. He's as dumb as any other man about that little simp. But liking Amanda Wycombe is one thing, and marrying her is something else. And make no mistake about it, lamb, marriage to my brother is what Amanda has her heart set on. Only I think it's going to be a bigger challenge than Amanda knows. Ty's funny. He'll go along playing by the rules for a while, and the family will be positively beatific—at least one of them turned out all right, they think—and then, when they least expect it, he'll go off and do something peculiar."

"You mean like shooting craps at a tea dance?" Kathryn didn't try to keep the sarcasm from her voice.

"Oh, no, that's perfectly acceptable. Drinking and that kind of thing are expected. Not for me, but for Ty. I mean really peculiar things. Like enlisting in the army."

"I don't see anything very peculiar about that. Except that it was the army. I'd have expected your brother to choose something more dashing—like the Lafayette Escadrille."

"It was the way he did it. The day after war was declared, he signed up—as an enlisted man. My dear, you can't imagine the shock —and embarrassment—of the family. Of course, Daddy started pulling strings immediately, and since Ty was a member of the City Troop, there was no problem. But it was a peculiar thing to do. Ty knew he could have been an officer right off, but he purposely chose to be an enlisted man. I still can't decide if he was trying to prove something or just wanted to shock the family. Anyway, he went quietly when they came for him, and now he's a proper second lieutenant."

"And I'm sure he'll go quietly when Amanda comes for him."

"Lord, I wish he wouldn't." Hilary was silent for a moment. "I have a marvelous idea. When Ty gets home, I'll have to keep throwing you two together. Lock you in the linen closet by accident, things like that. Why, I think I've just hatched the perfect romance."

"What you just hatched, Hilary, is a slight case of madness."

"I resent that, lamb. There is no insanity in the Enfield family. Weaknesses and eccentricities of all kinds, but no insanity."

Kathryn received only one letter from Johnny Witmer. It arrived the day the notice of his death appeared in the papers. Above the account of his heroic end in a flaming plunge to the earth and a history of his family and boyhood, there was a picture of Johnny Witmer. He was wearing an aviator's uniform, and the soft brown eyes were hidden behind goggles.

Kathryn was amazed, then horrified at how quickly her sorrow for Johnny Witmer turned to concern for Tyson Enfield. She was a fool, she told herself. Tyson Enfield had never written her a single letter. She remembered the picture of him on the *Leviathan*. He probably hadn't given her another thought after that day in the police station. Kathryn wondered if her father were right, and the possibility that he might be made her angry. She wouldn't make herself over for anyone. But even as she swore that, she knew with the same certainty she knew his hold on her that she would give up a great deal for Tyson Enfield.

The summer passed, a succession of war headlines strung together by long hot Philadelphia days. Early in June the American forces first went into battle.

GERMAN ARMIES TURN WEST TOWARD PARIS

GAIN SIX MILES, DO NOT CROSS THE MARNE

FIGHTING RAGES FIERCELY NEAR SOISSONS

The same week, Kathryn and Hilary met for lunch at Wana-maker's. Hilary said the family was leaving for Bar Harbor next week. It would be deadly dull, she insisted. "But that's why we go. It's so utterly safe. Mother figures even Daphne can't get into trouble in Bar Harbor. There's no one in Bar Harbor to get into trouble with. Although I suspect Daphne may give Mother a surprise this year. There's an adorable creature who works in the chandlery. Daf had her eye on him last summer, and this year she's just old enough to do something about it. And I don't blame her a bit. He's absolutely gorgeous, and a little of that rustic clean living goes a long way. Two and a half months without even a gramophone."

"Can't you take one up?"

"There isn't any electricity at the cottage. The whole point of Bar Harbor, Mother says, is leaving civilization behind. It would be the perfect place for an assignation, but as for summer hols with the family, I can't imagine anything deadlier."

Only when they talked briefly of the war did Hilary's brittle humor flag. "It's almost impossible to tell with all the censoring, but Daddy said he's sure Ty wasn't at Château Thierry. Lord, I hope not. He'd be just fool enough to try to play the hero."

There was some talk that year about not holding the Eighth Ward picnic, but since the war news was good, the ward leader with the approval of Mayor Owen scheduled the picnic for the third Sunday in July.

ALLIED DRIVE NETS 17,000 PRISONERS, 360 GUNS
FRENCH AND AMERICANS GAIN BELOW SOISSONS
CRUISER SAN DIEGO SUNK NEAR FIRE ISLAND

The tragic fate of the *San Diego* only served to keep the populace at home—after all, if there were U-boats off Fire Island, there must be U-boats off Atlantic City—and the ward leader congratulated himself on the biggest turnout ever.

Kathryn had not wanted to go, but Will insisted. "You've been going to the Eighth Ward picnic since you were in diapers, Katie, and you know what people will say if you don't go this year? They'll say Will Owen sent his daughter off to that fancy school and they put ideas in her head. Pacing, Katie, pacing is the thing. You can go as far as you want, but you can't go too far too fast. Remember that. Your children won't have to go to the Eighth Ward picnic. Oh, they'll be part of the Eighth Ward, all right"—he meant the silk-stocking district, and Kate knew it—"but they won't have to go to the picnic. I have to go, and as long as it's necessary for me to go, it's necessary for my family to go. Why, if I went to all the trouble of arranging a weekend pass for Chris, I'm certainly not going to leave you at home. The Owen family will make its customary appearance. I regret to say that it will be without Bill's Louise this year, but people will understand that. After all, confinement is confinement, even in this day and age."

Will was delighted with his daughter-in-law's condition. In these unsettled days it was heartening to know that another generation of Owens was on the way. Neither did he worry that the times might take their toll and deprive his still-unborn grandchild of a father. He had no doubt that his influence was sufficient to keep both his sons on this side of the Atlantic for the duration of the war. Will might be roundly opposed to conscientious objectors, but there were many ways his sons could serve their country. He had managed to have Bill assigned to the naval yard at Hog Island, and whenever the mayor made his rounds these days, his elder son, looking appropriately brave and patriotic in his naval uniform, was at his side, as he was today at the ward picnic. The two men were cut from the same cloth, down to the deceptively open faces and easygoing manners that camouflaged a canny suspicion of their fellowman. If the son was a shade less wary, it was only that his youth had been more clement. Will Owen had never spoiled his children, but neither had he seen the necessity of subjecting them to the hardships he'd been forced to endure. There was more than one way to forge strength and character in a man—or woman, Will thought, looking at his daughter, who was circling the dance pavilion in the arms of one of his constituents. She had not wanted to come, but once here, she played her role to perfection.

There were times when Will thought it was a shame Kathryn hadn't been born a boy. Not that he wasn't satisfied with Bill, but Katie would have made a fine politician. They would have had to tame her a little, teach her to hedge here and compromise there, but she had the fire and the stamina. She even had the will. Kate was always wanting to manage and remake things. Will didn't entirely approve of his daughter, but he couldn't help admiring her.

If only Christopher were more like her and less like . . . well, less like himself. Chris didn't accept things the way Bill did, or fight for them the way Katie would, and he had a tendency to question too much, to turn things inside out until they didn't make any sense at all, but Will supposed even that had its advantages. He conjured up visions of a dedicated physician discovering new cures or a scholarly judge handing down precedent-making decisions.

Margaret was at Will's side, and it was not Chris who concerned her at the moment. "Kathryn has danced with that O'Neil boy for the past three dances," she said in an undertone. "I don't like it."

"Nonsense." Will turned back to the circle surrounding him, but as he accepted homage and considered requests, he kept an eye on his daughter and the red-haired Mr. O'Neil. Will saw him bend to say something in Katie's ear and saw his daughter look up and laugh. In the light from the Japanese lanterns, the smile was too warm, the eyes too bright. Will turned from the group around him and summoned Christopher. "I wish you'd cut in on your sister."

"But she seems to be having a perfectly good time." Chris saw the look his father gave him. "Oh, I see. That's the point."

Mr. O'Neil relinquished Kathryn politely, but unwillingly.

"I don't believe it," Kate said. "My own brother doing me the honor. I haven't felt so exalted since you let me into your Do or Die Society."

"Don't get carried away. I'm here on orders. The princess was dancing too long with one of the commoners. They're worried that the dashing Mr. O'Neil may turn your head."

"Lord knows he's turned enough of them."

"But not Katie Owen's."

"Oh, I don't know. Kevin O'Neil has a sort of charm. What my roommate, who's very up on these things, incidentally, would call sex appeal."

"That's exactly what worries them. They didn't bring you up for the Kevin O'Neils of this world, you know."

"Who did they bring me up for, the Roger Athertons?"

"For one."

"Well, Kevin O'Neil may not be much, but I'll take him over Roger Atherton."

"So you're shooting higher than Roger Atherton." Chris saw his sister color and knew he'd hit the mark.

"I didn't say I was shooting higher. I just said I didn't want Roger Atherton. And if you're supposed to be saving me from the dangerous Mr. O'Neil, we'd better get off the dance floor. He's about to cut in again."

They moved to a small corner of the dance pavilion. From there they could watch the picnic drawing to a close. "Good Lord, it's like a feudal court. Look at the way they trek up to pay their respects before they leave," Chris said.

"Laugh at it all you want, Chris, boy, but just remember who gave you the right to be so superior," Bill said, joining his sister and brother. "If he weren't such a darned good politician, neither of you would be in a position to look down your noses at all this. And if either of you had any sense, you'd see there's nothing to look down your noses at. These people love Dad. Every one of them is grateful to him for something."

"That's right," Chris said. "Take old Frankie Tatum over there. He's so grateful for a lifetime of handouts that every election day he casts half a dozen votes for Dad."

"Even if you're right about that, and I'm not saying you are, Dad doesn't need Frankie Tatum's half-dozen votes anymore. He'd win every time, with the elections completely on the up and up."

"Then why does Frankie Tatum wear himself out running from polling place to polling place?"

"Because it makes him feel important to think he's done his part in helping Will Owen win, and there isn't much else Frankie Tatum's good for these days, other than casting votes."

"Now I understand. His half-dozen votes are an altruistic gesture." Chris laughed.

"Bill's right," Kathryn said. "Maybe not about Frankie Tatum and his votes, but about the rest of it. These people adore Daddy, and he's done a lot for them. Even if we don't approve of the way he's done it."

"You're darn right he has." Bill warmed to the subject. "You see that baby he's holding now? I'm sure it looks like the old political game to you, Chris, but as a matter of fact Dad has a very real reason to be proud of that baby, and the baby's mother has reason to be grateful to him. If it weren't for Dad, that baby would never have been born. His mother, the blonde hanging on Dad's every word, was trampled by a horse when she was six. I think it was the horse from one of the lumberyard wagons, but that isn't important. What is important is that she needed several operations, and Dad saw she got them, all of them. I know what you're going to say, Chris, that's charity, and charity's out of date. There ought to be laws to take care of that kind of thing. Well, you ask that blonde or anyone else here if they think Will Owen and his charity are out of date, and they'll laugh you out of here. That is, if they don't run you out first."

"As far as I'm concerned," Chris said when his brother was gone, "the sooner they run me out, the better. Oh, I know what you and Bill mean about Dad. He's done a lot—for himself, for these people, most of all for us. But that's just the point. I'm not sure I want to have all that done for me. And I know I don't want all the things he's planning to do for me. As soon as the war's over, I'm getting out, Katie. Out of Philadelphia and out of that nice world they're planning for me. And if you have any sense, you'll get out too. You're going to end up married to Roger Atherton, and that's not for you. Or worse, you're going to end up eating your heart out over someone you couldn't have, because no matter how hard you try, in this city you'll always be Katie Owen whose father was born in the Neck and whose mother came over as a servant. I mean it, Katie. Finish school and go to New York or Europe or anyplace. Just get away from Philadelphia and get away from that hopeless dream they've woven for you. And take my word for it, it is hopeless."

For Margaret Owen, lying awake later that night in the darkness of the large front bedroom, the dream was not at all hopeless. She had always believed her daughter would dance at the Assembly and mix with the very best people, as her own mother used to say. And now the dream seemed close to realization. It was all within Kathryn's reach—if only she kept her balance. But the girl could be difficult. Margaret knew that as well as her husband. They had both been delighted by the appearance of the Enfield boy—and appalled at the circumstances that surrounded it. And then there was that business tonight with Kevin O'Neil, O'Neil with his shock of red hair and a brogue as thick as the Irish mist. *How those people*—they were always "those people" to Margaret—*can keep their accents for generations is beyond me*. And as if that were not enough, Margaret thought, he was as Catholic as the pope. Try as she might, and in fact she did not try at all, Margaret Montrose could not overcome the generations of fear and loathing that had been bred into her northern Irish blood.

From the next bed Will's even breathing sounded an accompaniment to her brooding. Sleep always came easily to Will. His days were busy, his nights serene. He awakened each morning refreshed and eager, fell asleep each night instantly and deeply. The same could not be said of his wife. Margaret was black Irish in her coloring, black Irish in her brooding. The sight of Kathryn with Kevin O'Neil had filled her with foreboding. The boy was raw, but there was a power about him that many a girl would find exciting. She wondered if Kathryn were such a girl.

Margaret remembered how she'd felt at eighteen. She hadn't been one to be swept off her feet by some strutting cock of the walk. She had cared more for what a man might become than what he was, and the first night she met Will Owen at a ward social she'd gone to with one of the other servants in Lady Fenleigh's, now Mrs. Morris's, new house, she had known his future. When he had taken her out the following Sunday in a rented rig and told her his plans, not bragged about them the way some did, but told her in a calm, certain voice, she knew her intuition that first night had been correct. Will had asked her if she would come out with him again on her next afternoon off, and she had said yes. The rig cost fifty cents for a Sunday afternoon. As frugal as she was ambitious, Margaret saw to it that Will Owen proposed before the livery tariff mounted to three dollars.

If Kathryn were as practical as Margaret had been, there was no need to worry about the Kevin O'Neils of this world. But Kathryn was reckless and headstrong, and Margaret knew her daughter might throw away in a moment everything she and Will had pursued for a lifetime. The fact that it might be everything Kathryn herself wanted made it more perverse, but no less possible.

As the summer passed, the war news continued to improve, and speculation mounted.

FRENCH GAINING ADVANCE ON A 15-MILE FRONT
BRITISH STRIKE ON THE LYS, ENTER MELVILLE
CAN WIN WAR IN 1919, SAY OUR ARMY CHIEFS

"And I sit on Long Island typing orders and waging war against the mosquitoes." Chris tossed the full-page headline away in annoyance.

"Not everyone can be a hero," Kate said. "They also serve who only sit and type."

"Very funny, I'm sure. But I still feel like a slacker. There's something immoral about being in uniform and not in danger."

"Only you could draw a conclusion like that, Chris. Bill doesn't feel there's anything wrong with wearing his down to Hog Island every day. Roger Atherton takes an absolute pride in living as well as possible in his uniform. Only you seem to think that baggy tunic—and incidentally it looks worse than ever since you lost weight—

means you have to put yourself under fire. But that's the point, isn't it? Putting yourself under fire. You want to test yourself, don't you?"

"It isn't a question of testing myself," he said quickly. "It's a question of doing my part. If I'm in the army I ought to be fighting, not sitting at a desk typing orders."

Kathryn could have told Chris why he had been chosen for safety. When he had enlisted more than a year ago, he had announced to his father that he wanted no influence to be used, no undue consideration. He did not want to be an officer and he especially did not want a soft job in Philadelphia like the one his father was arranging for Bill. Will had pretended to comply. He had allowed Chris to remain an enlisted man. It was not unhelpful in the wards to have one son a doughboy while the other was an officer. He had permitted Chris to be shipped off to the wilds of Long Island. He would not, however, let him be sent to the front. Whatever his patriotic sentiments, Will Owen, like the song that had ceased to be popular the day war was declared, hadn't raised his boy to be a soldier, or at least not a fighting one.

Kathryn had overheard enough conversations between her parents to know that her father had given in up to a point only to convince his son that he had given in entirely, but she would not tell Chris that. She didn't want to see her brother off to war any more than her father did.

Kate thought of Tyson Enfield. She had been thinking of Tyson Enfield all summer, thinking of him and worrying about him, but she had not permitted herself to ask Hilary for news. Finally, Hilary's last letter had brought word. She had gone on at length about Bar Harbor and how unbearably dull it was. She and Daphne had been confined to the house after she had helped her younger sister sneak out for a meeting with the boy who worked at the chandlery. Since she hadn't had any of the fun, Hilary complained, she couldn't see why she had to share the punishment. At the end of the letter she had added, almost as an afterthought, that her brother Ty was in a base hospital in France recuperating from a wound he had received in a patrol near someplace called Roye. They had taken thirteen German prisoners. It never occurred to Hilary to add anything more about the wound. Kate pictured Tyson Enfield's classic features and elegant body maimed beyond recognition and cursed Hilary for her insensitivity.

* * *

By September the headlines were beginning to shape the peace.

AMERICANS WIPE OUT ST. MIHIEL SALIENT
TAKE 13,300 PRISONERS AND MANY GUNS
HURTLING CALLS FOR PEACE, NO CONQUESTS

But another danger had begun to threaten, a danger at once so virulent and surreptitious that the newspapers refused to record its progress. Small children, however, were less timid and skipped rope to the chant:

I had a little bird and its name was Enza.
I opened up the window and in-flu-enza.

An epidemic had flared last spring, then tapered off during the summer. Now it was building again. People walked the streets in face masks looking like grim surgeons. Every ship that arrived from Europe, South America, or the East had its complement of dead men. Hospitals overflowed. By necessity as well as choice—the hospitals were centers of infection—Louise Owen delivered her baby in an upstairs bedroom of the house in Mount Airy. William Owen III entered the world with a sharp squawk that seemed to deny there was an epidemic or a war, and at political clubhouses throughout the city the faithful removed their face masks to toast the little fellow and savor the cigars Will Owen arranged to have passed out.

In the large second-floor bedroom Will looked down at his namesake, a fat red baby with the determined face of a wizened old man who would have his way, and pronounced him a chip off the old block. From that day the third William Owen was called Chip.

A week after the baby's birth Samuel Enfield paid a visit to Mayor Owen. He was the first person to enter the office in seven days who did not congratulate Will.

"And how's the rowing these days, Mr. Enfield?" It was the only small talk Owen ever made with his old unwilling supporter.

"No time for rowing these days. The war. This cursed epidemic."

"Now, I wouldn't say epidemic, Mr. Enfield." Will Owen, like the newspaper editors, followed the official line. If they did not call it an epidemic, an epidemic did not exist.

Samuel Enfield looked down at his hands, one splayed on each knee, and Will Owen followed his gaze. They were the hands of an old man, gnarled and dotted with liver spots. He's frail, Will thought with a flash of delight. For all his rowing and riding and moderate living, he's weaker than I am. Samuel Enfield is overbred, like one of his own hounds. He can pick up the scent, provided it's the scent he's been trained to, but send him out into the woods with the mongrels and wild bitches, and he wouldn't last a minute. The Enfields need new blood.

But Samuel Enfield traced his exhaustion to a more immediate cause. "Last week, Mr. Mayor, the death rate in this city was five hundred percent above normal—and it's still climbing." He raised his eyes from his hands to Will Owen's face. "I don't know what you call that if not an epidemic."

"Now, talk like that," Will said, looking straight at Enfield—he felt no need for either evasion or reflection—"does very little good and may do a great deal of harm. We don't want a panic as well as an epidemic, do we, Mr. Enfield?"

Samuel Enfield looked at his hands again. "What we want is for the city to take a few positive measures."

"We've set up makeshift hospitals wherever possible. The trolley company has been good enough to stop production of new cars to meet the need for coffins. Face masks are required in all public places. If you have any other suggestions, Mr. Enfield, I'd be happy to hear them."

"Apparently you didn't extend the same courtesy to Dr. Stotesbury."

"Stotesbury . . . Stotesbury . . . oh, yes, young fellow who came by yesterday afternoon. Mr. Lemuel Stotesbury's boy, isn't he?"

"Dr. Stotesbury said he came to you with a special request for quarantine. The ship that came in from Brazil yesterday had thirty-five dead men on it."

"And nine hundred and sixty-five live ones."

"Most of whom are probably sick or at the least carriers of the disease."

"So Dr. Stotesbury seemed to think. I wasn't surprised to hear such a rash statement from a young fellow like Stotesbury, Mr. Enfield, but I would expect a little more sobriety from you."

"A death toll that is five hundred percent above normal is very sobering, Mr. Mayor."

"Exactly. That's why we must not quarantine this ship. I don't have to tell you what this outbreak of sickness has done to production. Between the men who are sick and the men who are afraid to go to work for fear they'll get sick, this city is barely functioning.

That's bad enough for us, but think of what it means to the country. That shipyard on Hog Island is the largest in the world. I'm sure I don't have to remind you of that, Mr. Enfield, or what it means to the war effort. Without those nine hundred and sixty-five able-bodied workers, the construction on Hog Island is going to fall even further behind."

Enfield knew it was not only the shipbuilding on Hog Island that worried Will Owen. The railroads, the mines, and the steel mills needed cheap immigrant labor, especially since the war industries had stolen their regular workers. Why would a man toil on the railroad for ten cents an hour when he could make five dollars a day in a munitions factory? So it was up to the politicians to see that the state's regular industries, the ones that would still be there in peacetime, found workers to replace those the war had stolen. Enfield understood their interests as well as Will Owen did. A good part of Samuel Enfield's practice involved representing those interests. At the moment, however, he felt the health of his city was a more pressing problem than the availability of cheap labor, but then, he could afford to feel that way. He looked down at his hands again. Samuel Enfield disliked innuendo of any kind. "To say nothing of our friends in the rest of the state."

Will was not embarrassed. "You can't win a war without coal and steel, any more than you can win it without ships, Mr. Enfield."

Samuel Enfield wanted to shout that it was not the war effort, but peacetime political support that worried Will Owen. Instead he said quietly, "We aren't helping the war effort by allowing several hundred sick men to fan out through the city and the entire state, spreading this terrible pestilence, and Dr. Stotesbury assures me they *will* spread it."

"And does Dr. Stotesbury say we're going to put an end to the epidemic—that's right, Mr. Enfield, I'll admit that's what we have on our hands—by keeping these laborers locked up in the hold of that ship for two weeks or a month? Does he blame those men for last week's death rate?"

"What Dr. Stotesbury says is that those men are bound to exacerbate the situation."

Exacerbate the situation, indeed. How could you exacerbate a plague? Will knew the figures better than Samuel Enfield. The death rate was not five hundred percent above normal last week, but five hundred and fifty percent. There wasn't a house in the city that didn't have its victim. When Will spoke, his voice was low and even. "What those men are bound to do, Mr. Enfield, is keep the economy of this city and state functioning and keep the war effort going. What those men are going to do is turn out ships and ammunition and a lot of other things for our boys overseas. And you can tell Dr. Stotesbury that I think that's just as important as not *exacerbating* the situation."

Samuel Enfield stood abruptly. "Then there's nothing more to say, Mr. Mayor."

"I'm always grateful for your advice, Mr. Enfield." But Samuel Enfield had already passed through the door into the outer office, crowded with supplicants waiting for a moment of the mayor's time. Will stood to welcome his next appointment, but he was only half listening to requests for a small park amid some tenements in one of the most notorious sections of the Neck. He was thinking that he'd tell Bill to stay away from the actual construction sites at Hog Island for a while. The boy had a habit of roaming among the workers—he said it was good practice for politicking—and Will decided to tell him to stick to his routine job in the naval office for the next few weeks. Moreover, he'd be sure to tell Margaret not to come downtown for any reason, and to keep Kathryn at home as well. And he'd reinforce the ban on visitors. There would be plenty of time to view the new baby after the weather turned and the epidemic broke.

Will's precautions for his family were comprehensive but not complete. He cursed himself for allowing Chris to be stationed at Upton. When the boy had first received his orders, Long Island seemed safe enough, but the epidemic had turned every military base into an ambush. The disease spread through the camps as easily as a fire might through the makeshift wooden barracks. As Will listened with half an ear to his petitioners, he began to think of ways to have Chris transferred to Philadelphia and a position that would allow him to live at home. With the war drawing to an end, it should not be difficult to arrange.

Chris heard the buzzing behind his ear and slapped at his neck. He looked at the palm of his hand smeared with his own blood. Still the buzzing whirred. He wondered if he were going mad. He wondered if for the rest of his life he would hear the infernal buzzing of Long Island mosquitoes. It seemed impossible that when he had arrived at camp last January the cold, damp air had been free of the sound.

He looked down the long mud street steamy in the September drizzle. He could walk for three miles and see nothing but drab wooden buildings and wet soldiers too dispirited to be angry. Morale had never been lower. Everyone knew the war was drawing to an end, and still the sergeants shouted threats on the drill field as if the men would actually get overseas, and Chris sat at his desk and typed meaningless orders.

The war would be over soon, and now he'd never know. For the rest of his life he'd worry and speculate, but he'd never be sure how he would have stood up under it.

It was Monday morning, but the weekend seemed days behind. It had been a curious weekend. Chris had got a pass, but he hadn't gone into New York or home to Philadelphia. Yaphank was an ugly little town in the middle of Long Island, but it wasn't far from the north shore and some of the most beautiful countryside in the Northeast. Chris knew it was, for the most part, a rich man's countryside— the rolling green hills were horse country, the deep coves and bays yachting territory—but he knew that even among such opulence, especially amid such opulence, he might pass a quiet end-of-summer weekend. He longed for the early-morning swim in the sound, an afternoon walk through a deep green wood. He longed to be away from the swarm of buzzing brown humanity of Camp Upton, as irritating as the swarm of buzzing insects.

He had found a house, standing clean and proud if somewhat shabby, in a small village that catered to the great estates surrounding it. Mrs. Trexler didn't usually take transient boarders, but since he was in uniform—although that wasn't always a recommendation these days, the way some of them behaved on leave, she said—and looked like a quiet young man, she agreed to give him a room for the weekend.

A tree-shaded road curved up from the village along the bay, and Chris set out on it Saturday morning. There was little traffic, and since he wasn't looking for company, he hadn't paid any attention when a red Stutz roared past him. He did take notice, however, when the car braked abruptly about twenty yards from him and began to back up. Chris recognized a man he'd known at Princeton. They had moved in different circles but had shared certain literary interests and pretensions, thrown into relief by the glaring lack of interest of the other men in their classes. A certain carefully circumscribed friendship had sprung up between them.

"I'd know that walk anywhere," Geoffrey Barker said. "What on earth are you doing around here, Owen?"

Chris was surprised at the pleasure he felt at Barker's greeting. He had thought he wanted to be alone this weekend, but the unexpected appearance of a half-friend from the past delighted him. He remembered long hours of good conversation in the local coffee shops or along the leafy paths of the Princeton campus, suddenly more immediate and vivid than the despair of Camp Upton.

"Serving Uncle Sam," Chris said. "I'm over at Upton."

"I hear it's a hellhole. The worst of the worst. Should have joined the navy, man. They've got me in Brooklyn. I get home every weekend. That's what this is, incidentally, home. And now that you're here, I can see we're going to have to entertain you."

Chris knew that before the war Geoffrey Barker would never have ventured off campus with him, let alone invited him home for the weekend.

"There's a polo match this afternoon and a bash at the Whitmores' tonight for their returning hero. You'd think he won the Croix de Guerre rather than just picked up a piece of shrapnel near Soissons. But who am I to talk?"

"Thanks anyway, Barker, but I think I'd be a little out of place." Chris indicated his enlisted man's tunic.

"Nonsense, man. We can fix you up with something to wear. You can probably fit into my flannels, and as for a dress shirt—what's your collar size? fifteen? I thought so—you can borrow one of Dad's." Geoffrey Barker looked at the thin face, sallow above the khaki uniform. "Seems to me you could use some taking care of, and believe me, the women in the family will be happy to do that. Mother loves to entertain our boys in uniform, and my sister, Alison . . . say, you're from Philadelphia, aren't you, Owen? Well, that settles it. Alison has a friend up for the weekend. Little girl from the City of Brotherly Love, and maybe I shouldn't say this, but I can tell you the girl takes that particular appellation absolutely literally. I don't know what it is this war's doing to girls, but I'm all for it. Well, what are you waiting for? Get in."

Chris followed orders, as he had been doing for the last year, and found himself in the front seat of Geoffrey Barker's Stutz speeding toward the Barker hospitality. It turned out to be as warm as promised. Mrs. Barker seemed not to notice his enlisted man's uniform, though Mr. Barker did look slightly relieved when Chris reappeared before lunch in one of his own soft shirts and his son's flannels. Apparently if Geoff chose to bring a friend home from school, even by such a circuitous route as Camp Upton, the friend was by definition acceptable.

Only his fellow guest, the girl from Philadelphia, appeared to disagree. Caroline Bullins was a thin, wiry girl with a sharp chin and a tongue to match, or so she told Chris. "I always say exactly what I think," she said after she had instructed Chris that he'd be much better-looking if he didn't wear his glasses and stood up straight. His limitations, however, did not seem to seriously deter Caroline, since she had proffered this advice in a rowboat that had been pulled up into a grove of trees at the end of the Whitmores' private beach. In the distance Chris could hear the music from the party celebrating young Whitmore's safe return, and beside him through the soft cloth of Mr. Barker's dinner coat and the thin organza of Caroline's dress he could feel the warmth of her deceptively angular body.

"I quite agree," Chris said. "Honesty is the best policy." He disliked Caroline Bullins, and her smug little statements that were meant to shock, as much as he enjoyed the almost tangible waves of feeling that emanated from her body. Once again Chris's instincts were at war with his intelligence, and the latter didn't stand a chance.

"You know, if you were really from Philadelphia," she said in her drawling, self-satisfied way, "I wouldn't be doing this."

"But I am from Philadelphia," he said absently, and moved his hand experimentally along her body.

"You know what I mean. Really from Philadelphia. If I knew you from the Saturday nights and my mother knew your mother and all that, I wouldn't be doing this." There was a mean light in her eyes, bright enough to see even in the dark shadows of the trees, and it seemed to kindle an angry fire in Chris's brain. But there was another fire in him, and it burned more fiercely.

"Then isn't it lucky," he said, sliding the soft fabric from her shoulder, "that I'm not really from Philadelphia."

The passion, if not the hunger, of Saturday night had passed, and in the steaming rain of Monday morning the words rankled. He remembered the conversation he'd had with Katie at the Eighth Ward picnic. As soon as the war was over, he'd get out, and he'd try to convince her to get out too. He thought of writing to her now, but he felt too tired. He'd felt that way ever since yesterday morning. He'd awakened with an aching head and throbbing muscles, and ascribed them both to a hangover—strange, since he hadn't thought he'd had that much drink. It must have been what he was drinking. Champagne always made you feel rotten the next morning.

Chris realized now as he stretched out on the narrow cot that it couldn't be a hangover. Not even champagne could wreak that much havoc. He heard the buzzing in his ears but felt no sting. His throat was on fire and his limbs were heavy, too heavy to lift. He'd probably caught cold on Saturday night. That's what he got for spending half the night in a damp rowboat. He thought of Caroline Bullins and her smug superiority. He hoped she'd caught cold too.

"Hey, Owen, you look like hell."

Chris opened his eyes and saw the man in the next bunk staring at him.

"You're white as a sheet and you're shaking."

Chris realized the man was right. His throat and eyes burned, but his body was ice cold.

"You better get yourself over to the hospital."

"Nothing wrong. Just a little cold." His own voice sounded strangely distant.

"Cold, nothing. You got that damn flu, and I ain't sleeping next to a man with that damn flu."

"Just a cold," Chris mumbled. "Girl in a rowboat."

"Sure you got the flu. You're talking crazy just the way they say the guys in the hospital do. When they get real sick, they start seeing things."

"Not crazy," Chris murmured. "Just tired," and he closed his eyes in exhaustion.

The man looked at the waxy face covered with a film of perspiration. "I ain't sleeping next to no one with that damn flu," he said to himself, and went off to find the sergeant. He'd get Owen out of the barracks.

An hour after Will Owen learned of his son's condition, a city ambulance was on its way to Camp Upton. Before the day was out, Chris was installed in his own room under the watchful eye of a private nurse. Louise had complained about the danger to the baby, but Will had silenced her immediately. Her room and Bill's was at the other end of the house, and there was no need for her to enter Chris's room or him to leave it. Besides, the baby was healthy. There was no reason to assume Chris or his disease would present any threat to Chip. In fact, the surprising thing about the flu was that it struck not the old or very young, but men and women in the prime of life. Will showed Louise the surgeon general's report that had been printed in *The Record*. "The husky male either made a speedy and rather rapid recovery or was likely to die. Infection, like war, kills the young, vigorous, robust adult."

The trouble, Kate thought, as she sat beside Chris's bed while the nurse had her lunch, was that Chris was neither vigorous nor robust. He had always been slender, and now his body, beneath the thin sheet that was all he could tolerate, looked frail. His condition reminded her of an incident she hadn't thought of for years. She must have been seven or eight at the time, because she remembered they had just moved from the tiny row house in town out to this big one in Mount Airy. Kate liked the house. She had her own room now, and there was a big front porch with a swing where she could sit and read, and a backyard with rosebushes. Everything about the house was wonderful except having to move into it. Kathryn had left all her friends behind and was sure she would never make another. On this particular day she was walking home from school, a frightened new girl on the block. When she saw Harry Johnson, whose name she had learned immediately because he was such a bully, and two of his friends, she had crossed to the other side of the street. They followed, and Kate knew with an awful lurch of her stomach that she was in for something terrible. Harry's henchmen grabbed her arms and held her while she screamed and kicked ineffectually at their shins, and Harry with a horrible leer had pulled her head forward and dropped a handful of worms down her back. Then they let her go and she ran home screaming.

Chris was on the front porch with his stamp book, and when he heard her story, he ran from the porch, leaving a whirlwind of unpasted stamps and an overturned bottle of glue. He returned twenty minutes later, his nose still bleeding, his shirt torn, an eye that was bound to turn ugly by morning, and a huge grin. "You won't have to worry about them anymore," he'd said.

It was shortly after that incident that Chris let her into his Do or Die Society. Actually it wasn't much of a society, since Chris was its only member, but in the adoring eyes of his younger sister that made it only more exclusive. Potential members were those who through a sense of honor and loyalty would stand up for each other no matter what the danger. They would, simply, do or die. Nonmembers were the cruel, who teased or bullied, the cowardly, who tattled, and the merely unsuitable, who had shown a lack of understanding of these higher principles valued by Chris and now his little sister, Kathryn. Bill was a nonmember, as was Roger Atherton. In fact, in the entire history of the Do or Die Society, the permanent membership had never grown beyond Chris and Kathryn. For almost a year there had been a boy named Brian in Chris's class at school, but when Brian had turned tail and run in the face of an onslaught by two older boys whom Chris had refused to back down to, Brian was stripped of his membership. There was a neighborhood girl, a year older, whom Katie had very much admired but her pending membership was blackballed after she admitted to her mother that yes, she was responsible for the snow that had been placed in Mrs. Cole's milk bottles, but she had been incited to the act by Kathryn Owen, who had been stuffing milk bottles with snow for years. And so the membership of the Do or Die Society had fared over the years. Sometimes Kate found herself still judging people in terms of its standards. When she first met Tyson Enfield, she had wondered about him, but after that day at the demonstration, she was sure. Tyson Enfield definitely ranked as a potential member of the Do or Die Society.

The sound of Chris's voice, low and incoherent, called Kate back to the present. His fever had climbed to 104 degrees last night, and for the last twelve hours he had been hallucinating. Kate couldn't understand most of what he was saying, but he seemed to be insisting on the fact that he really was from Philadelphia. A curious obsession, she thought.

The doctor called regularly each afternoon, but there was little he could do. "We're not sure what causes it, and we don't have a cure for it," he told Will. "The only thing I can prescribe is good nursing care, a light diet, and plenty of liquids. And don't let him out of bed. Influenza weakens. We've had cases where patients have died from turning over to let the doctor use a stethoscope on their back." Kathryn remembered the doctor's words and wished Chris would stop tossing and turning.

She took her eyes from Chris's face and looked around the familiar room. There were few signs of the man Christopher Owen had become. Only the books in a small case under the window had changed since he'd left for Princeton four years ago. Now slim volumes of Rupert Brooke and Wilfred Owen sat next to a high-school yearbook and a boy's illustrated edition of Kipling. "The trouble with this war," Chris had told her once when she had chided him for being as bloodthirsty as all the others in his eagerness to get overseas, "is that it's being fought by a generation that was raised on Kipling. Including me."

On the next day, the fifth since Chris had returned home, his fever broke. The doctor predicted a speedy recovery, and dinner that night was a restrained celebration. It was too soon for real rejoicing, but there was no mistaking the air of relief that permeated the room as surely as the aroma of roast meat.

When Louise brought the baby down later that night after his nine-o'clock feeding, Will took him from her. "You see, Louise," he said, looking down at the small thing in his arms, "there was no reason for worry. Chris is going to pull through, and little Chip here is fit as ever."

Louise took the baby from him quickly. Will's words seemed a needless tempting of fate.

The next day Louise was too tired to rise from her bed. Chip was put on a formula, and the private nurse was busy shuttling between Chris's room and Louise's. On the following day Chris's temperature returned to normal and Louise's soared to 103. Bill was relieved that his wife remained lucid—he didn't think he'd be able to take it if she began to rant and rave as Chris had—but he shuddered at the blue tinge that crept across her lips. It gave her pale face the look of a death mask. Little Chip cried constantly for his mother.

The following day Chris was permitted to come down for dinner. The nurse interrupted the meal by calling Bill to his wife's room. Louise was dead.

Chip's tiny fist pushed the bottle of formula away, and for weeks after that his cries echoed through the Owen household. Chris, recuperated but not yet returned to base, heard them as clearly as his own conscience.

In the street the neighbors waved flags, and on the front porch the fragment of black crepe on the door contrasted cruelly with the red-white-and-blue bunting. It was Armistice Day.

Kathryn watched her brothers at the window. When they turned back to the room, the look in both their eyes sent pain surging through her. Kate looked at Bill and knew he would never forgive Chris, but she looked at Chris and knew he would never forgive himself—for the child he had orphaned, for the war he had never fought.

3

By May the pandemic, as it had come to be called during its last outbreak in March, was a horrible memory, the war over—though the peace was still being fought—and life back to normal. Or back to abnormal, more than one preacher lamented. It was time the young people who had fought the war settled down to the peace, they said, but a songwriter wondered how you'd keep them down on the farm after they'd seen Paree, and thousands of veterans agreed.

It was Hilary's favorite lyric. "It's so trashy," she said. "And it drives Mother and Daddy absolutely wild. You can tell it's exactly what they're thinking about Ty."

Lieutenant Tyson Enfield had returned from France handsomely and elegantly intact. The first time Kathryn had seen him, he was sitting in a Marmon with Amanda Wycombe. *I should have known nothing could happen to him,* Kate thought.

"And they ought to worry," Hilary continued. "He's going to the devil in a barrel. He got off the ship with a bedroll stuffed with a dozen bottles of French cognac. He told me he'd already drunk one bedroll full, but he won the second one playing poker. He said that's all they did all the way home. Play poker and drink. He won five hundred dollars—besides the cognac. But that's the least of it. The army sent him to some swell hotel in Cannes to convalesce, and did he ever raise hell. Mother almost died when she heard he'd taken Elsie Janis to dinner one night. 'But she's an *actress,*' she said in that awful voice that told exactly what she thought of actresses. But that's nothing. It wasn't the stories Ty told, but the ones he wouldn't tell. I heard him talking to Uncle Nicholas in the library one day so I just skulked around in the hall for a while."

"You mean you eavesdropped."

"Listen, lamb, given the family, if I didn't eavesdrop I'd never hear anything of matters sexual. Anyway, according to Ty, the Riviera was just crawling with Red Cross girls. He told Uncle Nicholas the parties were *in-credible.* One night he ended up with two Red Crosses—one was a nurse and the other an ambulance driver—and, well, the rest of the story would curl Havelock Ellis's hair." Hilary had flunked Latin, as expected, but she was deep in psychology.

"I would have given anything to have signed on as an ambulance driver. If only I'd been a couple of years older. But of course I couldn't even lie about my age. The whole darned Red Cross recruiting team knows Mother. The opportunity of a lifetime, and it passed me by."

"Well, cheer up. The troops are home. Maybe you'll get another crack at decadence."

"In Philadelphia? Don't make me laugh."

On a Friday afternoon in May Kathryn got her own chance to welcome the conquering hero. It never would have happened if Amanda Wycombe in another of her attempts to make Ty jealous had not stood him up. He had been an hour late getting out to the campus, and Amanda had gone off with a Princeton senior whose lack of a war record was compensated for by a substantial reputation as a football hero. Kathryn didn't learn any of that until the following Monday.

It was about four o'clock when Kate set out for the railroad station. As she was crossing Montgomery Avenue she heard an automobile purring along beside her.

"Hi, Bryn Mawr. Want a lift?"

She knew who it was before she turned and saw Tyson Enfield behind the steering wheel of the sleek Marmon. Hilary had said the family never would have bought him such a flashy car if he hadn't been wounded. Kathryn was not sure what reasoning connected a new Marmon with being wounded on an army patrol, but the Enfields appeared to have a logic of their own.

"We're not supposed to hitch."

"I won't tell if you don't." He reached over and opened the door. "Come on, get in."

The upholstery was soft, and the wood of the dashboard glistened in the late-afternoon sun. She felt Ty's eyes on her as he raced the engine.

"You look different, Bryn Mawr."

She let her eyes meet his for the first time. "So do you." He hadn't returned quite as elegantly intact as she had thought. His face was thinner and he looked older.

"I'm supposed to. *C'est la guerre*. But you look really different." He was still staring at her. "It's your hair. What did you do to your hair?"

"Just what everyone is doing. I bobbed it."

"Good Lord! A man goes off to war, risks his life for his country and womenfolk, and what do they do? Shear their heads."

Kathryn wondered what he had said when he first saw Amanda's hair. The car was moving now, and as he took his hand from the gearshift, he reached over and ruffled her hair. "Don't worry, Bryn Mawr. It'll grow in.

"Where are you headed?" he called above the noise of the wind and the engine.

"Home. For the weekend."

"Well, if you're not in a hurry, I'm headed for the University. There's a party at St. Anthony's. Feel like a fraternity party?"

"I've never been to St. Anthony's," she said, almost as a challenge. If he were going to cross lines, he'd better be aware of it.

"Then it's about time you went there, isn't it?" He reached over and brushed her shoulder lightly, and she looked at him questioningly. "Without the chip on your shoulder. I hate dancing with girls with chips on their shoulders. They never can follow properly."

The stone terrace of St. Anthony's was crowded with men and girls. What had begun as a tea dance had turned into a Friday free-for-all, and even the young husband and wife who served as chaperons looked a little the worse for wear—and whiskey. From somewhere inside a gramophone blared "Hindustan."

Kathryn recognized two men Hilary had introduced her to, and several other faces looked vaguely familiar. She had seen them around her own campus, though she didn't know them by name. Most of the men she knew from the University belonged to less-exclusive clubs. Ty parked the Marmon on a small patch of grass next to the house. Then he was introducing her to people and his hand was in hers as if he thought it belonged there. "Drink and dance," he shouted down at her above the noise. "That's what we need." He handed her a glass of punch. It was heavily laced with whiskey, and she tried to stifle a grimace.

Ty laughed. "I see my sister hasn't corrupted you entirely." He was holding the glass in one hand, and the other arm was around her waist, and they were moving around the room in time to the music. Other couples kept jostling them, and there was a good deal of noisy conversation. Ty seemed to know everyone. A short wiry man called him a crasher and told him to go back to Princeton. The girl he was dancing with looked Kathryn up and down coldly. "Where's Amanda, Ty?"

Ty laughed and shrugged his shoulders. "Beats me."

Kathryn recognized the chubby boy with the pink cheeks standing behind Ty. "Can I steal your girl for a dance, Ty?"

"Only if you promise to take good care of her."

He said his name was Tim Wharton, and she said she remembered it from the tea dance before the war, but she hadn't remembered his name at all, only the fact that he had tried to steal Ty's dance with Amanda Wycombe and hadn't succeeded. His weight was deceptive, and he moved lightly about the floor. Another man cut in on her, and then several others. Ty let them have their turns until the music slowed and someone turned down the lights.

He had left the glass behind this time, and he was holding her closer. He danced her through the door to the terrace. In the gathering dusk couples moved in time to the music or sat on the low stone wall. The gramophone played more softly now, and the conversation was quieter, except for an occasional outburst of laughter.

When the dance came to an end Ty held her for a moment. Her head came just to his chin, and his mouth was pressed against her forehead. She shivered. "Cold, Bryn Mawr?" She shook her head, but he put an arm around her shoulders anyway.

Somewhere around midnight Tim Wharton decided sandwiches were in order. Someone suggested a roadhouse out beyond Manayunk, and a caravan of automobiles was snaking its way north through the quiet Philadelphia streets. Tim Wharton had folded himself into the rear seat and was serenading them with a ukulele.

The knowledge that when she returned to school Monday morning she would have to report herself for the trip to the forbidden roadhouse did nothing to dampen Kate's spirits. Monday morning was a lifetime away.

Ty seemed to be reading her mind. "Say, I just thought of something. You're not allowed in there, are you?"

"That's right," Tim said. "The old sacred seven." And he began to strum the restaurants where young ladies of Bryn Mawr were permitted to dine unchaperoned. Every college man in the area knew them. "Cheri's, Ferriston's, the Green Dragon," he sang.

"It's okay," Kate said. "I need a few reprimands. My record's embarrassingly pristine this semester." She hoped it sounded as if her record had not been so other semesters.

"Won't hear of it," Ty said.

"Won't hear of it," Tim echoed. "We'll go back to town." He leaned forward, his curly blond head against hers, and began to strum again. "Cheri's, Ferriston's . . ."

"Got a better idea," Ty said. "We'll picnic. Wharton here, sterling soul that he is, is going to serve us dinner *al fresco*."

When they got to the roadhouse, Tim climbed out of the rumble seat and walked, a little unsteadily, Kathryn noticed, to the restaurant. "I'd go with you, old man," Ty called after him, "but we can't leave the lady unattended."

In ten minutes Tim emerged from the roadhouse carrying a large bag. The rest of the party marched behind him with similar bags, except for one man who carried a platter with a chicken on it. He placed it on the hood of the car next to them with a flourish. "Need a tablecloth," he announced, and then everyone was producing lap robes from various cars and spreading food out across hoods and rumble seats. Someone had a bottle of bourbon and someone else a bottle of rye, and Ty seemed to remember there was a bottle of cognac someplace in the car, and it turned out that Tim had been sitting on it, but it was none the worse for wear.

There was a great deal of noisy conversation and much exchanging of food and drink, and the wiry young man from the next car shouted that it was the best party ever and everyone agreed. The girl beside him, the one with the mean eyes, looked directly at Kathryn. "Yes, isn't it a shame Amanda had to miss it?"

Kathryn, drunk more on Ty than the cognac, returned the girl's gaze. "Yes, isn't it a shame? Mandy would have loved it."

Ty seemed to choke a little on the cognac, and then he began to laugh as if Kate had said something very funny.

By the time they started back, Tim Wharton had drifted off to grace someone else's rumble seat. Kathryn was keenly aware of his absence. As the car raced through the spring night, she felt very much alone with Tyson Enfield. They said little on the drive back, and when they turned off the main road she directed him the last blocks to her house. The street was dark, but a light had been left on over the porch and another in the front hall.

"They sure do keep the candle burning for you, don't they, Bryn Mawr?" And then, as if it were the most natural thing in the world, he leaned over and kissed her. His mouth was soft and tasted faintly of cognac. She was aware of his arms around her, and then, without meaning to, her own were about his neck and she was kissing him back.

When he released her, she saw he was smiling.

"I'd better go in," she said quickly. She watched him get out of the car and stroll around to open her door. As they walked up the path, Kathryn thought she saw a shadow move behind the parlor window.

"It was a real party, Bryn Mawr. Thanks for the company." And then he was down the porch stairs and into the car in a few strides. As she stood alone in the front hall she heard the engine start up, then grow fainter as he headed down the street back toward the Main Line.

Kathryn was in her nightgown when she heard her mother knock softly on the door. She had been expecting her.

"You went to a party with Tyson Enfield." Margaret could scarcely keep the excitement from her voice. Her mind had been racing ever since Kathryn had called to say she'd be late, racing and praying that this time her daughter's behavior would prove more acceptable. According to Margaret's lights, it had not.

Margaret walked to the window and stood looking out at the street where the car had been only minutes before. When she finally spoke, her voice was stern. "You learn a great many things in service, Kathryn Margaret. You learn, for example, that young gentlemen, and often those who are not so young, will take their pleasure"— Margaret pronounced the word carefully—"where they are permitted to." She heard Kathryn begin to speak. "Don't tell me times have changed since the war. Some things never change." Margaret turned from the window to face her daughter, and Kate was shocked by the intensity of her expression. "Don't ruin it now, Kathryn! For the love of God, don't ruin it now!"

* * *

The next time Kate saw Tyson Enfield he was leaning against the Marmon that had been pulled into the archway between the dorms, talking to Ann Sommers. Ann had been engaged to an enlisted man from St. Louis who had been killed in the Argonne. She was not the only one on campus to have felt the war's impact so directly, but she attracted more sympathy because hers had not been a wartime engagement. Ann and her fiancé had grown up together and known from the time they were fifteen that they would marry.

When Ty saw Kathryn he raised his hand in a casual wave. Kate, coming from the gym, was suddenly conscious of her bloomers and middy. She waved back but kept walking toward the dorm.

"Hey, Bryn Mawr," he called. "Aren't you going to come over and say hello?"

She approached reluctantly.

"I'd better be going," Ann Sommers said. "This essay isn't going to write itself."

"Remember, Ann, if you need . . ." Ty hesitated for a moment. "Oh, I don't know, a lift, anything, let me know." When Ann was gone he turned back to Kathryn.

"How about a ride, Bryn Mawr? I need company." His tone was not as light as it should have been. She wondered if this time Amanda had succeeded in annoying him.

"Thanks, but I'm not allowed off campus in these."

He looked her up and down slowly. "I don't see why not, but I'll wait while you change." It was more order than request. Ty's customary arrogance was verging on surliness today.

She was into her blue skirt and a pale spring shirtwaist in minutes. When she emerged from the dorm he was sitting in the car waiting for her. He leaned over and opened the door from the inside. "You're faster than most girls, Bryn Mawr. I'll give you that."

She thought of that night in front of her house and wondered if he were making fun of her.

Ty started the car abruptly, and they were heading out beyond the school through the rolling green countryside. He was driving much too fast for the narrow dirt road, and his face in profile looked angry. He seemed to have forgotten she was beside him. After several minutes Kathryn broke the silence. "You're awfully quiet for someone who needed company."

"I said I needed company, Bryn Mawr. I didn't say I'd be good company."

"Maybe you should have told me that before."

"Do you want me to take you back?"

She didn't want to go back at all, but his arrogance inflamed her pride. "Yes."

He was silent for a while, but he didn't turn the car around. "Look, Bryn Mawr, I'm sorry. It has nothing to do with you. I just seem to be in a rotten mood today."

She looked at his profile again and saw the pain there as well as the anger. "Ann Sommers's fiancé?"

"He was in my company. Last time I saw him they were taking me to the hospital. He was laughing and saying with any luck he'd be with me soon. Instead a German bayonet got him in the stomach. By the time they got him to a hospital, he didn't need one."

"Neither did Johnny Witmer."

"Or Jim Savage or . . ." And he listed half a dozen names in a voice that didn't sound at all like his own. It was sharp with rage, impotent, undirected rage.

The old childhood test came to mind. Tyson Enfield was a Do or Dier all right. Kathryn was sure Chris would agree.

"I'm sorry," she said. It seemed an inadequate response to his outburst.

"Forget it. Doesn't do any good to talk about it. That's what's wrong with the world. Too many old boys sitting around jawing about the war. Too many people living in the past. All I care about is the present."

"*Carpe diem.*"

"I keep forgetting you're all such darned intellectuals. That's right, seize the day and wring the living daylights out of it."

"And what about tomorrow?"

He looked at her for the first time since they had left school, and his eyes were not especially kind. "One of the nice things about being a man, Bryn Mawr, is that you don't have to worry about tomorrow. There are always plenty of women doing that for you."

"If only I were a man," Hilary said. She had scraped through exams for another year, and she and Kathryn were packing for the summer. "Ty gets away with murder. Just wait and see. I give him about one week in Bar Harbor before he comes up with an invitation to Newport or Long Island. Mother will protest, of course, but he'll mention the war—ever so casually—and that'll be the last we see of Ty for the summer. And I'll be stuck for another two months in no-man's land.

"He lost the big battle, though. They're going to make him finish school. Ty said he had no intention of going back for his last year. Said going back to Princeton after the war would be like going back to St. Paul's after Princeton. You can imagine the row. I have to give Ty credit. He pulled out all stops. Said after he's spent six months in the trenches up to his knees in water and rats and lice, ugh, never knowing where or when the next German was going to turn up, he had a right to decide what he wanted to do with his life. Mother said the fact that he wasn't considering her wishes or anyone else's showed he hadn't any right at all, that he was still a child. Of course, Daddy was more practical. He said Ty couldn't possibly be a lawyer unless he got his degree first. Well, the lid really came off then. Ty said he'd never wanted to be a lawyer. *They* wanted him to be a lawyer. Mother got really angry at that one, but Daddy was the one who outsmarted Ty. He said Ty could have the rest of this year to do whatever he wanted—and you know what that's been—but by next fall he'd better have some idea of what he wanted to do, not just what he didn't want to do. I don't think Ty knows it yet, but he's going back to Princeton in the fall."

That first summer after the war, there was little peace in the Owen house. Bill did not wear a widower's mantle well. Louise had been dead for almost a year, and he felt the restless stirrings of a single man. He was only twenty-five, but he was also a father and a widower, and Will Owen, ever aware of propriety, insisted that he behave as such.

Twice that summer Will permitted his son a weekend in New York. Like many others in the city he governed, Will regarded New York as the safety valve that kept the machinery of a good many Philadelphia gentlemen functioning properly. And he could rely on Bill to see the wisdom of such an arrangement. The same could not be said for Christopher. Will Owen's younger son seemed to him particularly intransigent these days. He had turned down a minor position with the city to work for a newspaper.

"What I can't understand," Will said pointedly across the dinner table, "is how any self-respecting man can take a job where he's called boy."

Chris smiled down at his plate. "It's just a term, Dad. Copyboy. It doesn't mean anything."

"It means something. Titles always mean something, at least to the people who use them. I suppose you think it's exciting." Will started on another tack. "Big city room . . . All the news firsthand."

Chris wouldn't admit to his father just how exciting he did find the city room of the *Ledger*. It had a pace and feel of its own, and both suited Chris. In the early morning when most of the reporters were out on stories, it was a great cool vault, a haven from the hot city beyond. Here and there a typewriter sounded a single plaint, but there were few calls and Chris could lounge on the long bench in the center of the room and read or talk to the other copyboys. As the day progressed, the pace quickened. The typewriters played a symphony now to the accompaniment of constantly ringing telephones, and cries of "boy" came from every corner of the room. It was no longer a cool oasis, and as Chris and the other copyboys raced the stories along their assigned routes from editor to editor, the heat mounted and the smoke hung heavy in the humid afternoon air.

By five-thirty the entire city room, all forty-two men, were working at a frenzied but carefully orchestrated pitch. There were no wasted movements, no wrong steps. At six a bell sounded and everything stopped as suddenly as if someone had pulled the cord from an electric socket. A few minutes later the copyboys carried up the stacks of freshly printed papers, the acrid-smelling products of the day's toil, bearing news from all over the world. The peace treaty had been signed in the Hall of Mirrors at Versailles, a cat had walked from Chicago to Philadelphia to return to the home its masters had abandoned, four war aces accompanied by an equal number of Philadelphia's most attractive young ladies had staged an airborne fox hunt.

"Well, it may look as if you've got your finger on the pulse of things in that city room," Will continued, "but I can tell you nobody knows less about what's going on in this city, or any other for that matter, than the newsmen. Even when they think they've got a scoop, it's only the scoop we've decided to give them."

The point had been argued often enough for Chris to know debate was pointless. "You may be right, Dad, but I like it on the paper anyway."

"Well, I don't suppose it can do you much harm as long as it's only for the summer. At least you'll get to know the city. And the experience won't hurt you when you go back to Princeton."

Chris was familiar with this argument too, and until now there had been no reason to contradict his father, but now his plans were made, it was time to speak. He had lined up a job on the New York

Herald. It was barely a cut above copyboy. He'd be sorting letters to the editor and covering ladies' luncheons, but it was a beginning and, more important, it was an escape.

"I'm not going back to Princeton."

Chris remembered an article that had appeared in the paper the day after the armistice. "Here among the troops of the Rainbow Division there was no loud rejoicing, no songs, no cries of celebration. There was only silence. A thundering silence after the months and years of endless gunfire." Perhaps it was blasphemy to make the comparison, but that was the way the silence at the Owen dinner table sounded now.

"I don't think I heard you correctly, Christopher." Will's voice was even.

"I said I'm not going back to Princeton in the fall. There's no point."

"Are you telling me there's no point to a college diploma, a Princeton college diploma? In this town?"

"Well, that's the other part of it, Dad. I'm not staying in Philadelphia either. I've got a job lined up on the New York *Herald.* I start in September."

"You start Princeton in September."

"I'm sorry, Dad, but I start on the *Herald* in September. It's all arranged."

Arranged. The very word rankled Will. What did this boy know of arrangements? It had taken Will Owen a lifetime to arrange his family. It had taken him a lifetime to see their futures were properly planned, and now this ungrateful boy wanted to throw it all away, wanted to run off to a city where he was no one, to a job where he'd never amount to anything. It was something Will could not permit.

"Just like all the young men today. You think the mere fact of having been in the service gives you the right to do anything you please."

"Not anything I please, just the right to run my own life."

"Run it right into the ground."

"Maybe, but it'll be my funeral if I do."

"*Your* funeral. You speak as if you're not a member of this family, as if everything you did did not reflect on us."

Chris was smiling. For once he knew his father was impotent. He had made his plans, and no amount of threatening or cajoling would change them. "I wouldn't worry too much about that, Dad. Whatever mistakes I make, I'll be making them in New York, and I don't imagine that will embarrass you too much."

"But all your plans, Christopher." Margaret Owen spoke for the first time. "You were going to do important things, be an important person, a physician, an attorney."

"I'm sorry, Mother, but those were your plans, yours and Dad's, not mine." Listening to the argument, Kathryn remembered Hilary's report of a similar battle between Ty and his parents, but she could not believe her brother would yield so easily.

"Plans made in your interest," Will said.

"I know they were." There was no rancor in Chris's voice, only sadness. "But they weren't my plans. I don't want to be a doctor or a lawyer, and I don't want to live in Philadelphia." This last was blasphemy to Will Owen. "You've fought it all your life so that we could join it," Chris said, "but I don't want to join it, and I don't want to fight it. I just want to live my own life someplace where the Philadelphia Club and the Assembly and the Cadwaladers and Biddles and Enfields don't matter."

"Wherever you go, things like that and people like that will matter."

"Maybe, but not as much as they do in Philadelphia."

For once father and son were in agreement. That was precisely what made the city different. It was a difference Will Owen had pursued all his life, but one Christopher Owen was determined to escape.

Kathryn returned to school that year with a feeling of vague unrest. Chris's departure had discomfited her. "Remember what I said, Katie," he'd told her when she'd stood with him on the station platform waiting for the New York train. He was wearing a blue suit he'd bought before he'd left Princeton, and a straw hat, but even in the familiar clothes he looked strangely foreign, as if he'd already moved away. "Finish school and get out. It's the only way."

Waving from the train platform as it pulled out of the station, Chris looked happier than she'd ever seen him, but as she walked alone through the waiting room—both Will and Margaret had refused to put their seal of approval on Chris's departure by seeing him off—Kathryn felt only despondency. The emotion lingered through her return to school, and this time Hilary was no help, for the Hilary who returned to school was not the girl Kathryn had said good-bye to three months before. Hilary was in love.

She had discovered Carter Branch last June at Bar Harbor, or rather rediscovered him. Carter's mother was Mrs. Enfield's fourth cousin, and Hilary and Carter had met once as children. More to the point, as far as Mrs. Enfield was concerned, Mrs. Branch was a Charleston Middleton—one of the poor Middletons, but a Middleton nevertheless. Mrs. Enfield respected Middleton blood in others almost as much as she cherished it in herself. She thoroughly approved of Carter Branch. Had Hilary not approved of him so thoroughly herself, her mother's sentiments would have been enough to wreck the romance before it began.

Carter had come to Bar Harbor to rest after the ordeal of completing his last year at the University of Virginia law school.

"To rest?" Kathryn asked.

"That's the way Mrs. Branch put it." Hilary laughed. "You see, Carter's, well, slight. Slight, hell, he's two inches shorter than I am, and I outweigh him by at least fifteen pounds. There's nothing wrong with him, but Mrs. Branch, domineering old cow that she is, insists Carter 'isn't as strong as he might be.' So as soon as the term was over, she spirited Carter off to Bar Harbor 'to rest.' Carter said he hadn't planned to stay more than a few weeks, but then he met me.

"That's what's so amazing about the whole thing, lamb. He really likes me. Oh, sure, the Enfield money and the position with Daddy's firm help. Carter even admits that was what his mother had in mind when she dragged him to Bar Harbor—not necessarily me, but someone like me. But besides all the trappings, Carter likes *me*. Or at least he says he does. And I believe him. So I guess it's going to be the scion of the old impoverished family for little Hilary after all. What a shout! Hilary Enfield's going respectable. You aren't going to recognize me as Mrs. Carter Middleton Branch, lamb."

"I don't believe it, Hil. You'll be shooting craps at your own wedding."

"Nope, I mean it. I've reformed."

"Is that the way Carter wants you? After all, he fell in love with the old Hilary."

"That he did," Hilary agreed, and looked almost pretty for a moment. "But that was before we were engaged. Carter says now that we're going to be married, things are different. He says it's one thing cutting up when you're a kid, but now we've got to be responsible adults."

"And you agree with him?" Kathryn was incredulous.

"Why shouldn't I agree with him? What's so terrific about spending a tea dance shooting craps instead of dancing, or talking fast because everyone knows you aren't pretty or popular enough to be fast? Sure I agree with Carter."

"Well, in that case, Hilary, I hope you'll be very very happy. I mean it."

"I know you do, lamb. And don't worry. Just because I'm on my best behavior, it doesn't mean I'm going to turn into a stuffed shirt. Old Hilary's still good for a few laughs around the dorm. At least until Christmas. I don't think I'll come back after that. The family's going to announce the engagement in November—Mother wants to do it after Carter's established in Daddy's firm, though everyone will know the job was part of the dowry—and there's going to be a huge party Christmastime. After that, I plan to devote myself to being engaged. I had a rotten season when I came out, but I plan to have a perfectly glorious engagement—and marriage. Which reminds me. Set aside June 21, 1920. You're going to be a bridesmaid, lamb."

"You know what they say. Always a bridesmaid . . ."

"You're one bridesmaid who won't have to worry about that. As if you couldn't do it on your own, I've already got the bouquet signed, sealed, and addressed to you. Though you may have to wrestle Amanda Wycombe for it. Mother says I absolutely have to have her as a bridesmaid. I can't stand her, but Mother's determined to keep her under Ty's nose at all times."

Amanda Wycombe was angry. Her mouth pouted back at her from the mirror above her dresser. Just who did Ty Enfield think he was, anyway? Ty had promised last spring that he wouldn't stay in Bar Harbor, that he'd come down to Newport where Amanda was staying with friends as soon as he could get away, but instead he had gone cruising on someone's yacht for what was rumored to have been a two-week bachelor party, and when he finally did show up in Newport, he hadn't paid nearly enough attention to her. It was race week, and old Mr. Mallory had been short a hand, so Ty had crewed all week. After that he'd gone to Long Island to stay with someone he'd met in the war. Ty said he was going to play polo.

"But you don't play polo, Ty. Nobody in Philadelphia plays polo."

"That's why I'm going to New York, Mandy. To learn."

But a few weeks later Amanda overheard a joke Tim Wharton made to Ty, and she suspected Ty had gone to Long Island for more than polo. There was no doubt about it. Tyson Enfield had to be taught a lesson. She'd accept another invitation to the Yale weekend. When Ty finally got around to asking her, he'd find she was going with someone else. The question was who. If she went with Tim Wharton, she'd be with Ty all weekend, a constant reminder of what he'd lost, but of course Ty wouldn't be really jealous of Tim. Her mind combed the roster of Ty's club, selecting and dismissing at random. Doug Archer, the football player from Chicago, would be the best choice. Of course, if Amanda went with him, she stood the chance of having her escort put out of commission by the Yale team at the very height of the weekend, but it was a chance she decided to take. If Princeton won, she'd be on the arm of a hero—and right under Ty's nose.

Amanda hadn't bothered to answer Doug's last two letters. Now she took the writing paper from her desk and began to compose a letter. It was no more friendly than any she'd written him before, but the fact that she had written would be enough. His invitation to the weekend would be in the mail an hour after her letter arrived.

Amanda's plan didn't exactly backfire, but she was deprived of the pleasure of turning Tyson Enfield down. Doug Archer was so overwhelmed when he returned from practice one evening and found among his mail the envelope holding Amanda Wycombe's acceptance to the Yale weekend, he had not been able to contain his joy. By the time dinner was over, every man in Ivy Club knew that Amanda Wycombe, one of the most sought-after belles in the area, was coming to Yale weekend, not with Ty Enfield, who was generally thought to have the inside track, but with Doug Archer, the toughest end ever to come out of the Windy City.

"It's your own fault," Tim Wharton told Ty that night. "You waited too long to ask her. And you weren't exactly in hot pursuit last summer."

"I had better things to do last summer than dance attendance on Amanda Wycombe."

"Tell me that Saturday night of Yale weekend when you're cooling your heels on the stag line."

"What makes you think I'm going to be on the stag line?"

"Who are you going to ask? That Follies girl you told me about from the house party on Long Island? It's either her or one of the old regulars from the Saturday dances. And I can barely keep you civil at their coming-out parties. How are you going to put up with one of them for the whole weekend? You'll be drunk as a lord and twice as insulting. Face it, Enfield, you're not fit company for a nice girl. I wonder how Amanda puts up with you."

"If those husband-hunting harpies we grew up with are your definition of a nice girl, you're right. And the more I think about it, Doug Archer can have Amanda. She's getting just like them. Every time I talk to her, she tells me about another girl in her class or someone else from the Saturday dances who's got engaged. Her eyes light up like a damned engagement ring."

"If you don't want Amanda Wycombe, I'll take her."

"I didn't say I didn't want her. I just said I didn't want to marry her."

"Oh, you'll marry her, all right. Everyone knows that."

"How is it everyone knows something I haven't made up my mind about?"

"Well, at the moment you better make up your mind about the Yale weekend. You can always ask Cassie Latham or Linda Witmer."

"I told you, no one from the Saturday dances."

Ty sat in silence for a moment staring at the far wall. On it was a sign he and Tim had filched from a roadhouse in Manayunk the previous spring. He thought of that night and Kathryn Owen. For a moment he wondered how he'd forgot Kathryn Owen. Damn, but she was pretty. She reminded Ty of some of the French girls he'd known on the Riviera. For a time there while he was convalescing in Cannes, he had wondered how he'd ever found Amanda Wycombe's blond American-girl attraction so irresistible, but when he'd got home he'd found Amanda was prettier than he remembered after all. But so was Kathryn Owen, now that he thought of it.

She was more than just pretty. Ty remembered the way Cassie Latham had baited her that night, and how Kathryn had held her own. And he remembered the rest of the night. When he'd kissed her, she had kissed him back. Not like Amanda. Ivy Club gossip had it that Amanda Wycombe was untouchable. Ty knew that wasn't entirely true. He also knew that when he kissed Amanda she always put her hands primly on his shoulders as if to hold him at a distance. Afterward she drew back and said "there," as if she had just tied her shoe or parsed a Latin sentence.

"I'm taking Kathryn Owen."

"Who's Kathryn Owen?"

"Wharton, you have a remarkably short memory as well as a

remarkably bad eye for women if you can ask me that. The girl from Bryn Mawr I took to St. A's last spring."

"You're asking for trouble, Ty. House parties with chorus girls in New York are one thing but . . ."

"Kathryn Owen isn't a chorus girl."

"That's exactly my point. She's not a chorus girl, but she's not exactly one of us either, if you know what I mean. And that's where you're going to get into trouble, Enfield, my boy. With a chorus girl you play by one set of rules, with someone like Amanda Wycombe by another, but with some politician's daughter no one has ever heard of, you're right in the middle. You're sure as hell not going to marry her, and if you're even thinking of having an affair with her, you're out of your mind."

"All I'm thinking of doing with her is taking her to the Yale weekend. If, of course, it doesn't offend your social sensibilities, Wharton."

"It's not me I'm worried about."

"Well, I hope it isn't me, because I can take care of myself."

"I seem to remember your saying that on a patrol in Roye."

"And I was right, wasn't I? I ended up in a hospital on the Riviera, didn't I? While you were mopping up the last of the Germans, Timmy boy, I was up to my ears in Red Crosses. And next weekend when you're trailing around after Mandy Wycombe, I'm going to be having a perfectly swell time with that 'politician's daughter no one has ever heard of.' "

Of course Kathryn accepted. She had received another invitation to the weekend, but fortunately she had not yet answered it. Kate shuddered to think that if she were more prompt in her writing habits she would be spending the weekend with some obscure junior from Delaware rather than with Tyson Enfield.

On Friday evening Kathryn and a carefully chaperoned contingent from Bryn Mawr arrived at Princeton. On Saturday, somewhere between the third and fourth quarters of the football game, Kate noticed that Ty stopped calling her Bryn Mawr.

Doug Archer emerged from the game with a deep gash over his right eye. Amanda could not have been more solicitous. Once when she and Ty danced by, Kathryn heard Amanda call Doug her great wounded hero in tones slightly less modulated than usual. She looked up at Ty and saw that he was smiling.

When Timmy Wharton cut in on her, Kate saw Ty make his way across the room to Amanda. She tried not to watch as Ty's arms went around Amanda, and Amanda looked up at him with an expression that fell halfway between a pout and a promise.

But Ty hadn't danced with Amanda again, and when he and Kate, their hands twined together, walked back to the small rooming house off Prospect Street where two chaperons and six young ladies were to spend the night, he said he'd have to find a new name for her. "I can't go on calling you Bryn Mawr. I'll be calling school and asking for Bryn Mawr, and I'll find myself inviting the entire student body to go for a drive. Kathryn's too formal. What does everyone else call you?"

"Mostly Katie."

"Then Katie's out. And not Kate. Kate's a shrew. Kathy?"

"I absolutely forbid it."

"Then Kat. It's appropriate." He stopped walking and turned to face her. "Though I never saw a cat with blue eyes. At least not like yours." And then, although the willow tree they were standing under provided little privacy, he leaned down and kissed her. And despite the fact that a chaperon might easily have been watching out the window, she kissed him back, just as she had that night in front of her house.

A week later, when Amanda Wycombe saw the Marmon beneath her window, she went to the mirror and combed her hair. Then she pinched her cheeks, bit her lips to give them color, and sat down to wait the few seconds until the girl at the front desk rang to tell her she had a caller. When the summons did not come, she walked back to the window. She was just in time to see Ty helping Kathryn Owen into the car.

The week after Thanksgiving, Mr. and Mrs. Samuel Stratford Enfield announced the engagement of their daughter Hilary Tyson Enfield to Carter Middleton Branch. Mr. Branch was the son of Mrs. Branch of Charleston and the late George Tupton Branch. It was, the readers of the social pages agreed, a suitable betrothal. The families were equally matched. The groom had no fortune, of course, but then the bride was plain. The marriage was as carefully balanced as if it had been weighed in a scale of justice. Philadelphia approved and prepared to enjoy the festivities that would accompany the nuptials.

Mrs. Enfield was determined they would be splendid. She was pleased with the match and the change it had made in her daughter. She sat in the library of Highfield now, pondering the guest list for the engagement party. The front door closed and Emily heard Hatton, the butler, greeting her husband and his brother. She gave her gray chignon a perfunctory pat, though she knew it was perfectly arranged.

Samuel Enfield entered the library a step ahead of his brother, Nicholas. His spare frame and somber business suit were in marked contrast to his brother's portliness and casual tweed jacket. The man of self-denial, Emily thought, followed by the man of self-indulgence. Actually, her husband was not the ascetic his wife imagined him to be. It was not that she had mistaken his pursuits, but rather the pleasure he took in them. He enjoyed sitting on the boards of the railroad, one or two other gilt-edged industries, the hospital, the University, the Union League, and of course the Philadelphia Club, as much as his brother, Nicholas, enjoyed showing his horses, hunting the fox, and trotting up to New York for the theater, the art galleries, and assorted less acceptable pastimes. In the Enfield clan, pleasure wore a variety of masks.

"Either you're early, Sam, or I'm late," Nicholas said as he arranged himself comfortably in one of the two large leather chairs on either side of the fireplace.

"Samuel is always punctual," Emily said. "You must have ridden farther than usual, Nicholas."

"The far edge of the Radnor hunt is my customary afternoon trot, Emily. You know that."

"As a matter of fact, I left the office a little early," Samuel Enfield said.

"Glad you did," Nicholas answered. "You can join me in a whiskey before we dress. Can I interest you in some sherry, Emily, dear?" He looked at the papers on his sister-in-law's lap. "The very thing after a hard afternoon with a guest list."

"I'll ring for the drinks, Nicholas," Emily said. Give Nicholas half a chance and he would take over the entire house. Emily prayed her brother-in-law would move back to the studio his father had built him on the east edge of the property some twenty-five years ago when he had forced Nicholas to return from Paris, but now that Nicholas had given up painting, there seemed little chance of his choosing to rough it in the small cottage. Several years ago Emily had suggested the move to her husband, but Samuel had said in a rare display of impatience with his wife that there would always be a place for Nicholas in the main house at Highfield. Emily had not mentioned the move again, but neither had she stopped hoping it would occur.

"Well, how is it going, Emily?" Nicholas took the crystal glass with two fingers of whiskey from the silver tray Hatton held before him. "Has Cora Branch turned up any surprises? A skeleton in the Middleton closet perhaps?"

"Cora Branch has done nothing of the kind, Nicholas, and you know it." She turned to her husband. "But Hilary has presented something of a problem. I don't know what to do about it, Samuel."

Samuel Enfield rearranged his features to indicate interest in his wife's problem, although he had been considering a new fund-raising program for the University. "What to do about what, Emily?"

"Hilary insists on asking a girl named Kathryn Owen to her party. The girl is Mayor Owen's daughter," Emily added pointedly. "They shared a suite at school. I didn't think it was a good idea at the time, but I knew if I tried to stop Hilary she'd only do something twice as outrageous."

"Twice as outrageous as sharing a suite with this girl. I can hardly imagine what that would be," Nicholas said.

"This is no time for irony."

"Sarcasm, my dear Emily."

Emily tried to ignore her brother-in-law. "I simply don't know what to do, Samuel. I've told Hilary I won't invite the girl, but she's determined."

"Well, Emily, I don't welcome the idea of having William Owen's daughter in the house—though I'm sure she's a perfectly nice girl—but it is Hilary's party. I don't suppose it will hurt just this once."

"Of course it will hurt just this once, Samuel. If you let down once, you're bound to let down again. We've got to keep our standards. After all, this isn't New York."

"No, it certainly isn't," Nicholas agreed.

"It's not only the fact that the girl is a politician's daughter, Samuel. Do you remember who her mother is?"

"Margaret Montrose," Nicholas answered promptly. He was remembering when the little Irish girl had come over with Lady Fenleigh. Everyone had talked about what a beauty John Morris had captured in Lady Fenleigh, but Nicholas had thought the maid more desirable than her mistress.

"I don't remember the woman's name," Emily said, "but I do remember that she was Sybil Fenleigh's maid. The daughter of a politician and a woman who came to this country as a servant, that's who Hilary wants to invite to her party!"

"Everyone came to this country as something," Nicholas said. "In fact, if my knowledge of local history and genealogy serves me, the original Benjamin Tyson, the founder of your illustrious family, Emily, was colonial Philadelphia's most successful carpenter. A noble profession, but still a man who worked with his hands, so I don't think we ought to hold this girl's ancestors against her. In fact, we might see it as the realization of the American dream. A little Irish servant girl is now the first lady of Philadelphia."

"She is not the first lady of Philadelphia, Nicholas, and you know it. As for the American dream, I prefer a less vulgar one. I prefer the dream of the men who founded this country, including my ancestors —Benjamin Tyson's son was a judge—the dream of a people ruled by a group of enlightened gentlemen. Surely even you can't call William Owen a gentleman, Nicholas."

"I have to agree with Emily there," Samuel Enfield said. "But we seem to be straying from the point. I'm no more eager to encourage friendship with the Owen family than you are, Emily, but I don't see that we have a choice in this matter. It is Hilary's party."

"It is my party in honor of Hilary."

"Perhaps it isn't Hilary you're concerned about. Perhaps it's Ty," Nicholas said slyly.

"Don't be absurd, Nicholas. There's no need to worry about Ty so long as Amanda Wycombe is around."

"The Wycombe girl is a pretty little thing, I'll give you that, but if this Owen girl looks anything like her mother, I'm not sure I'd put my money on the Wycombe girl. On the other hand, if she is like her mother, I don't think we have to worry about Ty either." Nicholas was remembering a weekend he had spent at the Morrises' house in Cape May many years ago. Margaret Montrose may have been a servant, but she had her pride and her scruples. "No one ever took a liberty with Margaret Montrose."

"Really, Nicholas," Emily interrupted. "You are neither on the boulevards of Paris nor in the theaters of New York, and I'll thank you to take more care with your conversation."

"That means I missed something." Daphne Enfield stood in the doorway to the library. Hilary did not exaggerate when she said her sister was a beauty. Nature, the consummate artist, had spilled rivers of gold through the brown hair of the Enfields and spread a rich blush over her creamy skin. Daphne had high cheekbones and a perfect straight nose, but her eyes were cold for her sixteen years, and her mouth a little cruel. In those two features she resembled her mother, though neither of them realized it.

"And we must be thankful for that," Emily said, looking meaningfully at her brother-in-law.

"I miss all the fun. I'll probably die of boredom in this mausoleum before I'm seventeen."

"If you find life at home dull, Daphne, you should have taken more trouble to remain at school."

"All I did was get back about two minutes past six. I know lots of girls who've done a lot worse than that, and they weren't fired from old Miss Itty-Bitty's."

"It was not only getting back after six, Daphne. You should never have gone for a ride in the first place, and Blake Connigsby should have known better. I expected more of Nora Connigsby's boy."

"So did I," muttered Daphne, remembering the disappointment of the afternoon. Blake Connigsby wasn't half as wild as he pretended to be.

"I'm sure you'll find life here more interesting, Daphne, when you begin at Agnes Irwin's," her father said.

"Oh, just thrilling." Daphne was wondering which transgression would lead to her being asked to leave this time. She could imagine the gossip. *Have you heard? Daphne Enfield was fired from Agnes Irwin's. That makes four. What was it this time? Smoking or men?* She'd have to find a new crime.

"Cheer up, Daf," her uncle said. "Christmas is just around the corner. There'll be Hilary's engagement party, and a dozen others."

Emily Enfield's mind returned to the guest list on her lap. Her own children were impossible enough without inviting some upstart into the house. The girl might give Daphne ideas, not that the child hadn't enough of her own, and then of course there was Tyson. Nicholas had been on target there. Trust him to be contrary, give the girl what the young people called a *rush*. If only Hilary would be more reasonable—she seemed to be about everything else these days—but of course she wouldn't, and Emily supposed she'd have to invite the girl. All she could do was hope . . . and put her trust in Amanda Wycombe.

After the Yale weekend, Ty began to drive out to see Kathryn regularly. One Sunday when he had driven over from Princeton and Carter had taken the train out from Philadelphia to see Hilary, they all went to dinner. Over roast beef and Yorkshire pudding Carter talked of his work in the firm, discreetly of course, and engagement plans, and people Kathryn did not know. Ty said it was an afternoon he had no intention of repeating.

"He's all right for Hilary. In fact, he's perfect for Hilary," Ty told her the following week. They had just come back from tea at one of the nearby inns and he had parked the car some way down from the dorm. "But I can't take him. I look at Carter and I see the family's dream come true. Father says he's diligent. That means he slaves from morning till night for the greater glory of Enfield, Willows, and Caset. And Mother talks about how responsible he is."

"To think Hilary would be marrying diligence and responsibility."

"Not so surprising. A lot of Hilary was just bravado." These Enfields were always so eager to explain each other to you. "No, Carter's fine for Hilary. She certainly seems happy enough. But he isn't fine for me. He gives me the creeps."

"You mean you look at Mr. Diligence and Responsibility and see yourself in a few years."

He looked at her coolly. "Is that what you see?"

She laughed. "We were talking about you. You're the one he makes nervous."

"Don't tell me you like him?"

"I didn't say I liked him. I said he doesn't make me nervous. Bores me, annoys me, but doesn't make me nervous. Though I suspect I make him uncomfortable. He's sure I'm a suffragette."

"Are you?"

"More or less. Around here it's hard not to be, but I think I would be anyway. Why should you have the vote and not me?"

"If we gave you the vote, you'd only use it the way some man told you to." He laughed abruptly. "Though in your case I guess the man would be your father."

"I wouldn't be so sure. I'm not that easily swayed."

"What about me? Do you think I could make you vote the way I wanted you to?"

"Never."

His arm had been resting on the back of the seat and now he moved it around her shoulders and pulled her to him. "You're absolutely sure of that?"

"Couldn't be more positive."

He pressed her to him, and her mouth was warm and yielding against his. Sometimes she talked like a bluestocking, but Ty had never met a bluestocking with a demanding body, and the combination excited him.

* * *

A week before Christmas the weather turned cold and a punishing west wind brought heavy curtains of snow. By nine o'clock that night the campus looked like a desert in the moonlight, the buildings shadowy high-rising dunes, the shrubbery slumbering camels. By the next morning the mirage had evaporated in the sharp December sunshine and the snow glistened white and shiny on every surface. There was a tree just beyond Kathryn's window, and from her bed she could see the branches sagging under their new-fallen weight.

A snowball made a dull thud against the window. Kate thought of going down to join the prebreakfast fight—she was sure Hilary was the moving spirit—but an experimental foot on cold floorboards sent her back under the comforter. Another snowball splattered against the window, then a third. Dragging the comforter behind her, Kathryn moved to the window seat and knelt. She could see the Marmon pulled up in the lane beneath her window, and Ty. He was bending over to make another snowball, and in the big fur coat he looked like an ungainly, slightly unkempt animal. Until he straightened. In the morning sunshine, his face was a finely wrought mosaic of smooth planes and shadows. When he saw Kate at the window it turned into a smile. She opened the casement window, and the air was an icy shock against her face.

Ty tossed the fresh snowball in his hand menacingly. "You've left yourself wide open. Totally vulnerable."

"You wouldn't dare."

"I will if you're not down in ten minutes. It's cold and I want breakfast."

"I have a nine-o'clock class."

"Cut it."

"I can't."

"If you don't, I'll personally see to it that you get nothing for Christmas but coals in your stocking."

Even with the top up the car was cold, but there was a fur lap rug that Ty tucked around her.

"You must have got up at dawn to get here at this hour."

"Actually, I never went to sleep."

"One of those nights."

"Perfectly harmless, I assure you. Mere boyish pranks in the snow."

They were heading along Lancaster Pike now, and Ty handled the car surely despite the snow and the frozen ruts in the road. "Where are we going?"

"First we're going to have breakfast. Then Christmas shopping."

"For anything special?"

"Toys. Only toys. That's all anyone should ever shop for."

Yesterday's storm seemed to have reminded everyone that Christmas was indeed on the way, and the stores were filled with short-tempered women and whimpering children eager to purchase the first miraculous fruits of a peacetime economy. Ty and Kathryn were asked to leave Wanamaker's after Ty derailed an electric train and sent a model of a Spad biplane careening into flight. Ty promised to behave, and the floor manager, taking in his clothes and bearing, relented.

In one corner of the department a blond doll sported an elaborate lace wedding dress. "Is this what little Kat would have wanted for Christmas?"

"I think I'd rather have had the electric train. Or even the Spad."

"What do you have against brides?"

"Nothing. Only, what do you do with them?"

"Play wedding?"

"That's what I mean. I'd rather have the electric train."

"You're the darnedest girl, Kat. Don't you want to get married?"

"I assume that's a hypothetical question, not a proposal." But the appearance of Roger Atherton silenced whatever answer Ty had in mind.

Kathryn hadn't seen Roger since summer's end. He had purposely stayed away from her. Kate's coolness had begun to irritate him. She was taking him for granted, and no one took Roger Atherton for granted. He'd decided to disappear for a while, make her think she'd lost him. By Christmas or early spring at the latest, he'd have her—and on his terms. It was almost Christmas now, and the appearance of Kathryn with Tyson Enfield rearranged Roger's schedule, but did not shake his confidence.

"Hello, Katie," Roger said. "Enfield." He barely nodded to Ty. "It's been a while, Katie. I've been meaning to get out to see you, but I've been pretty busy."

The three of them stood for a moment, making awkward small talk in the middle of Wanamaker's toy department. Ty did not miss the way Atherton looked at Kate, or his parting sentence. "I'll try to stop by over the holidays, Katie."

A half-hour later, when they were seated in the small dining room at the end of the Bellevue Stratford lobby, Ty was still thinking of Roger's words—and his own unanswered question.

"You still haven't answered me."

"The hypothetical question, you mean." She laughed. "Of course I want to get married, Ty. Eventually. I just don't want to be a bridal doll. You know, the kind that walks down the aisle and then never does anything else for the rest of her life, or more to the point, goes on being a doll for the rest of her life, presiding over the dinner table, presiding over the tea table, presiding over the children." She thought of her parents. "All my life people have been trying to turn me into that kind of doll. And it all sounds so dreary. That's why I'd rather have the electric train."

But for Ty the conversation had passed the realm of toys. "What about Roger Atherton? Does he want to turn you into a doll?"

"Oh, you know Roger . . ."

"Apparently not as well as you do."

Kathryn remembered how she'd felt every time she'd seen Ty with Amanda Wycombe. It had never occurred to her that he might be jealous of her, just as she was of him. For a moment Kathryn could almost forgive Roger Atherton his boyhood cruelties.

4

Hilary's engagement was to be celebrated as splendidly as possible on New Year's Eve. Emily Enfield had planned every detail down to the exact moment and precise wording of her husband's announcement and toast. Four days before the party, however, a single flaw remained in the carefully planned evening.

"I knew this Owen girl would present problems," Emily said to her daughter. "And Carter agrees with me, don't you, Carter?" It was Saturday lunch.

"I do if you find it inconvenient, Mrs. Enfield."

"Kathryn won't be a problem, Mother," Hilary said. "There'll be scads of people here. You won't even notice her."

"I can assure you I will notice her very much, indeed, but that isn't what I meant. Have you even thought about an escort for the girl? She'll have to have one, of course."

"I'd be happy to serve," Nicholas said.

"If you can't be serious about this, Nicholas, I'd appreciate your refraining from the discussion."

"Perhaps Miss Owen has a beau of her own who might escort her." Nicholas saw Hilary and Ty exchange glances.

"No," Hilary said. "There's no one. Really."

"I should say there is no one," Emily said. "It's bad enough

Hilary insisted on inviting the girl. I won't have her dragging her own sort in with her."

"Her own sort, Mother?" Ty spoke for the first time.

"That's what I said, Tyson, and you know exactly what I mean."

"Yes, I do, and just to make sure that doesn't happen, I'll escort her myself."

"Stop being facetious, Ty. You're as bad as Nicholas. You'll escort Amanda, as planned. I won't have Hilary's selfishness in this matter upsetting you and Amanda and everyone else in the family. Still, we'll have to find someone."

"I know she's a friend of Roger Atherton," Hilary said.

"Sara Atherton's boy? Well, we haven't invited him . . ."

"Then I don't see how you can ask him now," Ty said quickly.

"There are always ways of arranging these things when necessary. I've never particularly liked Sara Atherton, but we do need someone to take care of that girl. All the same, I hate to give Sara an ounce. I've never approved of the way she made up to Boise Penrose. Just because one loses a fortune, it doesn't mean one ought to lose one's dignity as well. What do you think, Samuel?"

"It was foolish of Jack Atherton to lose the fortune in the first place. He oughtn't to have gambled with the family money."

"Well, then," Ty said, determined to get his parents back on the track and head off Roger Atherton, "if you don't like his parents, I can't imagine why you'd want to invite him."

"Because we need an escort for that girl."

"Timmy Wharton will be happy to take that girl." Ty was thinking Tim would be only too happy to take Amanda home after the party and leave Kat to him.

"Do you think he would, dear? As a favor to Hilary."

"In this case I think it's Hilary who will be doing Tim the favor."

Emily heard her son's words and remembered Nicholas's warning. That girl was bound to make trouble. Emily Enfield could feel it.

After lunch it was decided that the younger members of the family would go down to the pond formed by a small dam across the stream below the house for some skating. "You can use the exercise, Hilary." Emily eyed her daughter's waist pointedly. Though Hilary had been dieting strenuously, there was little chance of Emily Enfield's presenting a slender bride to Philadelphia society.

"I wish Mother wouldn't make such a fuss about Katie's coming to the party," Hilary said as they started toward the pond.

"I can understand your mother's being upset," Carter said. He did not miss the look Ty shot him. "Your friend Kathryn may be a perfectly nice girl, Hilary, but she doesn't really fit, you know. Your mother said her mother was a servant."

"I wonder why Mother never told me that," Hilary said.

"Because she didn't think it would change your mind, but she was hoping I might."

"Personally, I like the idea." Daphne swung her skates as she walked. "And if she has any brothers, I think you ought to invite them too. They're bound to be more interesting than Blake Connigsby."

"What's wrong with Blake Connigsby?" Ty asked. "Besides the fact that he got you fired from school."

"Everything's wrong with Blake—except his car. He's got that perfectly gorgeous Stutz, and all he does is drive around in it. What a waste."

They had dropped a few steps behind Hilary and Carter, and Ty looked at his sister carefully. "If you mean what I think you mean, baby sister, you'd better watch it. You're a little young for talk like that."

"Talk like that." She laughed. "It isn't the talk that worries you."

"That's right, it isn't. But I'm assuming at your age it's just talk."

"No one can stop you from assuming, big brother."

"But maybe I can stop you from doing anything about it."

"How? By tattling to Mother? She watches me like a hawk anyway. And you wouldn't tell on me, because someday you might want me to return the favor." She flashed a brilliant smile that had been known to convince older men than Ty to do what they had no inclination to.

After they had been skating for almost an hour, Ty stopped for a cigarette and Hilary skated over and sat next to him on the log. "Did you know about Katie's mother, Ty?"

"What about Kat's mother?"

"You know. What Carter said. That her mother was a servant."

"No," he said without any particular interest. Kat's family was not what concerned him.

"I wonder why she never mentioned it to me."

"Would you have mentioned it in her place?"

"I guess not."

"Suddenly Kat's background seems awfully important to you."

"That's not fair, Ty. Katie's been my best friend."

"You know, you just used the past tense."

"Well, she still is. Sort of. It's different after you're engaged. When you're going to get married, you don't need a best friend so much." "I'll keep that in mind when Tim finds someone. And now that Kat's your former best friend, you don't have to worry about the fact that her mother was a servant."

"I don't care about that, and you know it. It's just that, well, I don't want her to feel out of place. Maybe Mother's right."

"You mean, maybe Carter's right. Dammit, Hilary, you've gone to a dozen tea dances with Kat. She didn't feel out of place there. Kat will fit in just fine at your hallowed party."

Hilary had been watching her brother as he spoke, and she knew the flush on his face had nothing to do with the cold. "Don't fall in love with her, Ty. You'll just be asking for trouble. For both of you."

"Nobody said anything about love. I just hate to hear you beginning to sound like Mother."

Hilary ground out her cigarette with the blade of her skate and stood. "Well, Ty, I'll watch myself if you will."

As Tim Wharton drove through the December night with Kathryn Owen at his side, he couldn't help thinking that Ty was inviting trouble. Tim could see what Ty saw in the girl. She was pretty, maybe even as pretty as Amanda Wycombe in her way. And she was quick. Timmy had seen her come back at Ty once or twice the way no other girl ever had. Amanda wheedled and threatened and pouted. This Katie sparred. But all the same, Ty was making a mistake. There wasn't any need to go cutting across lines. It didn't work for either side. There was no doubt about it. Ty was asking for trouble. Typical of Ty. Trust him to complicate things. And when Amanda Wycombe was practically throwing herself at him. Tyson Enfield was his oldest and best friend, Tim thought, but sometimes he was just a little crazy. There was no other word for it.

Tim stopped the car next to a small gatehouse. A man in uniform peered into the car. "Go right on through, Mr. Wharton."

Suddenly Kathryn's stomach felt strange, as if she had gone too long without eating. Hilary had told her once that her family wasn't really rich, at least not by the standards of some of the coal or steel or railroad families. "The point is," Hilary had said in a tone Kathryn had learned to recognize as Hilary's imitation of her mother, "not the amount of money, but its age. Though Mother doesn't like to mention money, she's fond of pointing out that both the Tysons and the Enfields—and when she mentions the families, she means their money—go back to before the Revolution. When the Revolution came, the Enfields split, but since the loyalists had the powder works, they came out of it as well as the rebels, who never lost their land. Don't ever mention it to Mother, though. She's convinced profiteering started with this war."

Hilary's jokes had served to keep the Enfield wealth and position within the bounds of Kathryn's imagination. She had been impressed, but not awed by it. Now, as Timmy Wharton's Cadillac moved along beneath the huge chestnut trees toward a galaxy of lights glittering in the distance, Kate tried to quiet her fear, and when they finally reached the house, she was relieved to see it was smaller and simpler than she had expected. But as a footman opened the car door and helped Kathryn out, she realized both the simplicity and the size of the house were deceptive. It looked unpretentious because it was a superb example of Georgian architecture constructed not to intimidate man but to house him comfortably, and this Highfield had done for almost a century and a half since the first Nicholas Enfield had built it as a refuge from the yellow-fever epidemic raging through the streets of Philadelphia. He'd chosen the site carefully. It would be located on the crest of a rolling hill that commanded a full view of the surrounding countryside and caught whatever cooling breezes might arise during the hot summer months. The house had been constructed on the highest point of the extensive property. Since then each generation of Enfields had added according to his interests and needs. One need not say "taste," since the Enfield taste had remained as sure and unswerving as the original Georgian dictates. The east wing had been built just after the War of 1812. The son of a rebel Enfield had married the daughter of the loyalist powder-works Enfield, and the new wing was their first issue. A generation later, when the land west of Philadelphia was worth a good deal to the newly formed Pennsylvania Railroad, Alexander Enfield managed to keep the original tract, trade some less desirable acreage for railroad stock, and emerge with enough clear profit to construct the vast west wing reaching far out behind the house to provide a view of the stream that flowed below. After the Civil War Colonel Enfield, who had emerged from the war with profit *and* honor, unlike the noncombatant uncle Ty had referred to, had torn down the old stables and built a larger, more modern facility, and subsequent generations had contented themselves with adding greenhouses, summerhouses, and the dam that formed the pond below the house. Just before the turn of the century, Marion Enfield had built the small studio cottage for his son Nicholas, who would be permitted to paint the countryside of Pennsylvania but not the boulevards of Paris. And Samuel Enfield had constructed a garage and chauffeur's quarters next to the stables. Arriving at the Enfield estate on New Year's Eve, Kate knew none of its history, but she did know that it was more vast and splendid than either Hilary's or Ty's manner had led her to expect.

In the spacious front hall Hilary and Carter stood with two women and a man before a towering Christmas tree that reached through the circular staircase to the second floor. The polished wood of the floor glowed dully in the light from the candles on the tree, and the Oriental rug felt soft under Kathryn's evening slippers. On either side of the hall hung large portraits, but Kate had no time to examine them. The real Mrs. Enfield commanded her attention immediately.

"Hilary has told us about you, Miss Owen," Emily Enfield said when Timmy presented her. "We've looked forward to meeting you." Kathryn did not miss the discordancy between words and tone.

Kate found it hard to believe that the girl standing in the shadow of this tall woman with eyes like steel-gray bullets was the same Hilary she had lived with for the past two years. It wasn't merely the unfamiliar pearls or the diamond on her left hand. Hilary was on her best behavior, and as she uttered pleasant, meaningless words, she seemed like a coarser, less successful version of her mother.

Kate passed down the receiving line and found Ty at its end, waiting for her with two glasses of champagne. "Miss Owen," he said in a tone loud enough for Emily to hear, "how nice to see you." Ty seemed to be enjoying himself immensely, but Kate didn't see why. She found neither the fact that they knew each other well nor the fact that his mother did not know they knew each other well amusing. "Okay, Wharton," Ty continued in an undertone, "you're relieved."

"Don't you think you ought to let me dance with Katie once? If only for appearances?" Tim said as they moved off from the receiving line.

"You can dance with me once, Timmy. It will give me a reprieve." Daphne Enfield stood beside them, looking very pretty, but fortunately, Timmy thought, very young.

"Reprieve from what, Daf?"

"Mother says my headband has to go."

"I think it's chic." Tim laughed.

"That's just the point. Don't you know, Mr. Wharton, it's vulgar to be chic. After all, this isn't New York," Daphne quoted her mother.

"Well, in that case, you go take off the headband and then I'll dance with you. I have a feeling your mother is going to be sufficiently angry with me before the evening's over without my undermining the morals of a minor."

"You mean turning Miss Owen over to Ty?" Daphne seemed to notice Kathryn for the first time.

"This is my little sister, Daphne," Ty said, "who is just on her way upstairs to take off her headband."

"Never fear, my lips are sealed. I adore intrigue," Daphne said.

"I'll do my best to provide as much as possible." Kathryn tried to sound lighthearted, but she didn't think the situation nearly so much fun as the others seemed to.

"According to Mother, your being here is enough for the moment."

"Daf," Ty interrupted. "I thought you were going to change that headband."

"I don't understand all the fuss about a little piece of satin. I admit there are other pieces of satin that I might wear—or *not* wear—that might be distressing—"

"Daphne! Cut it out and go do what Mother says."

"Very well, big brother. I'll be a dutiful daughter—at least as far as the bandeau is concerned." Daphne flounced up the stairs with a movement somewhere between an angry child and a woman who knows exactly how desirable she is.

"My little sister is studying to be a vamp."

"She's very pretty," Kathryn said.

"Too pretty for her own good." Suddenly Ty saw his mother and Amanda Wycombe bearing down on them. "Well, Wharton, you've got your work cut out for you," and taking Kathryn's hand, he led her into the large room that had been emptied of furniture for the dancing.

Over Ty's shoulder Kathryn could see Amanda looking up at Tim with huge brown eyes that said he was the only man in the world, but next to them Mrs. Enfield was white with anger. Kathryn saw her turn to talk to another guest, and marveled at the way she rearranged her features into a gracious smile. Mrs. Enfield's control was almost more terrifying than her anger.

She was, moreover, not easily outwitted. Kathryn did not know if it was an accident, but she saw Mrs. Enfield turn from the guest to a young man at her side, and then the young man cut in on them. After that it seemed that every time Kate saw Ty start across a room toward her, Mrs. Enfield was beside him. Men cut in on Kathryn one after another, but it was after eleven before she felt Ty's arms around her again.

"I'd love to get through just one dance with you before the year's out," he said, drawing her close. "But between the stags and Mother, I was beginning to think that was impossible."

"Well, I've been here all along."

"Been here all along with Marshall Latham and Greg Childs and . . ." Ty listed half a dozen men Kate had danced with in the last hour. "But I've thought of a way to put a stop to it. We're going to have a moment alone at midnight if it kills me."

Mrs. Enfield would be the one it would kill, Kathryn thought.

"What do you say? Are you up to a secret assignation?"

"If you mean your car, I think it's a little cold for that."

"Give me some credit, Kat. I've got more imagination than that. At the end of the second-floor hall there's a small library. The last door on the right. You go up now," he said as the song came to an end, "and I'll be up in two minutes. And don't let any of those stags waylay you."

Kathryn found the room without any trouble. It was small and book-lined and very pleasant. There was a fireplace in the center of the far wall, and in it fresh logs had been laid, just waiting to be ignited. Kathryn thought that if she had grown up in this house, she would have spent a good deal of time in this room. It was more inviting than the formal library downstairs. And more private, she thought, wondering when Ty would arrive.

The music from the orchestra below drifted faintly into the room. "Alice Blue Gown" turned into "Mandy," then "Mandy" gave way to "Whose Little Heart Are You Breaking Now?" She was getting angry, angry with Ty for keeping her waiting, angry with herself for allowing him to. Why didn't he simply shake off that well-manicured hand Kate had seen Mrs. Enfield lay on the sleeve of his dark evening suit a dozen times that night?

Another song came to an end. One more, Kate swore, then I'm going back down. She heard the familiar strains of "Auld Lang Syne," then bursts of laughter and shouts and cheers from below. The windows on either side of the fireplace threw back a reflection of Kathryn standing alone in the center of the room. She walked to one of the windows and looked at her own image. Even in the dark, makeshift mirror the blue *crepe de chine* made her eyes look luminous. "Happy New Year, you fool. Happy 1920."

"And the same to you." The voice was deep, deeper than Ty's, and laced with a Southern drawl as smooth and rich as molasses.

She hadn't heard anyone enter above the noise from the celebration but now in the window she saw a tall man, almost as tall as Ty and twice as broad, standing just inside the doorway. Kate turned around. His face was as round and ruddy as Timmy Wharton's, but there was nothing cherubic about it. Tim gave an impression of being soft and chubby; this man was big, with the bigness of powerful muscles and rock-hard sinew. Everything in his appearance belied his soft lazy voice, everything except his eyes, which looked tired under half-closed lids, tired but not especially kind.

"If you're waiting for Mr. Enfield," he said in that voice that floated across the room like a wisp of soft white cotton, "the last I saw our hostess was telling him to take that blond girl in the lavender dress in to supper. Since he didn't have the chance to make his own apologies, I decided to stand in for him. He's terribly sorry." The man was very smug.

"I wasn't waiting for anyone."

Randy Curtaine saw no reason to argue. He had made enough clandestine escapes from enough parties to recognize what had happened when Ty and Kate had parted after the dance and Kate had gone immediately upstairs, but he did not want to humiliate her. It would be poor strategy. "I see. Just stealing a quiet moment. Can't say I blame you. Awful lot of partying going on downstairs."

"And I think I'd better join it." Kathryn started for the door, but the man reached out to catch her hand and stop her. Kate pulled away, but neither his eyes nor his voice changed.

"My name's Randy Curtaine. Cousin of the bridegroom. Up from Kentucky, as if you couldn't guess. You Yankees have been mocking my accent all night."

"It is rather hard to miss."

"Not if you live down my way, Miss . . . You haven't told me your name."

"Kathryn Owen," Kate said, starting for the door again.

This time he did not try to stop her. "Well, Miss Owen, perhaps you'll let me take you in to supper." He did not add the phrase "now that Mr. Enfield has taken someone else," because he knew she was thinking it.

They had reached the top of the wide circular stairway, and Kathryn was about to decline, but then she saw Ty standing at the bottom of the stairs. Amanda's arm was tucked neatly in his. When

Ty saw Kate, he excused himself and came up the stairs two at a time.

"I'm sorry, Kat . . . Mother . . . Amanda . . ." Ty tried to say with his eyes what he could not explain in front of this stranger, but Kate would not accept that silent apology.

"Mr. Curtaine was just going to take me in to supper, Ty. Perhaps you and Amanda would like to join us."

The only thing worse than being alone with Amanda at this point, Ty thought, was being with Kat *and* Amanda. He declined and rejoined Amanda at the bottom of the stairs.

After supper, when the dancing had started again, Ty went from room to room looking for Kate. She was not dancing, she was not in the library, she was not even in the small second-floor study where he'd dared to hope she might return.

"Looking for Miss Owen?" Daphne asked after Ty had made his third tour around the dancing room.

"Have you seen her?"

"Last I saw her, she was saying good night to Mother and Daddy. Mother couldn't have been nicer. That Mr. Curtaine was going to drive her home. You better watch out, big brother. He's absolutely devastating, if you ask me."

"No one asked you, Daf."

"And something of a parlor snake, I think. If the line he uses on your Miss Owen is half as good as the one he used on me, you're in trouble."

"Why don't you run along upstairs, Daphne? It's past your bedtime."

"Don't get angry at me, brother dear. I'm not the one who ran off with Mr. Curtaine. More's the pity."

Daphne had not misjudged Randy Curtaine. Kate's only salvation on the ride home was that he accepted her rebuffs as genuine. After Kate had removed his arm from her shoulders a second time, Randy Curtaine realized she had agreed to let him drive her home only because she was angry with another man. The realization produced disappointment but not anger in him. Randy Curtaine was a realist. If Kate was unwilling, other girls were not. He wondered idly if the party would still be going on when he returned. The bride's sister was young, but Randy Curtaine was not particularly scrupulous about a girl's age. Randy Curtaine was not a scrupulous man.

* * *

Will Owen was alone at the table when his daughter came down for breakfast the following noon. "I was beginning to wonder if we'd see you at all today. Happy New Year, Katie. Did you have a nice evening?" His manner was offhand. Will would have liked to know every detail of his daughter's treatment at the hands of the Enfields, but he knew that a close cross-examination would be sure to drive her to silence.

"It was all right."

"Just all right? I should think a party at the Enfields', a New Year's party in honor of their daughter's engagement, would be more than all right."

"It was splendid, if that's what you mean. Champagne and caviar, a huge midnight supper, a big orchestra, and scads of footmen." These were not the details her father wanted, and Kathryn knew it.

"And lots and lots of young people, I imagine. That Wharton boy seemed a nice-enough young man." Will had watched his daughter when Tim Wharton came to call for her the night before. He had seen immediately that there was no future there. "The Enfield boy was there, of course, the one from the police station. I trust you didn't get him into trouble this time."

Will had been trying to make a joke, and the anger in Kathryn's voice when she answered told him a great deal about the evening. "No, Daddy, I didn't get Ty into trouble. He was good as gold. Mrs. Enfield saw to that."

Will said no more about the evening, and Kathryn did not mention it again, but Will could put his daughter's tone together with his knowledge of Emily Enfield, and he didn't like the sum he totaled. The Enfield boy had clearly shown some interest in Kate, and Mrs. Enfield had tried to sabotage it. Will was not surprised, but neither was he acquiescent. The incident stayed in his mind like a small seed of discontent, and a week later, when Kathryn and Ty had already patched up their argument, he found fertile ground for planting.

The article, buried on the fourth page of the morning paper, excited little interest in the rest of Philadelphia. Abigail Starksby was merely another eccentric old lady who had died, leaving her fortune, which was, strictly speaking, no longer a fortune but was called so because the money had passed through many generations of Starksbys, to an aging Siamese cat, called Fritz after an early German lover, and the humane society. The small house in a section of the city that had long ceased to be fashionable or even safe was bequeathed to a nephew, along with the few pieces of good furniture

left, and the pictures to the museum. Among the pictures were two
by Thomas Eakins, a friend of Miss Starksby's late father. Will Owen
knew nothing about art, but he recognized the title of one Eakins
painting. It was a picture of rowers on the Schuylkill. One of the
rowers was said to be Samuel Enfield as a young man.

Will Owen had a superb memory. He listened to what other men
said, to both the words and the meaning behind them, and stored it
away for future use. There was nothing that might not come in handy
someday. And this morning Will was remembering a story he'd heard
some years ago. A Harrisburg man, a client of Samuel Enfield with
whom Will had his own dealings of a different sort, had amassed a
great deal of money and decided to storm Philadelphia society. He
was not a mean man and was willing to part with considerable sums
of his newly acquired wealth to achieve his end. Since the indus-
trialist's wife had certain pretensions to artistic achievement, he decided to start there. He would build a new wing for the museum.
Samuel Enfield did not tell his client that no amount of money could
buy him the place he sought—that, as Enfield saw it, was not his duty
as counsel—but he did advise the man as to where the contributions
might do the most good. He recommended the hospital and the University to begin with. It was not merely that Enfield served on the
boards of both these venerable institutions, he assured his client, but
rather that they were venerable institutions. If the man must have the
arts, let him endow the symphony. It was more appropriately Philadelphian. The museum, Enfield explained, had never mattered much.
"And that's as it should be. Pictures are meant to be lived with, not
hung in some mausoleum where people troop by and gape for a moment."

The man from Harrisburg had quoted Samuel Enfield to Will as if
to show how far he had moved up the social ladder, but Will remembered the words now and put them together with Miss Starksby's be-
quest. If Samuel Enfield did not approve of pictures being hung in
public places for the masses, how much more distressed would he be
at the thought of his own picture by Mr. Eakins being so hung. Will
told his secretary to get him the curator of the museum.

The curator sounded somewhat intimidated. He had never been
telephoned by the mayor before.

"I wanted to congratulate you on that fine acquisition from Miss
Starksby," Will said. "I'm looking forward to seeing the paintings.
When will you have them hung, Mr. Blake?"

"Of course, you can see them anytime, Mr. Mayor, but we plan to have most of them on display by the end of the month."

"Most of them?"

"Well, all but one. We've had a fine offer for one of them."

Will mentioned the title of the Eakins painting.

"Why, yes, that's the one. It's an excellent example of his work, but I must say I didn't expect it to bring quite that much."

"And who made this offer, Mr. Blake?" Will knew the answer before it was spoken.

"We don't know the individual, sir, but it came through a reputable dealer."

"I'm sure it did. Nevertheless, I don't think we want to sell what was left to the museum as a gift."

"We can hardly afford not to sell it at the price offered." The curator's voice was growing decidedly more nervous. "Why, at that amount we can buy something far more valuable than an Eakins."

"There are few paintings more valuable to Philadelphia, Mr. Blake, than those of her own sons. Leave the Michelangelos in Rome. I want the Eakins here in our museum. Tell the dealer the painting is not for sale—at any price."

"But, Mr. Mayor"—Will could hear the man swallow—"it's hardly a reasonable decision in economic terms. How will I justify it to the board?"

"I'll take care of the board, Mr. Blake, and you take care of the Eakins. I look forward to seeing it at the end of the month."

It was scarcely a major triumph, Will Owen thought as he hung up the telephone, but it was a small retaliation.

The cars began arriving from town and the nearby men's schools early in the afternoon, and by the time the last classes let out, the campus resembled a ghost town peopled only by the plainest or most bookish girls. Of course prohibition couldn't last, but it was a marvelous excuse for a party. Even the dormitory wardens, who wouldn't miss spirits, bemoaned the infringement of civil liberty and prepared to look the other way just this once when girls staggered in a little late and a bit unsteady.

Ty and Kathryn had started out early in the afternoon at a nearby inn, but by seven o'clock Ty decided this was an event that had to be celebrated among one's own.

"If we drive to Princeton, I'll never get back by curfew," Kate pointed out.

"Of course you will. I can get the Marmon up to eighty."

"Marvelous. A wrecked Marmon *and* a missed curfew."

They compromised on a party at the University.

On the lawn in front of St. Anthony's three young men lay uncon-
scious. It was a brutally cold night, and when a dry snow began to
fall, someone suggested dragging them in.

"Let 'em lie," someone else yelled. "They're Zeta Psi's." But Tim,
who was there with a freshman who would have been pretty if her
chin hadn't receded quite so abruptly, said that one University fraternity was as bad as another, and he and Ty half-dragged, half-carried
the three men inside.

"At least they're sober enough not to let them freeze to death,"
the freshman said.

"Just barely," Kate answered, not feeling very steady herself, and
then the sight of Roger Atherton across the room threw her further
off balance. He saw her immediately and began to push through the
dancing couples.

"I thought I might find you in here when I saw Enfield out there
playing good samaritan," Roger said.

"I notice you didn't bother to help."

"And head off a good case of frostbite. I've never seen a case of
frostbite, and I think that's a particular deficiency in my training."

"Perhaps you'd like to examine them now."

"I'd rather dance with you, Katie."

Kathryn started to refuse, but she saw Ty dragging the last of the
drunks in and remembered his jealousy that day at the Bellevue
Stratford.

They had been dancing only a moment when Ty appeared at their
side. "Okay, Atherton, time's up."

"Why don't you go rescue some more Zeta Psi's?"

"Because I'd rather dance with my girl." Perhaps it was the alcohol, but Kathryn noticed Ty's voice was not as bantering as it should
have been.

They had stopped dancing, and the three of them stood together in
the middle of the room. "What about it, Katie? Are you Enfield's
girl?"

Both men were watching her, and she looked from Roger to Ty
and flashed what she hoped was a playful smile. "For the present."

Kathryn hadn't known the truth of her statement, Roger Atherton
thought as he walked away from them. He had known Tyson Enfield
and his family since childhood, and he knew Ty would never marry

Kate. It was a shame Kate couldn't see that, but she would find out soon enough, and when she did, she'd come crawling back to him. He was certain of that.

Ty had laughed at Kate's answer to Atherton, but when Roger was out of sight, Kathryn looked up and saw Ty was no longer smiling. "Is that the way it is? My girl for the present?" The gray eyes were dark now.

"The nice thing about being a girl"—she laughed—"is that you only have to worry about the present. There's always some man who's willing to take care of the future for you."

He remembered the words and laughed with her, but for the first time since she had known him, Tyson Enfield looked as if he had been caught off balance.

By the time they left the party there was more than an inch of snow on the ground and it was still coming down heavily. Once in the Marmon, Ty tucked the lap robe around her. "Warm enough?"

"I doubt either of us could feel the cold at this point."

"Right. What we need is another drink to make sure it lasts out to Bryn Mawr."

"That's the last thing we need, Ty. Come on, if we don't get started, I'm going to have to find an open window in the dorm, and it's too cold for that."

"Can't have that happen." He started the car with a jerk and swerved into the street.

"I'd rather be late than not get there at all."

"Now, now, no backseat drivers. Enfield's at the wheel, and you're safe as a baby in a crib."

He was a good driver, Kathryn thought. She rested her head on the back of the seat and closed her eyes. The warmth of the car and Ty beside her and the alcohol pulsing through her veins made her drowsy, and she must have dozed off.

"Goddammit!" Ty's voice came crashing into her consciousness. She opened her eyes with a start and was blinded by two headlights. Then the car swerved and Ty's body was thrown across hers.

For a moment Kathryn was not conscious of anything; then she realized that the other car had passed, and they were in a ditch at the side of the road. At first she thought the car had turned over; then she realized it was only the angle of the ground. Ty's body pinned her against the door, and she could feel the handle cutting into her side.

He pulled himself up. "Are you all right? Kat, are you all right?"

"I'm all right. Are you?"

He didn't seem to hear her question. "Damn idiot drunken driver! Are you sure you're not hurt?" He had braced himself against the other door and was lifting her to him. "I could have killed you."

Suddenly she began to cry. "I'm all right," she said. "Really, I am."

"I'll never hurt you, Kat. I promise you. I love you, and I'll never hurt you."

She heard the words and told herself he was drunk. They were both drunk and shaken by the accident, but he drew back a little, and she could see the gray eyes clear now in the darkness.

"I mean that, Kat. I love you. And not just for the present."

The time for sparring was over, and she wanted to tell him she loved him too, but his mouth was on hers and they were clinging together, and there in a snowy ditch on the side of the road in the aftermath of an accident that could have killed them both, Kathryn felt safer than she ever had in her life.

On the first day of prohibition Ty awoke with a hammering headache and the vague feeling that something had happened. Then he remembered the accident and his words to Kathryn. He hadn't expected to tell her he loved her, hadn't even admitted it to himself before last night. He knew he looked forward to seeing her more than he ever had another girl, knew he wanted her with a fierceness he tried not to think about, but he'd never admitted he loved her. Until the shock of the accident. He had been angry, as much at himself as the other driver. The other car had been in the center of the road, but Ty knew his own reaction had come too late and been too extreme. He had been drunk, and angry at that drunkenness because it had endangered Kat. In the first flash of thought after they had careened off the road, he had cared only for her. It was all very well to say he could feel that he was not hurt, so of course his first thought was of her, but in fact, in those moments he could feel nothing at all except the overwhelming fear that he might have hurt Kat. For that single moment it had nothing to do with liking her or admiring her or even wanting her. It had to do only with loving her.

He went down to the telephone in the enclosed booth on the first floor and called her. The girl who answered the phone was gone for some time, and when Kat's voice came over the wire, it sounded sleepy.

"Kat, it wasn't the whiskey last night."

She prayed he meant what she thought, but when she spoke, her voice was even. "I know the accident wasn't your fault, Ty."

"I didn't mean the accident. I meant what I said."

"Oh." She had lain awake for hours last night remembering his words, remembering them with a terror that in the morning when the alcohol and the accident and the dark intimacy of the car were only memories, he would no longer mean them.

"I love you, Kat. Drunk, sober, crazy, sane, awake, asleep, any way at all, I love you."

"I'm glad."

"Is that all you can say!"

"I said it all last night."

"You were tight too. Say it now when you're sober."

"You know how I feel, Ty."

"I want to hear you say it."

"It's an open phone."

"I don't care. Say it."

"I love you, Ty."

"Then everything's perfect."

5

Kathryn knew, even as she agreed to take Ty to the meeting, that her parents would be furious. "Now, I'm not suggesting that you lie, Kathryn," her mother had once warned her, "but there are certain things a young lady need not reveal about herself." In the mouth of another mother those words might have many connotations, but for Margaret they had a single meaning. And taking Ty to a political rally clearly flew in the face of it.

Kate wasn't sure why she had agreed to it in the first place. It wasn't merely that he'd asked her to. She couldn't quite sort it out, but her willingness to take Ty to the rally had something to do with her parents' eagerness to keep him from such things and with the memory of New Year's Eve. It seemed very much a matter of pride that Ty see her father and, more important, Kathryn herself at this meeting.

The rally was not for Mayor Owen. Will had been reelected with the predictable landslide the previous fall and begun his third term as mayor. Now he was campaigning for the members of the newly created city council. He was determined to see his own men, hand-picked, loyal, party men, on the council. Joseph Thomas, a reliable fellow who had run his ward as tightly as a good captain runs his ship for as long as Will had been in office, was such a man. Unfortunately, Thomas's opponent, the kind of young man with a passion for political reform that the city had a tendency to spawn and then subdue at regular intervals over the years, had a war record. It was that record that Will Owen's presence at the rally tonight was intended to counteract.

The auditorium was full when Kathryn and Ty arrived and took seats at the rear. It was a poor neighborhood, proud, hardworking except for the usual number of drunks and malingerers, and entirely Irish. Kate felt at home in the audience of lean, hard-eyed men and worn-looking women, but Ty had never seen anything like it before.

On the platform Will sat with Margaret at his side and half a dozen men. The men were perfectly average in appearance and differed only in dress. The candidate, the ward boss, and his two assistants wore dark suits. Father Flaherty and Father Kean were attired in the cloth of their calling. Margaret did not always accompany her husband to these rallies, but in this particular district her obviously Irish good looks were a definite advantage. The audience responded to them wholeheartedly and without an inkling of the disdain Margaret felt for them or their religion. Margaret Montrose's northern Irish views were one of the best-kept secrets of Will Owen's career.

"My friends," Will began when the applause had subsided. "I've come here tonight to speak to you on behalf of Joseph Thomas. Now, I know you all know Joe Thomas. He's been a familiar face in this neighborhood for . . . well, perhaps we'd better not say exactly how long. Joe might not appreciate that, and I know Mrs. Owen here will give me a piece of her fine Irish temper for revealing any such thing about us." Will waited for the expected ripple of laughter to run its course.

"The point is, my friends, that with all the fanfare over what's been going on overseas, some of us may have forgot what's been happening right here at home. Now, don't for a minute think that I want to take anything away from our worthy opponent and his record in the Great War. No matter that Robert Fenster was never fortunate enough to get to the front and was forced to spend the duration of the war in Paris. We all know that he served his country with dignity and honor. But, my friends, *but* so did our Joe Thomas. While Mr. Fenster was sorting intelligence information in Paris—and I'm sure he felt the danger just as intensely as Joe's own son did at Château Thierry—Joe was taking care of things here at home. Taking care of your needs.

"Now, I won't even begin to list all the fine things Joe Thomas did to keep our city running smoothly during the war," Will said, and proceeded to catalog a host of activities ranging from official launching of ships at the Hog Island yard to organizing the quarantine during the flu epidemic. "As grateful as we all are to Joe Thomas for these things, what we're here tonight to consider is not what Joe has done for you in the past, but what he can do for you in the future." There was a good deal of murmured approval at this point.

"Let's begin with the water supply. Mr. Fenster charges that our city's water is undrinkable." More murmured appoval. "And he's right." Surprised silence. "That's right, my friends, the water that comes from our own Schuylkill River is no longer fit to drink. Mr. Fenster tells you that, but does he tell you what he plans to do about it? No! Because Mr. Fenster may know a great deal about the wines of Paris, but he doesn't know where to begin when it comes to the waters of Philadelphia. But Joe Thomas, Joe Thomas knows where to begin, because at my request he has been working for the past six months on a plan to improve the water that you and your children and every Philadelphian drinks. That's right, Joe Thomas has experience!" Kathryn remembered at this point, but did not mention to Ty, that the bottled water that was delivered by the city to the house each week was brought by Joe Thomas's son-in-law.

Will went on to list half a dozen other advantages that would accrue from Joseph Thomas's experience, and then paused. Ty, like many in the audience, thought this was the end, but Kate knew Will was winding up for the grandstand play.

"Now, I know, and Joe Thomas knows, my friends, that these things concern you. Jobs for our boys coming home. A policeman at the corner of Father Kean's school to keep your children safe from the growing number of automobiles. Clean drinking water. But I also know, just as Joe Thomas does, that these are not the only things that concern you. As both Father Flaherty and Father Kean will tell you, 'Man doth not live by bread alone.' And if the good Fathers were to continue that passage from Deuteronomy for me, they would tell you, 'For the Lord thy God bringeth thee into a good land.' A good land and the freedom to live well in it. We here in this room can give thanks to the Lord for that, but there are others who are not so fortunate. What of our brothers across the sea? Are our Irish brothers free to live well in their own good land? You know as well as I do they are not. At this moment as I stand here speaking to you, our Irish brothers are fighting for the right to rule themselves in their own land in their own way. And for that they must have not only our respect, but our support.

"My friends, Joseph Thomas stands where I do on this question, where each and every one of us stands. Ireland must be free! Ireland must be free!"

The room exploded, as Will knew it would, in cheers and shouts. Cries of "Free Ireland!" echoed and reechoed off the drab green walls.

"Is it always like that?" Ty asked when they were in the car driving back to school. Kathryn had taken him up to see her father after the speech, and she could see Ty was fascinated by the crowd that pushed and shoved around him, eager to shake his hand or merely offer a greeting.

"Not exactly. In South Philadelphia there's no mention of Ireland. There it's more likely to be another statue of Mother Cabrini and more construction jobs on city projects."

"Well, he was brilliant just the same."

"Brilliant?"

"He took them full circle and had them eating out of his hand by the end. He began by wiping out Fenster's war record and bringing the fight down to a local level, and ended up campaigning for the city council on the basis of a free Ireland. It was marvelous."

"You mean Machiavellian."

"I guess that's what I do mean." It was, in fact, what Ty had been thinking. It was a shame such skill couldn't be used along more honorable lines. If he could win them over with pie in the sky, imagine what would happen if he promised them something real and followed through on it.

It was not a question that occupied Ty's thoughts for long. He had been fascinated by the evening—it was like nothing he'd ever seen— but of course it had nothing to do with him. Ty had liked Kathryn's father and been impressed by his manipulation of the crowd, but it was his very cleverness and fancy verbal footwork that at once intrigued and offended Ty. Will Owen might be many things, but he was clearly not a gentleman. It was as if he were from another world, a world Ty had entered for an evening, and now he and Kat were returning to their own.

Emily Enfield sat staring at the picture on the third page of the *Morning Ledger*. There above the story of a political gathering of some sort was a photograph of her own son. He was standing in the background and his face was half-hidden by, of all things, a priest, but it was unmistakably and unbelievably a picture of Ty. And next to him stood that girl. The caption under the photograph did not list Ty's name—one must be grateful for small blessings, Emily thought —but gave the names of several men in the foreground, all congratulating each other at the conclusion of a rally for Mr. Joseph Thomas, candidate for the new city council.

Emily brought the picture closer to get a better look. Her thumb covered Ty's face, as if by covering his photograph she could blot out his presence at the rally, and she peered at the girl standing at his side. She was pretty, certainly, but common, Emily decided, definitely common.

Emily had been a fool to let the girl in the house, but it wouldn't happen again. She'd learned her lesson. Hilary would be told in no uncertain terms that the girl would not be invited to the wedding. And she must speak to Ty as well. That, however, was a more delicate matter. Like many women of her kind, Emily treated her daughters very differently from her son. With the girls she commanded, with Ty she cajoled.

Emily watched him now as he entered the dining room. She was glad he'd come home for the weekend, glad she'd waited until late to breakfast so they could be alone. She waited while the serving girl found out how Ty wanted his eggs.

"And I'd like some ham this morning, Hannah, and some biscuits too."

"You must have been riding," Emily said.

"I'd planned to, but I couldn't drag myself out of bed when Uncle Nick went off."

"Perhaps if you got in a little earlier in the evening—or should I say morning?" Emily smiled indulgently. She intended the comment to sound more like an affectionate joke than a reprimand. "Of course, I know how much in demand you are—in some of the most peculiar places." She handed him the newspaper folded open to the photograph.

"Not very flattering, is it?" Ty handed it back without interest.

"Whatever induced you to go there, Tyson?"

"It seemed a good idea at the time," he said noncommittally as he began to attack the ham and eggs the girl had placed before him. Ty knew exactly where his mother was headed, but he was determined not to help her along the way.

"Well, I can appreciate your wanting to be kind to Hilary's friends from school, dear, but don't you think something like this is a bit extreme? What will people think?"

"That I'm running for office?"

"I wish you would be serious for a moment."

"There's no need to worry, Mother. None of your friends will recognize me."

"Actually, Tyson, it's more than a question of what people will think. It's what that poor girl will expect." Emily forced herself to keep the disdain from her voice.

"What Kat will expect?"

"Kat?" Emily pronounced the word as if she were discussing some flea-ridden animal she insisted Ty remove from the house.

"Kathryn Owen."

"Well, at the risk of being indelicate, dear, a gentleman does not trifle with a lady's affections, even if she is not quite a lady."

"You sound like something out of Jane Austen, Mother. This is 1920, you know."

"A gentleman is always a gentleman."

"I'll keep that in mind."

"Fine, dear. And I'll see that the girl is crossed off the wedding list. We don't want to have the poor thing getting ideas."

"Ideas about Hilary's wedding?"

Emily was beginning to get angry. Tyson knew exactly what she meant, but he was being purposely obtuse. He seemed to want to force her to state the problem openly, and it was always so much better to do these things subtly. "Ideas about you, Tyson. Expectations, if you like, based on misguided kindness on your part."

"My feelings for Kat are not misguided, Mother."

"I wish you wouldn't use that vulgar nickname, Tyson, and now that you mention it, I'd like to know what your feelings for Miss Owen are."

Ty smiled at his mother as if it were the simplest question in the world, and the whole misunderstanding could have been avoided if only she had asked it before. *Really,* Emily thought, watching his expression, *he's being too difficult.*

"Strong, Mother, very strong."

"You mean sexual." She pursed her lips primly as she pronounced the word. She never would have used it with her daughters, and she didn't like using it with her son, but she wanted him to know that she understood the nature of his attraction.

"Now you sound like 1920, Mother."

"Well, at least we've clarified the issue. I can't stop you from seeing the girl—especially if she's that kind of girl—but I won't have her in the house and I certainly won't have her at Hilary's wedding."

"We haven't clarified any issue, Mother. You've merely jumped to a conclusion. A rather unseemly one, I think. My feelings for Kat have to do with more than sex"—Ty smiled to show that he had no trouble with the word—"and you might as well invite her to the wedding, because I'm going to bring her anyway."

"I should think the girl wouldn't want to go where she's not welcome."

"But she is welcome. I'm going to *make* her welcome, and so are you, because if you don't, I won't come to the wedding either."

"I won't be threatened, Tyson."

"I'm not threatening you, Mother. I'm merely telling you my plans."

"Well, your plans do not meet with my approval."

"I'm sorry about that, but they're still my plans. If you like, I can go back to school tonight and not come home for spring vacation. This summer I'll get a place of my own. I have the money Grandfather left me outright—not the trust. It isn't much, but it will be enough."

"There is no need for that, Tyson. This is still your home. I don't like the idea of your bringing that girl here, but I'd rather you bring her here than to an apartment. And I have no doubt your Miss Owen would go unchaperoned to a man's apartment."

"I'm not even going to bother to get angry at that, Mother, because you know nothing about Kathryn. But you're going to know quite a bit about her before I'm through."

Emily started to answer, but saw Nicholas standing in the archway to the dining room. She did not want to continue the argument in front of him. It was more than the fact that she knew he'd be on Ty's side. This was a personal matter between Emily and her only son.

"Am I interrupting something?" Nicholas asked.

Ty stood. "Not at all, Uncle Nick. I was just on my way out."

"Driving into town?" Nicholas asked. "If you'll wait a moment, I think I'll catch a ride with you."

"Sorry, Uncle Nick, not into town." Ty looked directly at his mother. "Just out to Bryn Mawr."

"I must say, Emily, you don't look pleased," Nicholas observed when Ty was gone.

"Have you had breakfast, Nicholas?"

But Nicholas would not be deflected. "It's that Owen girl, isn't it? Hilary's friend who was here for the party."

"Just a passing flirtation, I'm certain."

"If I were you, Emily, I wouldn't be so sure."

"Ty is obviously infatuated, but it won't last. It never does with girls like that. He will get over Miss Owen—and her attractions—and marry Amanda Wycombe."

"With your assistance, of course."

"If necessary."

"Be careful, Emily. You may push Ty just hard enough to make him fight. And you may find Ty learned something about fighting in the war."

"I have no intention of pushing Tyson. At least, not for the moment. And as for Ty's learning anything overseas, Nicholas, he knows nothing about wars of attrition."

On an April afternoon when the grass was wet underfoot and the rain pelted the classroom windows, Hilary drove out to school in Carter's new Ford. Mrs. Branch had bought it as an engagement present, though Hilary said it could scarcely be considered a present, since Cora Branch had saved a year of dividends from Carter's own minuscule trust fund to purchase it.

"The campus is just too depressing in this weather," Hilary said to Kathryn. "Come on, I'll take you into town for tea." The car jerked along under Hilary's inexpert maneuvering. "Carter's been teaching me. He says I'm not a very good student, but I have to learn. We won't be able to afford a driver at first, not on what Daddy's paying him."

"My heart bleeds for you."

"No need to, lamb. We're going to live on love."

Once in the tearoom, Hilary chain-smoked feverishly. "It's unfair. You've had three of those"—Hilary looked longingly at the buttered scones—"and you won't gain a pound." She lit another cigarette. "But I'm determined not to weaken. I'm going to be a svelte bride if it kills me. I want Carter to be driven mad with desire for this lithe white body."

"I thought he was."

Hilary blushed. "Those stories I told you about Bar Harbor, lamb, well, I exaggerated a little. Darn it, I exaggerated a lot. I'm still pure as the driven snow."

For as long as she'd known Hilary, Kathryn could not understand the ease with which she discussed what she called matters sexual. To Kate, it seemed too serious a subject to treat so lightly, but Hilary seemed to share neither her fear nor her fastidiousness. "You really are a sketch, Hil. After all those lectures. 'Virginity is a middle-class prejudice. The upper and lower classes don't have any patience with it.' " Kathryn imitated one of Hilary's discourses.

"Well, Carter made me see things differently."

"You mean Carter opened your eyes to the middle-class view."

"All right, Katie, you can laugh all you want."

"I'm not laughing." Kathryn wasn't laughing, but she was feeling a little sorry for Hilary. It seemed a shame to give up your convictions for someone whose own were so bloodless.

The bootleggers made their deliveries early the Friday of prom weekend, and by teatime the bar of every eating club on campus was fully stocked. By six the parties had begun to spill out of each house over the porches and across the broad green expanses of lawn and merge into a single gently flowing celebration. Young men and girls carrying whiskey-filled teacups drifted from one club to another like blossoms carried on the soft spring breeze, and Kathryn, her hand secure in Ty's, moved along with them, feeling inexpressibly happy. At the third club they visited she was amazed to find her brother Chris on the veranda.

"What are you doing here?" Kate demanded, throwing her arms about his neck.

Over Kate's shoulder Chris saw Tyson Enfield looking bleak. "I think an introduction is in order."

Kate introduced them and Ty looked clearly relieved. He remembered the man vaguely as someone he'd seen around the campus, but he hadn't known his name.

"But what are you doing here?" Kate asked again.

"Human-interest story. The graduating vets, what are they like, all that sort of thing. I got the story because I'd gone here. Well, what about it, Enfield, do you have any comments for the readers of the New York *Herald?*"

"You can tell them that I am entirely in favor of prohibition," Ty said as he refilled Chris's cup, then excused himself and moved off across the veranda to where Tim Wharton was summoning him.

"How long has this been going on?" Chris asked when Ty was out of earshot.

"Has what been going on?"

"You and Tyson Stratford Enfield."

"You know him. I mean, who he is."

"It was hard not to know Tyson Enfield when I was here. Very important man. Top club, Triangle, Senior Council. If only he weren't too light for football, he'd be perfect. But I see from your expression that you think he is perfect."

"There's no need to be nasty."

"Merely listing his qualities. He's a sterling fellow, a legend in his own time. In fact, around here he is something of a legend. Did he ever tell you about his sophomore year?"

"What about it?"

"End of first semester he was flunking out. Hadn't passed a course. Well, the powers that be in the Enfield family must have had something to say about that. Whatever it was, Ty came back in February, made up all the work from the first semester, carried a normal load for the second semester, and finished the year with the highest sophomore average in the history of the school. After that he went back to his gentleman's C's."

"Is that why you don't like him?"

"I never said I didn't like him. In fact, until now, I did."

"You mean until you saw him with me."

"That's exactly what I mean. The story about his marks wasn't the only one that followed Tyson Enfield around. There was something about a girl in an Atlantic City hotel. I just thought you ought to know."

"It would be hard not to know about Ty's checkered past. I roomed with his sister, and she was very proud of it."

"It's not his past that worries me, Katie. It's your future. He'll never marry you."

She flushed. "You're the only one who's mentioned marriage."

"I bet I am. Who are you trying to kid, Katie. It's written all over you. You're crazy about him. Well, I can't do anything about that, but I can try to make you see things the way they are. I know Tyson Enfield and I know his friends. They've got good manners, so they'll be friendly up to a point—but only up to a point. And that point stops short of marriage." Chris remembered that weekend on Long Island just before he'd got sick. "Keep it in mind if you ever start to think about Atlantic City."

"If you weren't my brother, I'd slap you for that."

"If I weren't your brother, I wouldn't have bothered to say it."

Around three in the morning Tim Wharton began to organize a

party to drive to the coast to watch the sunrise. "Nothing more romantic than the Jersey coast at dawn. Puts the Riviera to shame."

"You never got to the Riviera, Wharton," someone said.

"But I know all Ty's stories by heart."

They started out with a caravan of five cars, but no one was in a mood to follow anyone else, and finally they agreed through shouts and signals to meet at a certain spot in Deal. It was still dark when Ty pulled the Marmon up to the edge of the beach. Fifty yards away a white stucco palace loomed against the ocean, its orange roof shimmering in the moonlight.

"It looks as if we won," Ty said.

"Either that or we're in the wrong place."

"Are you questioning my navigation, Miss Owen?"

"Never. Only Tim's directions."

"Well, that's the Wyndham place. You can't miss it. It's the only house up this far."

"Then we'll just have to wait for the rest of them."

"And with any luck they'll never find us. How about sampling the water? You can leave your shoes in the car."

When they got to the edge of the water, Ty rolled up his trousers. "You'd better take off your stockings." Kathryn didn't look at Ty as she rolled her stockings down, but she knew he was watching her.

The water was icy against her legs. Once or twice Ty saw a wave coming and pulled her back before it could splash over her dress. They walked for a while along the edge of the water, and when they were past the large stucco house, Ty spread his jacket on the sand and they sat side by side staring out at the Atlantic.

"During the war I used to swear that once it was over I was going to take a tramp steamer around the world. I was going to go places where people had never heard of Philadelphia and see things no one from Philadelphia had ever seen."

"Why didn't you?"

"When I first got home, all I wanted was to sleep in a dry bed, eat food that was hot and didn't come out of a tin, and never take another order."

"And then you were back at school, and it was too late?"

"And then I'd met you and it was too late." He turned her face to him, and his mouth was warm on hers. He kissed her a second time and a third, and they were lying side by side on the sand. His mouth was soft and his tongue sharp with the taste of whiskey and desire. She felt his hand through the lace bodice of her dress, then warm and gentle against her skin. She wanted to go on kissing him, to go on holding him and being held and touched by him, and she pressed her body to his and felt the length of him lean and hard against her. His lips traced the line of her neck, following the path of his hands to where he'd undone her dress, and the touch of his mouth against her skin made her catch her breath. He heard the change in her breathing.

"I love you, Kat," he murmured against her skin. "I love you."

She heard the words but they had less meaning now than the warmth of his mouth against her breast, the excitement of his hands against her skin, the desire she felt rising within her until it seemed like a giant wave that would come rolling over the beach and drown them both. He raised his face to hers again and kissed her again, and she tasted him again and wanted him. Then the touch of his fingers against her thigh cut through the desire. It should not have, and perhaps at another time it would not have, but she heard Chris's words from earlier in the evening, and for a moment it seemed as if she could see him standing there on the beach looking down at them, and the cool sardonic eyes revealed their tangled bodies in a light sharper than the soft moonlight.

She pulled away. "I think we'd better go back."

Ty looked at her closely, as if trying to see if she really meant it. When he spoke, there was no anger in his voice, only sorrow. "Whatever you say, Kat."

Everyone agreed the wedding went off with a minimum of mishap. A few guests in rear pews noticed that the bride stumbled on the runner as she started down the aisle, but the kinder among them blamed it on nervousness rather than a lack of grace. Sally Reed, the bride's cousin, fainted in the church and had to be revived with Mrs. Reed's smelling salts, but Sally was known to be a girl who liked to attract attention. The most serious problem occurred early in the reception when the bride's father was summoned to the telephone. The manager of the West Philadelphia Railroad yard called to report that someone had scrawled a nasty word on the side of the private railroad car that had carried Drew Middleton and his branch of Middletons up from Charleston.

"Where was the guard?" Samuel Enfield demanded.

"He can't be everywhere at once, Mr. Enfield."

"Perhaps not, but I should expect him to be within view of Mr. Middleton's car. What did you say your name was?"

"Curry, sir." Mr. Curry did not know for certain that Mr. Enfield was on the board of directors of the Pennsylvania Railroad, but he did know that if he were not, his friends were.

"Well, Curry, see that the word is removed before Mr. Middleton returns this afternoon."

"It's being done right now, sir."

"And see that the car is watched more carefully as long as it's in the Philadelphia yard."

"Yes, Mr. Enfield. I'll have a man stationed on it for the rest of the day."

Samuel Enfield saw no reason to mention the incident to Drew Middleton, but he did make a mental note as he returned to the garden, where the reception was unfolding like a well-directed play, to look into the security system in the West Philadelphia yard. The rest of the city might be crumbling in a dirty, lawless heap—that was why Samuel had sold the house on Rittenhouse Square right after the war —but on railroad property, discipline must be maintained.

A wooden dance floor had been erected on a level piece of land just beyond the house, and Samuel Enfield was in time for his first dance with his daughter. He thought as he watched Hilary turn from Carter to him that she looked prettier than he'd ever seen her, not pretty of course, but prettier than he'd ever seen her. Samuel Enfield was pleased. It was a good match, and one that seemed to make his daughter happy.

For Kathryn the wedding was a pleasant surprise. She had expected a repetition of New Year's Eve, but Mrs. Enfield seemed content to let Ty spend as much time at Kate's side as he wished, and when Kathryn had passed through the receiving line Emily Enfield had greeted her warmly and said wasn't it nice to see her again. Nevertheless, several times during the reception when Kate looked up, she found Mrs. Enfield watching her closely. Nicholas Enfield, standing with Kathryn under an old willow at the end of the garden, noticed his sister-in-law's interest.

"You seem to have caught Mrs. Enfield's eye," he said to Kathryn.

"I'm glad you noticed it. I was beginning to think it was my imagination."

"Far from it, my dear. You have Mrs. Enfield worried. But try not to let her worry you." Nicholas sipped his champagne. "She's a dragon, but"—he looked at Kathryn meaningfully—"young men have been slaying dragons for centuries."

Ty returned balancing three glasses of champagne. "I hope you haven't been bringing the family skeletons out of the closet, Uncle Nick. You'll scare Kat off."

"As a matter of fact, I was telling Kate—I may call you Kate, mayn't I—about young men slaying dragons."

"Slaying dragons?"

Nicholas laughed. "Kate knows what I meant, Ty." He turned to Kathryn. "Don't let him backslide, my dear. You keep him up to the mark, and he'll make a fine knight. And now, if you young people will excuse me, I hear the strains of a waltz, and Mrs. Morris has promised to waltz with me this afternoon."

"He likes you," Ty said as he and Kate moved onto the dance floor.

"I like him."

"What was all that about knights slaying dragons?"

"Your uncle has a chivalrous view of you."

"You say that as if you don't."

"Perhaps I'm reserving judgment."

"Just find me a dragon and I'll slay it."

Kate could hardly keep from laughing when she saw Ty's mother standing behind him.

"Excuse me, children. I'm sorry to interrupt your dance, but, Ty, have you seen Daphne? The last I saw of her she was dancing with Mr. Curtaine, but that was more than half an hour ago."

"Perhaps she's helping Hilary change, Mother." Both Ty and Emily knew that was unlikely.

"Well, if you find her, dear, please tell her I'd like to see her."

Even when Hilary stood at the top of the great circular staircase looking flushed and happy and tossed the white bouquet over her shoulder, and it literally fell into Kathryn's hands, Emily Enfield remained calm and cordial, although she did mention to Cora Branch later in the afternoon that she had always found tossing the bouquet a vulgar tradition. "But girls these days seem to insist on it." In any event, Emily had little time to worry about Kathryn Owen that afternoon. Chaperoning Daphne was work for more than one woman. Emily Enfield thoroughly approved of Randolph Curtaine and the attention he was paying her daughter. She only hoped Daphne wouldn't do something wild and ruin things before they started. Daphne would come out next year, and it was Emily's intention to marry her off as soon as possible. Perhaps with the aid of a husband the girl could be controlled.

By late afternoon Carter and Hilary were on their way to New

York and a suite at the St. Regis—tomorrow they would sail on the *France*—the Drew Middletons had returned to their carefully cleaned private railroad car, and Emily Enfield sat with her husband and Cora Branch in a state of extreme satisfaction. Through the open windows of the downstairs sitting room they could see Hatton, the two gardeners, and half a dozen maids removing every trace of the festivities.

"I thought Hilary looked sweet," Cora Branch said.

"Everyone just adored Carter," Emily answered.

"They looked happy," Samuel said.

"Of course they looked happy, Samuel. They are happy. It was a splendid wedding," Emily pronounced.

Emily Enfield basked in her own satisfaction and the admiration of Cora Branch. She had pulled off a good match and given a superb wedding. Mentally she kicked off her shoes and relaxed. For the moment even the problems of Tyson and Daphne seemed remote.

Emily would not have felt so serene had she seen Ty take a bottle of champagne from one of the buckets in the kitchen, where a last two dozen were still cooling, and two glasses. "Now that's over, we can enjoy ourselves," he said, taking Kate's hand and leading her across the garden. The shadows were lengthening, and in the wooded glade beyond the garden it was cool and dim.

"Where are we going?"

"For a walk. It will sober us up."

"Is that what the champagne's for?"

"The champagne is for after we've sobered up."

Hand in hand they walked through the trees and down the hill to the little pond below the house. "Is this all yours?" Kate asked.

"It's all Enfield, if that's what you mean. Beyond those trees"—Ty pointed to the west, where the sun hung like a garish orange ball above a line of elms and spruces—"there's a fence that marks the border. On the other side it goes down to the main road."

"And whose is that?" Kathryn pointed to a small brick cottage half-hidden in a clump of trees. It was all but invisible from the big house.

"That's Uncle Nicholas's studio. Come on, I'll show you."

Inside the cottage was cool and damp. It was obvious that the rooms were cleaned regularly but never used. On the first floor there was a sitting room and a small pantry. A winding wrought-iron staircase led to a second floor. "There's a studio and another room upstairs, but Uncle Nick keeps the studio locked."

"A locked room. It is like a family skeleton," Kate said.

Ty took a cretonne throw from the sofa. "Sit down, my child, and I will tell you of the Enfield curse." He poured a glass of champagne for each of them and sat next to her on the sofa. "Actually, it's rather a sad story. Grandfather build the cottage for Uncle Nicholas when he came home from Paris in the nineties.

"After Uncle Nick finished Princeton, he was sent on the grand tour, as befitted a young man of his time, but Uncle Nick's conduct was far from fitting. He had the audacity to write home that he planned to stay in Paris and paint. Of course, Grandfather wouldn't hear of it. He said Nicholas only wanted to stay in Paris to drink and cavort with fancy ladies—and if I remember Grandfather correctly, he would use that term. He said if Nicholas wanted to paint he could come home and paint what he knew best, Philadelphia. I imagine mention was made at that point of his friend Mr. Eakins."

"So your uncle came home."

"He put up a bit of a fight, or so the story goes, but when Grandfather's checks stopped, the battle was over. Uncle Nick came home, and Grandfather built this cottage for him. He was supposed to paint here, and he could even live here if he liked. Apparently he did for a few years, but ever since I can remember, the place has been closed up. Mother has it cleaned and aired regularly, all except for the studio upstairs. Uncle Nick keeps that locked."

"What do you suppose happened? I mean, why did he stop, and what's locked in the room?"

"I don't know, and of course no one in the family is ever going to say. Maybe Grandfather was right. Maybe Uncle Nick didn't care about painting at all. Maybe he did want to stay in Paris to drink and cavort with fancy ladies. Any maybe there's nothing in the room but blank canvases."

"I don't believe that."

"You two certainly hit it off."

"There's another thing I don't understand. After you grandfather died, after your uncle had money of his own, why didn't he go back to Paris? Especially if all he wanted was the wine and the women."

Ty thought for a moment. He had asked himself the same question. "I guess it was too late. Whatever the dream was, it was just too late."

"That's so sad," Kate said quietly.

Ty refilled their glasses. "Oh, Uncle Nick's happy enough. He's got his horses, and he's a great old bachelor—everyone's favorite extra man."

"But that sounds so lonely." She was toying absently with Hilary's bouquet, and Ty's fingers twined with hers through the baby's breath. "Maybe that's what's wrong with Uncle Nick. He never fell in love. He never found anyone like you. It would have made all the difference."

His words were soft against her ear, then his arms were around her, holding her to him, and she could feel the bridal bouquet crushed between them. She was lightheaded from the champagne, and each time he kissed her she could taste it again on his tongue. His hands against the thin chiffon sent wave after wave of warmth through her. She felt his fingers at the tiny buttons that ran down the back of her dress, his hands sliding the dress from her shoulders, then the straps of the chemise, drawing it down her body as easily as he had the dress, and she was sure it could not be happening to her. It was someone else's body there on the couch in the dimly lighted room, someone else who watched Ty undressing her, but then his hands were on her skin, and the sensations were hers and she knew the hands that moved slowly and searchingly were Ty's, and what was happening was happening to them. She thought dimly, distantly that she ought to stop him, but she didn't want to stop him, and then she felt his mouth against her skin, the lips smooth and warm, and she was left without a will to stop him.

"Ty . . ." she said. "Ty, don't," because the words had been imprinted in her mind long ago, but he felt her body moving against his and knew she did not mean it.

His stiff shirt was rough against her skin, but then the shirt was gone and his skin was smooth against hers. His body was slender and felt hard against the softness of her own, and she felt him guiding her hands and marveled at the pleasure of touching him, as fierce and exciting as being touched by him, and they were tangled together hands and mouths and breasts and thighs until it was not her flesh or his but the two of them moving together as one. And just as there was no distinction between her body and his, there was no thought and there were no words such as right or wrong, but only the two of them who had now become the one of them, and the sensation of that, the trembling, terrifying, inexplicable sensation that made her cling to him in the shock of it.

When Kathryn opened her eyes, it seemed impossible that nothing in the room had changed. In the dim light that filtered through the leaded windows, the room looked bare and unforgiving.

"Ty . . ."

"Mmm . . ." Her head lay on his chest, and his answer sounded like the rumblings of his heart.

"All those stories Hilary told about you . . ."

"What stories?"

"About the Riviera. Red Cross girls, Elsie Janis. This isn't like that, is it?"

"Kat," he whispered into her hair, "this isn't anything like that." And it was true, he thought. Making love to Kat had been nothing like sex with those girls he hadn't cared about. Everything about her was different—the smell of her hair, the taste of her skin, the way her hands moved on his body—and everything he'd felt with her had been different. "It's different with you because I love you." He closed his eyes for a moment and the sensations of the last half-hour rioted in his mind, a heady echo of the pure physical passion. When he opened them, he found he was staring at the bridal bouquet that glowed like an incandescent flower in the dimness. "I love you, Kat, and I want to marry you."

"You don't have to say that because . . . because of this."

"I'm not. I want to marry you. I promise I won't try to turn you into a doll, Kat. I don't want a doll. I just want you."

She lifted her head and looked at him. The gray eyes were softer than she had ever seen them, almost like velvet.

"What do you say, Kat? Will you marry me?"

"Yes," she said quietly. "Yes," she repeated with her mouth on his.

The house was dark downstairs by the time Ty returned that night, but Emily, sitting up in bed reading, heard him climb the stairs to the second floor and start down the hall past her room. "Is that you, Ty?" she called quietly. "Come in and say good night."

"I thought you'd be asleep by now, Mother," he said as he entered. "It was a long day."

"And a fine one. Don't you think it went well?"

"I think it went very well."

"The dress was becoming to Hilary, don't you think?"

"Very becoming, Mother."

"And Daphne looked lovely in the yellow chiffon."

"She always does."

"That Mr. Curtaine seemed quite taken with her. I must make a note to see that he's invited to her dance."

"I'm sure Daf will remind you when the time comes."

"Well, I'm not going to worry about that for a while. Hilary's wedding went well, and now I'm going to take a rest before I begin to do a thing about Daphne's debut."

"Is that you, Ty?" The door to Samuel Enfield's room had been left ajar, and he entered his wife's bedroom now, tying a silk robe around him.

"I hope we didn't wake you, Samuel," Emily said.

"Wasn't asleep yet." It was one of the problems of age, Samuel thought, but didn't say. Exhaustion did not necessarily bring sleep.

"I was just telling Ty," Emily said, "that I plan to take a rest before I do a thing about Daphne's debut."

"A good idea," Sam said. "It's a great deal of work, marrying off a daughter."

It was the perfect opening, Ty thought. "But not a son. You won't have to do a thing this time around, Mother. Kat's agreed to marry me." His smile invited congratulations, though he was fairly certain none would be forthcoming.

"She's agreed to marry you! I should think so," Emily said. "I should think she hasn't stopped scheming toward it for a moment. Nevertheless, it won't happen."

"But it will, Mother. We're going to be married. As soon as possible."

"Now, listen to me, Tyson. I've put up with your whims and your bad manners for long enough. I've allowed that girl in my house and treated her like the lady she definitely is not. I did because I thought you'd tire of her. Men always do of that type. But instead of tiring of her, you've simply lost all your senses. Well, I have no intention of putting up with this ill-mannered joke any longer. You are not going to marry her."

"I have the feeling we've had this conversation before," Ty said. "I told you then that I was going to go on seeing Kat with or without your approval, and I'm telling you now that I'm going to marry her with or without your approval."

"You have every right to."

"Samuel," Emily cried. "What are you saying?"

"I'm saying that if Ty has made up his mind he loves this girl and wants to marry her, he ought to. I'm not saying I approve of his choice entirely, but I am saying the choice is his to make. After all, he's a grown man. If he was old enough to fight for his country, and be wounded in its service, then I guess he's old enough to choose his own wife."

The color had drained from Emily's cheeks until her complexion matched the white lace ruffle of her bed jacket. "Samuel, you don't mean that."

"But I do, dear. Ty is old enough to know his own mind."

"Well, thank you very much, sir."

"There's only one thing that worries me," Samuel continued. "And that's the girl. This Kathryn." He went on quickly before Ty could interrupt him. "Oh, I don't mean your mother's objections. It's a pity she isn't one of us, but as years pass I imagine people will forget that. And personally I rather like her. That's why I'm worried, Ty. I don't want to see you make her unhappy."

"If you mean I won't be able to settle down, you're wrong. I'm ready to. As long as it's with Kat."

"That's good to hear, Ty. I suppose you have some position in mind."

"Well, not exactly."

"Surely you don't expect me to support you and your wife? After all, if you're old enough to choose a wife, you're old enough to support her."

"I should have known you didn't mean it," Ty said. "About not minding."

"You're being unjust, Ty. I did mean it. I would never try to force you to marry someone you didn't want to, or prevent you from marrying someone you did, but neither do I intend to let you walk into marriage like some undergraduate lark we'll have to bail you out of in a year's time. I'd like to know how you intend to support your wife. And I expect the girl's father will want to know the same thing."

"There's the money from Grandfather. Not the trust fund, but the rest."

"That won't go very far."

"And I'll get a job. Right after graduation."

"What sort of job?"

"I don't know. I hadn't thought about it. But that doesn't mean I won't be able to get one. Other men do."

"I see. Perhaps you'll sell stocks and bonds. No, I see from your face that doesn't appeal to you. Insurance? No, I don't think that's for you either. I'd hate to see you choose the wrong career just to make some quick money. And while we're on the subject, Ty, the money isn't going to be nearly as quick as you think it is. It's one thing to walk into a family firm and quite another to work your way up from the bottom. You may not be aware of it, but you pay your bootlegger more a month than you're going to make in any job you get. And I'm not thinking only of you. Miss Owen may not have any family or background, but she's always had some money. I don't think she's any more suited to living in a small flat and doing her own housework than you are to selling insurance or bonds."

"We'll manage," Ty said.

"I have a better suggestion," his father continued. "One that will satisfy all of us, except perhaps your mother"—he smiled at Emily—"though I expect she'll adjust eventually. Why don't you start law school in the fall? I know you said you didn't want to, and I was perfectly willing to give you a year or two to decide what it was you did want to do after college, but it seems Miss Owen has changed all that. I suggest you enter the University in the fall, with an understanding with Miss Owen, of course. You'll complete law school while you're engaged, and then you can be married as soon as you're graduated."

"But that's three years!"

"It's up to you, Ty. Either you're responsible enough and love the girl enough to want to take care of her properly, or you're simply rushing into this thing on the spur of the moment to fulfill some . . . shall we say desire of your own. Excuse me, Emily, but I think Ty knows what I mean. If you're half the man I think you are, and if you care about her as much as you say you do, there's only one answer."

"But three years," Ty repeated.

"Your mother and I were engaged for two," his father said. "And one more thing, Ty. I think it would be better if we didn't announce the engagement right now. I think you'll find her family will agree. There's no point in having an announcement in the newspapers three years before the fact. Perhaps during your last year of school. It seems to me that's an appropriate time. But for the moment, allow me to congratulate you, and you can tell Miss Owen, Kathryn, I wish her good luck."

Kathryn had expected to feel some remorse the morning after Hilary's wedding, but it was the single emotion she didn't experience. Exhilaration, longing, surprise, pride, chased one another around in her mind so that her answers to her mother's questions were confused, and when her father commented that she was looking well this morning, she felt the color rise in her cheeks. Later, on the porch, with no one for company except Chip, whose childish dialogue with himself provided a soothing background to her thoughts, Kathryn thought of Ty and the time alone in Nicholas's studio and felt a tightening in her stomach as sure as a physical contraction. She supposed she should feel remorse, but there was nothing but an overwhelming eagerness to see him, to be with him.

They drove down to the Corinthian Yacht Club that night. Uncle Nick, Ty explained, kept his yacht there. "It isn't terribly large, but it is comfortable. When Uncle Nick takes to the water, he likes to be as comfortable as possible. No single sculls or small-class racers for him."

The boat was, as Ty promised, luxurious. The rugs and furnishings, Kate guessed, were more valuable than those in her own home, and there were several very good paintings. "Uncle Nick changes those every month," Ty said. "He's afraid the dampness will ruin them, but he says he can't stand to be anywhere there aren't good pictures."

"Absolutely cramped," Kate said after Ty had shown her through the main saloon, galley, master stateroom, and another smaller one.

"Well, it couldn't be too small." Ty laughed. "After all, Nicholas is on a pretty large scale himself."

Kathryn had noticed a picnic basket in the rumble seat of the car, and now Ty took two bottles of champagne and a cold chicken from it. "The wine comes with the compliments of Mr. and Mrs. Carter Middleton Branch. The chicken is from Ellen, the cook."

"Does she always do things like this for you? The cook, I mean."

"Whenever she gets the chance. She's crazy about me."

Kate took the glass of champagne he handed her. "Aren't all of us poor besotted women?"

He sat next to her. "But there's only one I want to be crazy about me." He took her hand. "I hope you don't mind about the picnic, Kat, but I didn't want to go out. I wanted to be alone with you. I haven't been able to think of anything but being alone with you all day."

"I don't mind, Ty. I'd rather be alone with you, too."

"I was afraid you wouldn't want to. I was afraid you'd be sorry."

"So was I, but I'm not." She traced the line of his mouth with her finger. "Not in the least." She leaned over so that her mouth was on his, and she could feel the familiar stirrings within her. When he took her hand and led her into the forward cabin, she did not hesitate. The only light in the stateroom was reflected from the main cabin, but she could see his face clearly and read the emotion in the soft gray eyes, an emotion that seemed to mirror her own. She started to unbutton her dress, but he stopped her.

"Let me," he whispered. It was a repetition of last night as she felt his hands deft at her clothes, then warm on her skin, but it was different too because there was no struggle within her. She worked quickly at his clothing, but she was inexperienced, and he had to help her, and they laughed for a moment at that, but only for a moment, because his mouth was on hers again, then moving over her body, touching it, tasting it, and her hands were tracing his own from the broad shoulders down the long, clean line to narrow hips. And it was different, too, because instead of the narrow sofa there was the wide bed made for lovemaking, and instead of the rush of the first time there was the pleasure of all the time in the world, and she could move slowly, exploring the wonderment that was Ty's body, feeling the network of muscle and tendon beneath the smooth skin, twining and untwining in the long arms and legs, and she could feel the same luxuriant ease in him as if he would spend the rest of his life exploring her with his hands and his mouth and his eyes. But then he was inside her and their instincts quickened until they were racing heedlessly through sensation and pleasure, driven by both, beyond both to an end that left them clinging together in exhaustion and amazement.

"My God," he whispered. His voice in the half-darkness sounded incredulous, and Kate was very glad.

Later she started to dress, but he wouldn't let her put on any more than her chemise. "I can look at you in a dress anytime," he said, and bent to kiss her shoulder.

They took the champagne to the cockpit and Ty stretched out with his head in her lap. It was a clear night and the stars were distinct overhead, while the lights of the city made a faint corona on the distant horizon. Kate had been staring off toward the lights, and when she looked down she saw that Ty was staring up at her. The gray eyes were soft rather than bright now, and she reached down and brushed the hair from his forehead. It was hard to keep from touching him.

"I almost forgot," Ty said. He reached into the pocket of his trousers that looked unnaturally white in contrast to his suntanned chest.

"Let me have your hand," he said. "Your left hand." She gave it to him, and he slipped a small ring, not on the third finger, as she'd expected, but on the last. "Of course, it's not a real engagement ring, but we can pretend it is for a while."

Kathryn looked at the delicate gold band. It was old and so small it must have been a baby's ring at one time. "It's beautiful, Ty. More beautiful than any usual engagement ring."

"I'm going to get you one of those too. If only for everyone else. I want every man who looks at you to know 'hands off.' As soon as I can, I'm going to march down to Bailey, Banks, and Biddle and buy a huge vulgar diamond that flashes 'hands off, everyone, Kat belongs to me.'"

She ran a hand over the smooth skin of his chest. "And until I get that huge vulgar ring, I still belong to you."

"Do you mean that, Kat? Even if it takes a while?"

She started to ask if what takes a while, but suddenly she knew the answer without being told.

"I talked to the family last night. I decided there was no point in putting it off. I told them we were going to be married." Ty felt the hand that had been tracing a lazy pattern on his chest stop. "I didn't ask them, Kat, I told them."

"And what did they say?" Her voice was flat, as if she were asking the time.

"They said it was fine," he lied.

"Ty, your mother said nothing of the kind."

"Well, Father did. He even said I was to wish you luck for him. He congratulated me and wished you luck."

The perfect gentleman, Kate thought. Never forgets his manners, even in a crisis, and she was sure she'd caused a crisis in the Enfield house last night. Emily Enfield had been polite at the wedding, but she would not have been polite last night.

"But he did bring up one point," Ty continued.

"I thought he might."

"Well, he's right, Kat. If I'm going to marry you, I ought to be able to support you."

If it were happening to someone else, she would have laughed. Tyson Stratford Enfield was worried about supporting his wife. They sat on this yacht, this small yacht according to Ty, that probably cost more than her father's official salary, and talked about whether or not he'd be able to support her. Sell the Marmon, she wanted to say, and we'll live for a year. Sell one horse, Ty, the one that you get home to ride so rarely that the groom has to exercise him, and we'll live for two.

"So he came up with a perfectly logical solution," Ty went on, as if marriage were a perfectly logical business to begin with. "He suggested that I finish law school and . . ."

"Finish law school! You haven't even started law school."

"Well, I'll start in the fall, and as soon as I'm finished, we can be married."

"Excuse me." Kathryn disengaged herself. "I think I'd like to be a little more formally dressed if we're going to continue this conversation."

He followed her below. "Listen, Kat, I know how you feel. I was pretty angry myself at first. And to tell you the truth, if it had been Mother who'd made the suggestion I would have expected a trick. But . . . well, he's right. I don't have any right to ask you to marry me if I can't support you. Maybe it's something only a man can understand. . . ."

"Oh, no, I understand it perfectly," Kate said, straightening her dress and climbing the three stairs back to the cockpit.

He didn't know if she meant it or not. "Will you please stop running away from me?"

She sat and smiled up at him. "I'm not running away now or during the next three years." She held up her left hand with the delicate antique ring. "You're stuck with me, Enfield. Whether you like it or not, you're stuck with me."

"I like it all right," he said, drawing her to him. "I like it more than I've ever liked anything in my life. I love you, Kat, and nothing, not three years, not anybody's family, nothing is going to change that."

She felt his arms holding her to him and heard the reassuring words, and over his shoulders she could see the faint haze of lights that was the reflection of the city. It would be a long battle, she thought, but she looked at the lights of the city and knew she would win. There was a time when she wouldn't have, there was a time when Emily Enfield and her kind owned those lights and everything they illuminated, but that time was gone, and it was gone partly because of the fight Will Owen had waged. Well, she was Will Owen's daughter, and she knew something of battles herself. Hadn't Will kept her in training most of her life? She had never fought for what Will wanted her to fight for because she had never wanted what he wanted for her, but she would fight now. She would fight Emily

Enfield and Samuel and three years of law school, three years of waiting and three years of worrying that she might get pregnant, because no matter how careful they were, that would always be a possibility, but she'd fight all that because if she won—no, when she'd won —she'd have Ty.

"You'll be the prettiest girl there," Margaret Owen said. "The prettiest girl, bar none."

"You don't have to sound as if you're going to cry about it, Mother," Kate answered, but she was only trying to keep her mother from making too much of it. For Margaret, however, it was an occasion for celebration. To think that her daughter was going off to the Devon Horse Show looking as lovely as Lady Fenleigh herself in the pale flower print dress and the wide-brimmed hat with the blue ribbon that echoed the color of her eyes. To think she was going off there looking like that and engaged to Tyson Stratford Enfield. To be sure, it wasn't an official engagement yet, but he'd spoken to Will, and Margaret was satisfied it was only a matter of time.

The look in Ty's eyes when he came to pick Kate up that morning mirrored Margaret's admiration. He said she looked much too good to waste on the crowds at the Devon Horse Show, and if they had any sense at all they'd go off alone for the day, but now as she sat in a first-tier box with Emily Enfield and watched Amanda Wycombe looking like a perfect mannequin of a girl as she circled the ring in her tight-fitting black riding coat and shallow-crowned derby, Kathryn felt less confident of her own appearance. Amanda was riding sidesaddle, a position that struck Kate as decidedly precarious, but Amanda's small body seemed very much at ease, and her face, so far as Kate could see it beneath the tightly drawn veil, looked completely confident.

"Amanda does sit a horse well," Emily said. "Don't you think so, Kathryn?"

"Amanda does everything well, Mrs. Enfield," Kate answered, and heard what could only be Daphne's snicker behind her.

"And she does look handsome," Emily continued. "That's one of the things I've always admired about Amanda. She doesn't let down her standards. Not just on an occasion like this, but always. Now, in the autumn at the hunt, some of the young people, and I'm sorry to say that includes my own children, turn up in all sorts of tweeds, but not Amanda."

"Never Amanda." Daphne laughed. "Why, I've heard her say she owes it to hounds to dress properly."

"It would not hurt you, Daphne, to take a lesson from Amanda," Emily said.

Daphne looked up at Randy Curtaine, who was sitting next to her. "Do you think I should take a lesson from Amanda?" she whispered.

"You don't need any lessons at all, honey chile," he drawled.

If the sight of Amanda straight-backed and graceful on her chestnut mare was disconcerting, the appearance of Ty was disarming. Kate had never seen him on horseback before, and it seemed impossible that this dashing stranger dressed like an English squire from another era was the same Ty who loved her and wanted to marry her. It seemed impossible that the graceful body that took every jump with ease was the one she knew so well.

It was Nicholas, however, who carried the day for the family. Despite his girth, his performance on the jumper White Lightning assured that he'd walk off with the cup. When he came over to their box after the competition, his face florid and beaming, his manner almost strutting, Kate couldn't help thinking he looked like a child who'd won the prize at his own birthday party. "There's an air of absurdity to these things," he whispered to her, "but I can't help loving them. Especially when I win." He took a seat next to Kathryn after that, and kept up an irreverent running commentary on the other events and contestants.

"Fine form, your young man," he said to Kate at one point, "but not the will to win.

"There's the will to win," he added later, when Amanda appeared for her last event. Even at this distance Kate could sense the concentration in Amanda's body and saw the force with which she spurred the horse. And she felt a little sick when, as Amanda passed their box on the way out of the ring, she saw the stain of fresh blood on the animal's flank.

"I hate to see that," Nicholas said quietly.

Later that night in the great tent that had been set up for dinner and dancing, the Enfield table was the center of considerable celebration. Everyone stopped by to congratulate Nicholas, and even Emily went out of her way to be nice to him. For once he'd brought glory rather than disgrace to the family.

Kathryn saw Amanda approach their table, say a few words to Nicholas, then move on to Ty. It was just at that point that Randy Curtaine, sitting on Kate's other side, asked her to dance.

"I wouldn't worry about her," he drawled.

"About whom?" Kate asked coolly.

"The little blond one. She's pretty enough, I'll give you that, but she's all ice. No fire there. Now, I don't imagine that's your problem."

Kate wondered if she wore some magical scarlet letter on her chest that could be seen by men like Randy.

"Though ever since we met, you've been going out of your way to make me think it is. I'm getting real discouraged, ma'am."

"In that case, I'm making progress. Anyway, I thought you came up to see Daphne."

"I don't see that one thing has anything to do with the other."

"And how does Daphne feel about that?"

A slow, lazy smile crept across his mouth. "Well, now, you might say that Daphne and I understand each other. You might say we understand each other perfectly."

If Randy Curtaine were right, and Kathryn suspected he might be, it seemed a terrible shame for Daphne.

In the summer of 1921, a year after Ty asked Kate to marry him, the social pages of the Philadelphia papers carried a variety of announcements that affected Kathryn in one way or another. In May there was an account of Daphne Tyson Enfield's debut. Kate read the report of the ball the following morning and had to smile to herself at the gulf between the description of Daphne as a delicate beauty destined to be the debutante of the season and the reality of the restless young girl sure to be the scandal of the year. Kathryn remembered a conversation she'd had with Daphne when the younger girl, at loose ends again having been fired from another day school, drove over to Bryn Mawr. She'd finally convinced the family that there was no point in enrolling her in still another school, especially since she'd be coming out in a few months.

"But what are you going to do now?" Kate asked.

"Do?" Daphne asked. "Well, I'm going to try to convince Daddy to get me an automobile, preferably a Stutz, so I don't have to beg to borrow Uncle Nick's, I'm going to go to parties, and I'm going to get married as soon as I possibly can because then I'll really be able to do what I want."

In June the papers announced that District Attorney William Owen, Jr., would marry Miss Helen Schron. The social page did not say, though everyone who knew Bill agreed, that Helen Schron bore an uncanny resemblance to Louise in both appearance and disposition. Bill had made a good choice again, and it was time little Chip had a mother.

In July the papers ran a brief paragraph stating that a daughter had been born to Mr. and Mrs. Carter Middleton Branch, and later that same month Mr. and Mrs. Samuel Stratford Enfield announced the engagement of their daughter Daphne to Randolph Middleton Curtaine. The social announcements seemed to rain down on Kate that summer, but at no time did the papers carry news of her, unless you counted the list of the graduating class of Bryn Mawr College, 1921.

Three days after Hilary returned home from the hospital with the first member of a new generation of Enfields, Kathryn took the train out to the modest house in one of those new developments where young couples like Carter and Hilary stopped for a few years on their way to the great estates of the area.

Hilary received her—received was the only word for it, Kate thought—in the small master bedroom. She was stretched out on a chaise and looked smug and a little incongruous in a frilly pink morning gown. Ruffles and lace never were Hilary's long suit. A few minutes after Kate arrived the nurse brought the baby in, and Kate thought the small squirming thing with the bald head looked as foolish in her white lawn dress as Hilary did in the pink gown. The nurse announced we'd taken our whole bottle, Hilary began to talk baby talk to the bundle placed in her arms, and Kathryn felt as if she'd suddenly been dropped center stage in the middle of a very bad farce. But that was nothing compared to Hilary's talk after the baby was taken offstage. Kate had been prepared for a flow of information on midnight feedings, layettes, and, given Hilary, the aftereffects of childbirth, but instead Hilary ran on about dancing classes and putting Camilla's name down for day school and Emily's arrangements for her invitation to the Assembly. It seemed to Kate that the child had come into the world with a dance program on her wrist. More immediately, there were the plans for the christening. Carter's first cousin was coming up from Baltimore to serve as godmother. Only a momentary quickening of speech indicated that Hilary even remembered announcing to Kate several months ago that she was going to be a godmother.

All told, it hadn't been much of a morning, and Kathryn was glad she could not accept Hilary's invitation to stay for lunch. She had an appointment in town at two, and she just had time to catch the Paoli local back. Hilary did not ask where she was going. After all, Kate's appointment had no bearing on Camilla's future.

When Kate was ushered into the office of Addison Wales at five minutes past two, she felt as if she were back at Highfield or another of the dozens of houses Ty had taken her to in the last year. The man's austere features, the carefully trimmed brown hair, the dark business suit, and stiff collar all screamed of Ty's world. And the tasteful, dark-paneled surroundings carried out the motif. Even the view of Independence Square and the side of the historic building from the window beyond Addison Wales's head contributed to the aura of old Philadelphia. Kate had thought a magazine would be different, especially one like this glossy weekly, but she might as well be in the offices of Enfield, Willows, and Caset. Then Addison Wales began to speak.

"Have you finished your great American novel, Miss Owen, or is it still a work in progress?" The voice was kinder than the words.

"Excuse me, Mr. Wales, I thought you were looking for a secretary."

He laughed. "I am, but you girls always have a manuscript up your sleeve. I hire a new secretary and within a week she's rewriting everything that crosses my desk and slipping excerpts of her work into the morning mail. And you Bryn Mawr girls are the worst. Why does every one of you have such a passion to be discovered? But I suppose you can't help it. What's that motto again? 'Only our failures marry'?"

"It's 'Our failures only marry,' and I can assure you, Mr. Wales, I have no literary talents I expect you to discover."

"Does that mean you're planning to be one of their failures, Miss Owen? I don't want to train you, only to have you run off in six months to marry some parlor snake."

Kathryn hesitated for only a moment. "I'm not planning to marry in the immediate future."

"Well, that's good enough for now. We don't ask for a lifetime commitment. At least not at the first interview. Perhaps later, but not at first. We will make you work, though, I promise you that, and there won't be anything glamorous about it. Being a secretary at a magazine is just as dull as being a secretary anywhere else, Miss Owen. You'll have to type and file and all those things my colleagues and I consider ourselves too important to do, though just between us, I think half of us haven't mastered the alphabet yet, which tends to inhibit our success in both those areas. And when you've finished that, I'll give you junk to read—and most of it will be junk—and then, assuming you picked up the rudiments of the English language at that school of yours, I'll let you start editing some articles.

"Oh, yes, there's one more task. More important than all the others. Your primary function as my secretary, Miss Owen, will be to protect me. From intruders in the office, from people I don't want to speak to on the phone, from irate authors, from the powers that be both here and in New York, and from a great many others you'll get to know in time. How does it sound to you?"

She said it sounded just fine.

"In that case, only a few more questions. My present secretary, the delightful Miss Indy, who is leaving to answer the call of love, has ascertained the fact that you know the alphabet and can perform the more menial tasks I've mentioned. So much for essentials. I see from the application, Miss Owen, that you're Mayor Owen's daughter, which would lead me to believe that you have no need of supporting yourself. And we've agreed you're not one of those lady poetesses waiting to be discovered. My question, then, is why are you here? What makes you want to cut short your parties and dances and whatever it is you do at night, to turn up bright-eyed and bushy tailed"—she looked startled, and he smiled—"every morning at nine?"

Kathryn looked around the office. The furnishings spoke only of the magazine, but the personal effects told a different story. Her eyes moved from a silver hunt-cup trophy over a photograph of Addison Wales with the Merion cricket team to the glass-front bookcase with the expensive leather-bound volumes.

"I might ask you the same question, Mr. Wales."

He looked surprised for a moment, then the narrow lips stretched into a smile. "How soon can you start, Miss Owen, because as far as I'm concerned, the sooner the better."

Ty was not nearly so enthusiastic. They were alone in the small apartment on Locust Street that Ty had shared with Tim Wharton for the last year. Tim was off to Cape May for the rest of the summer, and Ty had been talking about his absence for weeks. "It'll be almost like being married," he'd said more than once, but Kate knew it would be nothing like it at all. It would only be less awkward.

Ty's pleasure at their new privacy evaporated as soon as Kate told him how she'd spent her afternoon.

"But you didn't even tell me you were going." His voice was almost accusing.

"I guess I was afraid I wouldn't get the job."

"But you did."

"Mr. Wales said he wants me to start as soon as possible."

They'd been unpacking the groceries Ty had bought on his way home, and he stopped suddenly. "Wales? Addison Wales? You're not going to work for Addison Wales?"

"I liked him."

"That's exactly what I mean. Wales just divorced his second wife, and she was his secretary before he married her."

"You make it sound like one of the hazards of the job."

"Maybe it is. Maybe that's what he had in mind when he hired you."

"I don't think so, Ty, but even if he did, it doesn't matter because that's not what I have in mind. All I want from Addison Wales is a job."

"I don't see why."

"Now you sound like my father." They'd both stopped working and were standing in the small kitchen staring at each other.

"Maybe your father's right this time. It isn't as if you need the money."

"Then I'll save my salary and we can get married sooner."

"Not on your life. We're not going to live on your money while I go to school. I refuse to."

"That's a logical argument. We won't do it because you refuse to."

"Kat, can't you see how it would make me feel?"

The answer of course was another question. Didn't he see how their present arrangement made her feel? But if he did, he pretended not to, and Kate had no intention of explaining it to him. She'd made her bargain, agreed to the three-year terms, and she was determined not to whine about it. "Yes, Ty, I understand how it would make you feel, but then you ought to try to understand that I can't just sit around doing nothing."

"That's what other girls who are engaged do."

She smiled and started to unwrap the steak. "Then I guess I'm not like other girls."

The argument and the smile demolished Ty's offensive as abruptly as it had begun. "You've got me there, Kat. All right, go to work for Addison Wales." He took a step so he was standing behind her and reached his arms around her waist. "Work for him," he whispered, and his breath was warm against her ear, "but don't fall for him."

There was precious little chance of that, Kate thought as she felt

Ty's hands moving up from her waist to the row of buttons that ran down the front of her dress. Not a chance of that in the world, she knew as she left the unpacked groceries and let Ty lead her into the bedroom.

But later that night, alone in her room after Ty had driven her home, she wondered what would have happened if Ty hadn't given in. If he'd gone on being unreasonable, would she have given up the job? And she wondered, too, if Ty would be less proud about money and as satisfied with their arrangement if they'd never gone to Nicholas's studio after the wedding, but she pushed that thought from her mind as quickly as it had come. To contemplate it for even a moment was a betrayal of both of them.

"I should think Tyson would want to take his fiancée to the Assembly." Margaret looked uneasily at the door to the kitchen. Was the serving girl lurking behind it listening? "I certainly can't imagine his enjoying it without you."

Kathryn could imagine that only too well, but she did not say as much to her mother. Nor did she add that Ty had in fact asked her to go.

"I'll get Mother to wangle you an invitation one way or another. Of course, once we're married you'll go automatically as my wife, but until then we'll have to get you an invitation."

Perhaps it was the word "wangle" that did it. "I don't want to put your mother to all that trouble," Kate said, but Ty did not seem to hear the irony in her voice. "And I don't particularly want to go to the Assembly." There was no mistaking the surprise in Ty's face now. Men did not want to go to the Assembly, but girls always did. "I'll go after we're married," she added, "but not till then." Kathryn had a fairly good idea how she'd be received at old Philadelphia's most hallowed ball. It would be bad enough once she was married to Ty. Then she'd be a climber. If she went now, she'd be a crasher.

Will was not too busy carving the meat the girl had set before him to take up the thread of his wife's argument. Unlike Margaret, he suspected that Ty might have given Katie an opportunity to go to the Assembly, and she might have refused. It was exactly the kind of thing he was coming to expect from Kathryn. She'd managed to capture a prize beyond even his expectations, and now she seemed to be going out of her way to throw that prize away. Like that job at the magazine she'd insisted on taking. Will had raised his daughter to marry a gentleman, not work for one, and he'd told her as much the day she announced Addison Wales had hired her as a secretary.

"What will people think, Katie?"

"I don't imagine they'll think anything."

"You're wrong there. They'll think a great deal. They'll think I can't support you, for one."

Kathryn thought of the charges of graft that were raised every four years and laughed. "That's one thing no one's going to imagine for a minute."

"And they'll think you're some hard-nosed career woman."

"Won't that be just awful."

"You can joke about it, Katie, but it's no laughing matter. Do you think the Enfields want their future daughter-in-law working in an office?"

"The Enfields don't want their future daughter-in-law, so there isn't much point in worrying about that."

"Then what about Ty? I can't believe he wants you to work."

"I've got to do something while he finishes law school. I can't just sit around waiting to get married."

"Why not? Other girls do."

Kate did not tell her father those had been Ty's words exactly, but she did repeat her own. "Then I guess I'm not like other girls."

"It's that school," Will said. "You never would have dreamed of getting a job if you hadn't gone to that darn school."

"Maybe, but I never would have met Ty, either. And you have to admit you got your money's worth there."

"That's a vulgar thing to say, Kathryn Margaret," her mother reprimanded.

"Maybe, but Daddy knows it's true."

Will did, of course. If there was one thing he never underestimated, it was Tyson Enfield's value, which only brought him back to Kate's intransigence. "Perhaps," he said, looking down the dinner table at his daughter with eyes that were not especially kind and were not intended to be, "Ty doesn't want to take a working girl with ink stains on her fingers"—his eyes dropped to her hands pointedly—"to the Assembly."

"Perhaps this ink-stained working girl doesn't want to go to the Assembly."

Margaret made the same sound she did when one of the boys took the Lord's name in vain, but Will let out an angry bark of a laugh. He'd been right about Katie's refusing to go, but there was no satisfaction in the knowledge. "Oh, certainly, Katie. Next thing I know you'll be telling me you don't want to marry Tyson Enfield either."

Ty's fears about Addison Wales turned out to be entirely unfounded. He treated Kate in a variety of manners—professional in the morning, avuncular after lunch, undoubtedly his best time, intimate but straightforward when they were racing against a deadline—but none was even remotely romantic. Perhaps he'd learned a lesson from his second wife.

Addison Wales did, however, come to rely on Kathryn more and more. After six months he gave her a two-dollar-a-month raise and the lofty title of assistant to the publisher. She'd earned both, since by now Addison was letting her edit all the articles that didn't interest him, which meant virtually everything but a few pieces of good fiction. She'd also carried off something of a coup by badgering Addison into running a story that the entire editorial staff had sworn was too *avant garde*. The story had won an avalanche of praise from magazine readers.

"I've got to hand it to you, Katie. I missed that one by a mile."

"That's because you're so sure of your superiority. You knew you liked the story, but you were convinced most people wouldn't understand it."

"Does that mean you're not sure of your superiority?"

Kate laughed. "Don't forget my background, Addison. I'm a woman of the people."

Ty joked about the raise and said that now he could drop out of law school, but Kate knew he was really a little annoyed by it. What she didn't know was that Ty saw the raise as a vindication of his father's argument. Kat worked like a dog on that damn magazine, and if she were a man she couldn't have supported herself on her salary, let alone a wife, or so it seemed to Ty. Going up in the elevator of the handsome old building on Independence Square that housed the company publishing Kat's magazine and three others, Ty wondered how all these people managed to live on such meager salaries. "They don't drive Marmons," Kat had said to him once. She was right, of course, and it seemed a shame to him, because they all worked so hard to have so little. Ty guessed if you really loved what you were doing, it wouldn't matter that you weren't being paid much to do it, but how could these grown men and women really care about a magazine that published stories for small children or household hints for women or advice for would-be gentlemen? Even Kat's magazine, the largest and most important of the quartet published by the company, was no more than a mediocre rag that appeared each week with a different sentimental cover, though Ty admitted, when Kat pushed him, that they did publish some pretty good stories now and then. Still, he couldn't see devoting your whole life to it, and that's what most of these people seemed to do. Here it was six-thirty, Ty thought as he threaded his way through the labyrinth of offices and cubbyholes, and most of the desks were still occupied. Kat, however, was not at hers, though he knew she hadn't left. The desk was hidden under a profusion of papers, and in one corner the box of camellias he'd sent supported a stack of magazines. He heard her voice from behind the half-open door that he knew led to Addison Wales's office. Wales was moaning that this time they were finished for sure, they'd never make deadline, and Kat was laughing and reassuring him they'd make it this week just as they did every week. "Remember that Christmas issue with the story about the little boy and the lost dog? The author was drunk in a speakeasy, we had about fifty words to go on, and it was later than this, but we still put it together and closed the book in time. We did it then and we'll do it now."

"At least we had fifty words then."

"We still had to do the other eleven hundred and fifty, if you remember. Though I doubt you do. By the time we finished the story, you were as tight as the author. Tight as lords, both of you."

"Drunk as lords, Katie. 'Drunk as lords' is the expression. You young people get tight. I get drunk as a lord. Don't mix your metaphors—or are they similes?—well, more important, don't mix your drinks. That's the crux of the matter, Katie."

To Ty, standing alone at Kat's desk, the overheard conversation seemed more than intimate. It was conspiratorial.

They came out of Addison's office laughing, but Kate stopped when she saw him. "Oh, Ty, I'm sorry. I called the apartment, but Tim said you'd left. I've got at least two more hours here."

"Sorry, Enfield," Addison said as he passed. "We're going to keep your girl tied up here for a while. All for the greater glory of literature, you understand." Addison walked off laughing.

"He seems damn pleased by it," Ty said.

"Not at all, Ty. That's Addison's maniacal laugh. He always gets this way when he's afraid we're not going to make deadline."

"Well, that's Addison's problem. Mine is that if you don't hurry, we're not going to make the party."

"That's why I called the apartment. You go on without me, and I'll meet you there later. I thought this might happen, so I brought my things into town this morning. I can dress at one of the girls' apartments. That way I shouldn't be later than ten."

"And what should I tell everyone? Kat will be a little late? Oh, don't worry, only two hours or so. She's got more important things to do." The words had come out with more force than he'd meant them to, and Ty could feel heads at nearby desks turning, but he didn't care.

Kate led him into Addison's office and closed the door behind them. "I'm not going to miss the party, Ty. I'm going to be a little late for it, because whether you believe it or not, this is important to me."

"More important than Daphne's party?"

"Daphne's party! We've been to about fifty parties for Daphne and Randy this winter. Even Daphne says she's sick and tired of them."

"So this is your way of getting out of it. Why didn't you simply say so in the first place, and I would have told my aunt you were too busy for her party."

"Be reasonable, Ty. I'm going to the party. I'll just be a little late. With that crowd, no one will even notice. Two of the girls have an apartment on Fifteenth Street. It's only a few minutes from there to your aunt's."

"Addison Wales's place is right on the square. Why don't you dress there? It would be even faster." He was out of the office and moving down the hall toward the elevators before she had time to get angry.

"Is it all right for me to use my office now?" Addison asked. Then he saw her face and the tone changed. "Look, Katie, I can close the book without you this time. Why don't you go to that party or whatever he was so angry about."

She shook her head. "No, I'll stay. Besides," she added more to herself than to him, "it's too late to do anything else."

When Ty returned to the offices on Independence Square at ten-thirty, he found Kathryn and Addison in the latter's office. Wales was sprawled in the large leather chair with his feet on the desk, and Kathryn, curled up in a chair across from him, had kicked off her shoes. There was a silver flask on the desk between them and two cups. They both looked up when Ty appeared in the door.

"We were just talking about you, Enfield," Addison said. "I told Katie you'd turn up."

Ty stood in the doorway and glowered.

"Can I offer you two my office? I suspect I'm not needed in this conference."

"Keep your office, Wales. We're leaving. Get your coat, Kat."

"He's drunk, but I suppose he's harmless," Addison said in an undertone. "Good luck, Katie."

"Do you want to go back to the party?" she asked when they were on the street.

"Is that the way you work? Sitting around with a flask between you?"

"That's the way we relax after work. And if I were you, Ty, I wouldn't sound so superior. You aren't exactly sober."

"Pretty cozy there, shoes kicked off and all. Why didn't you take off your dress too? Or was that going to come later?"

Kate felt herself whirl on him, saw her hand crash against his cheek, and heard the sound it made in the cold night air, but she was not aware of willing any of it. She felt his hands on her shoulders as if they wanted to shake her, saw his face only inches from hers, taut with fury, and for a moment she thought he was going to strike her back, but he pulled her close and was whispering apologies in a voice that was closer to sobs than anger. He was holding her close, and she'd begun to cry, and when he kissed her she tasted the salt of her own tears on his mouth.

The square was deserted at this hour, and though it was a cold night that held the damp imminence of snow, they moved to one of the benches. "I'm sorry, Kat. God, I'm sorry. I didn't mean to say those things. You know I didn't mean them. It's only that"—he hesitated for a moment—"it's only that sometimes I have the feeling I'm losing you."

"Perhaps," she said quietly, "you want to lose me. Maybe we don't belong together." The words were out before she knew what she was saying, and she held her breath. He was going to agree with her. He'd only been waiting for a chance to break it off, and now she'd given him one. But she felt his arm tighten around her shoulders, felt the warmth of his body next to hers like a shield against the cold night, and heard the words, quiet but insistent, in her ear.

"Don't say that, Kat. Don't ever say that. There aren't two people in the world who belong together the way we do."

On the way back to the apartment, Ty said that Tim would be taking Amanda Wycombe home after the party and had decided to stay at his family's. When she got to the apartment, Kate called home and told Margaret she'd be staying with the two girls who shared an apartment on Fifteenth Street. She'd thought of it as the final lie and resisted it for almost two years, but she heard her voice natural and straightforward and knew it wasn't the final lie at all. There would be others.

When she awakened in the morning and found Ty beside her in his narrow bed, she forgot the lie. She looked at the face, not slack and stupid the way faces are in sleep, but as peaceful and beautiful as a Renaissance painting, and remembered Ty's words of the night before and knew he was right. She'd never belong to anyone but him.

That afternoon Charlie Finney, still driving for Will in Will's castoff suits, turned up at Kate's office a little after five. "The mayor's waiting downstairs for you, Miss Katie."

"Just Katie, Charlie. I keep telling you that."

"He wants you to drive home with him." It was like Will to send Charlie up with the message. Coming into the office himself would have been an admission that Kate worked there, and admission of the fact was too close to approval of it.

"I thought you might welcome a ride home, Katie," Will said as she got into the car. "You must be exhausted. Staying up so late that you had to spend the night with friends rather than have Ty drive you home."

"I had to be at the office at eight-thirty this morning. It just seemed simpler to stay in town. For everyone," she added lamely.

"I'm sure it was."

Will told Charlie to drive along the river for a while, and when they reached the spot where the boat houses stood, he insisted they get out. The wind off the river was cold, and Kate pulled her coat closer around her, but Will seemed not to notice. He was looking across the river to the other shore, covered with a light film of snow that had fallen that morning.

"The river's always a fine sight," he said finally. "No matter what the season. Do you remember that summer morning years ago when I brought you down here, Katie? We came here and then went over to old Senator Penrose's house."

"How could I forget? Roger Atherton was there."

"You've always been too hard on Roger."

"It isn't Roger you want to talk about," she said.

"No, it isn't. Do you remember who else I talked to that day? Who I came down here to see?"

"Ty's father, wasn't it? And his Uncle Nicholas. I was very impressed by Nicholas."

"He can be a very charming fellow. In that respect Ty takes after him more than his father. Lots of charm. Very appealing. I imagine Ty can be darn near irresistible when he wants to."

"I thought you liked Ty."

"I do. I like him, and I want you to marry him. I want it as much as you do, Katie. Maybe not for the same reasons, but as much. That's why I don't want you to do something foolish that will ruin your chances of marrying him."

"Like working at the magazine?" She knew that was not what her father had in mind, but she did not want to discuss what he did have in mind.

"Like making it so easy for Ty that he doesn't have to marry you. Like giving him all the advantages of marriage without any of its responsibilities. I think you know what I mean, Katie."

"You mean if I sleep with Ty now he won't marry me?" Kate knew she had shocked her father by the bluntness of her words, but she'd intended to. It was important to put him on the defensive.

Will looked off across the river again. "As a matter of fact, that's exactly what I mean. I only hope I didn't wait too long to have this conversation."

"You don't think much of Ty. Or of me, for that matter."

"Because I think you might do such a thing?"

"Because you think he wouldn't want to marry me if we did."

"Let's just say I know more about men than you do, Katie, and Ty's a man like any other. He may talk a good game—a lot of these young fellows do, especially since the war—but when it comes down to marriage, he'll revert to type."

"And which type is that?"

"I told you, Katie, he's a man like any other. And no man wants damaged goods."

"Even if he's damaged them himself?"

"That's the only way he knows for sure they're damaged."

"That's a horrible thing to say."

"I didn't make things the way they are, Katie. I'm just telling you the way they are. Warning you, you might say." Will turned from the river to Kathryn, and his eyes were stern now rather than embarrassed. "I'm assuming you did stay with friends last night and it's not too late for warnings."

"And if it is?"

Kathryn saw her father's face tense with anger. "Then you'd better tell me right now, Katie, because in that case, Mr. Tyson Enfield doesn't have a choice in the matter. He'll marry you immediately. I'll tell him that myself."

"You can put away the shotgun, Daddy. It's not too late," she lied.

He lifted her face to his so she was forced to meet his eyes. "Do you swear to that, Katie?"

Kathryn struggled against the impulse to pull away. "I said it's not too late. What more do you want?"

She saw the relief move across his features and relax them. "I'm glad to hear that, Katie. Very glad. Now, we'd better be getting home. But remember what I said."

"It's not something I'd be likely to forget."

Kate left the office early that afternoon and took the two-o'clock to New York. She telephoned Chris from Pennsylvania Station.

"I'll meet you at the Plaza," he said. "Do you think you can find the Plaza?"

"Don't treat me like a country bumpkin."

"You said it, Katie, I didn't."

Chris was waiting for her in the Fifth Avenue lobby. He was wearing a tweed suit that looked as if he'd been wearing it for several days too many, and the battered hat didn't help. The effect, in the midst of all that thick-carpeted, crystal-chandeliered opulence, was jarring.

"If I'd known reporters lived so well, I'd have tried newspapers rather than magazines," Kate said as he led her toward the high-ceilinged court where the afternoon tea dance was in full swing.

"This is strictly for you, Katie. I couldn't see you in my usual speakeasy. The whiskey's not bad, but the language is pretty awful. Where's the illustrious Mr. Enfield?" he asked when they were seated far enough from the orchestra to make conversation possible.

"He's staying at a friend's place for the weekend, but the friend is off to the country so Ty went over there to get the key and have a drink. He said he'll see you later at the party."

"Very discreet of Mr. Enfield to give us some time alone, but then Mr. Enfield is always discreet. Where are you staying this weekend, Katie?"

"Do you remember Nancy Bowdin from school? She has an apartment with two other girls on Thirty-sixth Street. Just off Madison Avenue. The other two aren't from Bryn Mawr, but I've met . . ."

"Skip the details, Katie. You're a rotten liar. Always have been. I suppose you know what a stupid thing you're doing."

She started to pretend as she had with her father, but it was no good pretending with Chris and she knew it. "You aren't exactly in a position to cast the first stone. Not with that steady stream of girls flowing through that . . . that Greenwich Village den of iniquity of yours. But it's the old story, isn't it? You're a man and I'm a woman."

"It may be an old story, Katie, but it doesn't happen to be that particular old story. There's one difference when it comes to that steady stream of girls you mentioned—and incidentally there aren't as many of them as you seem to think. You see, with us, nobody ever mentions marriage. Those girls don't want to get married."

"Of course. They all have their poetry or their art or whatever it is they're devoted to."

"You can laugh at them, Katie, and in a sense you're right. In five or ten years most of them are going to wake up one morning and find they've never sold a painting or published a poem and then they're going to decide maybe they ought to get married after all. But when that happens, they're not going to turn up at my apartment. You can be sure of that. That's the whole point, Katie. I don't lie to those girls and they don't lie to themselves."

"The implication, of course, is that Ty lies to me, and I lie to myself."

"It seems to me you've been—what is it you two call it?—unofficially engaged for an awfully long time."

"I hate to burst that superior little bubble of yours, Chris, but it's going to be official in another month. We're going to announce our engagement this Christmas and be married right after Ty is graduated in June."

He looked across the small table at her skeptically. "I'll congratulate you as soon as I read it in the papers."

"Sometimes you get me so darn angry."

"That, Katie, is my role in life. I've got to keep you on your toes."

"You have a particularly nasty way of doing it." It seemed to Kate that he'd spoiled everything. He'd deflated the holiday excitement of being in a strange town with no responsibilities, and almost soured the sweet expectancy of an entire weekend alone with Ty in the borrowed apartment. "Let's get out of here," she said, "now that you've done your best to ruin my afternoon." But when they were outside the hotel, standing on the carpeted steps under the red awning, she regretted her words, almost as much as she'd hated Chris's. He was so horrible about Ty only because he cared so much about her. Kate took his arm. "You'll still come to the party, won't you? I promised Ty I'd bring you."

"I bet he's just dying to see me."

"There'll be a lot of people you know. The host's from Princeton. You probably know him. Schuyler Mason."

"Mason? Let's see, that's the impeccable but impoverished one. Or almost impeccable. Wasn't his father disbarred for dipping into all those trust funds he managed? Quietly, of course. In the best Main Line tradition. I wondered why one of Ty's friends left Philadelphia for New York. Now I understand. You can get away with a disbarred father in New York but not in Philadelphia."

"And Ty said to tell you there'll be lots of pretty girls," Kate said, determined to keep him on the track. She wanted him to come to the party.

"I know the type," Chris said, turning to look at two girls entering the hotel. With their long legs flashing out from big furs, they looked like elegant cranes. "Those Park Avenue parties aren't my type, Katie." He glanced at the girls again as they disappeared through the door. "But I'll go for a while. It's always fun to see you Philadelphians letting loose in the big city. You could stay home and have the same parties, but somehow you feel you have to come to New York for a good time."

Chris steered her past the line of taxis at the curb and began walking east. "That Enfield character has spoiled you, Katie. We just had tea at the Plaza. You don't expect a taxi too? Come on, we'll take a bus. We can sit on top. The fresh air will do you good."

"But it's freezing."

"Don't go soft on me, Katie. What am I going to do if the only other member of the Do or Diers goes soft on me?"

Ty had not arrived when they got to the party, but Schuyler Mason said he was glad to see Kate again and that he remembered Chris from school and was glad he'd come, and steered them to the bar.

"Who's the blond beauty in the corner?" Chris asked.

"Ty's sister Daphne. And if that doesn't put you off, she's married. To that parlor snake leaning against the piano. So don't get any ideas."

"I wasn't. I told you, these parties and these girls aren't my type."

Daphne had crossed the room to them. "Ty's not here yet," she said to Kate, though her eyes were fastened on Chris as she spoke. "But we started early. This morning. Or maybe it was last night." She handed an empty glass to the man behind the bar as if she expected him to remember what she wanted. He did.

Kate introduced them. "You're not the district attorney," Daphne said, "so you must be the reporter. I don't think I've ever met a journalist before. Except for those ladies who write about weddings and things. And they don't count."

"We're no different from anyone else," Chris said. "Only poorer and maybe a little scruffier."

The wide gray eyes looked into his. "Oh, not scruffy, Mr. Owen. Not scruffy at all."

Ty arrived, and Daphne drifted off to grace the piano bench, where a short, handsome man was pounding out the latest tunes—"Indiana Moon" gave way to "Yes, We Have No Bananas" and ended in the dazzling virtuosity of "Dizzy Fingers"—but later when Chris was sitting alone in one of the window seats idly contemplating his drink and the party, she returned.

"You look bored, Chris. You don't mind the first name, do you? After all, we're almost related. And I can tell we're going to be good friends."

"I wouldn't be so sure," he said. He had not stood for her, and now he looked up at the figure leaning over him and thought she was probably as spoiled and difficult as she was beautiful.

"Oh, I'm quite sure. In fact, I thought we might get started right now. I know a quiet speakeasy just around the corner. Or we could have a drink at your place. I bet that's even quieter."

"I don't think your husband would like that."

She flashed a brilliant smile. "I wouldn't be too sure of that."

"Then I'm not sure I'd like it."

"Oh, you'd like it. I promise you that, Chris."

"Look, Mrs. Curtaine . . ."

"Daphne."

"You've got the wrong man. Why don't you go back to that fellow at the piano? Or better yet, your husband."

"But I know both of them, and I don't know you."

"That's right. And you've never met a newspaperman before. You're a collector, Mrs. Curtaine, but I don't like being collected."

"You should. It's quite a compliment."

"Thank you, but no thank you."

"I don't really think you have a choice, Chris. Does anyone ask the first edition or the watercolor if it wants to be bought?"

"But I'm not a first edition or a watercolor."

"If you were, I wouldn't be interested. The point is, I'm as good at my collecting as those silly people who collect first editions and watercolors. It runs in the family. There's an Enfield cousin who has the best collection of Ming vases in the Western world. One of them, one of the priciest apparently, wasn't for sale when he first saw it. He had to wait thirty years, but he got it."

"In that case, why don't we have this talk again in about thirty years?"

"I'm not that patient. But I am that determined."

She was still leaning over him, her face only inches away now, and he looked up at the flawless skin and the gray eyes wide with promise. She was very close and very desirable, and Chris removed the hand she'd rested on his shoulder and stood. "I'm afraid I have to be going now, Mrs. Curtaine. Good-bye."

"Not good-bye, Chris. We'll see each other soon. I feel certain of that."

The cold air felt good after the heat and noise of the party. Chris shook his head as if to clear it of the whiskey and the scent of Daphne's perfume. She was a bitch, he thought as he started downtown. A beautiful, spoiled bitch. Ordinarily he'd have felt sorry for her husband, but her husband looked as if he deserved her. It was a reassuring thought, Chris decided. Maybe there was some justice in the world after all.

It was still early, and he debated whether to stop at his favorite speakeasy or drop by the studio of a pretty and entirely untalented sculptress he knew fairly well. He was comfortable in her studio and comfortable with her, and he wanted something comfortable after the unsettling encounter with Daphne. He decided to go to the sculptress's studio, but when he left it early the next morning he was still thinking of Daphne.

By Sunday morning, however, her memory had begun to recede. Chris had worked late Saturday night, and that had helped, and on his way home he'd bought the early editions of all the Sunday papers, and when he got up a little after one and padded barefoot into the small untidy kitchen to make coffee, he was no longer thinking of Daphne. It was unnerving, therefore, when the bell rang, to open his door and find her standing there.

"You certainly take long enough to answer your door." She looked at the rumpled robe. "Hope I didn't wake you." Her smile suggested that the idea of her inconveniencing anyone was absurd. "Aren't you going to ask me in?"

"In a word, no."

"That's not very hospitable of you, Chris."

"I'm not a very hospitable person."

"I don't believe that for a minute," she said, pushing past him. She looked around the room. The sofa and the floor in front of it were covered with newspapers. On the coffee table there were half a dozen glasses, two with olives in them, a plate littered with cracker crumbs and a half-eaten apple, and two cups each holding the dregs of cold coffee and several cigarette butts. Half a dozen books were piled on one of the chairs opposite the sofa; two jackets, several shirts, a tie, a single glove, and a woman's silk scarf were strewn across the other. On a desk in a corner a typewriter was nearly hidden under a mass of papers, and an old tuna-fish can served as an ashtray. "God, you are scruffy after all."

"Now that you've discovered that, why don't you go back uptown?"

"Too boring. The party's still going on, but it hasn't aged well in two days. Aren't you going to offer me a drink?"

"I haven't got anything in the house."

"I don't believe that either. Just one drink, Chris. Give me one drink, then I'll be a good girl and leave."

"I doubt it."

"You're right, but I need a drink."

He went into the kitchen and returned with two glasses of whiskey. It was not very good whiskey and he had no ice and had added only a little water, but she downed it without a grimace.

"Now that you've had your drink, you can go."

"God, you are stubborn."

"That's right. I'm stubborn. And I don't like girls who collect one of every kind of man, or Main Line girls who go slumming, or married women. And you're all three of those, Daphne."

"But you like me."

"Not so long as you fit all those descriptions."

She smiled at him. "At least you'd like to sleep with me. You can't deny that."

"I might want to, but I wouldn't like myself much if I did."

She smiled again, her beautiful smug smile, and began to unbutton her coat. Chris had noticed it when she'd arrived. He didn't know what kind of fur it was, but it looked expensive. Everything about Daphne looked expensive. She unbuttoned the last button and shrugged the coat to the floor. She was suddenly naked. The cool gray eyes were fastened on his taking in the high round breasts, the smooth curve of waist and hip to long slender legs. They watched his eyes and read the defeat in them. She crossed the room to him and he felt the lovely smiling mouth against his, the delicate hands at the tie of his robe, then expert beneath it. She had sunk to her knees and she was drawing him down beside her on the floor and the smooth beautiful skin that felt like satin was warm against his and her mouth was hungry and her hands experienced, and it was some time before Chris returned to his senses and his defeat.

There was a knock at the door before nine on Monday morning. Chris left Daphne in the bedroom, and tying the same rumpled robe around him, went to see who it was. Kate was looking wide-awake and efficient in a gray coat and matching cloche. "I thought I'd take you to breakfast. You left so abruptly Friday night, and you either haven't been home or haven't been answering your phone since."

"I thought you'd be back in Philadelphia by now."

"Ty went back this morning, but I'm supposed to see some people today. For the magazine. Well, do you want breakfast or don't you?"

"Sure . . . only . . ."

Kate realized he'd opened the door only halfway and was standing with his arm against the doorjamb as if he wanted to block her entrance. She looked at his face, then the rumpled robe. "Oh, I see. One of your artistic friends who doesn't want to get married. I'm sorry."

"Don't be sorry, Katie." Daphne was standing behind Chris. She'd put on one of his shirts, but hadn't bothered with any more than that. She pushed Chris aside and led Kathryn into the room. "You don't have to go out for breakfast. We can all have coffee here. If you can stand the mess. How does Chris live this way?"

Kate stood there for a moment looking confused. "You hypocrite," she said finally. "You impossible, insufferable hypocrite."

"Now, don't blame Chris, Katie. He put up a good fight. I'll give him that. I'll let him tell you about it while I dress. You don't happen to have your suitcase, do you? I just remembered I don't have much to wear. Well, I'll comb my hair at least."

"Does Randy know about this?" Kate asked when Daphne had left them alone.

"How the hell do I know what Randy knows? I didn't know about this till yesterday afternoon. Why, is old Randy the violent type?" He laughed grimly.

"I just don't understand it. After all those things you said Friday afternoon. Or maybe I do. I guess girls who don't want to get married include those who already are."

"Look, Katie, I'm not denying my responsibility, but what Daphne said is true. She came down here wearing . . . well, let's just say she turned up uninvited with this in mind. And she can be very persuasive. Maybe it's a family trait. Maybe the Enfields always get what they want."

"Are you comparing this to Ty and me?"

"Merely citing a family characteristic."

"You're worse than insulting. You're crazy. You and Daf are nothing like us. We love each other. We're going to be married."

He was tired of the argument, sick of himself. "And Daphne's already married, and I'm not in love with anyone. You're right, Katie. This business with Daphne doesn't have anything to do with you and Ty."

That Christmas Kathryn received the promised diamond from Bailey, Banks, and Biddle. It was not as large or as vulgar as Ty had sworn that night on Nicholas's boat, because he'd had to buy it with his own money. Samuel had not offered to help, and Emily had never considered passing on one of the family heirlooms. Still, a chunk of his inheritance from his grandfather bought a handsome three-and-a-half-carat blue-white diamond. It was, Margaret pronounced, in perfect taste. Kate had never seen her mother so happy. If only Kathryn would let her give a party as well, but Kate said they'd have enough trouble when it came to the wedding.

In March, while Margaret was busy making wedding plans and Kate was beginning to believe she really would marry Ty after all these years of being sure it would never happen, Ty asked his sister Daphne to lunch.

Randy Curtaine was fortunate enough to have an income sufficient not only to his needs, but his tastes as well. He and Daphne had refused the Enfields' offer of a practical suburban house like Hilary and Carter's. Country living, they agreed, was not to their taste, although Randy returned to the family house in Kentucky every so often for no more reason, as far as Daphne could see, than to drink mint juleps rather than Manhattans or Bronxes. He and Daphne divided most of their time, however, between an apartment in one of those new buildings that were spoiling Rittenhouse Square, or so most of its older inhabitants believed, and an apartment they kept at the St. Regis in New York. On the day Ty asked Daphne to lunch, Randy was in New York. From what Ty had heard lately, it seemed that if one of the Curtaines was in Philadelphia the other was certain to be in New York.

When the maid showed Ty into the small solarium, he found his sister reclining on a white chaise. A man he'd never seen was stretched out on the black-and-white-tile floor with his back propped against the side of the chaise, and Daphne's arm was draped familiarly over his shoulder. The man's name, according to Daphne, was Frank Brown. He did not rise when he was introduced, and Ty did not extend his hand.

"My big brother is going to take me to lunch," Daphne said. "Will you take Frankie to lunch too, Ty? Poor Frankie, no one ever takes him to lunch." Her hand stroked the checked jacket in sympathy. "That is, nobody except me. And I don't do that very often, do I, Frankie?"

"That's all right, babe. I don't mind staying home with you." He ran a hand over dark brilliantined hair and smiled.

"If you don't mind," Ty said, "I'd like to speak to my sister alone."

Brown looked at him curiously but without hostility. "Sure, kid. Anything you say." He uncoiled his large frame and stood. He was a big man, and the tightly fitting clothes made him look even bigger.

"'Babe'! Good God, where did you find him?" Ty demanded when Brown had left.

"In a speakeasy," Daphne said. "He's a saxophone player."

"I should have guessed. Who else would wear a yellow-and-blue jacket?"

"I admit Frankie's taste in clothes leaves something to be desired, but in this case, brother darling, the clothes definitely do not make the man. Frankie has other attributes to recommend him."

"You talk like a tart."

"I'm not sure you'd know what a tart talks like, but if I'm going to be lectured, I'd just as soon stay home for lunch."

"You're going to be lectured, all right. I'd heard rumors, but that Brown character is worse than any of them."

"And if I'm going to be lectured, I need a drink. Can I make you a martini, Ty?" She walked to a cocktail wagon in a corner of the room. "That's another of Frankie's attributes. He's taught me to make marvelous martinis, though he drinks only neat whiskey and beer."

"He looks like a tough customer."

"Frankie? Don't be silly. He's a pussycat."

"Well, he's no good. You can tell that just by looking at him."

"Of course, he's no good, Ty. Why do you think I like him so much?"

Ty had come ready to confront Daphne with the rumors he'd heard, expecting her to deny them. He'd been prepared for every defense but no defense. "You must be crazy," he said helplessly.

"Not crazy, darling, only bored. Fortunately Frankie has helped a bit, but I don't suppose I can expect that to continue for much longer. His attributes are considerable, but his hidden resources are limited—if in fact there are any. Besides, he's started trying to borrow money, and that's always the kiss of death. It's not that I care about the money, but it's so tacky watching him try to think up ways of asking for it. Why is it people without money always think people with it are more stupid?"

"I wouldn't worry about any of that, Daphne, because you aren't going to see Mr. Brown any more."

"Do you have someone better in mind?"

"One more comment like that and I'll . . ."

"You'll what, Ty? I'm a married woman now. My life, including my sex life, is my own business."

"And Randy's. If I have to tell Randy to stop you, I will."

"Oh, you poor baby. You really don't know anything, do you? You can tell Randy if you like, but don't expect him to get too excited."

"It won't work, Daf. I know you move with a fast set, but I can't believe Randy would just shrug off something like this."

"You think I'm bluffing just to stop you from telling Randy? Well, let me tell you about Randy. Then you'll see whether I'm bluffing or not. You see, brother dear, Randy's the only man I've ever known who's as wild as I am. That's why I married him. I had to marry someone, and he was the best choice. I think Randy felt the same way about me. At first he agreed to marry me because he thought I was pregnant—after all, he's still a Southern gentleman, and when the lady gets pregnant a Southern gentleman does the right thing—but

when I found out I wasn't, he said we might as well get married anyway. He said we made a good team. And we do. The only trouble is,
both of us got tired of that team pretty quickly. I guess we knew we
would. At first we simply tried a few of each other's friends. As you
said, we move in a pretty fast set. But if you want to know the truth,
Randy's more exciting than most of his friends, and I guess he found
the same thing true of me and my friends. So you see, it was becoming a real problem. He tried watching me with other men for a while.
And we tried other girls too, all three of us together, but I didn't
much like that. I did it for Randy, but I don't much like crowds and
I really prefer men. I can see from your face that I'm shocking you.
Well, there isn't much more to tell. I like men, and for the moment I
like Frankie Brown. And the point of this little story is that I don't
think your telling Randy about him is going to do much good."

Ty had listened to her with a sense of mounting horror. At first
she'd merely sounded like the old Daphne, eager to shock, but as
she'd gone on he'd been repelled and, as Daphne sensed, appalled by
the things she said. "But you can't want to live this way, Daf. Maybe
when you're drunk or angry at Randy . . ."

"But I never get angry at Randy, Ty. We don't see enough of each
other to get angry."

"You know what I mean. Maybe there are times when you want
to do something wild, but you can't really want to live this way. I
don't see how you can possibly get up in the morning and face yourself in the mirror when you're living like this."

"In case you haven't noticed, darling, I'm very easy to face in the
mirror or anywhere else for that matter. Thank heavens nothing
shows on my face, and since I have no intention of having children,
nothing's going to show on my body. That's how I face myself in the
mirror."

"You sound as if you wanted things this way."

"Now you're beginning to understand. You see, Ty, I'm the only
real hell-raiser in the family. You and Hilary went through the mo-
tions. Who wouldn't with Mother and Daddy ramming old Philadelphia and Enfield and Tyson standards down our throats since the
day we were born. But for you and Hilary it was nothing more than a
reaction to all that. Hilary's the worst, of course. She's become Mrs.
Carter Middleton Branch with a vengeance. Sometimes I think she's
going to be harder on Camilla in that respect than Mother ever was
on us. And as for you, Ty, well, maybe you'll marry Katie. . . ."

"I'm going to marry her."

"But marrying Katie isn't nearly so shocking as the family has convinced you. And as for the rest, you'll finish school in a few months and slide right into Daddy's firm and the Philadelphia Club and all the rest. You cut up for a while, Ty, I'll give you that, but you were always eminently reformable. I think that's why Mother was convinced she could keep you from marrying Katie. But I really like raising hell. I don't do it to shock Mother and Daddy, I do it because I like it. I guess I'm the Uncle Nick of our generation."

"You make Uncle Nick look like a plaster saint."

"Well, Ty, darling, you know what Uncle Nick says. When girls go to the devil—at least, girls from families like ours—they're ten times worse than men. Besides, it's 1923, or haven't you heard? What was wild for Uncle Nick just isn't anymore, so I've had to break new ground."

"You've done a bang-up job of it."

"Thank you, darling. And now that I've had my lecture, would you like some lunch? I can have the cook make us something."

"Forget lunch, Daphne."

"You mean you don't want to eat with a fallen woman?"

"I'm just not very hungry."

"God, you are fastidious."

"I just keep remembering a blond kid who was sweet as hell."

"I still am, darling. Ask Frankie."

"Will you do me one favor, Daf? At least try to be a little discreet. Try to keep it from the family."

"Well, I can't promise discretion, but I'll try going to New York more often." She slipped her arm through his as they walked to the foyer. "After all, Ty, I don't want to hurt anyone. I just want to have a good time."

There seemed to be nothing to say to that, and Ty felt disgusted with his own futility, and with Daphne. He wanted to get away as quickly as possible, but the appearance of Hilary in the entrance hall stopped him. She looked as dumpy as Daphne did beautiful.

"I didn't think I'd be lucky enough to catch Daf in, but getting both of you together . . . What luck." Hilary began to take off the brown coat that was expensive without being in the least fashionable. The silk print dress she wore beneath it was exactly the same. "Now I can tell you both at the same time. You're going to be aunted and uncled again. I'm not sure if that's the proper wording for the announcement, but there it is. I've just come from Roger Atherton."

If the congratulations were less hearty than they might have been,

Hilary did not notice. She was too concerned with the details of the coming event. Roger said this and Roger said that. "Incidentally, Ty, tell Katie he asked about her. He always asks about her."

"Tell him she's engaged to be married," Ty snapped. "And next time he asks, you can tell him she's married."

Will Owen could tell from the way his son came striding into his office that Saturday morning that something important had happened. "I got a call about an hour ago," Bill said. "Fellow shot in his hotel room at Race and Twelfth. Jazz musician in hock to one of the big boys who runs the clubs. Apparently got in over his head—numbers, some of the big games—anyway, he was supposed to be working it off playing at one of the clubs. Well, the damn fool thought he could skip out on them. Lined up a job to play at a speakeasy in Wilmington. The news got back here before the guy could pack his saxophone, and the boss sent a couple of goons to make sure the man never left for Wilmington. Not much of a story, and I didn't think there was any news in it until I got the second call. There was a girl in the hotel room too. Those boys have some timing. Fellow's in bed with a girl, and they break in and start shooting. Neither of them had a chance. They don't exactly take aim with a submachine gun. The whole thing sounds like something out of Cicero or Chicago, but it happened right down on Race and Twelfth. And that's the point. The girl was Daphne Enfield. She's the younger one. The wild one, as if you couldn't guess."

"Do the papers know?" Will asked.

"They know about the shooting and that there was a girl involved, but that's all."

"Sam Enfield's going to have a hell of a time covering this up. We can say there was an unidentified woman with the man, and when they find the fellows and you prosecute, you can keep the girl out of the trial, but Enfield's still going to have a hell of a time. Too great a coincidence. A strange woman's shot in some musician's bed, and his daughter—how old was she? nineteen, twenty?—turns up dead. People are bound to put two and two together even if we don't say four."

"You don't sound too sorry about it," Bill said.

"The girl only got what she deserved. If she'd stayed where she belonged instead of fooling around with some two-bit hood, she'd be alive now. And as for any embarrassment to Sam Enfield, you know how I feel about that."

"I know, and I couldn't agree more. If you'd let me, I'd drag the whole damn Enfield clan through the mud when this thing comes to trial."

"That would only hurt Katie. She's going to be one of them, so we'll have to do our best to keep this thing quiet. All the same, it would be nice to strike back. After all these years, it would be such sweet justice to finally strike back. Well, I suppose I ought to call the car and get out to the Enfields'."

"Do you want me to go along?" Bill asked.

"No, that won't be necesssary. Sam Enfield and I have been at this game for a long time. We're not exactly friends, but we are accustomed to dealing with each other. Besides, I want you to make sure none of this about the girl gets into the papers. If any of the reporters have already got the story, you make sure it doesn't make the evening editions. You know who to call, Bill. Those smart-aleck reporters won't listen to sense, but their bosses will."

Samuel Enfield customarily spent part of Saturday morning in his library, and he was just about to leave it for lunch when Hatton announced that his Honor the mayor was here to see him. Samuel had no desire to see Will Owen, but he knew Will would not have come, especially without calling, unless the matter were important, important to Enfield as well as Owen.

"I'm sorry to interrupt you, Mr. Enfield."

"I know you wouldn't be here if it weren't necessary, Mr. Mayor. Although as you know, I'm no longer a resident of the city. Haven't been since I sold the house on the square."

"I'm not here on city business. It's a more . . . more personal matter. Concerns your daughter, Mrs. Curtaine. I'm terribly sorry, Mr. Enfield. The police found her body this morning."

Samuel's gray face turned white, but he said nothing. Will spared none of the sordid details, and through it all Enfield merely sat as if he were listening to the minutes of a meeting.

What did I expect? Will asked himself. Their grief, like everything else about them, is private.

"I appreciate your coming here to tell me," Samuel said quietly. "And I especially appreciate the trouble you and the district attorney have gone to in order to keep this quiet."

"It's the least we can do, Mr. Enfield. And I'd like to express my sympathies to you and Mrs. Enfield. A death in the family is a terrible thing. I can still remember my own father's, though I was only a boy at the time." Will looked at Samuel Enfield pointedly, but

Enfield was staring off into the distance at some truth more terrible than the one Will was recalling.

There was a knock at the library door, and suddenly Emily Enfield was standing just inside the room. "Lunch is ready, Samuel," she said without looking at Will. Hatton had told her who was with her husband.

Will stood. "I was just leaving, Mrs. Enfield. I'm sorry to have bothered you at home on a Saturday morning, but it was unavoidable."

Emily had a fairly good idea of what Will Owen would find so unavoidable that he had to invade their home. She turned, and the icy mask was gone. "I can tell you right now, Mr. Owen, that you have nothing to discuss with my husband or me. We are both unalterably opposed to this marriage and will do every thing in our power to stop it." Emily shook off the restraining hand Samuel had placed on her arm. "I don't care if the engagement has been announced or the date for the wedding set. I will continue until the last possible moment to do everything I can to prevent my son from marrying your daughter. And you can tell her as much."

Will's face was as flushed now as Enfield's was pale. "I came here to talk about your daughter, Mrs. Enfield, not mine. It was your daughter who was found in that hotel room. It was your daughter's body that was found with a saxophone player."

"Samuel," she said without taking her eyes from Will's face. "What is he saying?"

Will regained his composure. "There's been an accident, Mrs. Enfield. Your daughter Daphne. The police found her body this morning. She was—"

"That's quite enough, Mr. Owen." Though she'd been standing erect throughout their conversation, Emily gave the impression of drawing herself up. "My husband will give me the details."

Will looked at the thin face, the eyes cold but frightened, the narrow lips controlled to show no emotion, and he knew there was a struggle going on within Emily Enfield. He supposed he ought to feel some pity for that struggle, but he felt nothing but hatred. He supposed he ought to feel some compassion because behind that handsome disdainful face must be a mother's instincts, but he could feel no compassion. He felt only a terrible desire to slap that handsome face, slap it into humility and defeat.

Samuel Enfield stepped between them as if he'd read Will's

thoughts. "Thank you for your trouble, Owen. And now I'd appreciate it if you'd leave us alone with our grief."

And that, Will thought as he took his things from Hatton in the front hall, is about all you deserve.

The only people who did not know the real story of Daphne's death were those who relied on the newspapers for their information. A paragraph about her appeared in the obituary columns of all the papers, but not a single morning or evening edition mentioned her name in their front-page coverage of the gangland-style assassination.

Daphne was buried at a ceremony limited to the immediate family. Kate did not offer to attend, and Ty did not ask her to. For once he was willing to give in to his mother.

When Will first told Kate about Daphne's death, he could see she was shocked, but not by the conditions surrounding it. "Did you know about her?" Will asked.

"A little. More than I wanted to," Kate said.

"What about your brother?"

"Chris?" Kate tried to make her voice sound innocent.

"Well, I don't mean Bill."

"What does Chris have to do with Daphne?"

"You tell me, Katie. You know more about Chris than I do. All I know is that there was an address book in the girl's handbag, an address book with some of the most shameful people and places in it . . . well, it's not something I'd like you to know about, but your brother's name and address were there. Apparently he was one of Daphne's wide circle of friends. Just how good a friend was he? I want to know if any of this business is going to come home to roost. I want to know if my own son is going to bring disgrace upon our family the way Daphne Enfield did on hers."

"I don't think you have to worry about that. As far as I know, it was only a single weekend."

"And Chris told you about it? I don't understand young people today. That's scarcely the sort of thing a man would tell his sister in my day."

A man would do it, Kate thought, but not admit it. "He didn't tell me, Daddy. I found out. I went to Chris's one morning when I was in New York, and Daphne was there."

"I hope you left immediately."

Kate would have laughed if everything weren't so grim.

"Those Enfields certainly do a lot of damage," Will said.

"Only to themselves." Kate was remembering Daphne the last time she'd seen her. She'd been wearing a white satin dress. It had a low neck and a short skirt beaded with crystals and made Daphne look even more beautiful than usual. Kate pictured the white dress pierced by bullet holes and stained with blood. But that was as absurd as it was horrible. Daphne wouldn't have been wearing the white dress when she was shot. She wouldn't have been wearing anything. The image was even more terrible.

Will, however, was thinking of another member of the Enfield family. He was remembering Emily's outburst and an incident that had happened so long ago it should have been forgotten, but Will Owen was not one to forget his own family history. He might hide it from others, but he would not forget it himself.

"I suppose you know, Katie, that Ty's parents are not exactly in favor of your marriage."

"Ty tries to hide it from me, but it would be pretty hard not to know." She looked down at her hands folded in her lap. The diamond glittered next to the delicate gold band. "I don't care about them. I did in the beginning. I did when I thought they might convince Ty, but they haven't, and now they don't matter."

"Unfortunately, they do, Katie. Families always matter. Ty is a part of his family, just as you are of yours."

"Surely you're not against my marrying Ty just because of his sister?"

"No, I'm not against it, not even now, but I want to tell you something that you ought to think about before you do marry him. I never mentioned it to you before because I didn't think it was the kind of thing you had to know. Bill knows, but it was never necessary for you or Chris to. Until now. Something Mrs. Enfield said when I was at their house made me think I ought to tell you. And then this business with Chris and Daphne. There's more between our family and Ty's than there ought to be, and I want you to understand it all before you marry him. I want you to think about it seriously before you marry him.

"You never knew your Grandfather Owen, Katie. I barely remember him myself. I was eight when he died, but I was a good deal younger than that when he was sent to prison."

"You never told me he went to prison."

"It's not the sort of thing I enjoy talking about, though I can assure you it's nothing to be ashamed of." Will saw the look that crossed his daughter's face. "This isn't one of my political evasions,

Katie. There was nothing to be ashamed of. Your grandfather didn't steal anything or hurt anyone. All he did was try to support his family.

"My father worked in one of the tanneries in the foulest-smelling, filthiest section of Philadelphia. You can't imagine what the conditions in those sheds were like, Katie. They were small and dark, entirely airless, reeking with the smells of the trade, which, in case you don't know, and I'm pretty sure you don't, are awful. I can tell you about it, but neither of us can imagine what it was like to spend twelve or fourteen hours a day six days a week there. Still, your grandfather never complained. Until the year they cut the pay. You can't support a wife and four children on forty-five cents a day, Katie. Even then, even in the Neck, you couldn't do that. So your grandfather and some other workers went out on strike. But going out on strike wasn't enough, because for every man refusing to work at that price there were two more who would work at any price. So your grandfather and those men tried to discourage others from working. They picketed, and when men tried to cross their lines, there were the inevitable fights. Of course, the police arrested the strikers for those fights, not the men who were willing to work. Assault with intent to do all sorts of foul and terrible things. The charges never mentioned the intent to win a decent wage for a decent day's work.

"It's an old story, Katie, and I suppose you learned about it at that fancy school of yours. But there's an ending to it that they didn't teach you. Your grandfather and his friends were tried and found guilty. The judge decided to make an example of them. After all, if you let one group of tanners get away with it, pretty soon everyone will be thinking he deserves a living wage. The judge sentenced your grandfather and the others to ten years. The only problem was, after all those years of work in those foul, filthy sheds, your grandfather's health was not the best. He never served his ten years. He died in jail after two.

"That's all just terrible, you're thinking, but what does it have to do with Ty's family? The judge who decided to make an example of your grandfather was Ty's grandfather, the late—and widely respected—Judge Marion Enfield.

"That's the whole story, Katie, or the whole story up to now. I guess you'll have to finish it. I'm not suggesting you shouldn't marry Ty, but if you do, you ought to know what you're up against. It's more than a little polite snobbery. The hatred between our families goes back a long way. And it's not one-sided by any means. I've got in a few licks over the years—nothing really important, just an occasional reminder that we Owens aren't to be dismissed—and I don't imagine Samuel Enfield has appreciated them. So you'd better think seriously about marrying Ty. You'd better decide if your love is strong enough to overcome that legacy of hatred, Katie."

Kate was certain she knew the answer, or almost certain. It had happened a long time ago. She had never even known her grandfather. None of it had anything to do with her and Ty. And still some small seed of doubt remained. She'd never thought of herself as being family proud, but her father's story had struck some chord in her. She needed time to work it out for herself.

Her letter to Ty said only that a great deal had happened in the last few days and she wanted time to be alone. She would call him, she promised, as soon as she got back to town. To Ty the message was clear. Kate was put off by the scandal surrounding Daphne's death. Her message was clear and his answer was plain. Kat had to be made to realize that none of that had anything to do with them.

He called her house as soon as he got the letter, but Will did not know where she'd gone. "She said she was going away for a few days, but she wouldn't say where. I suspect she knows I would have told you." That much was true. Will had told Kate the story of her own grandfather and Ty's because he thought she ought to know, but he was still not opposed to the marriage. Dreams do not die that easily, at least Will's didn't.

Ty tried a few friends, but he knew it was hopeless. Kate would not tell Hilary, whom she rarely saw, or any of the girls in the office where she'd gone. Then it came to him. Addison Wales would know. He was sure of it.

Ty did not wait for the girl who was sitting at Kat's desk to announce him, and Wales looked momentarily startled by Ty's entrance into his office, startled but not especially surprised.

"Katie's not here, as you can see, Enfield."

"I know damn well she's not here. But I don't know where she is. And I have a feeling you do."

Addison smiled. "As a matter of fact, I do. But she asked me not to tell you."

"You'd better tell me, Wales, because if you don't tell me of your own volition . . ."

"Volition. I'm impressed. Didn't think you knew the word. Act your age, Enfield. Hitting me isn't going to do anyone any good. It will only make me less willing to tell you."

"What will make you more willing?"

"A few answers. Maybe it's none of my business, but I'm fond enough of Katie . . ."

"I can see that."

"Not in the way you mean, though I don't expect you to believe that. Anyway, I'm fond enough of Katie to care what happens to her. I won't ask if you love her. I wouldn't have had to put up with two years of histrionics in my own office if you two didn't love each other. What I'm really interested in is if you're going to marry her. I know that's a funny question coming from me, but just because I'm not very good at matrimony doesn't mean I've stopped believing in it. Especially for a girl like Katie. I know you say you're going to marry her, but it seems to me you're taking a hell of a long time getting around to it."

"If it's any of your business, Wales, we're getting married in June."

"Then why did she run away? What did you do this time?"

"That's just it. Nothing. At least, as far as I know."

Addison looked at him carefully. He was sure Ty wasn't lying. He looked too confused and lost for that. Addison thought of the rumors surrounding the Enfield girl's death. Whatever was going on between Katie and him wasn't going to be solved by not telling Ty where she was. He suspected Katie even wanted him to tell Ty where she was, though she'd said she didn't. "She's at my house on Long Beach Island."

"Your house! Christ, I suppose I ought to be glad you're not there with her."

"You know, Enfield, you'd be better off if you'd stop treating Katie like some object everyone's trying to steal from you and start treating her like a woman."

Ty did not bother to answer. If he left now, he could reach Long Beach Island before dark.

He made good time over the highway to the island that had been built just before the war, but the drive still seemed interminable. As he came off the bridge, he had a blowout in one of the rear tires. For a moment he considered walking the few miles to Wales's house, but decided it would be faster to change the tire. He swore steadily as he did.

The house was a weathered cottage almost hidden by dunes from the narrow road that ran the length of the island. At first Ty wasn't sure it was the right one, but the name on the mailbox told him it was Addison's. He knocked loudly several times, and when there was no answer, tried the door. No one ever locked doors on the island unless they were closing up the house for the week or the season.

"Kat," he called once inside the small living room cluttered with wicker furniture, some of it badly in need of reupholstery, and the sort of rustic woven carpets that could not be ruined by sand and salt water. There was no answer, and Ty began to wander from room to room. She hadn't gone back to town. He could tell that from the cold but half-full coffeepot on the stove, the ashtrays that had not been emptied, the clothes in the closet of the smaller bedroom. It was peculiar and a little galling to find Kat's things scattered so easily among those of Addison Wales. On the coffee table in the living room Kat's copy of Willa Cather's *A Lost Lady* rested on a large volume on cricket. Her blue sweater lay on the sofa next to an old tweed jacket she must have appropriated for her stay. In the single bath Kat's hairbrush sat on the windowsill next to Addison Wales's shaving cup.

Ty's hands were dirty from changing the tire, and he washed them and left the bathroom quickly. He walked through the living room and out onto the small porch that faced the sea. He'd wait there.

Kate had been walking for hours. She'd reached the tip of the island and was halfway back to the house before she realized how cold it was. The day had started out sunny, but the clouds had moved in as the afternoon wore on, and the air felt damp and smelled brackish. She was wearing two sweaters, but she wished she'd put on that old jacket of Addison's as well. She'd forgot how cold the island could get at the end of April. Still, she was almost glad of the physical discomfort. It kept her mind off Ty and her father's story for a while. She'd come away to think things through, but she hadn't been able to think them through at all, only to turn them around in circles.

Ty had nothing to do with that judge who'd decided her grandfather must be made an example. Ty wasn't rigid and hidebound and unforgiving. Except when she'd taken the job with Addison. That was unfair. Hadn't he given in on the job, given in with scarcely an argument? Until the night she'd worked late instead of going to Daphne's party. But he'd been angry only because he was afraid of losing her. If he were so afraid of losing her, why hadn't he married her as they'd planned? Because he'd given in to the family argument, bought the Enfield party line. She pulled the sweaters closer around her. The wind off the ocean was freshening. But he fought them too, had fought them simply by choosing her. Well, wasn't that brave of him? Chris would say. Wasn't that fearless, risking the Enfield wrath by sinking so low as to want to marry Katie Owen? No, that was unfair again. Nothing Ty said or did ever implied he thought there was anything wrong with marrying Kate. Except the fact that he'd let his parents talk him into waiting three years to do it. Around and around she went like the water caught in the small whirlpool formed by the jetty.

She saw the figure on the porch steps but couldn't make out the features. Perhaps Addison had come down to see how she was. It would be just like Addison to do that. She told herself it was Addison and prayed she was wrong.

The figure saw her and started down the beach. It was Ty. She saw him crossing the beach in his long easy strides, saw his body straining to hers, felt his arms around her as if she were coming home, and wondered how she had doubted him or them.

They stood that way for a few moments, holding each other without words or any need for them, then she shivered. "I didn't think you'd come," she said before she realized she was saying it.

His arm was still around her and he was leading her back to the house. "You didn't make it easy for me. Why did you run away, Kat? Because of Daphne?"

"Daphne? How could you think I'd be so narrow-minded?"

"I didn't know what to think. Your letter wasn't much help."

"It's a long story."

"Well, we've got all the time in the world. Why don't I make a fire and you find where Wales keeps his whiskey. There's bound to be some in the house, and then you can tell me all about it."

Ty built a fire and she found the whiskey and they sat on the musty-smelling sofa before the hearth while she repeated the story Will had told her. When she finished, Ty was quiet.

"It's funny," he said finally, staring into the flames. "All my life I've heard what a great man Grandfather Enfield was. Oh, there was the business about Uncle Nick, and some people admitted he might have been a little stern there, but on the whole Judge Enfield was supposed to be the closest thing to God Philadelphia had seen since Ben Franklin—and without old Ben's notorious weaknesses. I never thought much about him, but I never questioned their portrait of him either. And yet I know now your father's story is true. It's exactly like Grandfather. And there's nothing I can say, Kat, except that I'm sorry, sorry as hell, but it doesn't have anything to do with us. You say you don't really have any feeling for your grandfather. You never even knew him. Well, I knew my grandfather when I was a boy, and I never had much feeling for him one way or another except fear, and now I'm not going to let his cruelty and stupidity and intransigence or the accident of my being his grandson come between us. I haven't let my parents do that, and I'll be damned if I'll let the memory of our grandparents do it."

He was no longer looking at the fire and he lifted her face to his. "But you have to make up your mind."

She had, of course. The moment she'd seen Ty this afternoon, she'd known that her mind had been made up all along. She had been shocked by her father's story, then distressed by it, and that had made her question Ty, but now Ty was here, and there were no questions and no doubts. There was only Ty and a loving and wanting him that screened out the rest of the world and their problems and judgments. She told him as much, and then his mouth was on hers as if he wanted to taste as well as hear the words, and his hands were slow but searching beneath sweater, beneath blouse, beneath thin chemise, until they found her breasts. He could feel her body warming to his touch, turning to him, responding to him, and his hands moved more urgently, as if in realization of what they had almost lost.

She said they could go upstairs, but he said that was Wales's bedroom, and she started to say it was Wales's house, but she saw the familiar expression on his face and the flames reflected in his eyes and knew they had passed beyond discussion. She watched his hands on her body, the large graceful hands that had come to know her and her desires so well, and she saw his body long and lean and tawny in the firelight and through the desire and the pleasure came fear at what she had almost thrown away. The fear made her cling to him with what he took to be passion, then turned to passion as she felt his mouth on her breast and his hands hot on her body kindling flames as they moved, and she touched him and sensed the force of his own desire, matching hers, fanning hers to a white heat that could not be controlled. She wanted him, cried out that she wanted him, and then he was inside her and they were together and it was as if they would never be apart again.

"You know the first thing I want when we have our own house?" Ty asked. He had got up to put another log on the grate and cover them with an old patchwork quilt, and she felt warm and safe next to him on the worn old sofa. "I want an enormous bed. I think I'll have one specially made."

"And scandalize all Philadelphia?"

"Then every so often when I think you're getting spoiled by the luxury of it all, I'll drag you down to the living-room floor—not Wales's living room, but our own—or Uncle Nick's studio or the tack room and make love to you."

"For old times' sake?"

"To keep you from getting bored. I'm not taking any chances on losing you. Ever."

"I can see it all now. Being discovered by a brood of grand-children in the tack room."

"Good for the little beggars. Keep them from dismissing us as old fogies."

That night they drove down to the small fishing village at Barnegat and bought lobsters and clams, and Ty decided it was all right to ex-haust Addison's supply of whiskey since he was going to send him several cases in thanks for the use of the house as soon as they got back. They steamed the seafood and sat at the small table in the kitchen eating and drinking and making plans, some extravagant and some quite practical.

"A dozen children," he said.

"Never."

"Ah, my Kat is vain. Worried about that lovely body of yours."

"Just think how much of the time I'd be pregnant."

"Right. I've always believed in small families anyway. But a big old house in the country. Not on the Main Line, but really out in the country, with no one else around." He turned suddenly serious. "I suppose you're going to want to stay on with Wales for a while."

"Will you hate it if I do?"

He stared into his glass for a minute, then took a long swallow. "Darn it, Kat, I won't love it, but I won't hate it. I guess if I want you, I've got to let you be you."

She leaned across the table and kissed him.

"I love your lip rouge," he said. "What's it called? Essence of butter?"

"Are you going to mind the law firm?"

"It won't be so bad. And I'm not going to stay with it forever. Maybe I'll become a gentleman farmer at that place in the country. After I make our fortune, of course. Or I may do something else."

"Such as?"

He looked at her slyly. "Maybe I'll go into politics. After all, I've got a foot in the door."

"You're joking, aren't you?"

"Not in the least. A lot of attorneys do. Look at your brother Bill."

"Think of your family. I can see them now. Livid. And they'd blame it all on me."

"And they'd be right. You're going to turn me into a crusader, Kat. I can feel it."

"Well, if it's reform politics you're talking about, you're going to be running against my father."

"Don't worry about that. He'll be an elder statesman by the time I get around to all that. I have to make a fortune first, remember."

"Not for me, you don't."

"You mean you're going to fling the jewels and furs I bring you back in my face?"

"Well, I wouldn't want to hurt your feelings."

"A gold digger. I always knew it."

"It's what your mother thinks. That and a social climber."

He reached across the table and took her hand. "I told you, Kat. It doesn't matter what anyone thinks."

It rained during the night, but it was warm in the bed with Ty beside her, and when she awakened now and then she could hear the sound of the waves crashing on the beach and the rain pelting the porch roof below the window, and each time she'd touch Ty, brush the hair out of his face or kiss his shoulder or just touch his back to reassure herself he was really there.

The next day the sky was still overcast and there was a cold wind off the ocean, but Ty insisted they go for a walk on the beach. "It won't be a proper idyll if we don't walk on the beach." They walked for a mile or so, leaving sets of footprints side by side in the wet sand, and when they turned back their footsteps were still there because the tide was going out.

Later in the afternoon they drove down to the village again and bought more seafood and some greens at the small grocer's because Ty said he wanted a salad. On the drive back the sun came out in time to set. It warmed the air a little, and Ty made a fire on the beach because he said it was the only proper way to cook lobsters. They finished the seafood and afterward Kate lay back on the sand and said he was going to make her fat, and Ty put his hand on her stomach and said no but someday he was going to make her pregnant, just as he'd promised last night, and he rolled over, and she felt his weight on top of her and tasted the seafood and whiskey on his tongue and pressed herself against him, but he said no, beaches were for later, as he'd promised last night, and stood and held out his hand. Addison Wales's bedroom was no longer his but theirs, and as Ty rose above her she could see the silhouette of his body against the moonlit window, see the lovely long lean torso that disappeared into the two of them locked together, bound together forever.

They stayed at Addison's for fewer than forty-eight hours, but it seemed to Kate, even in later years, that it was one of the best times they'd ever had together.

6

Samuel Enfield was alone in the library when Ty entered. "Hatton said you wanted to see me, Father."

Samuel closed the morocco-bound volume and placed it on the table beside him. "Sit down, Ty. I'm going to ask you to do something for me, but before you say yes or no—and naturally I'm hoping you'll say yes—I want to explain things fully."

Feeling more like a client than a son, Ty lowered himself into a leather chair facing his father.

"You'll be graduated in a week and a half, and you plan to marry two weeks after that? Is that correct?"

"We've been through this before, Father. I plan to marry Kat with or without your approval."

"You have my approval, Ty. I've said that before, and I especially mean it now. You've finished law school, you've waited three years, you've proven that you're serious about this. I'm proud of you. I don't mind saying that. And I know you and Kathryn are going to be very happy." Samuel stopped for a moment and looked down at his hands, one splayed on each knee. "It's because I'm so certain of the lifetime of happiness that awaits you that I have the audacity to ask this favor." He held up one hand. "Hear me out before you say anything, Ty. I'm going to ask you to postpone the wedding for another month or two. That's all. Two months at the most. You and Kathryn can't object to that."

"We certainly can, sir."

"I asked you to hear me out, Ty. I'm worried about your mother. So is the doctor, if you must know. This business with Daphne was too much for her. I'd hoped by this time she would have begun to come out of it. The doctor assured me she would. Only she hasn't. You can see that for yourself. She doesn't eat, doesn't sleep, never leaves the house. We've got to do something. Before your mother makes herself seriously ill."

"I can't see how my postponing my marriage to Kat for another month or two is going to help Mother."

Samuel held up his hand again. "Please let me finish, Ty. The doctor has suggested that your mother go away for a while. There's too much here to remind her of Daphne." Samuel looked out the window for a moment and seemed to be recalling some memories of his own. "But it's more than the memories. Your mother's a proud woman. That's one of the reasons she won't go out. She's certain people are talking about Daphne, about her. She hates the scandal, but more than that, she hates the pity. That's why she must get away for a while. I'm convinced, and the doctor is too, that her only chance for resuming a normal life is to start among people who know nothing about her or this whole tragic incident.

"I've spoken to your mother, and she's agreed to a trip abroad, but she refuses to go alone. I can't possibly leave now. That coal case is sure to go to the state supreme court. Of course, Hilary's the logical choice, but unfortunately, or rather fortunately, Hilary is pregnant again. As for friends, well, they're the problem, not the cure. So that leaves you, Tyson. I'd like you to take your mother abroad. For a month or two. I realize it's a great deal to ask, but I wouldn't be asking it if I didn't think something more important was at stake. I'll put it as plainly as I can, Ty. You have a whole lifetime of happiness ahead of you. I don't think it's asking too much to beg you—that's right, Ty, beg you—to give up two months of that happiness to save your mother's life. And make no mistake, that's what it amounts to."

"You're a very good lawyer, Father."

"I'll pretend you didn't say that, Tyson, because I know it was only your disappointment speaking. I know that when you have time to think things over, you'll agree with me that taking your mother abroad is the only honorable, the only compassionate thing you can do. I'm sure Kathryn will agree. I'm sure she doesn't want to build her marriage on your mother's misery and illness."

"You know what they're doing, don't you? Go along with it if you must, Ty, but for God's sake don't go along with it blindly."

"Kat, be fair."

"Why should I? Your parents aren't being fair."

"Mother is ill. I spoke to the doctor."

"The doctor is one of your father's oldest friends. He'll say what he's told to."

"Are you suggesting they're lying?"

"I'm suggesting your mother is very unhappy about Daphne's death, and she's found a way to use that unhappiness to prevent another tragedy in the family."

"Don't say that, Kat. Please don't say that."

"What do you want me to say? *Bon Voyage?*"

"It's only for a month or so."

"I'm sure your mother has a somewhat longer trip in mind."

"I won't stay any longer than two months."

She looked at him, and the misery in his face cut the edge of her anger. "I know you mean that now, Ty, but just in case . . . well, I don't want you to feel tied down. It wouldn't be fair to send you abroad feeling tied down." She took the diamond ring from her third finger and handed it to him. "It's not as final as it seems, Ty. If you come home in a month or two, if things are still the same then, you can give it back to me. But in case you change your mind in Europe . . ."

"I won't change my mind, Kat. I haven't for three years, and I won't now."

"Well, in case you do, it will be better if you don't feel bound." She started to take the small baby's ring off her last finger.

"Not that one, Kat. Please keep that one."

She stopped, the ring halfway off. After all, it was only a keepsake, not a commitment. She slipped it back in place.

The letter was cold, and Ty cursed himself for its coldness, but he cursed Kat too for having given him back the ring. She shouldn't have done that. She could have tried to understand, but she'd been too proud to try to understand. Either that or she simply didn't care enough to try to understand.

He walked to the terrace and looked out over the canal. There was a gondola tied up in front of the hotel and the gondolier sprawled in it was singing quietly to himself, singing just as it said he would be in the travel brochures. And beautiful, romantic Venice was just the way they said it would be in the travel brochures. And every afternoon for the past five days Ty had toured beautiful, romantic Venice with a diamond engagement ring lying uselessly in his pocket.

He walked back to the ornate little writing desk, picked up the letter, and without rereading it, sealed the envelope. It wasn't much of a letter, but he wasn't going to get off a better one in his present mood.

Kate had read the letter five times, but there was no divining emotion where none existed. It wasn't a love letter, it was a Baedecker. She'd answer it, but not yet, not until she'd got her disappointment under control.

Her parents were at the table when she came down to dinner, and Bill and his new wife were there too. Kate had forgot it was Wednesday. Bill and Helen always came to dinner on Wednesday night. She'd forgot it was Wednesday because she'd lost track of days waiting for a letter from Ty. Her mother had called the office today to say it had arrived, though Kate had never told her mother she was waiting for it, but the letter that arrived was not the one Kate was hoping for.

"Roger Atherton called just before you got home," her mother said. "He said he'd call back later this evening."

"I'm not home."

"Don't ask your mother to lie for you, Katie," Will said. "And if you're no longer engaged to Tyson Enfield, I don't see why you can't see Roger."

"I didn't say I wasn't engaged to Ty."

"You didn't say anything," her father pointed out. "Except that there wouldn't be a wedding this month. But I don't see that ring on your third finger anymore. And the newspapers said that Mr. Tyson Enfield sailed for Europe more than two weeks ago."

"You shouldn't have let him go, Katie," Bill said.

"When I want your advice, I'll ask for it."

"Now, don't snap at your brother," Will said. "He didn't do anything. And whether you want my advice or not, you're going to get it. I think you ought to see Roger."

"He's doing very well," Margaret added.

"He delivers all the very best babies," Helen said. "And he's going to deliver ours."

"Fine, Helen, then you see Roger, but I don't want to."

"I just don't understand." Margaret shook her head sadly. They'd come so close, but close, she knew, was not enough.

Ty started looking for Kat's letter exactly ten days after he'd sent his off. He'd been looking all along of course, but he'd always known Kat wouldn't write first. Not after she'd given him back the ring. But now he'd written, and he was sure she would answer. He'd be getting a letter any day now, and each morning he went to the desk of whatever hotel they were stopping at and waited expectantly while the concierge checked to see whether there was any mail for Signor Enfield or Señor Enfield or Monsieur Enfield. On his first morning in Paris there were several letters for Monsieur and Madame Enfield, but since they'd got in late the night before, Ty slept till after ten that morning. Emily took the pile of envelopes from the concierge and retired to the writing room off the lobby to look through them. There were three for her and two for Ty, one from Tim Wharton and another from that girl. Emily considered opening it, but she did not believe in reading other people's mail. Instead she tore it in half, then in half again, and dropped it in the wastebasket beneath the desk. Then she went to telephone the Claridge. She must tell Amanda and Mrs. Wycombe they had arrived.

That afternoon Emily said she was tired and thought she'd take a nap, but wouldn't Ty go over to the American Express office himself and see about an automobile. If they were going to tour the battlefields they'd have to have one. Touring the battlefields had been his mother's idea. Ty wasn't at all sure he wanted to take in those particular sights. Still, he was here for his mother. On his way out of the Ritz, he checked the desk again. The concierge was sorry, but there was no more mail for Monsieur Enfield.

Ty was trying not to think of Kat and trying to remember the name of the little café where he'd got tight with another officer and two French girls one afternoon on leave, when he entered the American Express office. He was thinking of the girls and the long Paris afternoon and how they'd gone back to the apartment of one of the girls that night because, of course, it was wartime and nothing in Paris was open at night. He was remembering the other officer, who was from California, and the dark little French girl with the large eyes and the large breasts whom they'd both wanted, but who had chosen Ty, and thinking of what a terrible and wonderful time it had been. He was thinking a lot of things, but he was not thinking of

Amanda Wycombe when he looked up and saw her standing at the counter. At first he was surprised, then everything fell into place.

"Ty!" she cried. "Imagine running into you here. Of course, I knew you were abroad, but I had no idea you were in Paris. What a surprise! What a wonderful surprise!"

"Let's not be any more ridiculous about this than we have to, Amanda."

"My, my, what an ego. You can't really believe I'm following you around Europe. Well, the least you can do is say that you're pleased to see me."

"You're looking well, Amanda."

She told him that he was too, though it was a lie. "How is your mother?"

Ty had a feeling that Amanda knew only too well how his mother was, but he answered that she was feeling much better, thank you. And then, since it was teatime, it was only logical that he take her back to the Ritz, and when Emily came down from her nap she found them together and said wasn't it just the most wonderful surprise their running into each other that way. Remembering the war again, Ty thought of Elsie Janis and decided his mother could put on a pretty good act herself.

It was so fortunate that Amanda had turned up this way, Emily kept saying for the next few weeks, because things had been awfully dull for Ty and now Emily didn't feel in the least bad when she had an early dinner alone or with Mrs. Wycombe and spent a quiet evening, because she knew that Ty had Amanda to keep him company. The young people could stay up half the night and see what they wanted, because after all, that's the way young people are.

Ty never knew exactly when it happened, or perhaps he realized that it hadn't happened all at once, but a little each day. It would begin when he came down each morning and asked for the mail, and it got a little worse each night because he was drinking a lot, more than he had at any time since the war, and Amanda was working so damn hard at being nice. One night when they'd gone to three different clubs in Montmartre and he'd taken her back to her hotel, he'd kissed her, just for old times' sake he said, because after all, they did go back a long way together and they'd had some good times, or so it seemed when he was drinking. But it wasn't like old times, because instead of putting her hands on his shoulders and then pulling away quickly with a prim "there," she pressed her small body against his and opened her mouth and clung to him with a promise he'd never felt in her before. He'd kissed her again after that, and little by little it began to happen, though it had really happened, he supposed, that night they'd come back from Château Thierry. Emily had decided at the last minute that she didn't want to go, and Mrs. Wycombe had said she'd stay and keep Emily company. Ty said in that case he'd just as soon forget the whole thing, but Amanda said she'd really been looking forward to it because it was something she wanted to try to understand. And she'd been very understanding, asking the right questions, but knowing when to keep silent. She'd been, Ty told himself when he thought about that day and the night that followed, too damn understanding.

He'd begun to feel peculiar on the road out to Veuilly-la-Poterie. The villages looked the same, but they weren't the same because this time there were no crowds lined along the road to cheer them, only an occasional old man or group of children who eyed the big car curiously. But the closer he got to Veuilly, the more the old men and the children began to recede and the past take over. Instead of Amanda at his side there was Pastor, impossible, unlikable, talkative Pastor. All through the long march Pastor had kept up a barrage of criticism, about the filth of the French who kept manure piles in their front yard, about the general dowdiness of the girls who turned out to cheer them, about the old men at their sides who should have been at the front rather than home safe in their villages. Finally the man behind him had told Pastor to stop bitching or he'd start the fighting right here, but there'd been no force behind the words because they all knew Pastor was just scared, scared like the rest of them.

That was when they still had time to be scared. They'd had the long march through the night and most of the morning for that, then a few more hours after they'd dug in on the western flank of the German line. As Ty had lain there in the woods that smelled green and fresh in the hot June afternoon, he'd told himself this would be the worst part of it. The waiting and the fear would be worse than the reality, but he'd been wrong. There was nothing worse than the assault, wave after wave of Germans running at them, raining down on them from the dense black cloud of smoke. The smoke was the only thing you could see. After the first few minutes you couldn't see the trees or the sky or the sun, only a great black wall pierced by quick flashes of light. Then suddenly figures began to emerge from the smoke, running toward them, sending off more flashes of light as they ran, and as the figures got closer they'd fall, but behind them other figures would take shape from the blackness and keep coming and coming until Ty found himself among the group of men running through the forest, tripping on the underbrush, crashing into trees, cursing, screaming, and running all the way. Ty kept shouting to the men to stop, but all the time he was running as fast as they were.

When they reached a clearing, he looked around and saw in the faces of the men, his men, the same shame he knew must be written on his own. Then he saw Pastor, short, unlikable Pastor, running toward them, silent now, as if he were too busy concentrating on something to talk. He was only yards from the clearing when the top of his head flew off to one side, leaving Pastor with a startled foolish look on his face as he fell.

"Goddammit!" someone shouted. "We're going back." Ty didn't know who gave the order, but that night after the Germans had been driven out of the woods, someone said it had been his voice that had led the men back. He didn't remember giving the order, and certainly it was nothing to be proud of. Going back into the forest hadn't been heroic. It had merely been doing what he'd been trained to do, though after Ty had been through a summer of battles he came to realize that men didn't always do what they were supposed to the first time out. After he'd seen other raw troops panic until some animal hatred triggered by another man's death or just one assault wave too many turned them into the fighters they supposedly were, he'd come to realize there was nothing cowardly or even extraordinary about their retreat that first day.

Ty had forgot that particular truth because it was not one you especially wanted to remember after a war was over, but the memory of it came back now, and along with it memories of the fear and confusion, of the wall of smoke that turned the afternoon into night and the pinpricks of light like lethal little stars, and the filthy, acrid smell. The sensations flooded back, and with them the memory of Pastor and the startled look on his face as he'd fallen, and Thorpe lying a few feet from Ty sometime that afternoon holding his stomach and screaming, his inhuman screams mingling with Ty's calls for a medic, and the German who'd kept running after the bullets had torn through his shoulder and across his chest, kept running toward them until he'd fallen forward and his face had caught on a stump and twisted up so the lifeless eyes continued to stare at Ty until he'd moved on into the woods.

It had all come back, and for a moment Ty had felt the old nausea, but that had passed, just as the scars of battle had disappeared under the forest's new growth, and instead of the stinging, acrid smell of battle there was the rich, almost decaying smell of the woods on a hot August afternoon, and instead of Pastor and Thorpe and the dead German, there was Amanda, quiet and reverential at his side.

He and Amanda dined alone that night. Ty drank a great deal and said little, but Amanda went on being understanding, so understanding that when he took her back to her hotel suite, she went in to see that her mother was asleep, and when she returned to the sitting room she was wearing some sort of silk robe. She crossed the room to Ty and put her arms around him, and he realized with a shock that she was wearing nothing beneath the robe. He was very drunk, and the fact of his drunkenness was the last rational thought he had until afterward, when he had the distinct impression she'd taken advantage of him.

Ty awakened the next morning feeling sick. Too much to drink, he told himself, but he knew it was more than that. The room waiter brought his breakfast, but the *café noir* did no good. He tried to go back to sleep, but couldn't. He couldn't settle his head or his stomach, couldn't go back to sleep, couldn't stop thinking of Amanda. It had been a stupid thing to do. Well, he wouldn't make the same mistake twice. You could bet on that.

He was lying in bed debating which tack to take with Amanda— did he apologize for last night? did he pretend it had never happened?—when his mother knocked at the door.

"Ty, are you up?" she called quietly.

"Awake," he mumbled, hoping she'd go away and knowing she wouldn't.

Emily entered the room with that brisk manner that had always been a silent reproach to her children when she found them in bed at an hour she felt better suited to more active pursuits.

"I knew you wouldn't be asleep. Not with all the excitement. Amanda told me the good news. She telephoned first thing this morning. I'm so happy for you, Tyson. Though I'm not in the least surprised. I always knew you and Amanda would marry."

The pain in his temples he thought he'd conquered regrouped and made a fresh assault. "Amanda told you we're getting married?"

"Now, you mustn't be annoyed with her, Ty. She said she knew she should let you break the news, but she was just too excited. She said she hadn't slept a wink all night and couldn't wait to tell me. Apparently she woke Mrs. Wycombe in the middle of the night to tell her."

In the middle of the night. Ty wondered if that meant right after he'd left. He could picture Amanda going into her room, dressing again, putting on the layers of clothing she'd removed for him, then going to her mother's room to tell her the news. Or didn't she have to pretend? Were Mrs. Wycombe and his mother in on last night too? No, not last night. Both women would go to great lengths to bring off the marriage, but they wouldn't go that far. Amanda had brought off last night on her own. Well, not entirely on her own. Still, if she thought she were going to get away with it, she was wrong.

He started to tell his mother he had no intention of marrying Amanda, but stopped before the words were out. Ty could imagine the conversation all too well, or rather imagine its impossibility.

But I don't understand, his mother would say. *How did Amanda get the idea you were going to marry her, if you didn't ask her to marry you?*

She got the idea, Mother, because last night when I took her back to her suite she went in to see if Mrs. Wycombe were asleep and came out wearing this robe or gown or something like that—whatever it was, it opened pretty damn easily—and, you see, Mother, she was wearing nothing under it and I was pretty drunk, though not too drunk to notice that Amanda has a pretty good body, and not too drunk to do something about it . . .

It was not an explanation he could make to his mother. He'd talk to Amanda and tell her she'd have to tell her own mother and his that she'd decided not to marry him.

As soon as Emily left, Ty called the Claridge and asked for Amanda's room. Mrs. Wycombe answered the phone. He cursed Amanda silently as he listened to her mother telling him how pleased she was, assuring him he wouldn't have to write to Mr. Wycombe, since it was something the Wycombes, like the Enfields apparently, had always expected, asking him when he thought the wedding would be.

When Ty finally got Mrs. Wycombe off the phone and Amanda on, he asked her to meet him in a small café near the Boulevard Saint Michel. When they'd been there two days ago, there had been no Americans, and Amanda had said it was awfully clever of Ty to discover it.

"I knew you'd think of someplace romantic today, darling," she said.

She kept him waiting for half an hour, and the waiter brought a second aperitif, then a third disapprovingly. These Americans, they gulped food, drink, everything.

When Amanda finally arrived, Ty cut through her apologies and ordered a drink for her brusquely. "Why did you tell them we were getting married?"

"I'm sorry, darling. I know I should have let you tell your mother, but I just couldn't wait."

"You know damn well what I mean, Amanda."

He watched the small mouth purse as if ready to announce that she would not be cursed at, but then she seemed to think better of it. "I don't understand, Ty."

"No one mentioned marriage last night."

"I didn't think we had to in view of . . . in view of everything else."

"Listen, Amanda, I'm sorry about last night."

She smiled. Ty recognized it as her madonna smile. "I can't put all the blame on you, darling. It was my fault too."

Blame. Fault. Somehow she managed to make it sound like a great mishap. Well, the way things were turning out, it was, Ty thought.

"The best thing to do," she went on, "is to marry as soon as possible so it won't happen again."

"So it won't happen again?"

She dropped her eyes. "You know what I mean, Ty. So it will be *all right.*"

Oh, God, he thought. It will never be all right with you, Amanda. Life will never be all right with you. I don't love you. I don't even like you very much. He couldn't very well tell her that. "But marriage, Amanda. I just hadn't thought of marriage." At least not to you, he added silently.

"Perhaps you should have told me that last night," she snapped, then caught herself. "I'm sorry, Ty. But imagine how I feel." She sniffled softly, though Ty had not noticed any tears. "Last night may not have meant anything to you . . ."

"It meant something to me," he said lamely. "It meant a lot to me, Mandy."

"It meant everything to me. You know me well enough to understand that. You know me well enough to understand it's not the sort of thing I'd do unless I loved you and thought you loved me and we were going to be married. I can't believe you didn't know that, Ty." The tears had finally arrived, and she took a handkerchief from the pocket of her jacket and dabbed at them. "I can't believe you'd think I was one of those girls who'd do something like that . . ."

She let her voice trail off, but Ty filled in his own words. Do something like that out of simple love and desire. He remembered Kat in Nicholas's studio. "You don't have to marry me because of this," she'd said. But that was Kat, and Kat was gone. First she'd given him back his ring, then she'd refused to answer his letter. Kat was gone and Amanda was here beside him, dabbing at her eyes and blaming him for last night, no matter how much she pretended not to. And she was right. He knew what last night meant to a girl like Amanda. It didn't matter that she'd engineered the act. The consequences remained the same.

He felt sick and angry and trapped. Dammit, he wouldn't go through with it. He signaled the waiter for another drink. He'd find a way out. He didn't know how, but he'd find a way.

He didn't, of course. Every time he'd begin to explain things to Amanda, she'd cry or accuse him of taking advantage of her and not caring for her at all, and he'd apologize and assure her that was not what he'd meant, though it was exactly what he'd meant.

And all the time he went on looking for the letter from Kat. The letter, he knew, would give him the courage to break off with Amanda. But the letter never came, and by the time they boarded the *Aquitania* for the voyage home, he knew he'd lost Kat for good. And he knew too that he would marry Amanda.

Though they were engaged and though there is nothing more romantic than a sea voyage, that night in Paris was not repeated. It was ridiculous, Ty said, since they were going to be married, and hypocritical too, since it had happened once, but Amanda remained firm.

"It never should have happened, darling," she said. "And it never would have, but you were so unhappy that night and I loved you so much I just couldn't help myself."

"And you can now?"

"This isn't any easier for me than it is for you, Ty," she said, but it seemed to Ty that it was no hardship at all for her to pull away and straighten her clothes and say he had to be patient because they'd be married in no time at all.

Kathryn had gone up to New York that Friday on business for Addison Wales and decided to stay for the weekend. Ty had never answered her letter, and though she'd read of his return in the newspaper, he hadn't tried to see her, hadn't even telephoned. It was too painful to stay in Philadelphia waiting for him to.

Chris had moved onto the couch to give her his bedroom, and even cleaned the apartment. He'd begun to make a joke about its not being as posh as what she was accustomed to in New York, but caught himself.

They lunched on Saturday, then Chris went back to the paper and Kate walked around the city feeling more miserable than ever in the bright autumn sunshine. It seemed that every time she turned a corner she came face to face with some place Ty had taken her. There was the small restaurant on Thirty-sixth Street where they'd gone when they sneaked away from the rest of the crowd up for the Princeton-Columbia game. And somehow she managed to end up in front of the secondhand store in the shadow of the Third Avenue El where Ty had found the back issues of Kat's magazine. A little tight from the party they'd just left, Ty kept insisting that Kate autograph each and every one of them, and finally the sour-looking proprietor asked them to leave. She even recognized the balloon man in Central Park. Ty had bought his entire supply one afternoon, then liberated them all over the lake. They'd looked like bright-colored birds sailing higher and higher until they were out of sight. Kate hadn't thought she and Ty had come up to New York that often, but now it seemed they'd spent a lifetime here.

She got back to Chris's apartment a little after five and made herself a drink. She'd decided to go back to Philadelphia that night. She had been silly to think she could escape Ty that easily, and there was no point in visiting her misery on Chris. He wanted her to go to a party with him tonight, but a party was the last thing she felt like. When Chris burst into the apartment, Kate could tell from his breathing that he'd run up the stairs.

As soon as he saw her he felt foolish as well as angry. "I can't imagine why I'm in such a hurry. It isn't exactly good news." He handed her a newspaper folded open to the social page.

Kate was silent for so long that Chris began to think she was memorizing the announcement. "You have to hand it to Amanda," she said finally. "The wedding's next month. No three-year engagements for her."

"I wish you'd do something, Katie. I wish you'd cry or scream or something. Anything but just sit there and stare at that damn paper."

"I'm too tired to do anything, Chris. It was a long battle, and I'm much too tired to do anything about the fact that I lost it."

"That bastard!"

"I still love him."

"How can you? After all this?"

"It isn't that simple, Chris. I wish it were, but it's not. I can't stop loving him just because he's stopped loving me. Though I have to admit that for the moment, at least, I don't like him very much. I don't suppose I have ever since he went to Europe." She looked up at him and forced a smile. "Do you want to say I told you so?"

He sat on the arm of her chair and put an arm around her shoulders. "Don't, Katie, please don't." Then she began to cry.

Chris offered to take her out to dinner, but she said she wasn't hungry. "You can make me another of these, though." She handed him the empty glass. "Don't be so cheap. Fill it up. I plan to get as tight as possible tonight."

He poured a glass for himself. "We'll drink ourselves blind."

"No, Chris, you go to your party. I'd rather be alone. Really."

"I have no intention of letting you get drunk alone. Either we go to the party and drink or we stay here and drink."

"But that's not fair. You wanted to go to that party."

The argument went on while they finished their drinks, and by that time Kate didn't much care where she continued drinking so long as she did continue.

The party was in the garden apartment of an old brownstone on Eighth Street. There was a crush of people in the two small rooms thick with smoke, and some of the guests had spilled over into the garden. Kate downed the drink Chris had given her, then went to get another in the kitchen, where two men and a woman were arguing noisily about Russia and a couple was kissing in a corner. She kept her eyes from the couple while she refilled her glass from one of the dozen bottles on the table and left the room quickly. A man in the doorway said something to her, but she brushed past him and returned to Chris. He was standing with his arm around the waist of a slender girl with curly red hair and a wide mouth that gave her an air of abandon. Chris introduced them, but Kate wasn't listening to the girl's name, though she was aware of Chris's arm around her waist and hers draped possessively around his neck. Kate mumbled something and drifted off to the other room.

In the kitchen the trio was still arguing and the couple embracing, and Kate refilled her glass and went out to the garden. There was a low wall at the far end and the crowd was thinner there. Kate crossed the small patch of yard, stumbling a little on some uneven flagstones, and sat on the wall. She wished she'd brought one of the bottles from the kitchen. Then she wouldn't have to move all night. She could just sit here and drink herself silly, so silly that she couldn't remember Tyson Enfield's name.

"So you're Owen's sister."

She looked up and saw a man leaning over her. She narrowed her eyes until the doubled image blended into one. He was big, with a shock of reddish-brown hair. He reminded her of someone, but she couldn't remember who. Not Ty. He was nothing like Ty. Someone else. Someone unimportant. Kevin O'Neil. Kevin O'Neil and the Eighth Ward picnic. She'd danced with him too often for no reason other than he was a good dancer and she was bored, and her father had sent Chris to cut in. That was the night Chris had told her to go to New York. Something about going to New York because if she stayed in Philadelphia it would break her heart. Well, she'd come to New York and her heart was broken anyway and here she was with Kevin O'Neil again. No, not Kevin O'Neil, but someone who reminded her of him. Whoever he was, she wished he'd go away.

"I asked Chris who you were, and he told me to stay away."

"My brother generally gives good advice."

"Are you always so nasty, or is it just me?"

"Nothing to do with you," she said, and swallowed the last of her drink.

"If I bring you another of those, will you be nice? Or at least civil?"

She handed him the glass. "Civil. We'll settle for civil."

He returned in a moment with a full bottle. Whoever he was, he obviously had more foresight than she did. He sat next to her on the low wall and filled both their glasses. He said his name was Ross and she told him hers was Amanda. She didn't know why she told him that, but it gave her a curious sense of satisfaction. He watched her take a long swallow of the drink he'd just poured.

"You're hitting that stuff pretty hard," he said.

"Celebrating."

"What are you celebrating, Amanda?"

Kate thought for a minute. "My freedom. Celebrating my freedom."

"I'll drink to that," Ross said, and downed his own drink. "Everyone ought to be free."

He asked her about herself, and she said she wrote poetry and had a volume coming out next month. For some reason the fabrication pleased her as much as telling him her name was Amanda. She was one of those girls Chris talked about who lived for her art and her pleasure and had never thought of love or marriage. Or Tyson Enfield.

"Don't you think you've had enough?" One Chris, two Chrises, one Chris were standing over her.

"Not nearly enough," Kate said, and took another swallow.

"Don't be such a wet blanket, Owen," Ross said.

"That's right, Chris. No wet blankets tonight."

Chris looked at her carefully. He hadn't disagreed when Kate had said she was going to get drunk tonight. It was exactly what he would have done in her place. But he hadn't counted on Ross Thermon.

"Come on, Katie. It's time to go home."

"Name's Amanda. And you go home if you want. I'm having a good time."

"I can see that," Chris said. "Come on."

"Why don't you go take care of Daphne? You remember Daphne, don't you? Why don't you go take care of Daphne and leave me alone?"

There was no point in arguing with her, he decided. He'd keep an eye on her, and in an hour or so, at the rate she was going, she'd be beyond protest.

Ross Thermon did not wait that long. He poured the last of the bottle into Kate's glass. "Empty," he pronounced.

"Have to get a new one."

"I've got a better idea. There's a speak around the corner. Quiet little place and a lot more comfortable than this wall."

Kate hadn't realized she was uncomfortable, but now that he'd called her attention to it, she decided she'd like something to lean against.

"What do you say, Amanda? Just a quiet drink?"

"I say fine," Kate answered.

She stumbled once going up the stairs from the garden to the dining room, but Ross caught her before she fell. He kept an arm around her waist to steady her and was careful to steer her around the far end of the room so Chris did not even notice they'd left.

Kate was awakened by something rough against her shoulder, rough like a man's beard. She had been dreaming of Ty and turned to the roughness. Then she realized it was only a dream, she hadn't seen Ty in months, and opened her eyes. The broad face looked smug and not especially attractive in sleep. Kate turned away from it quickly. She hadn't. She couldn't have. Slowly, painstakingly, she tried to piece together last night, but it was a confused kaleidoscope of strange people and unfamiliar places and her head was throbbing. She turned and looked at the man again. For a minute she thought she was going to be sick, sick from the whiskey, sick from the knowledge of what she'd done.

She started to move away from him and became aware of her body. She was wearing nothing. She was sure she'd be sick. Not now, she prayed. Not here. She had to get out before he awakened. That was all that mattered now. She'd have plenty of time to be sick later.

She got out of bed carefully, keeping her eyes on him. The pale eyelashes fluttered and he moaned, but that was all. Her clothes formed a trail from the bed to a chair in the corner. Her dress was folded on the chair. Had he tried to be neat at first? Had she? Oh, God, what did it matter? She gathered them up quickly, went into the other room, and was into them in a moment. She closed the door behind her quietly.

In the small vestibule of the building there was a row of mailboxes. Kate let herself out without looking at them. She did not remember his name and did not want to.

"Where the hell have you been?" Chris was still in his clothes. She guessed he'd fallen asleep on the sofa waiting for her.

"Where do you think?" she said dully.

"That damn Thermon's?"

"Is that his name?"

"I went there, but no one was home."

"We went to some speakeasies first. At least I think we did. Do you have any aspirin? I'll listen to whatever you're going to say, but I've got to have some aspirin first. And some water."

Chris went into the kitchen and came back with a glass of water and a small bottle. "I never should have taken you to that party."

"It's not your fault, Chris. I'm a grown woman. A mess of one, though, that's for sure."

"Not such a mess," he said.

"What do you call last night?"

"Logical. You behaved the way any man would in your position."

"You mean now I'm one of the boys?"

"No, Katie. And I wouldn't want to see you make a habit of it, but don't punish yourself too much. It was a reaction to Ty and that damn announcement. Now you'd better forget it and him and start getting on with things. Why don't you move to New York? I told you that years ago, if you remember."

"No, thanks. I'm not letting Tyson Enfield drive me out of Philadelphia. I've got a job I like, and I plan to stay. At least for a while."

Chris had told her to forget that awful night; and the pain of losing Ty, losing him for good, made forgetting almost possible. Or at least it did for two weeks. At first she told herself it was impossible. It was the sort of thing that happened to other people, not to her. But in three weeks she knew that it was the sort of thing that happened to her, and in six the doctor confirmed the knowledge. It wasn't Amanda, it wasn't the poetess who would publish her first collection next month who was pregnant. It was Kate. Perhaps it was that other girl or those other girls who'd got drunk and gone to bed with a strange man, but it was Kate who ended up pregnant. And it was Kate who would have to find a way out.

Roger Atherton provided it. Roger had waited several weeks after the announcement of Ty's engagement to call. He did on the day after Kathryn had seen the doctor.

"Congratulations, Mrs. Taylor," the doctor had said. "From what you've told me, I'd say June, mid-June."

"I'd love to have dinner, Roger," Kate said.

He'd grown a mustache and looked very dapper. Helen said half his patients were in love with him. Looking at him, all sleek and sure of himself in his custom-tailored suit and silk shirt, Kathryn could understand their sentiments, understand but not share them.

They went to the Barclay for dinner. The restaurant, like Roger's clothes and the shiny new roadster, was intended to show Kate that he was no longer a poor boy with a brilliant future. The future had become the present, and he was Tyson Enfield's equal, not that Roger had ever considered himself Ty's inferior.

When he took her hand walking up the path to the house, Kate pulled it away instinctively. Then she remembered the small thing growing inside her and said yes, she'd like to go to the orchestra Friday night.

Kathryn saw Roger Atherton three times the following week. It wasn't exactly difficult being with him. Roger had always been quite a talker and he'd managed to acquire a certain surface charm in the last few years. His bedside manner, Kate told herself, taunted herself, knowing that sooner or later—and it had better be sooner—she would have to go to bed with him. She didn't see how. She couldn't bear to have him touch her. The slender well-manicured hand in hers or his arm around her waist made her skin crawl, and when he kissed her that night after the symphony it took every ounce of willpower to keep from pushing him away.

"No wool-gathering on magazine time," Addison Wales said. Kate had been sitting at her desk, staring off into space, and hadn't even realized Addison was there.

"I'm sorry, I didn't hear you," she said.

"You don't a good deal of the time lately, Katie. Do you want to talk about it?"

She smiled brightly. "Nothing to talk about."

"You look a little tired. If you want to take a few days off, you can. You're welcome to my house at the beach again. The season's over and it will be quiet on the island."

Addison's house at the beach. The happiest time she'd had with Ty, the last happy time she'd had with Ty. And now Ty was married to Amanda, and she was walking around with some stranger's baby inside her. And there'd be no running away to the beach because she had to concentrate on Roger Atherton.

"Thanks, Addison, but I don't think the beach will help."

"Can I?"

That all depends, she wanted to say. Would you like to marry me and give a name to my illegitimate child? Or perhaps you know a doctor somewhere who will take care of it for me. According to Ty, that's exactly the sort of thing you would know. No, no doctor.

"No, thanks, Addison. Everything's fine." Or almost so, Kate thought. Roger had already begun to talk casually about the future, as if it had always been understood that they had a future. It was clear that he assumed they would marry in time. The only problem was that Kate didn't have time. She had to let Roger—no, not let him, convince him to—make love to her now, immediately, before it was too late. Then he'd believe it was his baby and be willing to marry quickly without the fanfare.

It was a simple solution, a logical solution, but every time Kate made up her mind that it was the only solution, she came up against the same wall. How could she seduce Roger Atherton when she couldn't stand to have him touch her? Ah, the fastidious Miss Owen, she chided herself. How did the fastidious Miss Owen manage to get pregnant in the first place? She'd have to get drunk. If she could sleep with a stranger drunk, she could sleep with Roger Atherton drunk. She was sure she could.

"Mother liked you," Roger said as they left the old Atherton house that had, thanks to Roger's practice, been rid of all boarders. "She was prepared not to because of your family," he added as he opened the car door for her, "but she couldn't help herself."

"What do you mean because of my family?"

"There's no point in pretending, Katie. The Owens aren't exactly old Philadelphia."

Kathryn wanted to reach out and slap that smooth, smug face. She wanted to get out of the car and start running and not stop until she was far away from Roger Atherton, but she thought of the baby and merely adjusted the lap robe he'd put over her.

"What if I didn't like her?" Kate fired her only shot, but Roger had started the car, and the sound of the engine drowned her words.

"Would you like a nightcap?" he asked. "It's still early. We could go to that little place near the mews."

Kate held her breath. She had to do it. She couldn't waste another night. "Do you have anything to drink in your apartment?"

He looked at her carefully, as if testing her words. "I think so."

Roger had a floor in one of the old town houses that had recently been broken up for apartments. It was furnished sparsely but well with a few good Atherton heirlooms.

"I was thinking of June," Roger said after he'd fixed a drink for each of them. "Mother says if we plan on a June wedding it will give people plenty of time to entertain for us."

No romantic protestations of love for old Roger. Mother had approved, and they were as good as engaged. Well, who was she, Kate thought, to demand romance.

"And there will be people who want to entertain for us, Katie. There wouldn't have been at one time, but in the last few years it seems everyone has remembered I'm an Atherton."

I'm afraid June is no good, Roger. You see, in June I'll be in the hospital delivering a baby. "But I'm still an Owen," she said, and took a long swallow of the drink.

"That won't matter. I'll see to that."

"June seems an awfully long way off." She took another sip of the drink. She'd been a fool to think it would work this quickly.

"You're quite a girl, Katie. For years you won't give me the time of day. Then all of a sudden you can't wait to get married." Suddenly his face assumed a closed, wary look. "This wouldn't have anything to do with the fact that Ty Enfield just got married, would it?"

No, not Ty. Just the baby. You understand about that, don't you, Roger? You understand all about babies. According to Helen, you deliver all the very best babies in Philadelphia. "It has nothing to do with Ty Enfield, Roger. It's just that once I make up my mind, I don't see any point in dawdling."

He was sitting beside her on the sofa, and now he reached an arm around her shoulders. "You made up your mind a long time ago, Katie, only you never knew it."

At another time she might have laughed in the face of his absurd egotism, but she felt his arm around her and saw his face coming close to hers and there was nothing to laugh about. Think of the baby, she told herself. Think of the baby, but his mouth on hers, the mustache bristly against her face, his tongue trying to force her lips apart, obliterated every other thought. It's for you, she screamed to the small thing inside of her. It's to keep you alive and give you a name and a father, but he was unbuttoning her dress, and the feel of his hands on her skin and then his mouth sent a shock of revulsion through her. She pulled away abruptly and began to button her dress.

"I can't, Roger." She stood and walked to the other side of the room. "I just can't."

"I don't understand." His voice was icy but controlled. "You're the one who suggested coming here. I naturally assumed . . ."

"You assumed correctly, or at least partly correctly. But I can't."

"Then we'll wait until we're married."

"You don't understand, Roger. I can't marry you."

"Of course you can marry me. A minute ago you couldn't wait to marry me."

She was tired, tired of Roger, tired of the argument she knew was coming. "I couldn't wait to marry you because I'm pregnant. That's the reason I was going to marry you. The only reason."

"I don't believe you."

"It doesn't make any difference whether you believe me or not." She walked to the closet where he'd hung her coat. "It's true."

"You were going to marry me because you were pregnant? Pregnant by someone else?"

"I couldn't very well be pregnant by you, could I?"

"You bitch! You whore!"

"You're right, Roger." She started for the door, but his hand on her shoulder pulled her back roughly.

"You thought you could use me that way!"

"It was a bad idea. I'm sorry."

The hand crashed against her face, and she felt the pain echo through her head. His face was white with rage and his body hovered over her menacingly. It flashed through her mind that he was going to strike her again, keep striking her until she lost the baby. She saw him raise his hand again and prayed silently for the beating that would end it, the beating that would take away the baby and punish her at the same time, but he dropped his hand and turned away.

"Get out of here. Get out of here and take your goddamn bastard back to Enfield."

The next morning Kate asked Addison if his offer of a few days off still held.

"You know it does, Katie. Best thing in the world for you." She listened to Addison telling her she needed a vacation, offering the beach house again, suggesting other places, and tried to fight back the nausea. It had begun four days ago, as the doctor had told her it might, but it had never struck this late in the morning. For the last four mornings she'd awakened feeling sick, but it always passed by the time she got to the office. It had passed this morning too, but now it had returned. She mumbled something unintelligible to Addison and ran down the hall to the ladies' room. There she coughed and gagged on the remains of Sara Atherton's dinner. Afterward she rinsed out her mouth, washed her face, combed her hair, and returned to Addison's office.

"I'm sorry, Addison. For a moment there I didn't feel very well."

He looked at her closely. "You're not exactly the picture of health now."

"I'm fine. Really I am."

"Sit down for a minute, Katie."

"I really ought to finish that Westlake piece. I can't go away until that's ready for the printer."

"It will wait." He put his hand on her shoulder and pushed her gently into the chair next to his desk. "I won't ask you what's wrong, Katie, because I have a fairly good idea what's wrong."

She looked at him in surprise. He couldn't possibly have guessed. It was too soon for anything to show. In fact, she'd lost three pounds. And this was the first time she'd been sick in the office.

"It's that Enfield character. First running off to Europe, then marrying the Wycombe girl. If it makes you feel any better, Katie, gossip has it that he was so stinking drunk at the wedding he could barely get back up the aisle. Well, he's a fool, but now you've got to stop being one. You've got to forget him. For God's sake, he wasn't half good enough for you in the first place."

"That's nice of you to say, Addison . . ."

"Dammit, Katie, I'm not being nice. In case you haven't noticed, I'm not a *nice* person. I'm simply telling you the truth. He's a weakling without an idea in his head. Just another handsome face and pretty set of manners masking a Main Line mind, which is to say no mind at all."

"That's not fair, Addison. You don't know him."

"I know him. Him and a dozen like him. Gutless little boys. Gutless little boys who want an omelet but are afraid to break a single egg. Dammit, Katie, for two years it made me sick to see you throwing yourself away on him, and now it turns my stomach to see you going to pieces because you lost him."

"I'm not going to pieces because I lost Ty." Her voice was as angry as his had become. "I'm going to pieces because I'm pregnant!" The words were out before she realized she'd said them, and now they hung between them like some terrible image from which they both wanted to avert their eyes.

"I've got to hand it to Enfield," Addison said finally. "He's a bigger bastard than I thought."

"It's not his fault."

"The hell it's not."

Kate knew Addison had misunderstood her defense of Ty, but there was no point in going into the details, the sordid details, as they said in the pulp fiction.

"Well, that's beside the point," Addison went on. "At least it is now that he's married. Anyway, I don't care about Enfield, Katie, I care about you. What are you going to do?"

"I don't know. I was going to marry Roger Atherton . . ."

Addison groaned. "Talk about out of the frying pan."

"It seemed the only way out, but I couldn't go through with it."

Addison rotated the swivel chair until his back was to Kate, and sat staring out the window at Independence Hall. The rain had turned the faded old brick a deeper red. "How would you feel about marrying me, Katie?" He turned the chair until he was facing her again. "It wouldn't exactly be a grand passion. I'm well aware of the fact you don't love me, and to be perfectly truthful, I'm a little beyond those all-consuming emotions myself. According to my first wife, I was always immune to them. Too cynical, she said. But you know all that, Katie. That's the point. We're used to each other. I know how stubborn you can be when you get one of those *idées fixes* in your head. You know exactly how much I drink—and don't seem to mind. I'm fifteen years older than you, but I'm not exactly over the hill. I'd be a reasonably good provider, even with two alimony checks going out every month. And I'm generally faithful. My former secretary who was also my second wife was an exception to that last rule. A case of familiarity breeding more familiarity. But you wouldn't have to worry about that. I'd want you to go on working here. I know most men wouldn't. I know Enfield didn't want you to, but I would. You're good at what you do, and I can't see your not doing it just because you marry. So there you are, Katie. Not exactly a romantic proposal, but a perfectly straightforward one."

Her eyes, not wanting to meet his, slid past to the view he'd been looking at a moment before. She adored Addison, but not that way, not in the way that would allow her to marry him. And if she tried to pretend she did, if she tried to be a wife to Addison, she knew the affection would turn to resentment and finally to hatred.

"That's kind of you, Addison, and I'm grateful . . ."

"But gratitude isn't enough. Is that it, Katie? At your age you want more than gratitude. I'm beyond the grand passion, but you're not. Well, I'm glad. Not that you won't marry me. I was beginning to like the idea. But that you still think there's something better in life. I just hope to God you don't still think it's Tyson Enfield."

That evening Kate caught the six-o'clock up to New York and went straight to Chris's apartment.

"Christ!" he said when she told him why she was there.

"No editorial comments. Can you help me or can't you?"

"Are you sure you want to go through with this?"

"I don't have much choice." She told him about Roger and about Addison. She was afraid he wouldn't understand about Addison, but he did. "And I can't see having the baby and turning it over to an orphanage. The awful thing is, I don't even want to have it. I tried to pretend I did, but I don't. I hate myself for feeling that way, but I do feel that way. Maybe if it were Ty's, but it isn't."

"I don't suppose you'd want to marry Thermon."

"I never know his name until you mention it."

"All right, it was a stupid idea."

"I've been over it again and again, Chris. An abortion is the only way out."

"It's too dangerous."

"Not if you find me someone good. I'm sure that shouldn't be a difficult task in your circles."

"I wish you wouldn't sound so casual about the whole business."

She looked up at him, and the blue eyes turned inky. "Please, Chris, please don't make things worse . . ."

"I'm sorry, Katie. I'll find you someone. Don't worry. I'll take care of everything. I've only got about thirty dollars in the bank, but I'll get my hands on some more. Thermon ought to be good for some."

"He's got nothing to do with this. I don't want his money, and I especially don't want him to know. I've got more than a hundred with me. That should be enough."

He agreed it should, and told her he was going to a neighborhood speakeasy to find a friend who would know the name of a doctor. It was true, but only part of the story.

He found the friend and got the name of an elderly country doctor near New Hope, Pennsylvania. He wasn't the closest, but he was the best. Chris wrote the doctor's name and telephone number in the little book he used for notes when he was working and left the speakeasy. It took him less than five minutes to walk to Ross Thermon's apartment.

"I'm going to beat the shit out of you," he said when Thermon opened the door.

"What are you talking about?"

"It doesn't matter what it's about. I'm just going to do it." And though Thermon outweighed him by at least thirty pounds and had boxed for a year at a small college in the Midwest, Chris did exactly that. And all the time he was hitting Thermon he kept pretending it was Tyson Enfield.

Two days later they drove to Pennsylvania in a car Chris had borrowed from a friend. The white clapboard house looked like dozens of others they'd passed on the road down. The man looked like the sort of kindly country doctor who appeared regularly on the illustrated cover of Kate's magazine. His manner was brisk but not unsympathetic. Chris's friend had assured him the doctor was in the business for his convictions as well as the money. "Lucky fellow," the friend had said. "The two rarely go hand in hand."

A woman dressed as a nurse told Chris he could wait in the living room and took Katie upstairs. He paced the living room for a while, then the porch, then the living room again. When he looked at his watch, he was amazed to see only fifteen minutes had passed. Somewhere in the back of his mind was the knowledge that he was the perfect caricature of an expectant father, but for once the irony of a situation did not amuse him.

He heard a cry from upstairs, then another, and controlled the instinct to run from the house to the yard, where Katie's screams could not be heard, but then the cries stopped and the silence was worse. She was dead. Chris was sure of it. He started up the stairs, but the woman in white was coming down.

"She's fine," the woman said, but from somewhere above, Chris could hear the sound of Katie crying. "Don't mind that," she said. "They always cry when it's over."

"Are you sure she's all right?"

The woman looked at him, and her eyes were hard. "If you're so darn concerned about her, why didn't you marry her? Or are you married already? Well, it's none of my business," she added. "They come and they go, and I don't want to know the stories. They're all the same anyway.

"Let her rest for a while. Then you can take her home."

Kate was pale when the nurse helped her into the room. "It's over," she said quietly.

Chris took her arm from the nurse and felt her weight against him. "It's over," she repeated, "and I'm still alive." She was crying silently, but he could feel the sobs racking her body as he helped her to the car.

She stopped crying after about ten miles. "That was an awful thing to say. I'm alive, but it isn't."

"There wasn't any it, Katie. There was nothing yet."

"I'm not sure you're right, but I was so scared for a while that all I could think about was me. I was sure I was going to die."

He didn't want to remind her that it had been a possibility. "I don't suppose it's much fun being a woman," Chris said finally.

"It has its drawbacks. The funny thing," she said—she was staring out the window, and he couldn't see her face—"if this had happened a year or two ago, if we hadn't been so careful, I'd have the baby now, and Ty. But we were careful, and now I have nothing."

"You've got your whole damn life ahead of you, Katie."

She turned and smiled at him, but it was not much of a smile. "Sure I do, Chris. And thank you. For everything."

"Do you want to come back to New York with me?"

"No, I'd rather go home. It may seem strange to you, but I want to go home now. We'll say you drove me down from New York."

Margaret said Katie looked pale and tired and must be coming down with something. "Either that," Margaret added bitterly, "or you're having second thoughts about breaking off with Roger Atherton." First Tyson Enfield, and now Roger. It was worse than unfair. It was unforgivable.

Kathryn said no, it wasn't Roger Atherton, probably only a cold, and went to bed right after dinner. She fell asleep almost immediately, but was awakened by pains clawing at her stomach like a great ugly beast. She turned on her side and felt the rush of blood. It was as if her insides were running out of her. Her life was slipping out of her just as the baby had that morning. She sat up carefully. If only she could get to the bathroom. She'd get to the bathroom, then come back and change the sheets. She couldn't let her mother see the sheets. But the door opened quietly, as if not to wake her, and Margaret was staring at the crimson stain on the bed and the blood that covered the entire front of Kate's nightdress, and she began to scream.

"It's nothing, Mother. Really, it's nothing. I'm all right," but she didn't have the strength to stand, and sank back on the bed, mumbling the meaningless words of reassurance. She could hear the sound of footsteps on the stairs, her father's voice, and Chris's, her mother's terrified cries, but it all came to her distantly as if they were arguing and shouting and crying in another room. Then their words came closer, then farther away again, and her mind was wandering in and out of consciousness, wobbling back and forth between the pain and confusion and nothingness.

Will went to the hospital early the next morning. He had forbidden Margaret to accompany him, though he could not stop Chris from going with him.

"Who was it?" he demanded as he entered the room.

"Can't you leave her alone?" Chris said.

"I want to know who it was."

"Does it matter?" Kate's voice was thin with exhaustion.

"It damn well does matter," Will shouted. "Was it Enfield?"

"It wasn't Ty."

"Then Roger Atherton."

Kate turned away from her father and stared up at the ceiling. "I don't know who it was."

"You're lying to me."

"No, I'm not." Without her meaning it to, her hand moved to her stomach. "I didn't even know him." Out of the corner of her eye she saw her father turn and felt his hand against her cheek. It was a lighter slap than Roger's, but far more painful.

Chris rushed to the bed and pulled him away. "Goddammit, not now. She's sick. Can't you understand that?"

"All I can understand is that she's a tramp."

"She's your daughter."

"Not anymore."

Margaret had packed Kathryn's things as Will had told her to. A trunk and several suitcases stood waiting for Chris by the front door. Margaret had cried while she packed them, but she'd stopped crying now. There was no point to tears. Will had made up his mind. And Katie had made her own bed, as the saying went. It seemed to Margaret, sitting now in the deserted living room, staring out the front window and trying not to stare at the baggage that stood like a barricade before the front door, that she had always known Katie would. She remembered a night several years ago. It was just after the war, and Katie had called from St. Anthony's to say that she was at a party and would be home later than expected. Margaret remembered standing at the window and watching the red Marmon pull up in front of the house. She had stood at the window and watched and disapproved, and later she had spoken to Kathryn, but Kathryn had not listened. Margaret had always known she would not listen. She felt a sudden surge of hatred for this willful girl who looked so much like her but was nothing like her. They had given her everything, and she had thrown it all away. They had given her the opportunities Margaret had always wanted, and she'd thrown them back in their faces. Margaret looked at the luggage piled by the door, the luggage she'd bought for Kathryn's trousseau, and felt the cruelty of it and the injustice and the heartbreak.

Prologue to Book Two

Washington, 1937

She'd forgot how handsome he was. There were pictures, and people said pictures didn't lie, but they did about Ty. Pictures didn't capture that softness in his eyes when he smiled, or the way he moved, or the sound of his voice. She'd looked at the pictures again and again in the past two years, but the pictures had missed all that, and now she was aware of the eyes and the body and the voice as he stood there only inches from her, and she felt the familiar current of desire.

A little awkward, a little at a loss for words and actions, Kate held out her hand, but Ty took it and drew her to him and kissed her, and for the moment at least there was no awkwardness to his return.

"Your hair is different," he said when he let her go. She'd let it grow in the last year and he'd never seen it up. "Very chic," he said.

"Does that mean you don't approve?" The old joke was familiar between them. In New York, Emily had pronounced more than once, people tried to be chic. In Philadelphia being chic was merely vulgar. She wondered if he found the white dress with the halter neckline too chic. She'd worn it because she thought it flattering, but now she remembered that Peter Lynnquist called it her *Vanity Fair* fashion-plate look. Peter always said he liked that look, but Peter had not grown up in Philadelphia.

"I approve wholeheartedly. You look wonderful."

"So do you." He was deeply tanned and she wondered if he'd gone someplace for the divorce or merely returned to Highfield and ridden and sailed and played a good deal of lawn tennis all summer. She wondered, but she didn't ask. She wasn't going to ask about the divorce.

"Do you want a drink?" she said. "The gin and vermouth have been in the icebox since this morning."

"That's my Kat. Once you learn something, you don't forget it."

Kat. Nobody had called her that for two years, unless you counted that time at Virginia Beach Peter had called her Kat, and she'd asked him please not to ever again.

Ty made the drinks in the small kitchen because he said he still remembered where everything was, though in fact she'd changed a good deal about the apartment in the past two years, and they settled in the living room that was not cool, but cooler because she'd kept the venetian blinds closed all day.

"I thought we'd dine on the Shoreham Terrace. It should be bearable after dark. Is that all right?"

"It's fine," she said, turning the glass in her hands. It was absurd to feel awkward. After all, this was Ty, Ty she'd known and loved for twenty years. What was a two-year absence after twenty years? But still there was the strain. It hadn't been there when he'd come back last time, and he'd been away for longer then, but it was here now.

He asked about her work, probably because he didn't know or was afraid to ask about any other part of her life.

"The first guide came out last spring," she said. "All the Eastern offices were furious. Imagine being upstaged by Idaho. It's a first-rate job, too. That's because of Vardis Fisher. You can see his mark on every page."

Ty tried to look interested, but Kate doubted he knew who Vardis Fisher was or cared about the job he'd done on the Idaho guide. Of course she was in the same position. She didn't want to ask about the divorce or Amanda or the boys, so she asked about his work.

"I'm still there," he said. "And still talking about getting out, but I guess that's all I do. Talk about it."

She remembered something Peter had said to her, said to her again and again actually. It was something the President used to say during those first confused days of the new administration. "Take a method and try it. If it fails, try another. But above all, try something." The sentiment was typical of Peter. He'd never spend twenty years talking about something. He'd simply do it. But then Peter wasn't Ty. Ty reminded her of a Greek statue, not so much the way he looked, but the impression he gave. Ty was proportion and balance and eternal grace. Peter was like one of those Diego Rivera murals that had so influenced all the WPA paintings. Not that Peter looked anything like those Mexican peasants, but he had the same directness and strength and simple vitality. He had all that, but he didn't have Ty's elegance or ease, Kate thought as she watched Ty at the sideboard refilling their glasses.

He handed her one, then began to wander around the room. The tables were covered with pictures. A few were of good friends, but most were of people she no longer saw but with whom she still exchanged Christmas cards—the author she'd convinced Addison to publish who'd now become quite famous, a girl she'd vacationed with in Havana one winter, a publisher and his wife she'd known in New York. Chris had told her once that she lived with so many pictures because she didn't have a family. Except for him, that is. He wasn't trying to be cruel, only to convince her she ought to have one.

Ty stopped before a photograph of Chris that had been taken on the *Normandie* when he'd sailed for Europe. "I read about the Pulitzer. The Philadelphia papers made quite a fuss. Hometown boy makes good. He must have been proud."

"You know Chris. He was convinced he didn't deserve it. Thought it should have gone to at least half a dozen friends."

"I read about the other, too. I'm sorry, Kat."

She said nothing, and he continued his tour of the photographs. On an end table there was a picture of Kate and Addison Wales that had been taken at a magazine Christmas party. Ty picked up the photograph and looked at it closely. "Poor old Wales. I run into him now and then at the Philadelphia Club. He's worse than ever. A real old rummy."

"Addison's all right," Kate said quickly.

"Sure he's all right—if you don't mind old rummies."

"He's a good friend."

Ty looked as if he were about to say something, then merely smiled and turned to the long library table behind the sofa that held a dozen other photographs. With the exception of Chris and a small boy he remembered as her brother Bill's child, Ty recognized none of the subjects. "All these people, Kat, all these people in your life, and I don't know any of them."

"They're just friends, and not very close ones at that, I suppose."

"Is there a close one, Kat? Is there someone else?"

She looked up at him and smiled. "No one else."

"Then that means you'll marry me?"

She wondered if he'd really doubted it or was merely trying to save the pride he'd broken so many times. "What about the baby?" she asked.

"I suppose you think I'm a heel. My leaving you then, my leaving the baby now."

She looked up at him again and wondered what she really believed. Did she think he was, as he said, a heel? Chris had said he was, never stopped saying he was, but she didn't think so. If she did, she couldn't go on loving him. Some women could, she knew, but she couldn't.

"I don't think you're a heel, Ty, but I think you do more damage than you mean to. I think you do more damage trying not to hurt people. Your mother, Amanda, the baby, even me. You wouldn't marry me until you'd finished law school and had enough money to support me the way you thought I should be supported, but it would have been better if you hadn't worried about that, if you'd . . ." She stopped abruptly. "There isn't any point in going over all that now. You did what you thought you had to—we both did—and I don't think you're a heel for that."

"Then it isn't too late?"

"It's late, Ty, but I don't suppose it's too late."

"It will be different this time. I promise. Anything you say, Kat, anything you want. I've changed. I swear I have."

She supposed they both had. She looked across the room to where he was sitting. She'd been struck by how handsome he was when she'd first seen him, but he was no longer a boy. He was a grown man with a former wife and three children. And what about her? She was a thirty-seven-year-old woman with a good job, the latest in a long line of good jobs, a room full of photographs, and entirely too many memories of Tyson Enfield. But the memories would begin to fade now, the bad ones as well as the good, because Ty was back and he still loved her and he still wanted to marry her and she was a fool to worry about the fact that things weren't as perfect as she'd expected them to be when she was eighteen. She was a fool to dwell on the slights and the disappointments and the pain, and a fool to worry that she didn't love him or trust him the way she had when she was eighteen.

All the way to the Shoreham he talked of the future. He'd seen a nice house near Ardmore, but of course if she didn't like it, they wouldn't live there. How did she feel about France for a wedding trip? There was talk of a war in Europe, but he was sure that was some time off, and he wanted to be married as soon as possible. He couldn't wait until she met the boys. Ty Junior was twelve and at St. Paul's. Little Sam was only nine and still at Episcopal Academy, but he'd be going away soon too. Of course, Amanda had got custody, but they'd have the boys for holidays and summers, and when the baby was old enough, she'd come too.

How's that for a family, Chris? Kate thought. Instant motherhood. Before, there were none, and now there are three.

"And Nicholas sends his love. He can't wait to see you."

"I saw him about a year ago. He called when he was in town, and we dined."

"That makes twice now. First in New York, then here, and he didn't mention it to me either time."

"He wouldn't."

Samuel had been dead for several years, even before *last time,* and there was no mention of Emily. She would be staunchly in the corner of the wronged wife. Kathryn wondered idly about Hilary. Where would Hilary come down in the case of the second Mrs. Tyson Enfield versus the first Mrs. Tyson Enfield? Dormitory plots to wrest Ty from Amanda's clutches were far in the past.

And what of her own parents? Peter had tried to help her patch things up, but the rents in the family fabric still showed. Would marriage to Ty take care of that? She doubted it. To Will and Margaret she'd always be a fallen woman, and the scandal surrounding Ty's divorce would only make things worse. For her parents, Kate knew, divorce was only a little less terrible than adultery and fornication.

None of it mattered. Not Emily, not Hilary, not even her parents. She'd have Ty, and that would be enough.

On the Shoreham Terrace Japanese lanterns glittered in the Indian-summer darkness, and there was the faintest whisper of a breeze.

"It hasn't changed," Ty said when they were seated at a small table at the edge of the terrace.

"What hasn't changed?" She thought he was talking about the Shoreham, but as far as she could remember, he hadn't taken her here that summer two years ago. She'd been here with Peter and Chris before Chris sailed for Europe, but never with Ty.

"What happens when you walk into a room. Every man in the place stares."

"Certainly. I'm surprised there was no riot."

"They do. I used to love it, but I used to hate it too."

"And now?"

"The same. It's all the same, Kat." He reached across the table and took her hand. "You still wear it." She'd told herself again and again that she ought to stop wearing the small gold baby's ring, but she'd never got around to taking it off.

He took a small black velvet box from his pocket and opened it. Kate recognized the diamond she'd worn so many years ago. "I still have it, Kat, but if you want another, I'll get another."

She didn't know why the ring surprised her so. What had she expected? That he'd given it to Amanda? That he'd exchanged it for another?

"I don't care about the ring, Ty. I always told you that."

He took the statement as an acceptance and reached over to place it on her left hand. It felt peculiar on her third finger, not too large or small, only peculiar. But then the orchestra returned and Kate recognized a song from a movie Peter had taken her to a few weeks ago—"Thanks for the Memories," it was called—and she felt Ty's arms around her. Unlike the ring, they felt familiar, just as his mouth on hers had when he'd first arrived. They didn't feel safe the way they had so many years ago, but they did feel familiar and warm and exciting, and she wondered how she had lived without his arms around her for this long.

Book Two

Washington, 1935 — 1937

1

Chris finally got his way. Kathryn moved to New York. Addison helped her to get a job with a literary agency, and Chris turned up an old girlfriend who had lost a roommate and was willing to share an apartment close enough to Gramercy Park to be fashionable but far enough from it to be affordable.

It wasn't a bad life. Kate met a lot of people. She went to a lot of parties. She was courted by several men. One of them who made three million on Wall Street in 1926 took her to dinner and the theater, treated her with what Kate found a somewhat tiresome respect, and proposed regularly. Another, a writer represented by the agency where she worked, cooked her exotic dinners in his apartment, forced her to read several books she didn't enjoy, and made frequent and unsuccessful attempts at seduction. The millionaire surprised her by turning up one day married to a chorus girl from the second line of *Funny Face*. A year later he lost everything in the Crash, but Kate heard that the girl had stood by him, and she was glad. The writer had held on for a year after that, then surprised Kate even more and caused a mild scandal in the literary world by setting up housekeeping with an editor who'd just divorced his wife. After that there were a few years of quiet. She was getting older, and most men were either married or worried about the money and jobs they'd lost, or both.

That was when McSorley turned up and asked her to go to Washington with him. She was in her office with a strange birdlike woman who claimed she'd had a child by Max Schmelling and wanted to write a book about it. Kate was low woman in the agency and always got the cranks, especially the women cranks. She'd been musing idly that they could call the book *The Blue Max* and trying to ease the woman out of her office when McSorley turned up and shooed the woman away.

"Come to Washington, Katie, and help me work on the Writers' Project." His round face beneath the mane of white hair was flushed with excitement, and his chins jiggled as he spoke. "They're setting one up, you know. And you're perfect for the job. More perfect than I am, come to think of it. I know about books, but you know about books and the people who write them. When it comes to writers, Katie, you wear the proverbial kid gloves. And I ought to know."

McSorley was a Columbia University professor who'd written a thick novel that had been well received by the critics and almost entirely ignored by the book-buying public. Kate knew he was grateful for the little favors she'd done him when everyone at the agency and his publisher were too busy to bother with the dying novel. She knew he was grateful and she knew he liked her as a professor might one of his brighter students, but she had never expected him to offer her a job, especially one like this with the WPA.

"The pay won't be much, Katie. Probably less than you're getting here. But we'll find you a nice title. Better yet, we'll find you exciting work. There'll be plenty of that. By the time this thing gets under way, there are going to be several thousand writers—and the way things are going, would-be writers. They're going to need a lot of care and feeding, to say nothing of editing. How would you like to come to Washington and help me do both, Katie?"

Kate gave notice that afternoon. The fact that Chris was in Washington provided another incentive, though she would have accepted McSorley's offer even if Chris hadn't been there. He was, however, and he told Kate, when she telephoned to tell him about the new job, that it was the only place to be these days. At least it was the only place to be if you had to be in this country. Chris still hadn't got over not winning the assignment to cover that mess in Manchuria.

Bill was in Washington too, but that was another story. Senator William Owen and his wife, Helen, lived with Chip and their three children in a rambling old house in Kalorama Heights. Once when Katie and Chris had been drinking late into the night in one of those dreary little bars Chris seemed to love—"bars, not speakeasies," he had to keep reminding her, because prohibition had been repealed only a little more than a year ago—he suggested they pay a call on Bill.

"Come on, Katie, we'll have a reunion. We'll go on up to the Heights and let old Bill and old Helen show us how the rich live."

"We're having a reunion right now. The fallen branch of the Owen clan."

"Fallen but undaunted. Did I ever tell you what he said to me when I left Philadelphia that first time right after the war?"

She knew Chris meant Will, and she knew what Will had said, but she knew too that Chris liked to repeat it.

"He quoted old J. P. Morgan. As if Morgan were someone you're supposed to listen to. 'You know what J. P. Morgan says about journalists, Chris?' he said in that campaign-rally voice of his. 'Either they end up drunkards or they remain journalists, and I don't know which is worse.' Those were his parting words."

"They don't have to be parting words, Chris. You can go back anytime you want. You know they'd love to see you."

"Tough. I don't go home without you, Katie. You know that and so do they."

"Old Do-or-Die Owen. Still, you're being silly. They don't have anything against you."

He laughed.

"Or at least not as much."

"Listen, Katie, don't worry about it. You're actually doing me a favor. If I went home, I'd only fight with him. I'm better off staying away, and you give me an excuse to."

It was Chris who introduced her to Peter. By that time Chris knew a good many important people in Washington and was known by a good many others. It was a Sunday night and they'd spent most of the day moving Kate into her new apartment on Wisconsin Avenue.

"Home sweet home," Chris said, putting the last few books into place on the newly painted shelves. Kate was arranging the flowers Addison Wales had sent. She still didn't know how Addison had got her new address so quickly, but he had, and the flowers had arrived only a little after she had this morning.

"Now, go and shower," Chris said, "and put on something devastating but informal. Informal is the keynote. I'm taking you to your first scrambled-egg supper."

She groaned. "The last thing I feel like is a party. I'm exhausted. Besides, I had eggs for breakfast."

"That has nothing to do with it. You're in Washington now, and in Washington anyone who's anyone has scrambled-egg suppers on Sunday night. What's good enough for the President and Eleanor is *de rigueur* for the rest of us."

There was a mix of guests that Kate in the next months came to know as typical. Young by government standards, but not really young. Men who did things you could never really understand in agencies that were only just being formed, a few journalists, perhaps a freshman congressman, wives, women with their own mysterious government positions or newspaper connections, and always a pretty secretary or two.

She noticed Peter Lynnquist as soon as they arrived. For one thing, he was taller than anyone else in the room. For another, he was the center of a small group that was hanging on every word of some convoluted story he was telling. When he finished there was a great explosion of laughter, and Peter's sharp bark was louder than all of them. He was big and fair-haired and brash, and Kate took an immediate dislike to him. She asked Chris who he was.

"Came down with the administration. Taught at Harvard before that, but he's more troubleshooter than brain trust, if you can distinguish between the two. Do you want to meet him?"

"No, thank you," she said, but it was too late, because by then Peter had crossed the room to meet her.

"I was just telling Katie about you," Chris said.

"Nothing much to tell. Simple farmboy from Minnesota."

"What kind of a simple farmboy teaches at Harvard, Mr. Lynnquist?" Kate asked.

"A smart one." He smiled at her, and the smile was kinder than the bark of laughter she'd heard a moment ago, but it was canny too. "I saw your piece on Black Monday, Owen. Darn good. Left all the other papers behind. It's a shame those Supreme Court justices don't think the way you do. We'd still have an NRA."

"Anytime the President wants to appoint me to the bench, I'm ready," Chris answered. "I never went to law school, but then again, law school didn't seem to do Hughes and his boys much good."

Peter Lynnquist turned to Kate. "And what about you, Miss Owen? Can we appoint you to something?"

"I've been appointed. Or at least hired. Writers' Project."

"Well, you know what Hopkins says. 'They've got to eat just like other people.' "

Kate had heard the joke too many times to be amused. "Does that mean you don't approve, Mr. Lynnquist? It's all right to use federal funds to subsidize laborers but not artists?"

"You're on the wrong track there . . ." Chris began, but Lynnquist interrupted him.

"Perhaps you could convince me, Miss Owen. At dinner tomorrow night?"

Kate looked at the strong-boned face that would have been handsome if the expression on it weren't so self-confident. "I doubt I could convince you of anything, Mr. Lynnquist."

"You think I'm too opinionated?"

"As a matter of fact, I do."

"Do you always judge people so quickly, Miss Owen, because if you do, I feel sorry for all those poor writers. You'll be tearing their work to shreds and giving them the hatchet before they even have a chance. And I'd like them to have a chance. I'm strongly behind Federal One even if you think I'm too much of a philistine to be. I agree with Hopkins. Artists have to eat just like other people."

"I warned you, Katie," Chris said. "Lynnquist was one of the earliest supporters of the arts project."

"In fact," Peter continued, "I'm so interested in seeing that writers eat that I'm repeating my invitation. Dine with me tomorrow night."

"But I'm not a writer, Mr. Lynnquist."

"That's another aspect of the program I support. Why limit it only to published writers? What about would-be writers and copywriters and all the rest? You see, Miss Owen, I'm democratic. I want everyone to eat. Especially you. Is seven-thirty all right?"

"You might as well say yes, Katie. It's a well-known Washington fact," Chris said, "that Lynnquist always gets his way."

He did. Kate dined with him the following evening. As they sat and talked on the open terrace of an old country house that had been turned into a restaurant, she began to see behind the brashness. He was quick and bright and very sure of his ideas, but not of himself, though he pretended to be.

"What did a troubleshooter teach when a troubleshooter taught at Harvard?" she asked.

"Economics."

"I never would have guessed."

"Why not?"

"You don't seem to care about money."

"How can you tell?"

"For one thing, you never mention it. And it isn't that kind of well-bred reticence where you're thinking about money all the time, but are too polite to talk about it."

He laughed. "Are you suggesting I'm ill-bred?"

"I'm suggesting you don't care about money at all. You proved it just now when the waiter brought the check."

"Because I ordered another bottle of wine after I'd paid it?"

"Because you paid it without looking at it. Most people don't. Most people look at what's on it and check the addition. That sort of thing."

"I don't think I approve of the men who take you to dinner. Either they're too poor to take care of you properly or they care too much about money."

She didn't like the turn the conversation was taking. "That was my original point. You don't seem to care about it at all. I shouldn't think that would make you much of an economist."

"It makes me a very good economist. If I do say so myself. You see, I care more about people than about money, so instead of trying to tailor people to fit the economy, I try to tailor the economy to fit people."

After that evening Peter began calling regularly. Occasionally Kathryn told him she was busy, more often she did not. She discovered almost immediately that he knew everyone who mattered in Washington and didn't seem to care that he did. Often he'd give her a choice between some fashionable party filled with powerbrokers or dinner alone at one of those terrace restaurants overlooking a quiet garden, and always looked relieved when she chose the latter.

When the parties were more informal, Peter was not unwilling to attend. On a soft evening a few weeks after she'd met him he took her to one in the garden of an old house on Massachusetts Avenue. Although it was a warm night, the heat was not oppressive, at least not by Washington standards, and in the gathering darkness the city felt like the sleepy Southern town it had been until a few years ago. The air was heavy with the scent of magnolia and honeysuckle and women's perfume, and as the night wore on the party got a little noisier, but not much. A little after ten Harry Hopkins arrived.

"There's your boss," Peter said.

"Mine and several thousand other people's."

"All the same, you have to meet him." Peter led her across the garden to the crowd that had formed around Hopkins. The older man noticed Peter immediately and seemed pleased to see him.

"He certainly thinks highly of you," Kate said on the way home.

"A top man," Hopkins had said to Kate. "With two cardinal virtues. He understands that we've got to have an economy of abundance rather than one of scarcity. And"—Hopkins laughed—"he can pick winners. At least at the track. I'd rather go to the races with Lynnquist than half the men in Washington."

"Only because last time I went down to Laurel with him, he won a bundle," Peter said.

"He won a bundle and you won whatever it was you wanted from Mr. Hopkins."

"How did you know?"

"As far as I can see, it's the only reason you'd go to Laurel. I've never seen you gamble, and you don't have any apparent love for horses. But you seem to have kept both facts a secret from Mr. Hopkins."

"Harry's crazy about the horses."

"And you. I couldn't miss that."

"You weren't supposed to, Katie. That's why I took you over to meet him. I'm trying to impress you."

"It won't do any good," she blurted out. "What I mean is, I think well of you too, Peter, but as a friend."

"Well, I don't expect you to fall in love with an enemy, Katie."

"I'm not joking, Peter."

"Neither am I."

Kate was surprised when she got the letter, and more than a little flattered. Would she come back for reunion weekend, the class of '35 of Bryn Mawr College wanted to know, and tell them about what was going on in Washington these days and what the opportunities for women were. She'd written back saying she hadn't been there long enough to know, but if they still wanted her, she'd be happy to attend.

Kate remembered the women who'd come back and talked to groups of girls during her own undergraduate days and felt a surge of pride, but that was while she sat in her office and contemplated the event from a distance. Once on the train to Philadelphia, she was uneasy. It had been more than ten years since she'd left, and ten years was a long time, but perhaps in this case not long enough. The closer she got to the city, the stronger the memories grew, memories of Ty and her parents, memories of what she had been raised to be, and speculation on what she'd turned out to be. She was staring out the window trying to make sense of it, though she'd been sure she'd made sense of it years ago, when she noticed a billboard, obviously a leftover from the last administration. WASN'T THE DEPRESSION TERRIBLE? the billboard demanded. It had been put in in 1932, Kate knew, as the worst year of the Depression deepened. It made her think of the lies people told each other and themselves, and though it should have made her feel worse, it didn't.

The campus hadn't changed much, though she and the students had, and they made her feel old and far removed. The effect of the other alumnae was even worse. She wondered if she were as much a shock to her classmates as they were to her. "You haven't changed a bit," they repeated to each other, secretly horrified at the slender flapper turned overweight matron, the smooth-cheeked face slashed by deep lines around the eyes and mouth, and, in the case of Hilary, the class clown turned stodgy bore. Though in the case of Hilary, Kate was less than surprised. She'd seen enough of what Hilary was becoming, before she'd left Philadelphia, to accept the final product.

She and Hilary ran into each other at the outdoor reception that first afternoon. Hilary looked enormous in a flower print afternoon dress that was cut very badly for a woman of her size, but the young girl at her side was delicate and lovely in a way that Daphne might have been if Daphne had not been set on self-destruction.

"And this is my Camilla," Hilary said.

Kathryn saw the girl cringe at the possessiveness of the introduction.

"Miss Owen and I were in the same class," Hilary continued, as if to dismiss Kate as quickly as possible.

"I remember when you were born, Camilla," Kate said, "though I can't believe it was as long ago as it obviously was."

"I'm fourteen," Camilla said seriously.

"Fourteen next month," Hilary corrected.

"And what about the other children? There were three, or was it four?" Kate asked, racking her brain and the columns of the alumnae bulletin for names or sexes or any identifying characteristics.

"Three boys and another girl," Hilary began, then stopped abruptly. Kate followed her gaze across the green to where Amanda was standing. She was watching them openly, and there was no mistaking the look of disapproval on her face. Hilary excused herself quickly, and without giving Camilla a chance for the polite good-bye that had obviously been ingrained in her, started toward Amanda.

Amanda turned away, but Kate continued to watch her over the heads of two graduates who were eager for jobs in Washington. Amanda had aged well. Kate had been sure she wouldn't. Those blond, little-girl types often didn't, but Amanda had. Her hair, a little darker now but still pretty, was pulled back in a smooth chignon, and she wore a blue silk dress that was, Emily must have agreed, handsome without being too fashionable. Amanda had changed little, and in one way not at all. She still had that self-satisfied air that was almost palpable, and later in the afternoon when she heard someone cry "Amanda Wycombe!" the way people do at reunions and heard Amanda answer "Amanda Enfield," Kate felt the old envy with new force.

"You'd better hurry and dress," Amanda said as Ty entered the bedroom. "I asked you not to be late tonight, but you probably weren't listening."

"I didn't know we were going out."

"That's exactly what I mean. I told you this morning we were dining at the Pennells'."

"I thought we didn't see them anymore. After all, he did support 'that man Roosevelt.' And I hear he's going to accept a position in his cabinet."

"We still see them because of poor Lydia. It must be difficult enough being married to a man like that without having your friends cut you."

"Poor Lydia! If that novel Pennell wrote a few years ago is autobiographical, I'd say poor Charles. What an icicle."

"The wife in that book couldn't have been Lydia, Ty. Lydia never lived abroad and she doesn't have an uncle who bought a peerage."

"Literary license, Mandy. Surely they taught you about literary license at that fine school of yours. And speaking of that, how was the reunion? How is the class of '20 fifteen years after the fact?"

"Very well, thank you." She ticked off a list of husbands whose bloodlines might have read by the blue book out of Dun and Bradstreet.

"I'm sorry I couldn't provide you with more spectacular credentials," Ty said.

"Your credentials, as you call them, are just fine, Ty. I'm perfectly satisfied with the marriage I made."

"That's nice to know. If only you didn't sound quite so much like one of my colleagues talking about a successful contract when you said it."

"Did you see the boys before you came up?"

"They were more interested in the radio. I can't hold a candle to Jack Armstrong, the aaall Aaamerican boy."

"I wish you wouldn't let them listen to those dreadful programs," Amanda said.

"If you don't want them to listen, you tell them. But before you do, I wish you'd tell Harris to bring me a drink."

"You don't have time for one."

"I'll drink it while I dress," he said, and closed the door to the bath behind him before she could answer.

"Hilary brought Camilla to the reunion," Amanda said when he returned to the room. "That child gets lovelier every day."

Ty took the drink from the table. "She looks exactly like Daf."

"Thank heavens she isn't exactly like Daphne."

"Cruelty doesn't become you, Mandy."

"I'm not being cruel. I'm merely saying what everyone thinks, including Hilary and your mother. They look at Camilla and remember Daphne and pray she won't be like Daphne."

Amanda moved from the mirrored table where she'd been sitting, to the large walk-in closet she used as a dressing room. A few minutes later she emerged in a chiffon evening dress. She looked very pretty, but not very desirable, Ty thought. Perhaps it was the fact that she insisted on dressing in another room. Perhaps it was the set of her mouth, as if she'd just made up her mind about something.

"I saw an old friend of yours at the reunion."

Ty was putting the studs into his evening shirt, and stopped as if he knew what was coming, but Amanda continued on her way to the dressing table and began to fiddle with a bracelet as if what she was saying wasn't in the least important.

"That Owen girl. You know the one I mean. The climber."

He wanted to slap her for that, but you didn't go around slapping your wife because she said something nasty about a girl you still happened to be in love with. He went back to work on the studs. "How did she look?"

"Hard. But then what can you expect?"

"What does that mean?"

"The sort of life she's had. Career woman. New York, Washington. Heaven knows what she's been through. I'm sure I don't. But it shows on her face."

"I don't believe it," he said without meaning to.

"Well, that's a foolish thing to say, Ty. You didn't see her. I did."

"Women never can judge what another woman looks like."

"I'm sure there are men who would find her attractive, if that's what you mean. But perhaps that's what I meant when I said she looked hard." Amanda walked to the mirror where Ty was struggling with a black tie. She pushed his hands away and tied a perfect bow. "It takes a husband and children to keep a woman from getting hard, darling. Everyone knows that. Thank heaven I have you and the boys."

On the way back to Washington, Kathryn told herself she was glad she'd gone, glad she'd proved to herself she could return to Philadelphia without going to pieces, glad she'd seen Amanda radiating contentment and self-satisfaction. That would stop her from thinking of Ty. It was foolish to be still thinking of him after all this time. It was worse than foolish. It was irresponsible. She had more important things to worry about—like the absurd directive to the regional offices that lay on her desk now. "Every writer is required to produce seventeen hundred words a week." At first Kate had thought it was a mistake, but she'd called the office responsible for the order and checked. There was no mistake.

She picked her way through the maze of cubicles that had been set up in the orchestra pit of the old auditorium. McSorley's office, four makeshift walls without door or ceiling, was located in one corner, and the peeling gilt paint from the tier of boxes above rained down on him and everything in the office with a slow and maddening regularity.

He looked up from the messy desk when she entered, but didn't smile. He'd lost weight since they'd come to Washington, and he looked tired. It was the political infighting, Kate knew. "I thought I'd seen politicking in academia," he'd said to her early on, "but I hadn't seen anything."

Kate handed him the paper. "Have you read this?"

"Of course I haven't read it," McSorley answered. "That's why you're here. So I won't have to read things like this."

"Seventeen hundred words a week. 'Every writer is required to produce seventeen hundred words a week.'"

"That doesn't sound like too much."

"Too much! It's nothing. They ought to be doing that in a day. They're not undergraduates writing research papers, you know."

"Now, don't get snippy, Katie."

"It's Bryant's fault, of course. They should never have let an advertising man draw up the directive."

"Let's not start on that." McSorley sighed. "The problem of who would qualify for the project was settled long before we got here."

"I don't mean that. I think copywriters and technical writers and all the rest ought to qualify. But I don't think a man who's accustomed to taking three weeks to get a hundred-word ad approved by an entire agency and a sponsor ought to determine how fast writers can write. I don't like the idea of a minimum number of words in the first place—you know that—but if they're going to set one, they ought to make it realistic. Asking for seventeen hundred words is asking for wasted time."

"You know who you sound like now, Katie? All those Babbitts who are horrified that the government is paying artists and are sure that the artists are only going to sit around and drink and make love —free love—on their money."

"You know that's not what I mean. It's only that you're going to sap a lot of energy if you tell people they're expected to turn out seventeen hundred words a week. A professional who's been writing for years knows his own pace, but a lot of these people aren't professionals. They're kids out of college and copywriters, like the misguided Mr. Bryant, and researchers and heaven knows what else. Why not encourage rather than discourage them?"

"And you want me to tell Bryant that?"

"Well, it's not my place to. Think of what it would do to the hierarchy around here."

"Why did I ever leave Columbia?" McSorley said.

"Because you can do more good here. By talking to Bryant, for one thing. Start with eight thousand words a week. That will give us a bargaining point."

"Any other orders, Katie?"

"No, just talk to Bryant."

McSorley did. The debate went on for weeks, and by the time it was finished, everyone including McSorley had forgot that it was Kate who'd started it. She wasn't surprised by the fact or even particularly dissatisfied. She had, as Peter pointed out when she told him about it, accomplished her end.

* * *

Ty told himself Amanda's mention of Kat didn't make any difference. He didn't need someone else to remind him of her. He'd never stopped thinking of her and remembering her, though he'd erected defenses against doing anything about her. Amanda was one. The boys another. Then there was honor, and somewhere along the way there was even fairness to Kat. In the days after Amanda's mention of Kat, Ty worked hard at strengthening those defenses, shoring up a gap here, fortifying a weak spot there, but he was building on a foundation of sand and he knew it.

Hilary suspected as much when he sought her out after lunch at Highfield the following Saturday. Emily and Amanda were upstairs with the dressmaker—she'd announced she didn't come to the house on Saturday afternoons anymore, but when Emily Enfield summoned, she came—and Carter had taken his own boys and Ty's to a cricket match. Ty was to join them later.

"I didn't think you'd be going to the reunion," he said casually as he eased himself into a wicker chair next to Hilary's. "Your fifteenth is next year, isn't it?"

"Mummy doesn't have a reunion," Camilla said. "She was never graduated. She married Daddy and had me instead."

"And a perfectly wise thing it was," Hilary said to her daughter. "I only hope you have as much sense." She turned to Ty. "I thought I'd take Camilla. Carter and I aren't at all sure we want her to go to college, but we thought we'd let her have a look. And then Mandy was going, so we tagged along."

Ty looked off toward the masses of wisteria that hid Nicholas's cottage from view. "I heard Kat was there."

Hilary took a long time to answer. "Kate Owen? Was she? I don't remember. It was such a crush."

"Of course you remember, Mummy. You introduced me to her. That dark pretty lady who said she remembered when I was born."

She would, Ty thought. It was the summer after his first year in law school, the summer she'd taken that job with Addison Wales, the summer Tim Wharton had gone off to Cape May for a month, leaving them that small cluttered apartment on Locust Street. The windows of the bedroom faced west and he could still remember the way the setting sun streamed across the bed and how Kat had looked in that light, her suntanned skin smooth as burnished gold, the dark hair tousled, the blue eyes bright but soft because they had just made love.

"So you thought she was pretty, Camilla?"

"For someone that old."

Ty laughed. "How did she seem to you, Hil?"

"I'm sure I don't know. We barely said a word. After all, I was with Amanda," she added pointedly.

"She lives in Washington," Camilla said. "I heard her telling some girls."

"I thought it was New York," Ty said.

"I don't see that it matters where she lives," Hilary interrupted. "She's nothing to do with us. And I wish you'd both stop talking about her."

"I only asked how she was," Ty said.

"I know how I'd feel if Carter asked about . . ." Hilary looked at Camilla. "You know what I mean, Ty, and I hope you aren't going to do anything foolish. Remember Amanda and the boys."

He heard Amanda's voice mingling with his mother's in the front hall. "How could I forget them, Hil?"

Ty couldn't forget Amanda and the boys, but their presence in his mind didn't stop him from picking up the telephone and calling Kat the following Monday. He was glad it was a long-distance call and he didn't have to dial. His hands were shaking too badly to dial.

Her voice at the other end of the line sounded exactly as he remembered it.

"Kat, it's Ty. Ty Enfield."

Was there any other Ty? She tried to light a cigarette and dropped the match into her lap.

"How are you?" he asked.

"I'm fine. That is . . . wait a minute." She brushed the sparks from her skirt and tried to calm herself. This was not the way it was supposed to be. This was not the way she'd always imagined it. She took a deep breath. "I'm fine, Ty," she repeated. "How are you?"

"I'd like to see you."

"Why?"

He hadn't expected the question, but knowing her, he should have. "Because I think of you all the time."

"I think of you too, Ty. That's why I don't think we ought to see each other. I don't think Amanda would like it. I don't think I'd like it."

"Please, Kat. Just this once. Someplace noisy and crowded and very public. I'll take you to dinner. Let me come down and take you to dinner."

"I don't think so."

"Then a drink. Think of it, Kat. We haven't had a legal drink together since 1920."

She wondered if he remembered that night as vividly as she did. It was the first time he'd said he loved her.

"You can't refuse me a single drink. Especially if I'm willing to come all the way to Washington for it."

"It won't be a single drink, and you know it."

He was silent for a moment. "It will be anything you want it to be, Kat."

"I wish you wouldn't."

"You don't mean that."

"I'm trying to."

"I'll catch the four-o'clock on Thursday." He hung up before she could say any more.

It started all over again that night. They'd both known it would. He took her for the promised drink, then to dinner, and then back to her apartment, and they'd sat and talked for hours. He told her how unhappy he was, though he didn't blame Amanda, told her how it had been a mistake to marry her in the first place, and he'd done nothing but regret it and think of Kat for the last ten years. She asked him why he had never answered her letter that summer and he pointed out that it was she who had broken the engagement and never answered his letter, and they railed against the European postal systems, and she cried. He held her then because it hurt so to see her cry, and kissed her, and they tasted the salt of her tears on each other's mouths and somewhere around dawn they made love.

The next morning they awakened and discovered each other and smiled because it was such a miraculous thing they had found each other again. Kate felt his hand pushing her hair back from where it had fallen over her cheek, tracing the line over neck and shoulder and breast, felt him turning her to him, drawing her to him, and she knew she'd come home.

Or had she? Kate wondered an hour later. She was in the small kitchen making coffee, and she could hear Ty in the shower, her shower, singing "Blue Moon" in an absurd parody of Russ Columbo. He sounded very happy.

The shower and the singing stopped at the same moment, then Columbo née Enfield started up again with "You Call It Madness." An image of Ty, only a few hours ago, his body naked and glistening with perspiration above her in the tousled bed flashed through her mind. She closed her eyes and tried not to think how quiet the apartment would be tomorrow morning, quiet and empty.

He'd stopped singing again and a moment later she felt him standing behind her. His arms went around her waist and his lips found her ear. He was wearing only a towel and his skin was smooth and still damp.

"How did you like my serenade?"

"Pretty soppy."

"Soppy! It was supposed to be romantic. I was wooing you."

"You've already done that."

"It's an ongoing process. I don't suppose," he said, nuzzling her neck, "you have a razor in the apartment. I know you don't have a straight razor—at least I hope you don't—but perhaps one of those safety things. I'm only thinking of you." He rubbed his beard against her cheek.

"There's one in the cabinet over the sink. And a fresh packet of blades. Do you want eggs?" she added as he was leaving the kitchen.

"Just coffee and toast, thanks."

As she took the bread from the metal box on the counter, she wondered if toast and coffee were his usual morning meal. He used to love enormous breakfasts, but he'd been younger then. Amanda would know what he wanted these mornings, of course, and the servants would have it waiting for him each day when he came down. Kate told herself again that she would have to speak to him. As soon as he was dressed, she promised, and began to carry the breakfast things to the dining table in the near corner of the living room.

"What would you like to do today?" He was standing in the doorway to the bedroom knotting a striped silk tie. Kate wanted to scream. The big things were painful enough, but the little ones were killing. Razors and ties and what he ate for breakfast. It was all so stupid and irrelevant and agonizing.

"What I have to do today, Ty, is go to the office."

"Won't hear of it," he said, sitting across the table from her.

"I'm afraid McSorley—that's my boss—won't hear of anything else."

"Then I'll go with you, sit at your feet all day, mooning up at you with calf eyes."

She had to straighten things out. Really. "Ty, be serious for a minute."

"I *am* being serious. I don't want to leave you for a minute. Take today off and we'll go away for the weekend."

He didn't want to leave her for a minute, at least not a minute of this weekend. "Last night was wonderful, Ty, but it was wrong, and it can't happen again."

He put down his cup abruptly and looked at her. He was serious now all right. "You know it wasn't wrong, Kat. It was right. We're right."

"Maybe we were once, but we're not anymore. You're married, and I don't think I can stand that. I don't think I can stand an affair with a married man."

"I never expected you to. I'll get a divorce."

"Isn't that what they always say?" She saw his face go rigid.

"I don't know what 'they always say.' I don't know what your experience has been. I only know what I'm going to do."

She opened the silver case he'd placed on the table and took a cigarette from it. He had no right to anger. "I wasn't speaking from my experience, as you put it. And there's no need to be nasty. Neither of us is in much of a position for moral superiority this morning."

"I'm sorry, Kat." His voice sounded as if he meant it. "But think how I feel. One minute I think I've found you again, the next you tell me I've lost you."

"It won't work," she said simply.

"It will, Kat. It will because it has to, because I won't let it not work." He reached across the table and took her hand. "Without you I have nothing. I've lived that way for ten years, but I won't go on living that way. It may take a little time, the legalities and all the rest of it, but I'll get a divorce, Kat. I swear I will. By a year from now we'll be married." He raised her hand to his mouth. "If you'll have me," he murmured against her palm, and it felt like a tangible promise she could hold on to.

"I'll have to think about it," she said lightly because she could feel her face collapsing the way it did when she was going to cry, and she had no intention of sitting here over breakfast with Ty sobbing about how unhappy she'd been and how happy she was.

He must have known what she was doing because when he spoke again his voice matched her own. "Now the least you can do is take the day off. I'm sure the Writers' Project isn't going to fall apart simply because you don't turn up one day. Besides"—he looked at his watch—"you're already far too late, and better never than late. If one of my secretaries comes in late, I assume she's lazy and begin to think of letting her go, but if she stays home sick, I just feel sorry for her."

"You're a tyrant. And anyway, I'm not a secretary."

"My apologies. All the same, I don't care if you're Roosevelt's righthand man—woman—the New Deal will keep on dealing without you."

"I suppose you're right." She hadn't taken a day off since she'd been here, and she didn't suppose one day would hurt.

"You know I'm right. Now, where would you like to go? There's a fellow I know in Virginia. Has a horse farm. He's got a guest cottage that's quite private and I have an open invitation. He won't ask questions or raise a single eyebrow."

It's started already, she thought and fought to push the idea from her mind. It was replaced by an equally unpleasant one. An open invitation. She wondered how many times Ty had used the guest cottage and how many times his friend the breeder had asked no questions and raised no eyebrows. "Please not Virginia horse country, Ty. All those station wagons with names on the side and dogs in the back and everything smelling of horses and everyone talking of horses all the time."

"It sounds as if you'd spent a lot of time there."

Kate started to explain that it had been a single weekend at the house of a woman who, by dint of a handful of poems she'd had published privately, thought she was qualified to run the local Writers' Project, but then decided she owed Ty no explanations. "Anyway, no matter how private the cottage is, we're still someone's guests."

"Where would you like to go?"

She thought for a moment. "Nowhere. We'll stay right here. I'll show you Washington—the way the other half sees it."

"Kat, you could show me Dante's Inferno, all nine circles, and I'd love every one of them."

"I thought there were more than that."

"Only nine, though that doesn't include the anteroom. I ought to remember. I went through every one of them in my sophomore year. It was pure agony."

"Is that story about your sophomore year true? The one about almost flunking out and then finishing with the highest average ever?"

"Absolutely, and I trust it impresses you."

"It must have if I still remember it."

"How did you hear about it? I know I never told you. Hilary?"

"Chris."

Ty looked surprised. He hadn't thought Chris would have told Kat anything flattering about him.

Kate could still remember the night Chris had told her the story. It wasn't the only thing he'd said that night. "He'll never marry you, Katie." It was the first time Chris had warned her, but not the only time. She wasn't going to think of that now.

"Well, if I'm going to show you Washington, we'd better get started. I bet you've never even seen Congress in session."

"I was hoping it wouldn't be. Haven't they adjourned for the summer?"

"They're held up on some bill. And the Supreme Court. I'll have to show you the Supreme Court."

"I've seen that, thank you," he said in mock indignation. "From behind the rail. Three cases."

"How did you do?"

"Won two, lost one." He smiled at the look that crossed her face. It wasn't exactly surprise. "Not bad for a gentleman lawyer."

"All the same, you haven't seen the new building. And the Smithsonian and the Lincoln Memorial and the White House." She stopped for a minute and grinned slyly. "Or perhaps we ought to skip the White House. At least as long as its present occupant is living there."

"I'll have you know I'm thought of as a wild-eyed radical in Philadelphia."

"I daresay you are—in Philadelphia. At any rate, we'll do all the landmarks today. We'll be properly patriotic and self-improving and go all the places the tourists do. And tomorrow I'll take you for a picnic in Rock Creek Park."

"And then I'll take you to a polo match. And Sunday we can go for a sail. They rent boats in Washington Channel."

It was like Ty to know that. Drop him in a strange town and within hours he'd know where to find boats, horses, the best restaurants, and the liveliest nightclubs.

Ty turned out to be an indefatigable and irreverent tourist. In the rotunda of the Capitol he was jostled by four noisy, ill-mannered children and sneered at by their mother for not looking on the little darlings more kindly. "You see, dear," he observed to Kate in an audible undertone. "I told you we should have brought the children. Everyone else does. And they would have enjoyed it so." He turned to the woman, who'd been listening carefully. "It's so difficult though —with ten. Still, I was determined to try it, but the missus said no."

The woman transferred her frown from Ty to Kathryn, the selfish wife, the incompetent mother, and shepherded her children off like a hen clucking after noisy chicks.

As they stood in line to tour the White House he defended the President stoutly against the slurs of a man from Alabama. "Aren't you proud of me?" he asked after they'd left.

"If only you believed half of what you said." Kate laughed.

"Now, now, you can't have everything."

But for all his clowning, he missed nothing. His eye was quick, and his mind, observing and judging, worked rapidly.

"You know," Kate said when they got back to her apartment that evening, "it's very nice seeing things with you."

He caught her hand as she was walking past him to the living room and drew her to him. "You're supposed to say that it's nice doing anything with me."

"Well, it is."

"That's better," he murmured with his mouth on hers.

"Do you want a drink?" she asked quietly, though she knew it was not what either of them wanted.

He shook his head and began to lead her into the bedroom. The shades were still up and in the late-afternoon light the room was all soft shadows and quiet privacy. He took her in his arms again and she could feel his hands working at the buttons at the back of her dress. "I only want you, Kat. All day, wherever we were, you were all I wanted. You're all I'll ever want." And his hands sliding the clothing from her, moving slowly over her body, exploring, arousing, promising, gave force to his words.

The sheets felt cool against their bodies, warm with desire, tangled together in the heat of wanting each other and having each other. He kissed her again and again and she tasted Ty again and again and felt his skin against hers and his hands that had not forgot the secrets of her body or her desires. And it was all familiar but new as well, the softness of his mouth on her breast, the strength of his body moving against hers, the sensation of holding Ty, of smooth skin and taut muscle, of Ty hard with wanting her. And in the shadows she watched him and saw him watching her and they were mouths and hands and whispered words and desire, climbing, growing, swelling to that moment when all consciousness exploded in the midnight blackness of pure pleasure.

"About that drink," he said. She didn't know how long they'd lain that way, her head on his chest, his arm holding her to him, but it had grown dark in the room and when she lifted her head all she could see was the outline of his profile and the glowing ember of his cigarette as he inhaled. She reached over and turned on the lamp beside the bed.

"A cold martini and a hot bath. I can't remember when I did so much walking."

"You take care of the tub and I'll take care of the martinis." He sat and began to rummage through the pile of clothing on the floor in search of his trousers. "Where would you like to dine?"

"Nowhere," she answered without thinking.

He turned to look at her and smiled.

She was embarrassed for a moment. "I mean I hadn't thought of any place in particular."

"Good girl. We won't budge."

She ran the water, eased herself into the tub, and lay back with her eyes closed. Through the half-open door she could hear Ty opening and shutting cupboards. He was doing his Russ Columbo imitation again.

"Any requests?" he called from the living room.

"You'd better be careful," she called back, "or I'll do my Dietrich."

"The legs are the same, but the coloring's all wrong."

She was startled by the closeness of his voice and opened her eyes. He was standing over the tub, smiling. "Come to think of it, the legs are better." He handed her one of the glasses he was carrying and sat on the side of the tub. "I was contemplating joining you but I don't think there's enough room. Nevertheless, I can still offer my services." He put his drink on the floor, reached over for the soap, and began lathering her back. His hands were slow and coaxing on her skin and she closed her eyes again. She felt his mouth against her shoulder and his hands moving over her back, then smooth and gentle as they reached around to caress her breasts. She caught her breath.

He heard the sound and when he spoke his voice was a hoarse whisper. "If you don't come out, I'm going to have to come in."

She laughed but it was a strange choked sound, and she watched him removing the trousers he'd just put on, watched the long lean body climbing into the tub, and felt his skin warm and slippery against her own. She was trembling from his touch, his hands on her breasts, at her thighs, and they were locked together in an awkward, impossible, irresistible embrace. The water moved around them gently, lapping at their bodies, washing over their desire, and she clung to Ty drowning in the power and pleasure and fulfillment of him.

He refused to let her dress for dinner. She stood at the stove in her chemise while he sat on a tall stool in the corner watching her. He kept up a steady commentary while she grilled the steaks and mixed a salad and fried some potatoes, but his eyes never left her.

As they were about to sit down at the small table in the living room, he decided they'd dress after all. He went into the bedroom and returned with his tie and a necklace he'd found on her dresser. He was wearing only trousers and he knotted the tie neatly around his bare throat, then fastened the necklace around hers. "Just like the British," he said. "We dress for dinner even in the jungles of Washington."

After dinner Ty insisted they go dancing. He crossed the room to the radio standing on a table in the corner. "Which roof do you prefer?"

She laughed. "Do I have a choice?"

"Probably not." He fiddled with the dial until he found dance music. Then he held out his arms and she crossed the room and went into them.

It was no use saying he was a good dancer. Ty was much more than that. He moved with the innate grace of an animal, and like an animal, his ease had to do less with confidence than with instinct. She'd noticed it the first time she'd seen Ty and she'd never stopped responding to it. Her body followed his easily, and she closed her eyes and leaned her head against his shoulder. His skin was smooth against her cheek. Through the thin chemise she could feel the hard strength of his chest and then he was sliding the straps from her shoulders and there was nothing between them, only warm flesh against warm flesh, and it had turned into another kind of dance entirely.

They slept soundly that night, but once in the early hours of the morning she felt Ty turning to her, and in half-sleep she clung to him, and she awakened to find that she had been making love to Ty in her sleep.

The next day they picnicked as Kate had said they would and they went to a polo match in West Potomac Park as Ty had promised, and they behaved, as Ty said, quite properly. "Not like that shameless couple last night." But at one point during the match when they were sitting quietly between chukkers, she felt Ty watching her and turned to him, and he reached out and touched her cheek with his hand. It was a simple gesture, but Kate felt herself color as if everyone around them saw the intimacy behind it.

They awakened Sunday morning to the sound of rain on the bedroom window. It was a nice steady rain halfway between the hesitancy of a drizzle and the intensity of a sudden shower. It was the kind of rain that would continue all day.

"Breakfast in bed," she whispered, moving closer to Ty beneath the covers. She rubbed her cheek against his shoulder. He smelled of sleep and of . . . of what? Kate wondered. Of Ty.

"Breakfast," he repeated, turning to her. "And lunch." His mouth traced a path down her neck. "And dinner."

Ty's visits after that were frequent but irregular. In the middle of July he took off another whole weekend. Kate knew that Amanda and the boys had gone to Cape May for the summer, and she knew that Ty joined them there on weekends. She didn't know what he'd said to Amanda about this weekend, and he didn't tell her, though he spoke of divorce frequently.

Ty rented a car and they drove along the Chesapeake to an inn he'd heard of that was pleasant but not fashionable. There would be no one there who knew him. It was still light when they arrived on Friday evening, and Ty insisted they go for a walk on the beach. It was a clear day, miraculously dry for that place and time of year, and the sea breeze was invigorating after the heat of Washington. Kate felt her spirits lifting. She'd been looking forward to the weekend ever since Ty said he could get away, but on the drive down she'd begun to feel somehow wary.

"Is it the inn?" Ty asked as they started along the beach.

"What do you mean?"

"Whatever it is that's bothering you. Is it registering at the inn?"

"No, that didn't bother me." It was true, for the most part. She'd felt a twinge of anger as she'd watched him sign Mr. and Mrs. Tyson Enfield, but it had passed quickly enough.

"Then the memories of that weekend at Addison Wales's house?"

"I've always thought that was one of the best times we've ever spent."

"So have I," he said.

"Then why does it hurt to remember it?"

"Maybe because we came so close that time." Ty stopped walking and turned to her. "We won't miss this time, Kat. I promise you that. And we'll make new memories. In a couple of years we'll sit around and talk about how wonderful that weekend on the Chesapeake was."

It usually didn't work that way—usually when you tried that hard it didn't happen—but it did that weekend. It was warmer than it had been at Addison's and they swam in the morning and again in the afternoon and on Saturday night Ty said it was time for another swim because midnight swimming was good for the soul, to say nothing of the body.

The night air felt cool on their wet bodies and they ran back to the inn. Once in their room they toweled each other vigorously, and Ty said they had to get out of their wet suits because everyone knew sitting around in a wet suit was dangerous and unhealthy. He peeled the bathing suit down her body gently but quickly, as if he were impatient, though they'd made love before dinner. His skin was damp against hers and cool at first, but then warmer. She could taste the salt on his mouth and knew he must taste it on her as he traced a line down to her breast, and the soft lips and hard teeth made her cry out, not from pain, but from the pleasure he gave her and the desire he aroused, a fierce hunger that drove her hands and mouth shamelessly, wildly over his body. And the more the desire was fed, the higher it mounted, until she was dizzy with wanting him. She could sense the same throbbing hunger in him, in the rush of his hands and the urgency of his mouth, and then when she thought she'd go mad with wanting him inside her, he entered her and she drove her body relentlessly against his, rushing toward something, racing heedlessly, breathlessly, greedily until it overtook her with wave after wave of pleasure.

It had been a perfect weekend, as Ty had promised, but it had been only a weekend. The following Saturday she was alone in her apartment, remembering it and agonizing over what Ty was doing this weekend. He'd be at the beach again, but he'd be at the beach with Amanda and the children, their children.

Kate was absurdly grateful when the phone rang. It was Peter. She hadn't seen him in weeks and she'd told herself she should tell him she wasn't going to see him at all, but she was too eager for company this morning to worry about that.

"How about a ride in the country, Katie? And by the country I mean run-down farms, not some fashionable watering hole. I'll explain the whole thing on the way. Be ready in half an hour, and don't look too well-heeled. We're on government business."

When she got into the car, he handed her a letter.

dear mr president

everybuddy say what good you do specaly for the farmer but you dint do me no good the bank leff me alone and i was alright until that man come by and say he from something call aaa and i cant grow nothin no more so now theres no crops and no money and now the bank is come by and bother me they say you a fair man but it dont look that way from here

elwood lanks

"Don't tell me we're going to see Mr. Lanks," Kate said.

"You guessed it. Those stories you hear about the White House are true, Katie. All those letters do get answered and all those problems are looked into by someone. And today that someone is me. Us."

"Chris said when we first met that you were a troubleshooter, but I thought that meant big guns."

"It usually does, but today I'm having my knuckles rapped. Being taught humility."

"What was your particular sin of pride?"

"I had lunch at the White House yesterday. Hash with a single poached egg as usual. A meeting about all these strikes for union recognition. Well, I was arguing with the President about something—he's a little afraid of unions himself, if you want to know the truth—and I was so caught up in my own argument that I didn't notice when he stopped saying 'I think' and started saying 'the President thinks.' I not only lost the point, but I'm being reprimanded in the bargain. Our visit will show Mr. Lanks that the President cares, and me that I'm not as important as I think I am."

"You don't seem particularly troubled by your penance."

"Someone has to see Mr. Lanks—though I'm not sure how much good we're going to do—and it gives me an outing with you. I'd be a lot angrier if my penance didn't include you."

She'd have to stop seeing him. Really.

The Lankses' farm was not very far from the Chesapeake resort where she and Ty had spent last weekend, but it seemed to Kate that the distance couldn't be measured by miles. Mr. and Mrs. Lanks lived with Mr. Lanks's mother, his two brothers, and six children in a two-room shack. In the front room there was a wood-burning stove, a table, two chairs, and half a dozen crates. Several mattresses spewing old newspapers were piled in one corner, and the single window that had been patched with cardboard let in little light. The stench of grease and sweat and urine was physically overpowering, and Kate was relieved when Mr. Lanks said they'd talk outside. He pulled up a crate for her, while he and Peter stood. Several children sat on the ground far enough from Kate for what they believed was safety, close enough to examine her. The two youngest children wore what must at one time have been sacks for some kind of food. None of them wore shoes.

Kate was too busy watching the children to pay much attention to Peter's conversation. She heard him explaining the AAA to Mr. Lanks, heard him telling the man that he'd misunderstood this and could get around that, and by the time they left, Mr. Lanks was smiling, if you could call that toothless grimace a smile, but Kate was still thinking of the children.

It was a little after three when they started back and Peter noticed her silence. "And you thought it was only Oklahoma."

"I've never seen anything like it."

"Makes those men selling apples on the streets look positively affluent, don't they? To say nothing of your penniless writers." He took his eyes from the road and looked at her for a moment. "I'm not making fun of you, Katie, and I'm certainly not blaming you. You saw the men with the apples and the breadlines and you suffered for them and did what you could, and I admire you for it, because too many people like you who were never touched by it directly didn't suffer or understand or even see. But you're not going to find people like the Lankses on the better streets of New York or Washington or Philadelphia. Even selling apples."

"Or in an ivory tower at Harvard."

There was a stand at the side of the road with a homemade sign that read FRESH FRUITS AND VEGETABLES, and Peter stopped the car in the shade of some trees a little distance from it.

"Are you hungry?" he asked.

"Not very."

"Have to eat, all the same."

He left her in the car and returned in a few minutes with a bag of peaches and two containers of strawberries. He put the fruit on the seat between them and took a peach. "I wasn't always in that tower at Harvard, you know," he said, as if there had been no break in the conversation. "There really was a farm in Minnesota."

"Not like the Lankses', certainly."

"No, not like the Lankses'. There was a decent house, not elaborate but decent, and a lot more land. That was the trouble. More land meant a bigger mortgage. It's all gone now, the house, the land —and my father. He was proud, too damn proud. He took money from me for a couple of years—it was as much as I could send, but still not enough—and he hated it, but he said he wouldn't take money from the government, and that was his only hope after he lost the farm. So one day he had an accident, or at least he made it look enough like an accident for the insurance company to pay my mother the small amount that hadn't been borrowed on."

"How awful."

"There are lots of awful stories, Katie. My father was only one of them."

"How you must hate them."

"Who?"

"The people who did it. The banks, the judges, all of them," she finished vaguely.

"I wish I could, Katie, but it isn't that simple. Oh, there are the big bankers and the Wall Street boys, the Insulls and the Henry Ford Juniors and a few others, and I hate them, but as for the men who took the farm away, some of them were only trying to do their jobs. Like the judge who signed the foreclosure. A bunch of vigilantes took him out one night. Not because of my father's farm. They had their own gripes. They beat him and threatened to kill him. He knew who all of them were, but afterward he refused to press charges. Somehow I can't blame him for the foreclosure."

He pushed the hair from his forehead with the back of his hand and shook his head. "Some outing this is turning into. I'm supposed to be cheering you up after the Lankses, not depressing you more. Here, have some strawberries. Or would you like a watermelon? I can go back and get a watermelon."

She laughed. "No, the strawberries are fine."

He took the largest, ripest one off the top and made her take a bite, then he ate the rest of it. She was startled by that.

"Did I ever tell you about my first day in Washington, Katie? That's comic relief, if I ever heard it." He had on his raconteur's face now, the one he'd been wearing that first time she'd seen him. She hadn't liked it then, but she didn't mind it now.

"I came down from Cambridge with all the flags flying. Forget the President, I thought. Washington was waiting for me. Stopped at the rooming house just long enough to drop my suitcase, then headed straight for one of those run-down old office buildings within running distance of the White House. They were still using them then. I'd been told they'd found me an office on the first floor. I could picture the staff assembled to greet me. Secretaries ready to take down every word, assistants eager to run here and there at my bidding. After all, I wasn't an obscure college professor anymore. I was a man of importance, a man who was going to get this country back on its feet.

"There was a welcoming committee, all right. One of those little bespectacled men who look as if they've been lost in the government files since Silent Cal, or before. 'Are you from Minnesota?' he demanded. It was a strange greeting, but I assumed he was an erstwhile little fellow who'd been checking into his new boss's history. I admitted I was. 'About time,' he said, and told me to follow him. I thought he was officious, but I wasn't going to argue with him on the first morning. The next thing I knew I was in the basement of the building. The electricity had been out for two days and they were waiting for someone from the Minnesota Wiring Company. The one state that doesn't have a street in Washington, so they have to name an electrical company after it.

"What really got me," he continued, "was that I'd walked in there looking like what I thought was a million dollars. No more scruffy tweeds, no more worn-out elbows with patches. Before I'd left Cambridge I'd gone in to Boston to Brooks Brothers and bought what I was sure was *the* man-of-importance suit. Double-breasted pinstripe that practically radiated power. But maybe it was just too dark without the lights for the little man to notice."

They stopped for dinner at a restaurant that overlooked the water, and by the time they got back to Washington it was almost midnight. She was laughing at another of his stories—absolute truth told without an ounce of exaggeration, he insisted—when they pulled up in front of her apartment.

"You see, Katie, I'm good for you. Like a patent medicine or something. Now I've got to get you in the habit of taking me more regularly."

She stopped laughing abruptly. "I've been thinking about that, Peter. I don't think we ought to see each other anymore." She could barely see his face in the darkness, but she could feel the change in him.

"What brought this on?"

"There's someone else. We're going to be married."

She saw the large hand on the seat next to her clench and unclench. "He's a fast worker."

"Not exactly. We've known each other for a long time."

"In that case, what took him so long?"

"It's a long story, Peter, and I'd rather not go into it."

The words and the fleeting embarrassment that crossed her face gave her away. The oldest story in the world, the oldest damn story, but it was new when he thought of it in terms of Katie. The guy was married.

"Well, Katie, you've always said we were friends. I guess we'll have to go on being just that."

It wasn't an easy task for Peter, especially when he called her apartment a few nights later. He could tell from her voice and the evasive sentences that kept drifting off that she was not alone. And then, as if that were not cruel enough, he heard a man's voice in the background. He couldn't make out the words, but he heard the voice, easy, confident, possessive.

Peter went to four different bars that night. In the last he ran into Chris. He'd suspected he would. He supposed that was why he'd gone there. If he couldn't be with her, at least he could talk about her.

"You know what's wrong with your sister, Owen?" he demanded.

"No, what's wrong with Katie?" Chris asked without any particular interest. He'd been hanging on the wire down at the newsroom all evening following the latest development in the Philippine revolution, and Katie was the last thing on his mind.

"Nothing, absolutely nothing." Peter was silent for a moment, contemplating some truth in his half-empty glass. "Except that goddamn guy who just walked back into her life."

Suddenly Chris was alert. "What do you mean?"

"Some joker she's known for a long time, she says. They're going to get married, she says."

"Tyson Enfield?"

"Don't know his name. Haven't had the pleasure." Peter signaled the bartender.

"Did she say anything else about him?" Chris demanded. "Did she say he was married?"

"She didn't have to."

* * *

"You can't be that stupid! Nobody could be that stupid! Didn't you learn anything last time?" Chris shouted.

"I wish you'd stop screaming. I have neighbors, you know." Kate tried to keep her voice calm.

"To hell with your neighbors."

"That's a civilized attitude."

"I'm not feeling very civilized, Katie. Tyson Enfield has a way of making me feel damn uncivilized. I suppose he's still married." She said nothing. "But talking about divorce, of course."

She could hear the cheapness behind every word, and it shamed her. Shamed and frightened her. "We've discussed it."

"I'll just bet you have. What's the catch, Katie? As soon as the children grow up? As soon as that old bitch of a mother of his dies? Or is it as soon as his wife dies? I might even believe that one."

"I don't care what you believe. And I don't care what you think about Ty and me. I'm sick of your preaching, Chris. It's like that business with Daphne. You make one set of rules for me, do whatever you please yourself, and then justify it by some intellectual somersault that says you want one kind of life but I'm supposed to have another. Well, maybe I don't want the kind of life you think I ought to. Maybe I'm perfectly happy the way I am."

"In other words, you like being a married man's mistress."

"I like being with Ty."

"Then stay with him. At least for as long as you can. But if you run into trouble again, do me a favor, Katie. Don't come to me. I don't think I'd have the stomach for it this time."

"I'll keep that in mind," she shouted, but he'd already slammed the door behind him.

When she entered the restaurant Kate was surprised to see another man at the table with Ty. As the *maître d'hôtel* led her across the room she recognized Nicholas's profile.

"I hope you don't mind, my dear." Nicholas stood and took her hand. "I'm on my way south to look at some horses and I decided on an evening in Washington. I admit I had you in mind when I decided on it. Ty didn't want to let me join you, but I insisted. After all, he's not the only one who's missed you. It's good to see you, Katie."

Kathryn was surprised at how good it was to see him. She'd always liked Nicholas, but it was more than that. His presence somehow transformed the whole evening. With a third person at the table she and Ty were no longer illicit lovers hiding from the world. Nicholas gave them a stamp of respectability and permanency and approval, though Kate was aware that no one, least of all Nicholas himself, ever associated him with those traits.

"You're looking lovely as ever, Katie. Haven't changed a bit. Though it's been . . . what . . . seven years?"

"Longer than that," Ty said.

Kate smiled and Nicholas laughed. "Longer than that for you, my boy, but not for Katie and me. We lunched in New York. The roof of the Ritz, if I remember correctly. And you were wearing a particularly fetching blue hat. Matched your eyes perfectly."

"I remember the Ritz but I'd forgot the hat," Kate said.

"You never told me," Ty reproached Nicholas.

"Do you expect me to tell you every time I lunch with a beautiful woman, Ty?"

"It was a wonderful lunch. I enjoyed it," Kate said.

"We had some good conversation, didn't we? Well, enough about the past. Ty tells me you're down here reforming the world."

"Not exactly," Kathryn said. "I'm with the Writers' Project."

"Ah, yes, all those starving writers scribbling histories of the states. Not a bad idea. To tell you the truth, my dear, I never expected Mr. Roosevelt to come up with so many good ideas. He wasn't such a liberal when he was younger, I can tell you that."

"Did you know him?" Kathryn asked.

"You should know by now, Kat, Uncle Nick knows everyone."

"Not everyone, Ty, but almost everyone. It's a result of being a peripatetic old bachelor. Yes, I've met Mr. Roosevelt off and on during the years. And I must admit that I was impressed by him, though, as I say, I never dreamed he'd go this far. Not only the presidency, but the kind of president he's become. You know what they say about him, that he may be an aristocrat, but he's no gentleman. It's not true. He's a gentleman in the best sense of the word. He's what Ty should have become. After all, the President was a bit of a hellraiser as a young man too."

"It seems to me," Kate said quickly, "that Ty's turned out just as well in his own way."

"Do you hear that loyalty?" Nicholas demanded. "More important, do you appreciate it? I tell you, Katie's a gem. Hold on to her, Ty. Don't let her slip away this time."

For a moment Kate was caught off balance. She'd forgot how direct Nicholas could be.

"Not a chance of that, Uncle Nick," Ty said. "I may not have turned out to be the man you hoped, but at least I've learned not to make the same mistake twice."

Nicholas had been like a gift, and for the next few days Kate felt better about everything. She even let herself believe Ty would get around to asking Amanda for a divorce as he kept saying he would. But the following week Ty brought her another gift, a real one, and it undid all the good of Nicholas's visit.

Ty arrived at the apartment with his small gladstone and a large box tied with silver ribbon. "It looks like Christmas," she said.

"Nothing that momentous. But I was walking through Wanamaker's and saw it hanging there and thought of you. Open it."

Inside the box hidden within clouds of tissue paper was a black satin nightgown. It was very beautiful and, Kate knew, very expensive. It was also the worst gift he could have brought her. Kate felt the tears welling up and knew how silly they were, but there was nothing she could do to stop them.

"Kat, what's wrong? What did I do wrong?"

"Nothing," she lied. "It's so silly. I'm so silly."

"I don't understand," he said, though he was afraid he was beginning to.

"It's beautiful, Ty, absolutely beautiful." She brushed at the tears with her hand, then blurted it out. "But it's a mistress's nightgown. I know it's stupid of me to cry about it, because after all, that's what I am, but . . ."

He dropped to his knees beside her chair, and his arms went around her. "I'll tell Amanda this weekend, Kat. I swear I will."

"I wasn't trying to force you to do anything, Ty."

"I know you weren't. You never do. But I am going to get a divorce, Kat. I promise you that. And I'm sorry about the nightgown. It was stupid of me, but I never dreamed . . ."

"It was nice of you, Ty. It was a nice gesture."

"But the wrong one." He took the box from her lap.

"What are you doing?"

"Getting rid of it."

"Ty, don't. It's beautiful, and I really do like it."

Ty wasn't listening. He was already halfway down the hall to the incinerator. Kate heard the heavy metal door squeak open, then bang closed. She knew it was as good as burning money, and that was an unconscionable thing to do these days, but she was glad.

* * *

It was a cool day for August, and Emily decided she'd call Ty at his office and ask him to dine that night. She'd enjoy the company. Not that she missed Bar Harbor. Without Samuel or the children it had ceased to be enjoyable, and she refused to go to Cape May with Amanda or Hilary. Cape May was not what it used to be—but what was since the war? Emily preferred the quiet of Highfield, but tonight she'd prefer Ty's company at Highfield.

"I'm sorry, Mrs. Enfield," Ty's secretary said. "Mr. Enfield has gone to Washington."

"How extraordinary," Emily said.

"Oh, no, Mrs. Enfield. Mr. Enfield goes to Washington at least once a week."

Emily hung up and dialed Carter's private number at the office. "Carter, does the firm have any clients in Washington?"

"Not that I know of, Mrs. Enfield, and I would know of them, I assure you."

"Would Ty be recruiting any?"

"It isn't likely, especially these days. Unless, of course, he were taking one of those test cases to the Supreme Court, but I assure you I'd know of that too."

Emily ordered the car to be brought around in half an hour. She reached Cape May just after lunch. The boys had gone off to their sailing lesson, and Amanda was alone on the broad wooden porch of the old house Samuel had bought for the weekends they weren't in Bar Harbor.

"Didn't you tell me last spring, Amanda, that that Owen girl was living in Washington?"

"I believe that's where she is. Why do you ask?"

Emily waited until the maid had placed the tray of iced tea on the glass-topped table and left the porch. "Did you know that Ty was spending a good deal of time in Washington these days?" There was only the slightest break in Amanda's motion at the tea tray, and anyone less observant than Emily would not have noticed it. "I spoke to Carter this morning. The firm has no clients in Washington."

Amanda handed her the glass of iced tea.

"What are you going to do about it?"

"I'm not sure yet."

"The boys are growing up, Amanda. They'll both be away at St. Paul's before you know it. Perhaps you ought to have another child.

I've always thought Ty ought to have a daughter. Though another son would do as well."

On her way to town the next day Amanda stopped in Atlantic City at a store she visited infrequently. The garments they carried were expensive but not to her taste. She was glad the shop girl did not know her. It was distasteful enough to be buying something like this without having one's regular shop girls know about it.

Ty was ebullient when he arrived at the apartment that Wednesday night, but Kathryn couldn't see why. It was one of those August nights that bring home with a sticky immediacy the truth of the British foreign service's designation of Washington as a tropical post. There would be a thunderstorm before the night was out, but the heat would linger. More than the weather, however, was troubling Kate that evening. The black satin nightgown had been thrown into the incinerator, but the memory of it still burned in her mind. She'd pretended to Chris that she didn't mind being a married man's mistress, but she did. She minded a great deal.

Ty arrived with a dozen roses. "I've told her, Kat," he said before she'd even taken them from the box. There was no need to explain what he meant.

"And what did she say?" Kate asked, keeping her eyes on the roses she was arranging in a crystal vase.

"She agreed to a divorce."

Kate could see her hands begin to shake as they moved around the flowers. It had been too much to hope for, but now Ty said it was true. "Just like that?" There had to be a trick. She was sure there was a trick.

"Well, not exactly just like that. She isn't happy about it, of course. She doesn't mind my leaving. Only the scandal. But she agreed to it all the same. Said she'd go away next fall. As soon as the boys return to school. Reno or someplace like that. It will be easier that way."

"She's being very decent about the whole thing."

"What else can she be? She knows the marriage is a failure. It was a mistake in the first place, and it's never worked." He crossed the room to where she was standing and turned her to him. "She knows I'm in love with you, Kat. She knows I always have been."

She tasted the words on his mouth and felt his hands molding her body to him, binding her to him. They moved to the bedroom, and it was as if they were moving into another realm, their own private world where nothing and no one could intrude. She clung to him, her arms around his neck, her mouth against his, as he undressed her, and when she was naked, feeling his hands on her, dizzy with his hands on her, she began to work at his things. The silk shirt was smooth against her skin, but his flesh was warmer and her hands trailed down him over the hard stomach working impatiently at his trousers.

He drew her down to the bed and they were moving slowly, lazily, luxuriating in each other, tracing familiar paths with eyes and fingers and mouths, and suddenly she felt the change in him, a sudden quickening, and she knew the laziness had turned to urgency. She sensed his excitement and it fired the same hunger in her.

"Kat," he said. It was no longer an endearment but a plea, and he entered her fiercely.

"Ty," she heard her own voice. And then "yes," and then "Ty," again in rhythm with their movements, quickening, racing until his name was a cry of pleasure and her own a soft moan that seemed to come from deep within him.

She felt his body relax on hers. "Kat," he said into her hair. It was a whisper now. "My Kat." It was a promise.

Ty had not lied to Kathryn. Amanda had agreed to the divorce, agreed to go away in the fall and divorce him with a minimum of fuss and scandal. He hadn't lied about any of it, but he hadn't told the truth in its entirety either. There was no point in telling Kat any of that. What had happened the night before he'd asked Amanda for the divorce had nothing to do with Kat or their future. It had no significance at all. It was merely a foolish, embarrassing mistake.

Ty had been surprised that night when he'd looked up from the book he was reading and saw Amanda emerge from her dressing closet, as surprised as he'd been when he'd returned from the office that evening and found she'd left the boys at the beach and come home for a few days. She was wearing a white nightgown of a fabric so thin it revealed every line of her body. Amanda still had a good figure, he thought, despite bearing two children. The straps of the nightgown were thin and the bodice small and low-cut. If Amanda's breasts were larger, it would not have covered her. It would not, Ty thought, have covered Kat.

He returned to the book and was only dimly aware of Amanda moving about the room, opening the draperies, raising the windows several inches.

"It's almost as cool here as it was at the beach. I'm glad I came home for a few days."

Ty looked up and saw that she was standing over him.

"Aren't you glad I came home, darling?"

He knew something was wrong. Even before she lifted the light linen comforter and got into his bed beside him, he knew something was wrong.

"It's been so lonely at the beach without you." She lifted her face to his expectantly.

Ty moved away, though there was little enough room in the narrow bed. "I think I'm getting a cold, Amanda. You know how annoying these summer colds are."

"Well, darling"—she turned so he could feel the length of her small body against his—"you know what the minister said. In sickness and in health."

He felt the pouting little mouth pressed against his, then, surprisingly, shockingly for Amanda, her hand beneath his silk pajamas.

"Amanda . . ." he said.

It had been a protest, but she took it as an endearment. "Darling," she murmured. "Darling." Her hands traveled over him as they never had before, and the small, slender body, suddenly free of even the slight restraint of the thin fabric, moved against his eagerly. Ty was surprised, but his body was not. It responded as it was meant to.

He had been caught off guard, Ty told himself afterward. It had happened only because he had been so sure it would never happen and hadn't bothered to erect any defenses against it. But it would not happen again. He swore to that.

It was all so distasteful, Amanda thought, lying alone in the cool freshness of her own bed. The vulgar nightdress, the whispered terms of endearment, the provocative behavior. She had actually touched him, as if she were some French tart. It was distasteful, but it was necessary. She only hoped she wouldn't have to repeat this ridiculous performance too many times before she found herself safe, pregnant and safe.

Amanda was at the breakfast table when Ty came down the next morning. She'd never been one to sleep late or indulge in breakfast in bed, and didn't approve of women who did. That sort of behavior smacked of vulgarity and new money and, as always, New York.

"Good morning, Ty. Did you sleep well?"

"I want to talk to you, Amanda."

She glanced through the arch to the tall English clock in the hall. "Perhaps tonight. You're a little late this morning, aren't you?"

"I want a divorce."

"I must say, you're not very amusing this morning, Ty."

"I'm serious. I want a divorce. I'll give you any grounds you want."

She refrained from observing that he already had. "After . . . after last night," she said quietly, and even managed a blush.

She was good, all right. Ty had forgot just how good she could be. "I'm sorry about last night."

"That's not very flattering."

"Let's cut out the games, Amanda. Last night has nothing to do with it."

"I suppose that . . . that tramp Kathryn Owen has something to do with it."

"Watch yourself, Amanda."

"Watch myself! I'm not the one having an affair with someone else's husband. It's your little climber, your little Katie Owen who's doing that. Katie Owen. Even her name sounds like trash."

Ty stood abruptly, and Amanda watched the untouched coffee spill over his cup and saucer onto the linen place mat. She'd have to remind the maid to soak it in cold water as soon as Ty left.

"I'm not going to argue about Kat with you. I want a divorce. I hope you'll give me one, because it will be easier on everyone, including you and the boys, if you do, but if you don't, I'm leaving anyway. You can reach me at my club when you decide what you want to do."

"Sit down, Tyson."

"There's nothing more to say."

"There's a great deal more to say, but I'm not going to say it while you stand there looking like a salesman on his way out the door." She waited in silence. Time was on her side. She watched him take his place across the table from her with satisfaction. "There's no need for you to go to your club, Tyson. It will simply give people something to talk about. I'll go back to the beach today and stay there until the end of summer. Just as if nothing had happened. When the boys return to school, I'll go wherever it is people go for this sort of thing. I have no interest in making things easier for you or that woman, but I don't want your sordid affair dragged through the courts here. I intend to go on living in this town, and the boys are going to grow up here, and having people know just how big a fool and philanderer you are won't help us."

Amanda looked at the clock again. "Now, you'd better run along. I have several things to do before I start back to the beach. And"— she smiled at him coldly—"I'm sure you'll want to call your mistress and tell her the good news."

He hadn't called Kat. He didn't want to tell her over the phone. He wanted to be with her when he told her, see her face, feel her mouth on his saying yes they really would be married, feel her body pressed against his denying they'd lost anything, promising all they'd still have. And when he told her, it was just as he'd known it would be.

Kathryn was surprised when Chris turned up at her office that morning. She hadn't seen him for more than a month, since the night they'd argued about Ty.

"Come on, you can buy me a going-away lunch," Chris said. There was no apology in his voice, only an embarrassed attempt at affection.

"I didn't know you were leaving."

"Neither did I till a few days ago. Special-feature stuff. With everything going on here, the paper decides I'm the one to cover the dust bowl. Now, there's a story for you. Dust in my typewriter and starving kids in my dreams. And do you think anyone is going to care? After two years of drought, no one cares except the poor devils living through it."

"That's why they're sending you, Chris. To make us all care." She was very happy to see him.

"Flattery won't get you off the hook. Lunch is still on you."

"Gladly. We'll do it up brown. I'll take you to the Mayflower."

Chris started to say that her tastes were getting rich again since Ty's return, but he caught himself, and neither of them mentioned Ty until they were standing outside the Mayflower two hours later. Chris couldn't resist a parting shot. "Take care of yourself while I'm gone, Katie. Better yet, let Lynnquist take care of you. He's dying to, you know. And he'd do a better job of it than Enfield."

"I'm going to marry Ty."

Chris narrowed his eyes as if to put her in focus. "It seems to me I've heard that before."

"It's true. Amanda has agreed to give him a divorce." He was still staring at her from behind the wire-frame glasses. "Don't you believe me?"

"Of course I believe you, Katie. I just don't believe him."

"He's never lied to me, Chris. We've had arguments and made mistakes—both of us—but he's never lied to me."

"I hope to God he doesn't start now." Abruptly, as if to cover the emotion behind the words, he bent to kiss her on the cheek, then was off down Connecticut Avenue. Without turning, he raised one hand in a brisk backward salute.

Amanda Wycombe Enfield never thought of herself as lucky. Deserving perhaps, but never lucky. Still, fortune smiled upon her that summer, and Roger Atherton confirmed the fact. There wasn't much more to it than that. Ty came down to Washington supposedly for the International Horse Show. He'd promised Amanda to exercise a certain discretion until the divorce was final. It was the least he could do for her and the boys, she pointed out. He'd come down for the horse show confident that Amanda was to leave for Reno in three days' time, and when he called his office and was told that Mrs. Enfield wanted to speak to him immediately, he was annoyed, but not worried. It would be just like Amanda to leave with some imperious instructions about what he must or must not do if he wanted her to go through with things.

Ty had called Amanda from Kat's apartment and received Dr. Atherton's good news. There was not much more to it than that. To be sure, when Kate came home from the Writers' Project office that evening and found him still in his riding habit, on his third whiskey but still not drunk, they went over it for hours. There were the usual accusations and recriminations, the usual tears and apologies, but when she looked back, Kate realized there had been no more to it than that. Amanda had called to say she was pregnant. There would be no operation and no ugly aftermath for Amanda. Amanda was pregnant and Ty would return to her. It was that simple.

2

"I didn't ask if you wanted to go, Katie." McSorley's chins jiggled. No matter how much weight he lost, his face remained the face of a fat man. "I said you were expected to go. We've got to clear up this mess in Philadelphia. I want to know what's going on with that director and I want to know for sure. My theory is either there's a woman in Bucks County or he's doing some research of his own. Well, he's welcome to either or both, but not on government funds. I want the trips to Bucks County stopped, and I want the man out, but we've got to be sure of our facts. Byer was handpicked by the local WPA boss, and I don't have to tell you what kind of a political bombshell that can turn into. I don't want another local war between the WPA people and us. And I especially don't want a scandal. We've got enough bad publicity as it is. So there you are, Katie. Go to Philadelphia. Find out what's really happening with Byer. Then find a way to get rid of him without antagonizing the local pols or giving the newspapers any grist for their anti-Writers' Project mill."

"Any other orders?"

"Have a good time. Visit your family. See old friends. And be back as soon as possible."

The train was late and it was after nine by the time she arrived at Thirtieth Street Station. Visit your family, McSorley had said. See old friends. Kate told the taxi driver to take her to the Bellevue Stratford.

It had not been snowing in Washington, but several inches had fallen in Philadelphia, and it was still coming down heavily. Funny that she had chosen the Bellevue Stratford. Kate remembered another snowstorm. They'd gone Christmas shopping, and Ty had taken her to lunch in the small restaurant at the end of the lobby.

The desk clerk told her she could still get something to eat in the dining room at the end of the lobby. Kate said she had dined on the train.

Early the next morning she called Addison and asked if she could stop by his office.

"Better than that, Katie. Let me take you to lunch."

She told him she'd love to but didn't have the time. She was eager to take care of things and return to Washington.

"But you have to lunch, Katie."

"Not with your style."

"Washington is ruining you, I can tell. Turning you into a drudge.

"Though I must say," Addison observed when she entered his office a little after ten, "you don't look any the worse for wear. Whatever you're doing down there seems to agree with you. What are you doing, Katie? It's not an idle question. You never know when I'm going to need your connections. What do you say? Do you think you'll have room for another aging dipsomaniacal editor down there? Though from what I've heard the booze part of it is a requirement rather than a deterrent. Rumor has it the entire project is rife with drunkards. But then again, what can you expect when you get a bunch of writers together?"

"All sorts of scandalous behavior. That's why I'm here, Addison. Do you know a writer named Martin Byer?"

Addison thought for a moment. "Art critic? Wrote a terrible novel based on the life of Gilbert Stuart?"

"That's the one."

"I've met him several times. A rotten writer but a nice-enough fellow. Not a drunk so far as I know."

"No, he wouldn't have to go to Bucks County just to drink."

"In other words Byer's been slipping off to Bucks County on government money and you're here to find out why."

"Find out and do something about it. As quietly as possible."

"Well, I can't help you do anything about it, Katie, but if you want my opinion, it's a woman. There was a fuss several years ago when he was teaching at the academy. One of his students, or maybe more than one. I don't remember the details."

"I knew I could count on you, Addison."

"I'm a fund of vicious gossip."

"No, just a source of background material. I knew you'd know something about him, and I didn't want to go in blind. It's always easier if you know what you're after. Besides, Addison, it gave me an excuse to see you."

"As if you needed one. You're sure you won't change your mind about lunch?"

"Positive. I want to get back to Washington tonight."

"You mean you can't wait to get out of Philadelphia?"

She felt no embarrassment at the question. No matter how infrequently she saw Addison, the old ease always returned. "Can you think of any reason I ought to want to stay?"

"Aside from lunching with me, not one."

The confrontation with Martin Byer was unpleasant but not difficult. Kathryn said Washington was spot-checking the progress of various regional projects and asked to see the research on Bucks County. The dark eyes that had taken her in carefully—and obviously, Kate thought—turned shifty. The research was really in no shape to be seen, Byer said. Kate explained that she was accustomed to making sense of rough notes. Byer admitted she might have a skilled eye, but these were too rough even for her. Kathryn asked for the outline of the Bucks County section. Byer said there was no outline. He was still getting the feel of the area. The game went on for a little longer; then Kathryn asked, with a directness that was intended to unnerve, what he was really doing in Bucks County. Byer said he was only combining a little pleasure with business, and in any event, the Pennsylvania guide wouldn't be complete without a detailed tour of Bucks County. The more he talked, the more damage he did. One minute he was threatening Kate with his political connections, the next begging her to do whatever she had to do quietly. He had a wife and four children in Philadelphia, and the woman in Bucks County was married too. Kate told the director not to worry. The Writers' Project could not afford bad publicity any more than he.

It was not a lie. Finding out what was going on had been the easy part of the job. Getting rid of Byer without antagonizing the local WPA man and having a dozen newspapers screaming about those immoral, Red-loving writers was something else. Still, there were methods, and Kathryn had already set one in motion by the time she checked out of the hotel that evening. She had taken the first step, and the rest would have to be done in Washington.

Kate was feeling sorry for Byer, but not too sorry, and pleased with her plan, when she turned from the cashier's desk. She was just in time to see Ty and Amanda Enfield crossing the lobby with another couple. The fur Amanda wore was fully cut, but it did not hide the fact of her pregnancy. She was talking to the other woman and smiling as they walked. Ty's hand was at her elbow, as if to protect her, her and the baby. He had not even noticed Kathryn.

Peter was waiting for her in Union Station. If he had asked whether she wanted him to meet her, she would have said no, but she was suddenly very glad to see him.

"I called Philadelphia, but the hotel said you'd just checked out, so I assumed you'd be on this train. I hope you didn't eat on the way down, but if you did, you can keep me company anyway."

She was tired and wanted a bath, but she also wanted not to be left alone with her thoughts. She'd had enough of them on the ride down. "I haven't eaten."

They went to a small Italian restaurant near her apartment. It was dimly lighted and boasted the obligatory red-and-white-checked tablecloths, but the warm air felt good after the cold night, and it smelled delicious as only an Italian restaurant can. Kate realized she was hungry. She'd been sure she was too unhappy to be hungry.

"How was Philadelphia?" Peter asked when they were seated.

Kate noticed that he'd looked down into his drink as he'd spoken. She wondered if there'd been a hidden question behind the obvious one. She didn't know if Peter connected Ty with Philadelphia. She didn't know what he knew about Ty, only that he had never asked any questions or shown any curiosity about Ty's disappearance. He had merely noticed and begun to take advantage of it.

"Philadelphia doesn't change," Kate said.

"But people do."

He must be asking about Ty. Either him or her feelings for him.

"Did you solve the mystery of Bucks County?" Peter went on.

"It wasn't much of a mystery. McSorley was right. There was a woman. Or rather, is a woman."

"What are you going to do about her?"

"I'm not going to do anything about her. That's up to Mrs. Byer. All I care about is the project. He has to go, but he has to go quietly."

"Will he?"

Kate smiled. "I think so."

"You look positively smug, Katie. I suspect you're up to no good."

"Not in the least. I did some very good work this afternoon. After I left Byer I stopped at the Art Project. An old friend from school works there."

"You wouldn't look so pleased about seeing an old school friend."

"Byer's an art critic as well as a writer. Used to teach at the academy, as a matter of fact. I mentioned what a gem he was to several people at the Art Project. Told them we couldn't get along without him. A top administrator. The guiding force of the Writers' Project."

"Did you mention that you hoped no one tried to steal him away?"

"No, I thought that might be heavy-handed. Though I might suggest McSorley throw it in when he speaks to some people down here."

"Byer will be working for the Art Project in weeks. I only pity the poor artists."

"Don't. I think Byer will behave himself. At least for a while."

"Ah, yes, the repentent husband returns to hearth and home."

Kate had been reading the menu halfheartedly, and now she looked at him sharply. But that was ridiculous. She was reading too much into Peter's words. He hadn't seen Ty and Amanda earlier this evening. But she had.

"Don't they always?" she asked.

"I suppose you realize this whole thing is crazy," Kathryn said.

Chris shrugged and smiled. Kate couldn't remember when she'd seen him so happy. "Someone's got to cover it."

It was almost a year since he'd gone off to do those articles on the dust bowl, and he had, as Kate had predicted, made people care. He'd gone beyond the descriptions of walls of rolling black smoke and Oklahoma streets where the lights remained on for three weeks straight and temperatures surpassed 105 degrees daily, and made people know what it was like to live under those conditions. They read Chris's articles and tasted the grit in the food and felt the dirt beneath their clothes and squirmed in the constant heat and darkness and knew the fear of losing the farm for certain. Chris had made people care and the Pulitzer judges take notice. He'd won the prize and found that he could now choose any assignment he wanted. He chose, as he put it, "the mess in Spain."

"There's no point arguing with him, Katie," Peter said. He'd come up to New York with Kate to see Chris off on the *Normandie*. They'd teased Chris about that.

"All that luxury," Peter had said. "Even a second-class stateroom is luxe."

"All that Lalique," Kate had added. "Can't you just see Chris dining amid all that Lalique elegance?"

"Obviously the Pulitzer has gone to his head," Peter said.

It wasn't a very good joke, really, but it served to keep them from talking about the fact that luxury was the last thing Chris was going to find once he reached Spain. He was mad to go, they agreed.

"With everything going on over here," Peter said, "and an election year to boot, he wants to watch a bunch of Spaniards killing each other. There's nothing new there, Chris. It's been going on since the Inquisition."

"This is different, Pete. It's more than Spain. In a couple of years the revolution is going to spread through Europe. And along the same lines."

"You mean we're going to have Germany fighting Russia?" Peter said.

"I won't swear to the countries, but it's going to be right against left. It's been coming for years, and if you'd just open your eyes, you'd be able to see it. In fact, if you'd just look beyond the next political poll, you couldn't miss it."

"Chris," Kate interrupted, "that isn't fair."

"The hell it's not. You're a good man, Lynnquist, but you're an isolationist."

"Is that supposed to be an insult?" Peter asked.

"Well, I can't say I have much admiration for you fellows who sit around screaming about neutrality. The generals weren't neutral when they sent those African troops in to overthrow the republic. And you can't tell me Hitler and Mussolini are neutral about this thing."

"And Stalin. Don't forget Stalin."

"At least he's supporting the right side. Or rather the left side, but the rightful government."

"I thought journalists were supposed to be impartial."

"I am," Chris said. "I'm as impartial as I was when it came to the people versus the drought."

"Time out," Kate said. She was tired of the argument. They'd been at it for weeks, but she'd known from the beginning no one was going to talk Chris out of going to Spain. "I thought this was supposed to be a *bon voyage* party, not a Senate debate."

"That it is," Peter said. "And personally I'm going to have a go at this champagne we brought, because once your news buddies get here, there won't be any left for anyone else."

"You know what J. P. Morgan said about journalists . . ." Chris started, and Kate laughed, and then the second-class stateroom was filled with a dozen reporters and their wives and girls and assorted hangers-on who'd come down to see Owen off to Spain. It was quite a party.

Toward the end of the summer Peter took Kate to a quieter, more fashionable one. The dinner would probably be dull, he said, but it was absolutely necessary. There would be several congressmen including the head of a committee who'd been bottling up some legislation in which Peter was especially interested.

The dinner was given by the wife of a congressman from Ohio, and Kate was surprised to see her brother Bill and Helen across the large Early American living room. "You didn't tell me it was going to be bipartisan," Kate said.

Peter followed her gaze across the room. "You mean Senator Owen? He votes with us often enough to be considered one of us. Almost. Why, do you know him?" It had never occurred to Peter to put the senator together with Kate. Owen was too common a name and Washington too small a town for any relationship between them not to have become known to him before this.

"He's my brother. Though we haven't seen each other in some time."

"He's planning to remedy that right now."

Kate was surprised to see that Peter was right. Bill was crossing the room toward them. She watched him greeting Peter and recognized the old political expertise.

"You know," Peter said, "it never dawned on me to connect Katie with you."

"And she never told you?" Bill asked. "Must be ashamed of her big brother. How are you, Katie? You're looking well."

"So are you," she answered. It was true. There was an air of prosperity and satisfaction that had not been present in the man she remembered. "How's Chip?"

"He's starting Princeton in the fall."

Her parents must be pleased, Kate thought. They'd lost Chris and they'd disowned her, but they had a third generation of Owens to be proud of. She wondered if Chip had turned out like Bill or if there were a streak of Chris or herself in him. It was impossible to guess. He might have turned into anyone.

"Strange," Peter said on the way home.

"The party?"

"You and Bill Owen. You and Chris are so close, but you acted as if you hadn't seen the senator for years."

"I told you, I haven't."

"He seemed happy enough to see you."

Kate had noticed the same thing and was surprised by it. She'd turned it over in her mind during dinner, and when the men emerged from the dining room after coffee and brandy and she saw Bill at Peter's side, it came clear to her. She didn't know how or why, but she knew that Peter could help Bill. And she knew her brother well enough to know he'd overlook a great many things, even herself, if it were politic to do so.

There was something else Kate noticed that evening. At dinner Peter had been seated next to a young and extremely pretty divorcée. The daughter of a senator and the former wife of a congressman, the woman was a far cry from the scores of pretty secretaries and typists who crowded the offices of every government building these days. She was a far cry from what Chris called the available girls. And yet her interest in Peter was as obvious as that of those other girls. Kate had noticed it immediately, and a few nights later she was reminded of it.

They'd gone to the movies to see *Dodsworth,* and something about the character or something about Walter Huston as he'd played the character reminded her of Peter.

"Why didn't you ever marry?" she asked as they were walking home.

"I never expected that question from you, Katie. You must hear it as often as I do, and you must realize how silly it is."

"No, it isn't. I used to think it was too, but now I realize why people ask it. It's only silly when you know the answer. I do about me, but I don't about you."

He stopped walking and turned to her. There was an awkward pause while a streetcar moved noisily past them, leaving a hot breeze in its wake. "I was married. I was married for three years and now I'm divorced."

It was absurd to feel betrayed. She'd never asked Peter if he'd been married and he'd never actually said he hadn't. It was absurd to feel betrayed, but she did.

Kate started walking again, and he fell into step beside her. "Aren't you going to ask me any more about it?"

She waited till the sounds of a second streetcar moving past them in the night died. "I don't know what to ask," she said quietly.

"You could ask why she left me. You could ask how bad it was. Dammit, Katie, you could ask anything. You could pretend to care even if you don't."

"Why did she leave?"

"I'd like to say it was my work. I spent too much time with it and not enough with her. Or she didn't like being a college teacher's wife or she wanted more money or something like that. But it wasn't any of those things. It was just another man. Not even someone special or different like the movie tonight. No Arnold what's-his-name or an Austrian count. Just another college teacher. An associate professor in the history department. He didn't even outrank me. As for the second question, it was hell. It took me a year before I started seeing people again, two before I spoke to another woman who wasn't a student or someone's wife. And even then it went on being hell. I thought I'd never get over it."

"But you did." She was sorry as soon as she'd spoken. It sounded as if she were trying to diminish his words.

He stopped walking again, and the quick intelligent eyes fastened on her. "People do, Katie. People get over these things. Unless they're masochists. That or damn fools."

Kate received one letter from Chris as soon as he arrived in France, then nothing until late in September. He'd been at Alcázar when they'd broken the rebel resistance, he wrote. He'd never imagined such horror and bloodshed. Until Badajoz. In Badajoz the rebels had herded thousands of peasants into the bull ring and butchered them, butchered them with less thought and certainly less ceremony than they butchered bulls.

I think that's the worst thing about this war, Katie. About any war probably. Not the bloodshed, but the inurement to it. My first day in Madrid, I saw a woman mowed down in the street just a few feet from me. I saw the body and the blood and heard the screams and I couldn't stop throwing up for the rest of the day. In Badajoz I saw the bodies of eighteen hundred people—women and children as well as men—and smelled their blood and heard their cries, but I wasn't sick. And maybe that's more terrible than the bloodshed.

He wrote of the horror, but not the pride, though Kate could sense it behind every word. He'd been sick at the sight of the woman, but not sick from fear. Again and again, she could tell, though Chris never said as much, he'd come under fire and had neither panicked nor run. Chris had found his war and proved himself. The damn fool.

There were no letters after that, only his dispatches in the newspaper. Kate swore she'd stop reading them—they only frightened her —but she continued to search for them.

MADRID. The city is cold and damp and thick with fog. The enemy stands at the gates, and the bombs rain down from the skies daily, but the real enemy is within the city. It isn't the cold or the damp or the fog. It's the assassins who streak through the streets spraying shells as they go. It's the informers who lurk behind every wall. Every *madrileño* walks with death.

And Chris dances with it, Kate thought furiously, and swore again she'd stop reading his dispatches. She was grateful for the sound of the phone.

"How would you like to have lunch in Vermont, Katie?" She wasn't surprised by the invitation. There was a time when she would have been, but not anymore. Peter was always running off on the spur of the moment, and he frequently asked her along. "Lunch in Vermont, and we'll be back in Washington in time for dinner."

"It sounds hectic—even for you."

"There's a Ford trimotor plane waiting at the airport. I'll bet you've never even flown. Come on, Katie, you'll love it."

His eagerness to take her up reminded her of someone. Who was it? Not Ty. And yet somehow she connected it with Ty. Johnny someone. Johnny Witmer. That dance during the war, the one Hilary had taken her to. It had been the first time she'd danced with Ty. She told Peter she'd love to have lunch in Vermont.

Lunch was not quite the pleasant outing Peter had promised, since they were joined by three aides and conversation was entirely strategic. The election was just around the corner. Things were not going well for the President. Peter asked questions, the three men answered, Peter made suggestions, the men vowed to carry them out. It was after three by the time the meeting broke up.

"We still have time for a drive before we head back to the airstrip," Peter said. "I'll get rid of the driver and show you some of the countryside. I know lunch was dull, but you won't be able to fault the countryside."

She did. The leaves had turned weeks ago and the trees looked barren and unforgiving beneath an overcast sky. There was a punishing damp wind and Kate wished she'd worn something heavier. It had been sunny in Washington that morning, and she hadn't bothered to put a coat over the light tweed suit.

"Are you cold?" Peter asked.

"Just a little."

"Stupid of me. I should have warned you to bring a coat. Here, try this." He took the battered trench coat he carried from September to June from the back seat and handed it to her.

By the time they reached the airstrip they could hardly see it. A dense wall of fog had rolled in from the sea. "No flights tonight, Mr. Lynnquist," the pilot told them. "But we'll get you out in the morning for sure. Supposed to lift before noon." They could go back to town and spend the night at the hotel, the pilot said, or there was a nice inn a little north of here. "A lot of people come up from New York and Boston just to stay there during the summer."

"How about the inn?" Peter asked when they were back in the car. "It's bound to be better than that hotel where we lunched."

"I don't suppose it makes much difference."

The inn was fashionable enough to be almost half full even this late in the season. All the man at the desk could offer were several small rooms, servants' rooms really, he said, on the top floor or—he looked them over carefully—two deluxe rooms on the second floor. Those were joined by a sitting room. The suite was more expensive, of course, but he really couldn't recommend the rooms on the top floor.

"I have the feeling we're being taken," Peter said when they were alone in the sitting room. The bellboy had started the fire for them, then gone off to get the bottle of whiskey and the ice Peter had ordered. "Well, I don't mind paying more if it means I'm being taken for a city slicker. Quite a compliment if you think about it."

The bellboy returned with the whiskey and ice, and Peter poured a drink for each of them.

"No, thank you," Kate said when he handed one to her.

"You'd better drink it. You got quite a chill this afternoon."

"I don't want a drink."

"Look, Katie, I'm sorry about the plane, but it's not so terrible. We'll be out of here by tomorrow morning."

"Oh, it's not terrible at all. It's very cozy. The fire, the whiskey, the adjoining rooms."

Peter smiled, but it was professional rather than genuine. "Would you have preferred the little servants' rooms in the attic?"

"Does it make any difference what I would have preferred?"

"I didn't do this intentionally, Katie. If you think about it, I didn't do anything. That fog rolled in all by itself."

"And without any warning. I'm sure they never give weather reports at that airstrip."

"As a matter of fact, they do. The one I got when we arrived didn't mention the fog. Or anything else."

"I'm sure."

She was sitting in a chair next to the hearth, her hands folded in her lap, her legs crossed at the ankles, like a prim schoolgirl at her first dance, he thought, and when she looked up at him her eyes were cold, as cold as her voice had been a moment ago. He downed the drink, then walked to the table where the bellboy had put the tray and poured himself another.

"I may be a fool about a lot of things when it comes to you, Katie, but I'm not that much of a fool. Oh, I'm in love with you, all right. Whatever that means. And I'll tell you one thing"—he took a long swallow of the drink—"it doesn't mean what I thought it would. For a long time I thought it would never happen again, and then when it started to, I thought it would feel terrific, but it doesn't. It feels like hell. Hanging around you all the time, hating myself for hanging around . . ."

He stopped suddenly, then took another swallow of the drink. "I seem to be straying from the point. You're right about a lot of things. You're right that I'm in love with you," he repeated. "You're right that I want to sleep with you. Want it so much that sometimes I can't even think about anything else. I'm forty goddamn years old, and I walk around like some goddamn kid thinking about sleeping with you. But I'm not a goddamn kid, Katie, because I only want you if you want me. That's where you're wrong tonight. You're wrong to think I'd try to trick you into anything. There's only one way anything's going to happen tonight, and that's if you want it to. I'd sell my soul for that, Katie. I'd sell my soul to have you walk into my room tonight and say, 'Peter, I love you.' I'd sell my soul to have you walk into my room and get into my bed and say, 'Peter, I love you and I want to marry you.' I'd sell my soul for that, but I wouldn't give a penny to trick you into some lousy seduction scene. I want you, Katie, but I don't want you that much."

He finished off his drink and filled the glass again. "So you might as well have that whiskey. No one's trying to get you drunk. Though I don't promise the same about myself." Without giving her another look, he walked into his bedroom and closed the door behind him.

She took the drink he'd left her. It made her feel warmer but no better. She'd been a fool, an arrogant fool, and she didn't blame him for his anger. The fire was beginning to die, and she got up and put another log on the grate and more ice and a little more whiskey in her glass. She was sipping it slowly, staring into the flames and trying to make it last, but by the time she finished it, Peter had not come out. There wasn't a sound from behind the closed door.

She walked to the door silently, as if afraid of being caught before she reached it, and knocked softly.

"It's not locked," he said.

He'd taken off his jacket and tie and shoes, and was stretched on the bed in his shirt and trousers. He didn't stand when she entered the room.

"I'm sorry, Peter. Really sorry."

He didn't say anything for a while, just lay there staring at her and not saying anything. Then he smiled, a thin, constrained smile. "Those weren't the lines you were given, Katie, but I guess they'll have to do."

The next morning Peter went down to telephone the airstrip, and when he returned to the small sitting room Kate could tell he'd had bad news. He was holding a newspaper that was open to an inside page, and for a moment the memory of Chris holding the announcement of Ty's engagement flashed through her mind. But that was silly. This was bound to be political bad news. It had nothing to do with her.

"Katie," he said, and she knew from his voice it did have something to do with her. "Katie, it's Chris." He handed her the paper.

It was a local paper, and the article was brief. It was a news-service story datelined Madrid. "Pulitzer-prize winning journalist Christopher Owen was killed in action here today." All the information about Chris was familiar, even the fact that he'd been shot while engaged in battle as part of the International Brigade. He'd gone over as a correspondent, but Kate had always known he wouldn't go on being an observer. She'd always known he'd fight for the side he believed right.

She heard someone screaming, but didn't realize it was her own voice until she felt Peter shaking her. "Stop it, Katie," he shouted above her screams. "Stop it!" Then he pulled her to him and held her until the screams stopped, and the sobs too, and then there were only the tears. He would have held her through those, but she'd pulled away finally because she knew those would go on for a long time.

"He found his war," she said finally. "He found his damn war and proved he was a damn hero. I hope he's satisfied."

There was a great deal of red tape involved, but between them Peter and Senator Bill Owen managed to have the body brought home. Peter never asked Kate if she wanted him to accompany her to Philadelphia for the funeral. He simply acted on the assumption that she did.

"I think I ought to warn you," Kate said on the train up, "my parents don't speak to me." If Peter wondered why, he did not ask.

It was a dazzling autumn day. At the far end of the cemetery two men raked at an easy pace, working futilely against the brisk breeze that blew the gold and orange leaves about. Kate wished it were raining.

The paper had said the funeral would be private, but Will's followers and Bill's constituents and the people who were suddenly proud to have known the dead Pulitzer prizewinner crowded the gravesite. If any of them disapproved of the circumstances of Chris's death, this was not the time to say so.

During the brief ceremony neither Will nor Margaret raised their eyes to Kathryn, but she could not help staring at them. Though Margaret's face was hidden by the dark veil and it was hard to tell, she seemed to have changed little. She held her head high and her back straight, as if she were daring anyone to pity her. Will's bearing made no such challenge. His face was creased with sorrow and his shoulders bent. He looked to Kate as if he'd shrunk. She wondered if her father's condition were the result of Chris's death, or if it went back further than that, to Chris's original defection, to her own betrayal, to the fact that he'd finally passed the mantle to Bill. He'd be proud of Bill, but Bill had been only part of the dream. Kate watched the men lowering another part into the earth now. Still another had been buried a long time ago.

The crowd drifted away quickly. The spectacle was over. Will looked up from the grave, and for a moment, before he realized where he was looking, his eyes caught Kate's. He turned before they could register any emotion.

"Mr. Owen," Kate heard Peter call quietly. She was surprised to see Will stop and turn back to them. Peter crossed the short distance between them and introduced himself.

It was obvious that Will recognized his name. "It was kind of you to come up for the funeral."

"I came up with Katie," Peter said.

Will said nothing, simply looked down at his feet, then slowly up at Kathryn. He stared at her for a long time. "How are you, Katie?" he said finally.

Without questioning or thinking Kathryn began to move toward him, but Will held out his hand in a gesture that was only partly a greeting. It was as if he wanted to keep her at a distance. Well, what had she expected, open arms and forgiveness? She took his hand briefly. It felt cool.

They stood for a few minutes talking of Chris. Will and Margaret had known he was in Spain, of course, though he hadn't written them. Kate told them she'd received two letters, and surprisingly Will asked her to bring them with her next time she came to Philadelphia. He didn't say home. Things had gone too far for him to say home.

Margaret invited them back to the house, and Peter accepted quickly. It seemed to Kate the house hadn't changed at all. Even the black crepe on the front door looked familiar, though now there was no red-white-and-blue bunting. She remembered how Chip had cried for days at a time after Louise's death. He was a young man now, down from Princeton for the funeral, looking very grown-up and self-sufficient and a little like Bill. She remembered Chris that day too, angry that the war was over, guilty that Louise was dead. He'd managed to make up for all that.

The visit didn't turn out badly, only less well than it might have. There was little to say, or perhaps too much. Will was quiet, quieter than Kate had ever known him. Several times during the afternoon she looked up and found him watching her, watching her as he might a stranger he didn't entirely trust. Well, she couldn't blame him for that. You couldn't blame people for not feeling what you wanted them to feel.

As they were leaving, Margaret told Kate to let them know next time she was in Philadelphia. Then she said the same thing in the same voice to Peter. It had been the instinctive gesture of a politician's wife, not a mother. On the way back to Washington Kate thanked Peter, but she couldn't help wondering if the silence hadn't been preferable, or at least less painful.

Kathryn didn't return to Philadelphia that winter. There was no reason to, nor was there time. The Writers' Project was in a state of perpetual chaos. Regional offices erupted in political squabbles, local newspapers screamed of communist infiltration, and chunks of manuscripts arrived late if at all. They were frequently not only unpublishable, but totally unintelligible. As an advisory editor now, only the last problem should have fallen within Kate's province, but lines were not so clearly drawn. When the early sections of the Calumet guide failed to arrive on the first three promised dates, she had to find out why before she could do anything about it. The Calumet group, it transpired, had split into two factions, neither of which spoke to the other. Kate convinced McSorley to appoint a new director who could bring both into line.

She enjoyed the problems, or at least she enjoyed solving them. Even when she was away from the project, Peter said, she wasn't really away from it.

"You're worrying about Winberg," he observed one night in the small Italian restaurant near her apartment. They'd just left a large, noisy cocktail party. "You were worrying about him all through the party."

"Did I miss much?"

"Not a thing. All the same, it would be nice if you were here occasionally. Winberg isn't going to commit suicide, you know. People who talk about it never do. And no one ever committed suicide because he had to spend his days labeling street maps when he wanted to be writing fiction."

"I know he isn't going to kill himself, and I know he wouldn't be ranting about it if he weren't drunk half the time, but that's just the point. Maybe he wouldn't get drunk every day at lunch and come back threatening suicide if he were writing more than street names on guide maps."

"He might stop threatening suicide, Katie, but he'd still get drunk."

"You've been listening to Addison Wales."

Peter and Addison had met only the previous week, when Addison had been in Washington and dined with them. Kate had expected the two men to dislike each other on sight. Addison the cynic would laugh at Peter the do-gooder. Peter the political idealist would despair of Addison the decadent aesthete. She hadn't been entirely wrong. They'd disagreed on almost every point and had a thoroughly good time doing it.

"I approve," Addison had said when Peter had gone off to find a taxi. "Of Lynnquist, I mean. If I were more of a romantic, I might even say he was worth waiting for, but since I'm not, I'll limit myself to best wishes. When's the wedding?"

"There isn't going to be a wedding, Addison."

He looked at her in the soft light of the restaurant foyer. "You aren't being coy, are you, Katie?"

"You know me better than that."

"Then you're a fool. If you weren't, you'd marry him in a minute."

"Maybe he doesn't want to marry me."

"Now you're being coy."

"All right, but I'm not going to marry him."

It was the first time Kate had seen Addison really annoyed with her, not just pretending to be to make her see what he wanted her to. "I thought you'd grown up, Katie. I was sure of it. But I was wrong."

"He's drinking more than ever," she'd said to Peter on the way home. It wasn't Addison's anger at her, though she wished she could blame that on the alcohol. His hands had shaken as he raised the first drink to his mouth, shaken enough for Kate to notice.

"He can handle it," Peter said. "If he's a drunk, he's a good one. Doesn't get hostile or sloppily sentimental. And from what you've said doesn't go off on binges. It may take a few years off his life, but then again it may help him get through the years he does have."

"Well, what do you plan to do about Winberg and all the rest of them?" Peter asked after the waiter had brought their drinks. "If you're going to think about the problem all through dinner, we might as well talk about it."

"I don't see there's anything I can do. Winberg wants to write his short stories and Arthur Lasher wants to write his poetry and the government wants them to write guidebooks."

"Why not let them do all three?"

"You know the answer to that as well as I do, Peter. The government wants something *useful*. But the real reason is the powers-that-be are afraid. Let those fellows write what they want, and the government will be paying for a lot of red propaganda. Or so they say."

"How left wing is it?"

"It varies. Lasher's poetry a little, but most of it is so obscure it doesn't matter. Winberg's not at all. You know what it's like. Someone writes about growing up without shoes or enough to eat, and some conservative senator sees red."

Peter looked thoughtful for a moment. "Katie, who puts out those guidebooks? Not the Government Printing Office?"

"You know they don't."

"You have to find sponsors for each one, right? A sponsor and a private publisher. A private publisher who doesn't need a congressional act to tell him what he can print."

She put down her drink. "How long have you been thinking of this?"

"I haven't. It came to me now while I was listening to you."

"It's so simple I can't believe we didn't think of it before. Winberg and Lasher and all the others are turning out the work on their own time anyway. Some of it very good work, incidentally. We've got the editorial staff to put it together. All we do is take it straight to a publisher. Since it won't be an official government publication, it won't need official government approval, only unofficial project sanction. You're a genius, Peter Lynnquist. An absolute genius."

"You might as well call McSorley now. You won't be able to eat dinner until you do." He took a nickel from his pocket. "There's a phone in the back."

She went to a booth hidden behind a coatrack in the rear of the restaurant. When Peter had finished his drink and she still hadn't returned, he followed her. Through the glass he could see her talking and gesturing excitedly. When she opened the folding door she was smiling and her face was flushed.

"I could kiss you."

"Only politely, Katie. After all, it's a public place."

Kate chastised herself later because she hadn't meant to be a tease, but it was hard to keep feeling bad because she kept remembering how nice it had been to kiss Peter Lynnquist.

McSorley had given the go-ahead on the anthology more than eight months ago. The first one would be out before the end of the year, and they'd already begun work on the second. Arthur Lasher had brought her several pieces for it this morning, and Kate had planned to get through them by the end of the day, but she hadn't succeeded because Ty had called this morning and said he was coming down on the four-o'clock to ask her to marry him, and all her plans and good intentions had fallen apart in the face of Ty's return. It seemed to Kate that her whole life had fallen apart in the face of Ty's return.

They'd dined on the Shoreham Terrace, though neither Kate nor Ty had eaten much, and they'd danced until after midnight. Ty asked if she'd like to go somewhere for a nightcap, but Kate said no, she wanted to walk for a while. She liked the way the deserted streets felt quiet and familiar in the Indian-summer night. A breeze had come up from the west.

"It feels as if the heat wave is finally going to break," Kate said. "Thank heavens. There's nothing worse than a Washington heat wave."

"I never could understand your living here," Ty said.

She laughed quietly. "You never could understand anyone living anywhere but Philadelphia." Kate remembered a boy who'd talked of taking tramp steamers around the world, but didn't mention him to Ty.

"You won't miss it, Kat. Washington, I mean. And you'll like coming home."

Home? The Main Line wasn't home. Ty's friends wouldn't be home. Her parents were no longer home. But Ty was home. "Yes, I'll like going home."

"When?"

"When?" she repeated.

"When can you leave here? When can we be married? As far as I'm concerned, we can drive to Maryland tonight."

Drop everything. Enfield is back. Again. "I'll need a little more time than that, Ty."

"A little more time! I've given you twenty years."

No, she thought. I've given you twenty years. "I'll have to give them notice."

"That means two weeks."

"It may take longer. They'll have to find someone else."

"I admit you're irreplaceable, Kat, but they'll find someone else." He was quiet for a moment. "It's about time you got out of there anyway. The whole project is crawling with reds."

"So the newspapers tell me."

"You don't belong there, Kat."

"Where do I belong?"

He stopped walking and turned to her. She felt his mouth on hers, then tracing a line to her ear. "With me. You've always belonged with me."

"What are you thinking?" he asked an hour later. They were in the living room of Kate's apartment and she'd been sitting with her head on his shoulder staring into the middle distance.

"I was thinking of Nicholas."

"I can't say I'm much flattered, but if it has to be another man, it might as well be Nicholas."

"Remember that time he took me to lunch in New York?"

"I remember hearing about it."

"He answered the great mystery that day. Told me what was in that room in his studio. It turned out to be no mystery at all. Only a lot of his paintings. Very bad paintings, according to him."

"Well, at least he did paint for a while."

"Oh, he did that, all right. Painted his heart out—and apparently broke it when he gave it up."

"Then why did he give it up?"

"That's what I asked him. 'Because I have too much respect for beauty,' he said. 'What I was creating was second-rate. No, tenth-rate,' he said. It's funny the way I still remember his words. 'I would have had to compromise to accept my own work, and I couldn't do that.' Those were his words."

"It sounds like Nicholas."

Kate was shocked at how quickly everything fell into place. She sat up and faced him. "It sounds like us, Ty."

"I don't understand."

"We've made too many compromises. Or rather we'd have to make too many now. At least I would. Whatever we had was first-rate once. I'll always believe that. But there have been too many mistakes, and it's not first-rate anymore. We've been pretending it is, but it isn't."

"Kat, what are you saying?"

"Go back to Amanda, Ty. She'll take you back, I promise you that."

"I don't want to go back to Amanda. I love you. I've always loved you."

"I believe you, Ty. And I've always loved you. A part of me probably always will, but it is too late. I said it wasn't, but it is. We're different people now. We were fools to think we weren't. We don't really have anything anymore. At least, we don't have anything first-rate. And I don't want to live with less than that. I guess I'm like Nicholas in that respect. I'd rather have the ideal of what we had than the disillusion of what we might have."

"There's someone else," he said. "There must be."

She started to tell him he was wrong, then stopped in mid-sentence. "I didn't think there was, but maybe there is."

"He'll never love you the way I do, Kat. And you'll never love anyone else the way you love me."

"I know that, Ty. But maybe I'll love someone else differently. Maybe it will never be as good as it was with you, but maybe it will never be as bad either. You hurt me too much. That's not an accusation, just a fact. You hurt me too much, and I'll never be able to forget it. But maybe if I start over with someone else, I won't think about it so much."

"I'll make you forget, Kat. I'll make it all up to you."

"You couldn't, Ty. There are too many years and too many memories, and there's no point in arguing about it."

There wasn't any point in arguing, but they did all night. He apologized for every pain he'd caused her, but she said you couldn't apologize for the past, you could only accept it. He swore they'd recapture what they'd had, but she said it would be like trying to recapture youth. He insisted they were right for each other, more right than any two people in the world. Thirteen years of marriage had taught him that. She said the same thirteen years had taught her a different lesson. He told her she was merely upset by the suddenness of his return, and when she thought about it rationally and calmly she'd see she was making a mistake by sending him away. She assured him she was quite rational and calm now. He railed against the unknown man who'd come between them. She said nothing.

He swore he wouldn't give up, would keep calling and writing, would never go back to Amanda because no matter what Kat said they belonged to each other, and when they stood at the door just before dawn, and he held her, and she felt his mouth on hers again, she thought for a moment he might be right, but she pulled away quickly, because the years had taught her differently.

After he left she looked at the thin gold watch he'd given her so many years ago. She'd have to get herself a new one. No, that was silly. She wasn't going to marry Ty, but she wasn't going to deny he'd existed or that she'd loved him.

The watch said ten after five. It was an unholy hour to telephone anyone. She dialed Peter's number. She told herself he wouldn't be there, but there was always the chance he'd taken the earlier train out of Chicago, or, given Peter, flown.

The voice was sleepy, but it was unmistakably Peter's. "Katie." He looked at the clock next to the bed. "Katie, are you all right?"

"Do you still want to go away for the weekend, Peter? Because if you do, I can be ready any time."

"What?"

"Do you always wake up so slowly? You suggested going away for the weekend. Virginia, you said. Though I know an inn in Vermont. I think we can get a suite—though I ought to warn you, I'm not sure I can be trusted. I might turn up in your room one night saying outrageous things."

"Katie, what are you talking about?"

"Don't you know?"

"I know what it sounds like, but I can't believe it."

"It's true."

"Where are you?"

"Home."

He had started across the room toward the closet, carrying the phone with him. "Stay there, Katie. I'll be right over."

It was more than a mile from his apartment to Kathryn's, but Peter ran all the way. It had still taken too long, he told her, and she agreed.

Epilogue

Washington, 1940

"Hello, darling, you're late." Kate raised a cheek to Peter and he kissed it. It was a familiar, almost perfunctory gesture. They both knew it, and they both loved the fact that it was.

"I assure you it couldn't be helped, Katie." It was true and they both knew that too. Peter no longer stayed late at his office unless it was absolutely necessary. He loved walking into the small living room, still filled with sunlight in the early summer evenings, darker in the glow of a winter's fire. He loved walking into it and finding Katie there waiting for him. She always arrived home before he did, and she always looked up eagerly when he came into the room. He looked forward to that moment all day. At first he'd thought he couldn't possibly go on looking forward to it so intensely, but they'd been married almost three years now and he still did.

Kate had wanted to put off the wedding. Everyone knew that business with the Dies Committee was coming up, and if she were called before it, and she was sure to be, it would be bad for Peter. The only sensible thing to do, she said, was to wait until the whole thing blew over, but Peter said he was tired of being sensible and especially tired of waiting.

"Good Lord, Katie, at our ages we can't afford to wait. Do you want your husband rolled up to the altar in a wheelchair coughing and wheezing 'I do'?"

They'd married less than a month after that night she'd said good-bye to Ty, and the following summer Peter had gone through the whole ordeal of the Dies Committee hearings with her. The day she was called to testify, he was in the room. The newspapers had a heyday with that. "Prominent member of administration and communist wife," read the caption under a photograph of the two of them arriving at the hearing. Peter had managed to laugh at that, but he hadn't laughed at her testimony. He'd been too angry at the committee for that.

Congressman Dies produced the by-now famous copy of *The People's Front* by Earl Browder and asked if that were Kathryn's signature halfway down the list of names. Kate admitted it was.

DIES: Were you aware of the inflammatory nature of the book, Mrs. Lynnquist?

KATHRYN: I knew it was a copy of *The People's Front*, if that's what you mean. It was the logical gift for Mr. Simms. Everyone in the project knew it was his bible. Or so he said until he turned it over to this committee.

DIES: Are you suggesting your signature in this book has no significance?

KATHRYN: It signifies I was present at the party that was held for Robert Simms after he was fired from the Writers' Project.

DIES: It does not signify your belief in the ideals expressed in this book?

KATHRYN: Not in the least.

The questioning continued in a similar vein for another hour. Dies produced a copy of the first anthology and turned to a long poem by Arthur Lasher. He asked Kate if she were responsible for selecting the poem for the anthology. She admitted she was. Dies proceeded to read several lines.

DIES: Are you telling this committee, Mrs. Lynnquist, that this description of a great red flame that will engulf our nation is not an open call to revolution, an open call to a communist revolution?

KATHRYN: I wish the passage were as clear to me.

A murmur of laughter ran through the room. The congressman didn't like that.

DIES: Do you often publish things you don't understand?

KATHRYN: Good poetry is open to interpretation.

Arthur Lasher loved her for that. He forgave her all her past transgressions and said she'd behaved well, for a filthy capitalist. Nothing much came out of the hearing, at least that year. After a while the public grew bored with the book that more than fifty members of the project had signed at a going-away party for the turncoat Robert Simms and the hidden meaning of literature they'd be unlikely to read under other circumstances. Nothing much came of it except the end of the Writers' Project. It was to be turned over to the states.

"What are you going to do now?" Peter had asked. "Can't sit around listening to the radio and eating bonbons all day, you know."

"I like that!"

"You'd hate it, Katie. You'd be bored in a month. And ripe for the first bachelor who came along."

"An unlikely to say nothing of an unseemly suggestion."

"Still, I can't take the chance. You'll have to find another job."

"Slave driver."

"What about that friend of Chris's? The one who's looking for someone to run the Sunday supplement?"

"I don't know anything about newspapers, Peter."

"But you know a lot about magazines. According to Addison, you know practically everything there is to know about magazines. And that's what a Sunday supplement is."

She'd taken the job and it had turned out well, almost as well as her marriage, Kate thought as she looked up at Peter standing over her chair now. He looked tired, but pleased to be home, as pleased as she was to have him home. It seemed strange to Kate that she'd lived alone for so long, strange that she'd made it through so many solitary nights. Now she hated it when Peter worked late.

"And even if I am late," Peter continued, "you shouldn't reprimand me in front of Chip. He'll think I'm henpecked." Peter crossed the room to the tall young man who'd stood when he entered. Like his father, Chip had a good-natured, open face and a ready smile, but there was an intensity to the eyes that was out of keeping with the rest of him. "Well, Chip," Peter said, shaking his hand, "what brings you down from that country club you call a college?"

"Not everyone can go to Harvard," the boy said. "And we thank God for that. Actually I came down to talk to Dad, and now that I have, I came over to talk to you and Aunt Katie."

"I suspect that means your father did not approve of whatever it is you came to talk to him about."

Chip sat. "That's the understatement of the year." He crossed and recrossed the gray flannel trousers.

"If you want to run off and join the Canadian Air Force, I'm on his side," Peter said.

"That's what I was telling him," Kathryn said.

"No, it isn't that. I agreed to finish school. It's less than a year. Then I'm going to enlist in the navy."

"In that case, what's the problem? Your father was in the navy in the last war, wasn't he?"

"It isn't the war. It will be when it comes—he'll try to get me some soft job here—but it isn't now."

"A girl?" Peter asked.

"You guessed it."

"And they don't approve?" Kate said.

"That's only half of it. No one approves."

"I assume the girl does," Kate said.

"There's no problem there, but her family's dead against it, and so are Dad and Helen. That's the strange part. I was sure they'd approve. There's nothing wrong with Camilla or her family, but . . ."

"Not Camilla Branch?"

Chip looked at his aunt eagerly. "You know her?"

"Her and her whole family. I roomed with her mother at school."

"Then maybe you can tell me what goes on between them and Dad. When I came home and told him I was going to marry Camilla Branch, he practically went through the roof. And that's nothing compared to Camilla's family. When they found out she was coming down for a weekend last month, they forbade her to see me ever again."

"I take it she hasn't listened to her parents."

"Not exactly," Chip said.

Kathryn thought of Daphne Enfield. No, that was unfair. Just because the girl looked like Daphne, it didn't mean she was like Daphne. And who wouldn't defy parents—especially parents like Hilary and Carter—to see the boy she thought she loved.

"I just don't understand the whole thing," Chip said. "I'm not surprised at the way her family feels . . ."

"Why should her family disapprove?" Peter asked. "There's nothing wrong with you as far as I can see."

Chip smiled. "Tell him about Philadelphia, Aunt Katie."

"I've heard about Philadelphia, thank you," Peter said, "but you're not going to let something like that stop you, are you?"

"I'm not going to let anything stop me," Chip said. "I'm just trying to find out what I'm up against."

"You're up against a family feud—you can both laugh, but it's true —that goes back four generations. To your great-grandfather and Camilla's."

"I don't believe it. That's why Dad's against my marrying Camilla? Because of some crazy fight between two old men who have been dead for ages?"

"It's a little more than that," Kate said.

"Well, you've got to talk to Dad. Both of you. That's why I'm here. He won't listen to me, but he will to you, or at least to Uncle Peter. Will you talk to him?"

"Of course we'll talk to him," Peter said.

"I don't know," Kate said. Both men looked at her in surprise. "I'm not sure that I don't agree with your father this time."

"You can't mean it. Not you," Chip burst out.

"It's not the old family thing." Kathryn could feel Peter's eyes on her and would not meet them. "It's the rest of it. The snobbery and the distinctions and all the little things that separate someone like you from Camilla Branch. You can go anywhere else in the country, and they won't, Chip. You look right and you speak properly. You've been to the best schools, and your father's a senator, and most places that would be enough, but it isn't in Philadelphia."

"Who cares about Philadelphia? By the time I finish school and marry Camilla, we'll be in this war, and there'll be a lot of places to worry about besides Philadelphia. Places like Dunkirk and Antwerp and Calais."

"Last time around they worried about places like the Marne and the Somme and a place called Roye . . ."

"I never heard of that one," Chip said.

"It doesn't matter," Kathryn answered quickly. "Once they got back to Philadelphia, none of them mattered."

"Maybe that was true of your generation, but it isn't of ours. And it isn't true of Camilla. She doesn't care about any of that. She isn't afraid of any of that." He saw his aunt smile. "I know you don't believe me, but it's true. Camilla isn't afraid of anything. You know what she did last fall? I guess that was when I first realized how much I loved her. It was the night of that stupid Martian broadcast. She'd been listening to *Charlie McCarthy*. Her family always listens to *Charlie McCarthy* . . ."

"I can believe that," Kate said.

"And when the commercial came on, they switched to *The Mercury Theatre*. That's why she didn't realize it was a hoax. All she heard was that Princeton was being wiped out. Now, most girls would start crying and run the other way, but not Camilla. She got in her car and drove all the way to Princeton. It took her half the night with all the confusion and traffic jams and stuff, but she got there."

"To be with you when the end of the world came," Kate said, but her voice was not unkind, and she had an inkling of what the meeting might have been.

"You can laugh if you want, but I think it was a terrific thing to do. She got hell for it later. The family threatened to take away her car. And that was before they knew I was the one she'd driven up to see."

"I think it was a terrific thing to do too," Kate said.

"Then you'll both talk to Dad?"

"I didn't say that. I just said I admired Camilla's courage."

Chip's fist came down on his knee in exasperation. "I don't understand you tonight, Aunt Katie."

"I don't think," Peter said, "we're going to come to an understanding about this thing tonight, Chip."

"Does that mean you're against me too?"

"I'm not against you," Peter answered, keeping his eyes on Kate, "but I think this is something we might want to think about for a while."

"I've been thinking about it for long enough. I'm ready to do something about it."

"I'm sure you are, Chip, but not tonight. Why don't we let it go for the rest of the evening, and we'll talk about it tomorrow. You're staying in Washington for the weekend, aren't you?"

"I'm going back first thing in the morning. There's a dance for someone at the Cricket Club tomorrow night."

"And Camilla will be there?" Peter said.

Chip smiled for the first time in a long time. "I'm glad someone in this family understands."

"Your aunt understands," Peter said when they'd reached the door. "In some ways she understands more than we do."

They avoided any mention of Chip during dinner. Peter told her the latest news about the drift toward war, and Kate pretended to listen, but they were both thinking of something else, and they knew it.

Afterward they went back to the living room, and Peter started the fire again. He asked if she'd mind if he looked at some papers he'd brought home, and Kate said of course not, she wanted to finish that Thomas Wolfe book he'd brought her, but when Peter looked up from his papers half an hour later, he saw that she was sitting in the same position staring into the fire. *You Can't Go Home Again* lay unopened on the table beside her.

She felt him looking at her, and her eyes moved from the flames to meet his. "Maybe I'd better tell you the whole story, Peter. It's not very nice, but it can't be as bad as what you're thinking."

He was surprised. He'd completely misread her. "Is that what you're worried about? What I'm thinking?"

"Shouldn't I be?"

He moved from his chair to the side of hers and reached an arm around her. She smelled of Chanel No. Five, but she smelled of it the way only Katie did. "Listen, Katie, if you feel like talking, I'll listen. I'll always listen to you, you know that. But if you've got some kind of confession on your mind, I'm not interested. Whatever happened to you in the past made you the way you are, and I love you the way you are."

She took his hand from her shoulder and held it against her cheek. "You know, sometimes you're just too good to be true. It's like living with a saint."

"That's not what you said last week when we were supposed to dine at the Stones' and I got tied up at the White House. You wouldn't even talk to me when I got home."

"I was asleep when you got home."

"Feigning sleep, I suspect, but at least you didn't lock me out of the bedroom. I was half-expecting you would."

She looked up at him in surprise. "You don't mean that, do you? You know me better than that."

He laughed. "No, I don't mean it, Katie. And yes, I know you better than that."

"Still," he said after a while, "you're wrong about Chip."

She pulled away a little, as if in reaction to something he'd put between them. "I just don't want Chip to get hurt. And he will."

"Because you were?"

"The story's too familiar."

"Every story is different, Katie. Times change. People change."

"You don't know Philadelphia the way I do."

"Neither of us knows this Camilla."

"Chris would have understood."

"Chris was one story, Katie. You're another. Chip and Camilla are   J 33 a third. Don't make them pay for your experiences." He pulled her to him again. "You did enough of that yourself. Now forget them."

"I had, until tonight."

He turned her face to him so he could see her eyes. "Do you mean that?"

"I didn't realize how well I'd forgot until Chip."

"Then I ought to thank him," Peter said.

"For reminding me?"

"For letting me find out you'd forgot in the first place. We'll have to do something nice for the kid."

"Like talk to Bill?"

"Sure we'll talk to Bill. And we'll be absolutely convincing. Think of it, Katie. If we can't make a case for love, who can?"

"You always were sure of yourself."

"Not when it came to you."

"Especially when it came to me. You always knew it was only a matter of time." And she supposed it had been.